DESIRE'S PRICE

"Please," Jessica whispered. "Do not hurt me."

At her words, the Duke stood in one, swift movement. He placed the rapier across a nearby table. "Contrary to what you may have heard, I do not make a practice of harming beautiful young women," he informed her as he advanced. "You need not be afraid."

Reaching out, he pulled her easily toward him and kissed her gently. Jessica was frightened, but his hands worked magic on her body, and made it come alive under his touch. A wonderful warmth enveloped her.

The feelings he was awakening in her were intoxicating. She wanted more, much more. Never had she realized that the touch of a man could be so magical.

"Are you still willing to pay my price, Jessica?" he asked in a hoarse whisper.

She let her eyes close. "Yes," she sighed . . .

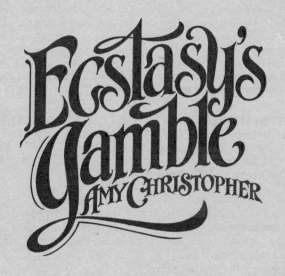

Ecstasy's Gamble

Amy Christopher

ZEBRA BOOKS
KENSINGTON PUBLISHING CORP.

ZEBRA BOOKS

are published by

Kensington Publishing Corp.
475 Park Avenue South
New York, NY 10016

First printing: August, 1990

Printed in the United States of America

To Ken, who is always there for me.
With all my love.

Prologue

England, 1804

The early morning mist swirled about the trees. Catching in their branches, it tore apart as a gossamer veil. A slow, light patter sounded against the leaves as moisture dripped from limb to limb. The call of the mourning dove echoed through the glen, amongst the trees, and across the fields and gardens. All else was silent.

As the veil of mist parted, a small group of men huddled beneath a towering stand of oaks. They were dressed for the dawn's chill dampness in greatcoats and hats. Nearby were several carriages, well-appointed and drawn by neatly groomed and well-matched teams of horses. The animals occasionally stamped and snorted indignation at being kept standing on such a morning.

The men spoke quietly, then, as the appointed hour drew near, they broke apart. Three individuals were left alone in the center of the clearing. As the others watched, two of those who were left in the center positioned themselves back to back. They had discarded their outer garments and wore only waistcoats over white shirts. The dark hair of the one and the light hair of the other contrasted sharply, even in the dim light of dawn. Shoulder to shoulder they stood, erect and tall, each with a brightly polished dueling pistol in hand. The eldest of the trio moved back to where the others stood waiting. Speaking clearly, he explained the gentlemen's rules.

"You will each walk ten paces on the count, turn, and fire," he told them. "Each man will be allowed one shot. Any man who turns and fires before the end of the count will be warned by the other's second and, if it is judged appropriate, will be shot by him. Do you understand the rules, gentlemen?" At a curt nod from each of the duelists, he went on, "May your honor be satisfied when this is finished. God go with you both. Are you ready?" When both men had indicated they were, he began, "One . . . Two . . . Three . . ." Each paced off at the count. "Four . . . Five . . . Six . . ." They marched on. "Seven . . . Eight . . . Nine . . ." The moment was at hand. "Ten." They turned and fired.

The explosions of the pistols was startling. The peace of the glen was broken. The sudden eruption awakened the birds. Rising from their nighttime roosts, they called an alarm. The pistol reports echoed across the fields and through the trees.

The light-haired man grabbed at his chest and swayed. Several of the onlookers rushed to his side and caught him as he fell. They lowered him gently to the ground. A dark, red stain began to spread across the white of his shirt.

The dark-haired man slowly lowered his pistol as his friends gathered about him. His expression was one of dismay and slight puzzlement. He turned to his second who was holding his coat for him.

"I aimed away from him," he said, shaking his head. "I could not possibly have hit him."

His friend glanced over at the fallen man and then back. He said nothing, but merely helped the duelist with his greatcoat and handed him his hat. Together, they walked to one of the waiting carriages. The

8

wounded man was carried gently to his own carriage and driven away. Slowly, the others dispersed.

Soon the glade was empty. There was no evidence a duel had been fought. The acrid smell of the gunpowder dispelled. The birds settled back to their roosts. The mists hung under the trees as the sun broke through the fog and cast golden rays into the peaceful glen. A dark figure, which had blended in with the murky undergrowth, skulked away to be swallowed up in the indistinct distance.

Chapter One

London, 1809

The room was quiet except for an occasional murmur and the hushed slap of cards being dealt around the table. Candles shone softly from the chandelier that hung over the green, baize-covered table. As silent as statues, the servants in their livery stood in their inconspicuous positions. Six people sat about the table. Six pairs of eyes tried to hide feelings of disappointment or elation as they scanned the cards they were dealt. One pair of startlingly blue eyes, made all the more noticeable by the black silk mask that surrounded them, appeared extremely indifferent as they looked at cards that could not possibly lose. Bets were made and play went on until only two people were left in the game. One of them shook his head.

"Well, that's it for me," he announced as he threw in his hand. "I say, m'lady, you've the Devil's own luck this evening."

Blue eyes peered out from under thick black lashes, and the lady addressed smiled sweetly. "Nay, Lord Hoxly, the Devil has none, for Luck is a lady."

There were appreciative chuckles around the table as Lord Hoxly smiled his defeat. "May I compliment Lady Luck on her choice of companions? It is not every evening I can lose to such a beautiful victor."

"Why, thank you m'lord. Perhaps next time you will allow me to win even more."

Guffaws came from the other players as Lord Hoxly shook his head in silent admittance of his vanquishment, both verbally and at cards. The other gentlemen card players appreciated Hoxly's situation for they all, at one time or another, had been hapless victims of the beautiful Lady Jessica Carlton.

After gathering her considerable winnings, Lady Jessica, or the Lady Fortuna as she was known at the gaming house, bestowed a dazzling smile upon the gentlemen at the table.

"If you gentlemen will excuse me," she said, rising, "it has been an exhausting evening. It is time I took my leave. Good night."

The men rose with her and murmured their farewells as she left. They watched her departure with varying degrees of interest—from gentlemanly appreciation to outright leering. Settling themselves back down into their chairs, they called for brandy and cheroot before they, too, would leave for their homes.

Lord Hoxly remarked with admiration, "That, gentlemen, is one damned good-looking woman." He turned to the young man who had been seated next to Jessica. "I say, Durham, how is your foot?"

"Ah, the price of temptation," Sir Raymond Dahl, another player, said dramatically. "The Devil will always get his due."

"You are merely jealous that you were not sitting next to the lady yourself," Lord Patterson smirked. "Come, tell us, Charlie, how is that dainty foot which the lady trod upon so harshly?"

Young Charles Bellingham, Marquis of Durham, smiled ruefully. Jessica's heel had come down sharply on his instep when his hand had happened once too often on her thigh. Although his foot pained him, he considered it a small price to pay for exploring the lady's charms.

"She deserves the name 'Ice Witch'," he grumbled. "I've never met such a cold-blooded woman with such luck. I would give almost anything to look behind that mask she wears."

"She is probably hiding some horrible scar that disfigures her entire face," Lord Patterson yawned.

"Perhaps she is related to the royal family and does not wish her identity known," Sir Raymond suggested.

"Or perhaps she is the Prince Regent's new paramour." Hoxly added his view.

"Then it is no wonder she wears a mask," Patterson laughed. "It might get around that good King George is stuffing the treasury with her winnings."

As the others chortled at this witticism, one older gentleman who had lost heavily offered direly, "She's in league with the Devil, if you ask me. Never did go for her type. All skin and bones. No flesh."

"Where do you suppose she came from, and how is it she can outplay every bloody one of us?" Lord Hoxly wondered. "The chit can't be more than seventeen or eighteen."

"What's the matter, Hoxly? Feeling a bit put out?" Sir Raymond teased.

"Heard she was the daughter of some earl or other," Lord Patterson informed the table. "Now, this is just gossip, but I heard he got himself killed somehow. Mother died in childbirth. She's just a tragic little orphan with no one to care for her." Melodramatically, he spread his arms wide and gazed with mock innocence about the table.

"How unfortunate," Bellingham commented as he smiled wolfishly.

"Hmph. Her father should have made arrangements to marry her off early," the older gentleman grumbled. "I'll not have my daughter carrying on like that. Got it all arranged. Soon as she turns eighteen, she'll be married."

"Good thing, too, old man," Lord Patterson teased. "If she takes after your side of the family, she'll run to fat by the time she's twenty."

Laughter erupted around the table as the men rose and took their leave to retire to their homes for what little remained of the night.

Had Jessica heard their conversation, she would have been very amused. However, at that moment, she was leaning wearily against the seat of the carriage that was taking her to her lodgings. She had done well playing cards this evening. Perhaps she would have to play only once more before she had to return home to Braeleigh. Jessica sighed at the thought. There was a time when Braeleigh meant everything to her. Now, she was not quite so sure it did. Of course, the painful memories did not help.

Her mother's death, her father's remarriage to Margaret, and then her father's sudden, tragic death six months ago had combined to turn a place of peace into one of grief. Yet, Jessica would have been content to stay and try to heal her wounds and those of her eleven-year-old brother, Jason, had it not been for Margaret's cruel demands. Because of their stepmother, Jessica was living a dual life—one of the adventuress out to win every penny she could, and one of the genteel daughter of an earl who dutifully traveled home from the city every month to visit her brother and stepmother.

Another sigh escaped Jessica's lips. She gazed blindly at the passing houses and storefronts. Normally, the excitement of the life she was living would cause her blood to pulse through her veins. The gaiety, the laughter, the concentration of the game combined to help her repress the true purpose of her

14

sojourn in London, at least for short periods of time. But tonight, for some reason, a depression lay heavy on her heart. It was as if something dire was about to happen, only she did not know what or when. Could it be that she was giving up the struggle of wits she sustained with Margaret? No, she would not let it happen! She would never let her stepmother be victorious in her little scheme.

Gazing out the window, Jessica saw they were nearing her lodgings. Her bed, hard and lumpy though it was, would be a welcome sight tonight. Her evening at the gaming house had drained her more than she realized. Lord Hoxly had been a formidable opponent; Bellingham, the Marquis of Durham, had persisted in his advances to the point of being crude. It was a different life she lived now. No longer was she cradled in the warmth of her father's love and the companionship of her younger brother. She missed Jason terribly, and she ached for him, for Margaret was a shrew, and cared only for herself.

The carriage stopped before the rooming house where she had been living for the past six months. It was not exactly a palace, she thought wryly as she noted the stained whitewash and paint peeling off the door. Next door was the Green Dragon Inn. The sign, hanging above the door from one hook and creaking back and forth in the night wind, pictured such a creature. The poor dragon's fiery breath had turned to pale yellow and many of his scales had flaked off with the paint. Not a very formidable dragon, she noted. She turned her attention back to her own lodgings. There was scant light coming through the street-level windows. The landlady was probably sleeping and would not be pleased to be roused at such an ungodly hour. Jessica would have to endure her dire looks and scathing comments once more. Even though the woman was paid extra

15

for her trouble, she felt obliged to scold. At least, Jessica thought, the place was clean. And inexpensive.

She stepped down from the carriage, paid the driver, and knocked. After several moments, she heard the bolt thrown back and the door was opened a crack. An eye peered at her through the opening.

"It is I, Mrs. Cooper. Jessica."

There was a grunt and the door swung wide. As soon as Jessica stepped across the threshold, the door was slammed behind her and locked. Muttering, Mrs. Cooper shambled back to her room. Relieved that she had been spared a tongue-lashing, Jessica started for her room. The front parlor was deserted except for a rather mangy dog sleeping before the dying fire. He barely opened his eyes as she walked past. The candles in the sconces on the staircase had burned low and gave testimony to the late hour.

Jessica smiled as she thought of Donny waiting up for her. The woman would, no doubt, have something to say on the matter of the lateness of the hour. She usually did. However, had it not been for Donny's matter-of-fact acceptance of the situation and her constant mothering during the time they had been in London, Jessica doubted whether she would have been able to go through with her scheme.

Quietly, she opened the door to her room. It appeared deserted. There was a single candle burning low on the table beside the bed. The fire, however, crackled brightly. Jessica tossed her wrap on the bed and went to stand before the fire's warmth. The carriage ride from the fashionable section of London to the less respectable area of the city had been chilly and damp. Jessica had not wished to spend the few extra coins for a warming brick for her feet or an extra carriage blanket.

"Aye, and 'tis a God-forsaken hour ye be comin'

16

in," a voice Jessica knew well spoke from a dark corner.

Jessica laughed lightly. "Oh, Donny, stop complaining." She threw a pouch onto the bed. It landed with the heavy clink of money. "See what these late hours have brought us."

Mistress Donlin harumphed and rose from a chair in the shadows. Walking to the bed, she picked up the pouch and hefted it in her hand. "And a good thing 'tis, too, what with ye havin' to make payment soon."

Moving to a spot near the fireplace, she lifted a loose floorboard under the threadbare rug and emptied the pouch into a box nestled in the hiding place. Carefully, she replaced the board and smoothed the rug.

"Better I should have to return to Margaret every month with a payment than marry that fat, middle-aged baronet with thinning hair and red veins across his nose." She shivered delicately. "He made my skin crawl."

"Aye," Donny agreed. "Sir Percival Lowry was no great catch for any girl. But he would've saved Braeleigh for ye."

"If my father were still alive, he would never have consented to the marriage. He would never have even considered it. He wanted a love-match for me, and would have lost Braeleigh sooner than have me unhappy."

Donny straightened and turned to help Jessica undress, something she had done every night of the girl's life. "The Earl was soft where his daughter was concerned."

Jessica turned on Donny. "Just because you have been my nanny all my life, Mistress Donlin, does not give you the right to criticize my father!" Even as she said the words, she knew that Donny was right. Her father would never have given up his an-

17

cestral home. Was it not for just that reason that she was in London, living a precarious existence?

"Go on with ye," Donny told her sternly. "Ye know as well as I that ye father was never in his right mind after his lady died. All that gamblin' and racin' and schemes to make money. 'Twas the racin' that killed him and the schemin' that put ye here in the city."

Jessica shrugged and turned her back so Donny could unbutton her dress. "With Napoleon rampaging all over the Continent and England's shores threatened, the idea to build a new shipyard was the thing to do for a man loyal to the Crown. It was not his fault that the other investors ran off with the money and left my father with none to meet the Admiralty's orders."

"Hmph. Left yer father and you and yer brother with none, not to mention Margaret. Or have ye forgotten what it is yer about here in London?" Donny slipped a warm nightgown over Jessica's head.

"I've not forgotten. I believe I will only need one or two more evenings at the card table this month before I have enough for Margaret. The fifteenth of the month is almost a fortnight away. I may be able to begin on next month's stipend before we leave for Braeleigh. Perhaps there will be enough left over for some of that marvelous scented soap I saw at the perfumer's."

Donny's heart ached for the young girl. She should not have to hoard every penny, nor live such a precarious existence. Instead of giving her sympathy, however, she grumbled, "Seems to me y'ought to stay in and try goin' t'bed early. Ye be too thin. Next thing ye know, ye'll be gettin' sick, and then where'll ye be?"

"I'm fine, and I am not going to get sick," Jessica answered firmly as she sat before the small dressing table so Donny could brush out her hair. "Margaret will get her stipend."

"Ye ought to find yerself a husband to take care of ye. Ye shouldn't have to go to that gamin' place." Donny pulled the pins from Jessica's hair and began to brush the long, ebony tresses.

"I'll not marry till I'm ready. I'll not marry someone whom I don't love." It was an old argument, and Jessica said the words by rote, but she meant them.

"If yer father had lived, he'd'a found yer a husband," Donny said with conviction. "And ye would've married him whether ye loved him or not. It's a husband's place to take care of his wife an' her family. Ye wouldn't have t'be runnin' around like some strumpet all night."

Jessica climbed onto the bed and slid under the covers as she hid a smile. "Are you suggesting, Donny, that I should have been a dutiful stepdaughter and wed Sir Percival?" Jessica knew her nanny's feelings about Margaret and her scheme, but she loved to tease her.

Donny glared at her charge. "Yer stepmother had only herself in mind when she came up with that one."

Jessica giggled. "Come, Donny, I thought you wanted me to wed."

"Aye. To some nice lord who'll take care o'ye for the rest of yer days." She tucked the blankets around Jessica.

Jessica sighed. "I don't think I'll ever find one of those. The men who frequent the gaming houses are not looking for wives, for the women there are not— shall we say—acceptable."

"Seems t'me a young girl with a decent name and good looks ought t'be acceptable," Donny grumbled.

Jessica only smiled as she snuggled down into her pillow. "This girl with a decent name is tired, so if you are through your grumbling, I'll go to sleep," she murmured. "And blow out the candle when you leave, please."

Donny gave the blankets one last pat, then did as she was asked. On her way out the door she noticed the brightening of the sky in the east. Shaking her head, she headed for her own bed.

Chapter Two

A lone rider cantered through London's deserted streets. His magnificent stallion belied the man's shabby and bedraggled appearance. His clothes were wrinkled and mud stained, and his long, black cloak and soft, wide-brimmed hat pulled low over his eyes gave him an ominous, villainous mien. Yet, he did not have the bearing of cowering peasant or skulking outlaw, for he rode tall and proud.

As he reached the marketplace, the sun had just topped the buildings, and the peddlers and hawkers were selling their wares. The rider smiled in enjoyment as he wended his way among the various carts and milling people. He turned his horse down a quiet street lined with large, expensive homes. Turning through the gate of one of the larger, more impressive houses, he rode around the back to the stables. A grizzled, wiry little man came out of the stable building as the rider dismounted. His eyes ran over the familiar horseflesh, then took in the rider's shabby appearance.

" 'Ere now, what ye be doin ridin' 'is Grace's 'orse?" the little man demanded.

The rider turned to him and grinned. "His Grace gave me permission, Davy," he answered.

At the rider's words, the little man paled. "Yer

Grace!" he exclaimed, completely mortified. "Is it yerself?"

"None other, Davy. Didn't you receive word that I would be arriving?"

"Aye, but not so soon." Davy, out of respect for the master of the house, only gave a quick squint at the disreputable appearance of his usually immaculate and very fashionable Duke, then turned his attention to the Duke's horse.

His Grace, the Duke of Wyndham, caught his groom's glance at his clothes and realized he must look like something that had washed up on the banks of the Thames. He ran his hand over several day's stubble covering his chin. "Mr. Bonaparte's troops decided to race me to Dover," he said dryly. "It was not convenient to attend to my usual grooming."

"Aye, Yer Grace, but I bet ye gave them Frenchies a run they ain't soon goin' t' ferget," Davy chuckled appreciatively. Having been a groom for the Duke's family all his life, he felt a strong loyalty to the Wyndham name, and had been rewarded with the knowledge that his Duke was involved in some sort of secret mission in France.

"Let us hope they do forget, Davy," the Duke told him. "I would not want them to remember my tricks and capture me if I return."

Davy shook his head and grinned. "Ye'll jest think up some new ones, Yer Grace."

"Hmm," was the Duke's only response to Davy's comment as he sniffed the air appreciatively. A delicious aroma wafted from the kitchen. Tossing the reins of his horse to Davy, he said, "Give Apollo extra rations, Davy. He deserves them. It's been a while since my last meal. I think I will pay my respects to Aggie." Walking with purpose, he headed toward the kitchen.

Davy watched his Duke's retreating back and shook his head. God only knew what hornet's nest the Duke had been involved in for the last six months. He hadn't been leading the good life, that was for sure. Lost some weight, too, by the look of it. He sure was a strange one for a member of the ton. Weren't many other gents who'd risk their lives by living by their wits in an enemy country. Had to hand it to him, though. Slipped from one life to the other as if it were the most natural thing to do. He'd disappear for months at a time, then show up, pretty as you please, as if he'd only been gone overnight. The head groom shook his head. He certainly couldn't figure it out. He'd better stick to taking care of the horses. Turning, he bellowed for one of the stable boys.

The Duke arrived at the kitchen door and stepped inside. A very plump woman in a crisply starched dustcap was wielding a rolling pin with great enthusiasm. She spoke without looking up.

"Now, y'git yerself back out t'the stables, Davy Cooke. I'll let ye know when th'muffins be ready."

"Can't I stay and wait, Aggie?" the Duke asked softly.

Aggie looked up and her mouth dropped open. "Ooooh, Yer Grace! Beggin' yer pardon." She dropped a small curtsy of apology, then her face broke into a grin. Placing her hands on her hips, she looked the Duke up and down. "Ain't ye a sight fer sore eyes? Looks like ye haven't eaten or washed fer weeks. Haven't changed none from when ye was just a young whelp."

The Duke laughed at the observation of the family's lifelong cook. "You're not far wrong, Aggie." He walked over to the woman and put his arm around her plump shoulders. "How about some of your famous muffins when they're done?"

Aggie blushed with pleasure at the Duke's compliment. "Looks like ye need more'n jest muffins. All skin 'n' bones ye be." She felt his ribs and shook her head. "All skin 'n' bones."

At her words, the Duke deftly swiped an orange from a bowl on the table. As he peeled it, he turned to one of the scullery maids who stood gawking at him. "You there, girl."

The young girl hurriedly dropped a curtsy. "Y-Yes, Y-Yer Grace?" she stammered, suddenly terrified that this tall stranger who seemed to be the master of the house had noticed her.

"What's your name?" the Duke asked. Evidently there had been new additions to the household staff since the last time he was home.

"M-Mary, Yer Grace."

"Well, Mary, go rouse my manservant, Wilson, and inform him of my return. Tell him I would very much like a shave and a bath."

"Yes, Yer Grace." Mary dropped another curtsy, then relieved to be out of the fearsome Duke's presence, she sped out the door.

The Duke watched her hasty retreat with amusement, then walked down the central hallway into his study. His eyes ran over the familiar room with its massive walnut desk, its book-lined walls, its deep, red leather chairs. Everything was unchanged. A decanter of brandy caught his eye, and he contemplated having a drink to chase away the chill in his bones. Thinking better of it as he remembered the only thing he had eaten in the last thirty hours was the orange he was munching, he crossed the thick carpet and stood before the fireplace. The portrait hanging above the mantle was what drew him.

His father. Except for the color of the eyes and the wig his father wore, it might almost be a painting of himself. The jaw had the same squareness as his own, and the nose was arrogantly aquiline and straight. But where the portrait's subject showed the slightest hint of softness about the mouth, the Duke's showed a hardness and determination. The expression of the eyes was the same, however. They looked out with a certain recklessness, daring the world to do what it would.

He smiled wryly. He wondered if his father would have put himself through the hardships that he had just endured for six months. Probably. His father would have thrived on the uncertainty and risks. It had been his father who had suggested a commission in the army for his restless younger son. If he had not been born into the nobility, his father probably would have been a pirate. The Duke gave the portrait a casual salute, then left the room.

He climbed the stairs two at a time and turned to the right. Walking to the end of the hall, he opened the door to his own room. As he entered, a figure emerged from the corner and bowed to him.

"Welcome home, Your Grace," Wilson greeted him. "It is good to have you back, Master Damien."

Damien smiled at his longtime valet. "It is good to be back, Wilson. How have you fared in my absence?"

Without changing his very proper expression, Wilson answered, "It was rather boring, Your Grace."

Shaking his head in mock disappointment, Damien said sadly, "Ah, Wilson, I fear you are a rogue at heart. A good man's man would never approve of the life I lead."

Wilson nodded once. "As you say, Your Grace, a good man's man would never approve. I fear, should I ever leave your employ, that I would never be hired as a *good* man's man."

"Ha! Spoken truly, Wilson." The Duke sat on a chair and held out a booted foot. Wilson tugged at the jackboot until it slid off Damien's foot. "Ah, Wilson," Damien sighed, as he wiggled his freed toes. "I can not decide between the bed or the bath. I am tired to my very bones." The Duke stood and began to strip off his clothes. He tossed each piece to

Wilson, who caught them deftly.

"May I suggest, Your Grace, the bath first, then a bite to eat? You will rest easier with a shave and a satisfied belly."

"You are a better manservant than any I have encountered, Wilson. You have decided for me." Damien stepped into the steaming tub that had been prepared. He sighed in contentment as its warmth enveloped him. Having been awake and on the run for the past several days, he decided coming home to all its comforts was comparable to being in heaven.

"There, Wilson. Massage that spot will you? There's a good man," he said as Wilson scrubbed his back. The Duke wriggled his shoulders to get out the kinks as Wilson kneaded his tired muscles. "Ah, that's wonderful, Wilson. Perfect. I fear I am getting too old for being chased about the countryside by Napoleon's man, Fouché. Damn, if he didn't almost succeed in capturing us this time."

"If I may say so, Your Grace," Wilson ventured, "It appears that you have seen some inhospitable times."

"An understatement if I ever heard one, Wilson." The Duke shook his head. "That Minister of Police, that Fouché, he's a sly one. He spread false information that led us right into a trap. The old tart we kidnapped turned out to be one of Fouché's men in disguise. Left a trail behind him big enough for a blind man to follow, right up to our hideout door. We escaped by the skin of our teeth."

"I assume you led Fouché on a merry chase through the French countryside, Your Grace." Wilson came as close as he had ever come to smiling as he considered the French soldiers being outwitted by his Duke.

"A very merry chase. Well, enough of that. I'm quitting, Wilson. Finished."

"Finished, Your Grace?" Wilson was so surprised

he stopped in the middle of rinsing off his master.

The Duke squinted at him. "Wilson, do you mind?" The soap was running from his hair into his eyes.

"Oh, sorry, Your Grace. Forgive me."

When he was completely rinsed off, the Duke stood and his man wrapped a large, fluffy towel about his middle and another about his shoulders. "Yes, I'm finished. No more spending my nights in damp forests or musty hovels. It's time I spent my nights in featherbeds with a warm, curvaceous companion. Eh, Wilson?" He winked suggestively.

"Your mother is most anxious for you to sire an heir, Your Grace. She will be quite relieved that you have come to this decision."

"Yes, I know she will be relieved," the Duke agreed with a hint of impatience. "She never lets me forget my duty." He shook his head. "Damn my brother for getting himself killed in that duel."

"Your Grace!" Wilson exclaimed, scandalized.

The Duke stopped drying his hair and looked at his valet. "Wilson, I loved my brother. Ever since we were children, I admired him, looked up to him, but to get involved with that woman was pure idiocy. She was years older than he and married besides." He shook his head again, this time in grief. "It should have been Brian who is called the Duke of Wyndham, not I. He was the elder."

"Yes, Your Grace." Wilson agreed not because he thought the older brother would have made a better duke, but because he, too, missed him. Before he had become the valet of the present duke, he had been the valet of the older brother.

"Well, enough of this," the Duke said briskly as he strode to stand before his cheval mirror. Picking up a bristle brush, he began to straighten out the mess of short golden curls atop his head. "Wilson, just lay out something suitable for lounging for now. I will

27

dress later, after I sleep."

"Yes, Your Grace." Wilson bowed and retired.

Immediately, a knock came at the door. "Enter," the Duke called without thinking. The young maid, Mary, came in with a tray laden with food.

"I brought your breakfast, Your Grace" she said as she dropped a curtsy. Her eyes widened, and she blushed at the Duke's state of undress. Only a towel tied about his waist kept him from being completely naked. Desperately, the young girl tried not to stare at the muscular physique displayed before her.

"Thank you, Mary," the Duke said, not paying full attention to her. He was busy brushing his hair into place. When he realized she still stood with the tray, he turned to her with some impatience. "Well," he asked with a raised eyebrow.

Mary curtsied again. "Beggin' pardon, Your Grace," as she became even redder, "where would you like this?"

The Duke gestured to a small table by the window that overlooked the rear gardens of the house. "Over there will be fine." Realizing finally he was scantily covered, he hid a smile of amusement at the girl's obvious discomfort. Very different from the maids of France. Those girls were used to seeing their masters unclothed and their mistresses step out in public in the flimsiest of clothing. When Mary had placed the tray on the table and turned to leave, the Duke smiled warmly at her, making her blush even more. He was in awe that someone could get so deep a shade of red. "Thank you, Mary. That will be all."

She curtsied quickly and almost ran out the door. Chuckling to himself, the Duke threw down his brush and attacked his meal. It took little time for him to devour almost everything Aggie had sent up to him: the fluffy eggs, scones, coddled cream, slices of ham, kippers, and wonderful coffee from South America. When he had eaten his fill, he fell into bed and immediately went to sleep.

It was mid-afternoon when he awoke. He felt refreshed and eager to resume the more normal side of his life. Dressing quickly in the clothes Wilson had laid out for him, he went to pay his respects to his mother. He found her sitting at her desk in her room. She was dressed for travel.

"Damien!" she exclaimed with pleasure when she saw him. "Wilson told me you had arrived home."

Damien walked to where she was sitting and bent over her outstretched hand, then he kissed her lightly on the cheek. "How is it that every time I come home, you look younger than before?" he asked with a grin.

"You are a sweet-tongued rogue, Damien Trevor, Duke of Wyndham," she laughed. "Just like your father."

"Evidently not enough to keep you from running out as soon as I return home." He looked pointedly at her travelling clothes and the small valises still scattered about her room.

"Ah, yes," she sighed. "I would love nothing better than to remain here and reacquaint myself with my only child, but there is a problem with one of the tenants at Wyndham, and I understand that there are other things that need to be seen to there. Besides, I have had enough of the city. I need to be home with the fields and trees around me."

"I can understand that," he said gravely. "For me it is the very opposite."

His mother noticed the deep lines of fatigue about his mouth as he turned his head. "Was it so bad this time, Damien?" she asked with concern. "You look so tired."

He shrugged, walked to the window and rested on its sill. "Not so bad," he answered offhandedly. "I just have not had very much sleep lately." He smiled wryly. "All those balls and masques, and the mad so-

29

cial whirl, you know."

"Don't you give me that rot," she scolded. "I know you were chasing about France ferreting out some important bit of information for His Majesty. It seems to me you could expend your energy here at home and find yourself a decent wife and sire an heir."

With a mischievous glint in his green eyes, he said, "Perhaps I already have, mother."

The momentary shock on the Duchess's face made Damien laugh. "Oh, Damien," she complained, "I am serious. You have been living a dangerous life. The only way the title will be continued is if you father a son—legitimately."

"What of Cousin Harry? The name could go on through him."

"Cousin Harry is a ninny. Would you truly want him to carry on the line?"

"No, I can't say that I would," he grinned. Then becoming serious, he said, "That is why I have come home. I am home to stay."

The Duchess said nothing for a moment. What her son did not say told her more than any explanation he could have given.

Forcing herself to look away from the exhaustion and cynicism that had suddenly appeared in his eyes, she asked, "Will you be staying here in town?"

"Yes, for a while," he told her.

"Good. Have an affair of the heart. You need someone to help you forget. But please, no children from the wrong side of the covers."

"What?" he asked in mock surprise. "No scandal to set the local wags gossiping? I rather thought I might pursue the daughter of that wealthy merchant again. She was a delectable piece of fluff."

"She has been married off to the third son of Viscount Somebody-Or-Other. Thankfully," she said as she straightened a hat on golden hair streaked with grey. "There was a child six months after the nuptials."

"A premature birth, to be sure," Damien murmured wickedly.

The Duchess gave him a look of annoyance and rang for her maid. The woman must have been eavesdropping, for she appeared almost immediately. "I am ready to leave, Randall. Have Jacobs get one of the footmen to carry down the rest of these valises." Randall disappeared again to do her mistress's bidding. The Duchess turned back to her son. "Come, see me off."

Damien held out his arm to his mother, and they left the room together. As they descended the wide, curving staircase to the front hall, Damien glanced down at the woman at his side. She was still very attractive, and although her hair was streaked with grey, her face was unlined and her green eyes sparkled. Despite the sorrows she had seen, first of her husband dying, then her eldest son being shot in a duel, she still carried a zest for life. Her figure remained girlish, and if seen at a distance, she would be taken for a much younger woman. His mother was an amazing woman.

When they reached the bottom of the stairs, Jacobs, the majordomo, greeted Damien solemnly and announced that Her Grace's carriage was waiting. The Duchess turned to Damien and placed her hand to his cheek.

"Enjoy yourself, my son," she said with tender concern.

Damien captured his mother's hand and gave it a squeeze. "Do you doubt that I will, madam?" he asked with his green eyes glinting mischievously.

His mother smiled back. "Not one bit," she laughed, and swept out the door.

Damien watched the carriage rumble down the drive and out into the street before he turned from the door. His eyes swept the majestic foyer of his London house, and he breathed in deeply. Home. He was home. A tiny smile lifted the corners of his mouth, and he headed in the direction of his study. It was time for that long-awaited brandy that he had denied himself that morning. He would settle himself before the fire and wait patiently for the evening to arrive.

Chapter Three

Jessica entered the establishment of Madame du Barré. After greeting Jacques, Madame's very large majordomo, and handing him her cloak, she stood and looked out over the elite of London society who had come to titillate their excitement and slake their thirst for more than the usual round of balls, dinner parties, and theater. The establishment of Madame du Barré was neither coffee house nor club; it was a gaming house, one with a reputation for fairness at the tables and wickedness elsewhere within its walls. Madame du Barré's was not for the faint of heart or pious of nature. Although many of the forms of entertainment were illegal, nothing had been done to close the doors, for many of the guests were members of His Majesty's government, including the Prince of Wales on occasion.

Jessica smiled at Jacques, who had murmured that Madame was most anxious to speak with her this evening. Not everyone was allowed past the front door by Jacques, but to be told that Madame wished to speak with one was indeed an honor. Of course, once inside, it was customary to pay one's respects to Madame, but it was not always the rule that a person would be warmly welcomed or even acknowledged.

A burst of laughter carried over the noise of the

crowd, and Jessica turned her head in its direction. It came from the gold salon where Madame usually spent her evening. There must be an exceptionally witty crowd this evening, Jessica thought. She moved through the crowd toward the sound of the laughter. Gentlemen, clad in the latest of fashions, bowed to her, and women in the most daring of gowns nodded their greetings. The ladies for the most part wore dominoes, half-masks, as Jessica did, to conceal their identities and preserve their reputations. Yet, it was usually not difficult to discern the better known members of society.

It was to this establishment that Jessica came when she first arrived in London. Strangely, it had been from Margaret that Jessica had learned of Madame's establishment. On one of the few times that Margaret had talked about her life previous to becoming Lady Carlton, she had mentioned going once to Madame's. She had told Jessica how exciting it had been to wear a mask and mingle with such a rakish crowd. Jessica, in her innocence, had been fascinated with the story. When she had asked her father if he had ever been there, he had become furious with Margaret and had told Jessica that should she ever find herself in London, under no circumstances was she to go near the place. The matter had been forgotten until her father's death and Margaret's insistence on Jessica's marriage.

When Jessica had first conceived of her plan to outwit her stepmother, she had decided that the gaming house of Madame du Barré was exactly the type of place that would best suit her needs. She had gone to visit Madame during the afternoon, when no one else had been there. The name of her father had gained her entrance and a meeting with the woman.

As Jessica moved toward the gold salon, she remembered her first impressions of the house and the woman who inhabited it. She had been led upstairs and only caught glimpses of darkened rooms that contained gaming tables and other shadowy shapes of furniture. The room where she was finally brought, however, was bright with sunlight and decorated in expensive velvets and brocades and furniture imported from France. An attractive, middle-aged woman dressed in a lavender silk negligee reclined on a chaise.

Jessica stood at the door to the gold salon and watched that middle-aged woman flirt outrageously with the men around her. Madame had accepted the frightened, eighteen-year-old girl and her desperate scheme to make money; she had even given Jessica money to get started and helped with her wardrobe. All Madame had asked in exchange was for Jessica to deliver letters to a certain Monsieur Montaigne who lived not far from Braeleigh, and to keep these letters a secret. Madame had been more than generous.

Jessica's career as a professional gambler had been launched. She visited Madame's establishment with great frequency and became well known to everyone. To the patrons, however, she remained a mystery. To their inquiries Madame imparted little information about her, and Jessica herself imparted even less. The only information they had concerning her that they knew to be true was the strange name she gave herself—that of Lady Fortuna—and the fact that she was a very shrewd card player who rarely, if ever, lost. It had become somewhat of a contest among them to see who would be able to defeat her at the card table. It also had become a contest to see who would be able to break down her virtue, for she always carried about her a very cool and aloof demeanor.

Catching sight of Jessica, Madame waved her lace fan at her. The men about her, wishing to know who it was that Madame was waving to, opened ranks as they turned around to see. The gap in the crowd allowed Jessica an unobstructed view to the woman who sat royally among her fawning subjects.

Jessica's eye was caught by a stranger who stood slightly behind and to one side of Madame's chair. One hand rested almost possessively on its back. The stranger was tall with hair the color of spun gold, and his skin was unfashionably tanned from being in the sun. He stood easily, appearing confident of Madame's attentions while the others about him jostled nervously for a word or a glance from her. What struck Jessica the most, however, were his eyes. Even from across the room, she could tell they were the color of bright emeralds and seemed almost as hard. He watched Jessica approach Madame with a speculative look that Jessica found terribly unnerving. She wished he would turn away.

"Ma petite," Madame greeted her as she held out both hands. *"Très ravissante,"* she approved of Jessica's appearance.

Jessica smiled in thanks as she kissed Madame on both cheeks. She knew the dress she wore, which Donny had made for her, was becoming. It was a simple, black, watered silk gown cut quite low over her bosom with a high waistline defined by a gold ribbon tied beneath her breasts. The sleeves were long and tight and ended in a point that covered the back of her hand. Her hair was piled in curls on top of her head and entwined with another gold ribbon that matched that on her dress. She wore no jewelry but for a simple gold locket that teased the cleavage between her breasts.

Madame turned to the stranger who stood beside her chair. *"Monsieur le Duc,* do you not think *la petite fille* beautiful? Ah, but where are my manners? You have not met our enchanting gambler. May I present the Lady Fortuna? *Ma petite,* this is His

36

Grace, Damien Trevor, Duke of Wyndham."

Jessica, despite her wish not to, was compelled to look up into those green eyes. They seemed to mock her very existence. An aura of self-possession emanated from him and a strange magnetism demanded one's attention. He was dressed simply, yet elegantly, in a coat of rich, brown velvet with tight, fawn-colored breeches that just missed being indecent. His waistcoat was a pale yellow satin embroidered in white silk, and it covered his white silk shirt. A very large topaz winked out from the folds of his intricately tied stock. He was easily the handsomest man Jessica had ever met. She curtsied politely and extended her hand.

"A pleasure, my lady," he smiled slowly, as he bent over her fingers.

"Damien has just been telling me news from the Continent," Madame sighed. "It is so long since I have been home."

As Jessica smiled sympathetically in Madame's direction, she felt the Duke's lips touch the back of her hand. It was a bold, improper action, one that should not have surprised her in Madame's establishment. She jerked her hand away as the shock of his touch on her skin sent a strange, thrilling sensation up her arm. Sending him a cold glance of warning, Jessica was unprepared for the intense, calculating look in his eyes. It was gone immediately, replaced by an amused, mocking glance, but Jessica had seen something beneath the gentlemanly exterior of the man before her. It frightened, yet fascinated her. Her mind searched frantically for something to say to give herself time to regain her composure. She focused on Madame's words.

". . . because of that man, Napoleon," she was saying. "Bah. He is a wily one. He says *Liberté! Fraternité! Egalité!*, and then he makes himself emperor."

"But he is conquering Spain and Italy for France,"

Jessica argued. "Do you not wish to see your homeland grow more powerful, Madame?"

Madame smiled at her. "Not at the expense of so many lives, *ma petite. Mais,* I do not live in France any more, eh? I am here, in England, with all my friends."

"And we are so very glad that you are here, Madame," the Duke bowed graciously. "Where else would we find so charming a lady as yourself?"

Madame flipped open her fan and held it coyly before her face. "Ah, *Monsieur le Duc,* you have a golden tongue. Did you learn that from Monsieur Napoleon himself, or did the angels bless you at birth?"

The Duke smiled at Madame but his eyes looked at Jessica as he said, "It was not I who was blessed by the angels, Madame."

Madame saw his glance and pouted. "Naughty boy," she scolded as she snapped shut her fan and tapped him on the arm with it. "It is impossible to flirt with two ladies. You will make them both sad, and then you will be left with none."

"Madame, with you, I wear my heart on my sleeve," the Duke said gallantly. "But I find I cannot ignore the charms of this quite intriguing lady." He took Jessica's hand and, this time, kissed the inside of her wrist.

Jessica was aghast at his brazen action. Although dealing with men who made advances was not new to her, for some reason the Duke caused her a great deal of apprehension. Summoning up her courage Jessica gently disengaged her hand.

"You are too kind, Your Grace," she said coolly. "But surely, you have met other women more intriguing than I in your travels? Did not Madame say that you have just returned from the Continent? I have heard that the women of Spain are hot blooded beneath their demure facades, and the women of Italy will take two men to their beds."

"I'll wager after those women of Italy have had Damien, two men wouldn't be enough," someone said from the back of the group.

The Duke bowed his acceptance of the compliment in good humor, and the others standing about chuckled.

"And the women of France?" Madame asked with a smile. "What have you heard of them, *ma petite?*"

Jessica smiled at Madame. "That they are urbane and witty and set the fashion for the rest of the women of the world."

"Perhaps that is so," the Duke said, "but none has the beauty of the English rose."

His eyes caressed the features and figure of the young woman before him. In spite of her wish to remain cool, Jessica felt herself blush.

Madame saw Jessica's discomfort and took pity on her, yet she did not wish to interfere in the Duke's interest in Jessica. "There is a game just beginning in the green room, *ma petite.* Perhaps, Your Grace, you would be interested to join in also?"

"That sounds intriguing," Damien answered her without taking his eyes from Jessica. He offered his arm to her. "Lady Fortuna, may I have the pleasure of escorting you?"

Jessica had no choice but to take his arm. At least he was not Sir Percival, the man her stepmother would have her wed. At the thought, she looked up at the Duke to compare the two men, which was silly. There was no comparison. The Duke was handsome and charming, where Sir Percival was ugly and vulgar. Realizing the ludicrousness of her comparison, she smiled to herself.

Damien caught her smile and raised an eyebrow. "Is there something that the lady finds amusing?"

Caught off-guard, Jessica blushed again and was surprised into telling the truth. "No, Your Grace. I was just comparing you to someone I know."

"I see. And this other man, do you find him attractive?"

Jessica laughed at the idea of Sir Percival being found attractive by anyone. "Not at all, sir. It was a ridiculous thought." Not wishing to say more about it, she quickly changed the subject. "I have never seen you here before, Your Grace. You do not come here often?"

"As you heard before, I have been on the Continent for quite some time. When I am in London, I am an occasional visitor to Madame's, but, perhaps, I may begin to come more frequently." He turned his gaze on Jessica in speculation.

"Do not come to Madame's only on my account, Your Grace, unless you wish to lose at cards," Jessica told him. "I am not looking for any amorous entanglements."

"Really," the Duke murmured, not at all put off.

Jessica was relieved to find that they had at last arrived at the green room. She did not like the Duke's last murmured comment and the hint of challenge it held. The man was too handsome and too charming for her tastes. She had never heard of him before, and that was something quite unusual. Gossip about this baronet or that earl, this vicomtesse or that duchess was always making the rounds at Madame's. Yet, he and Madame had acted as if they were old friends — or lovers. Something was not right. She would have to question Madame about him as soon as she had the chance.

Jessica and Damien entered the green room, one of the smaller gaming rooms in Madame's establishment. It was only large enough to hold one table for seven or eight people. There were several chairs and a settee at one end of the room where the players could relax during breaks in the game. The room was, indeed, green, from the patterned carpet on the floor, to the dark green brocade on the walls, to the various shades of green satin covering the furniture. There was a sparkling crystal chandelier that cast its light over the whole, and crystal wall sconces helped illuminate the room. Jessica had gambled in this room many times and won quite large sums. She considered it a good omen that Madame had suggested this place on the evening she had met such a man as the Duke of Wyndham.

The other gamblers, all men, were already seated about the table, but play had not yet begun when Jessica and the Duke arrived. There were only two empty chairs at the table. Jessica breathed a silent sigh of relief that they were not next to each other. She did not wish to have to sit next to the Duke all evening. She needed to concentrate on the game, not some skirt-chasing man intent on making a conquest.

The men greeted the two newcomers as they seated themselves. Jessica was relieved to discover that everyone knew His Grace—relieved and intrigued. Who was this man that he was so well known by everyone but her? However, she put it out of her mind. The less she had to do with him, the better.

There was something about him that was different from the other men she had met at Madame's. It was not that he was so handsome, with his darkly tanned aquiline features and dark golden hair, for she certainly had met other handsome men. It was not even his charm or his smile, though she found his smile devastatingly winning. It was, rather, the aura about him of an untamed animal, taking what he wanted when he wanted it. Yet, he was not vulgar or uncouth, for in the few minutes she had been with him, his manners had been flawless, and he had shown her every respect, despite the boldness of his kiss on her hand. However, he gave the impression of being slightly uncivilized, that perhaps he should have been a pirate instead of a Duke. In short, he frightened her.

After a few pleasantries, the game commenced. Jessica played well at first, winning most of the hands. After the first hour of play, however, her luck seemed to leave her. She was having trouble concentrating, for every time she looked up, a pair of brilliant green eyes seemed to be mocking her. As the hours passed, the pile of money before Jessica grew smaller, while the pile of money in front of His Grace multiplied. In desperation, she tried to bluff with a very large bet on the next hand. The Duke was not fooled. He held better cards and won the round. Nervously, she placed her hand over the few coins still before her. There was barely enough to pay for a hired carriage to get her to her lodgings.

She decided it would be wise to leave the game before all her money was gone. She had lost a considerable sum, almost a third of what she owed to Margaret. It would take several more nights at Madame's to make up the amount needed to pay her stepmother.

She tossed her cards into the middle of the table. "I believe you gentlemen have outwitted me this evening," she told them with a smile. "You have repaid me in kind for my winning so much from you on previous evenings. I bid you good-night, sirs."

The gentlemen stood and consoled her with, "Bad luck, m'lady. Next time will be better. The cards were against you," and similar things. As she accepted their condolences, she noticed that the Duke called one of the ever-present servants over and spoke to him in a low tone. The servant nodded and left the room quickly. Jessica thought nothing about it, as she listened to the comments and words of sympathy from the other players. Only the Duke said nothing as he sat back in his chair and watched her with a curious glint in his eyes.

Finally able to take her leave, Jessica walked with her usual dignity out into the main gaming room. Blinking back the tears in her eyes, she kept her chin up as she maneuvered through the people milling about the tables of chance. Fortunately, no one stopped her to greet her or pass the time. She was greatly relieved when she finally reached the entrance hall and was able to ask Jacques for her cloak and to fetch her carriage.

While she waited, she tried to push her depression to the back of her mind, but her thoughts invariably turned to Braeleigh and her brother. Oh, Jason, she promised, I'll make back the money I lost tonight. Margaret will not have any reason to use you for her own ends as she did me.

With one last sigh, she pushed away her dark thoughts as Jacques returned through the doorway.

"Pardon, Mademoiselle, but your carriage is gone," he said.

Jessica frowned at him. "That's impossible," she argued. "I paid the driver extra to wait for me. Let me look." Impatiently, she pushed past the majordomo and stepped out the door. She looked up and down, but only a few private coaches waited silently for their wealthy owners. Her carriage was gone! It was impossible to find a carriage for hire at this time of the night. What could she do? How was she to get home? It was very dangerous to walk, for gangs of thieves and cutthroats roamed the streets seeking out vulnerable victims. It was out of the question to go back inside Madame's and ask someone for a ride. Her pride had suffered enough for one night. She could not face anyone after losing so badly. She was sure the news of her loss had spread as soon as she had left. It was too difficult to act as if losing meant nothing to her.

As she stood wondering desperately what to do, a

deep voice spoke next to her. "Is there some difficulty, m'lady?"

Jessica jumped at the sound. She had heard no one approach. Turning, she discovered the Duke at her elbow. He smiled engagingly.

"I apologize if I startled you, but you seemed troubled by something," he said.

The Duke of Wyndham was the last person she wished to see at that moment. Jessica pasted a smile on her lips as she spoke flippantly, "It would seem my luck has fled me completely this evening. My carriage seems to have left, so I am without a ride home."

"Then it is fortunate indeed that I also decided to leave Madame's early. I will give you a ride home." He spoke as if there was no other alternative. It was almost an order.

"That won't be necessary, Your Grace," she told him. "I am sure Jacques will be able to find me some means of transportation."

"Nonsense. Besides, Jacques is occupied with other matters at the moment." He turned and gestured through the door.

Inside, Jessica could see two gentlemen challenging each other to a duel, and the lady for whom they fought had fainted into Jacques' very capable arms. She glanced up quickly at the Duke's strong face and found him watching her as he waited politely for her answer. Immediately, she dropped her eyes in order to think more clearly. She could not make a decision while looking into those shards of emeralds. The Duke did have a point. Truly, what other choice did she have? Knowing that she was placing herself in jeopardy, she resolved she would be very alert for any improper action on the part of the Duke. That decided, she began to tell him she accepted his offer, but he was already summoning his coach.

As she watched the dark, shiny vehicle pulled by four matching bays approach, she had a moment of panic. He could not learn of her poor lodgings. It would begin to dispel the air of mystery she had so carefully built around herself. He would realize that she was no better than an adventuress, out to win riches and perhaps a husband or benefactor, even though that was not the truth. What if he told others where she lived? Would the men still wish to have her gamble at their tables? Would the women still include her in their gossip? She sent a furtive glance in the Duke's direction. His hard profile was turned to her. He did not seem the type to be spreading tales.

The carriage stopped before her, and she found she had little choice left. The Duke had his hand beneath her elbow and was propelling her up the small step and into the dark interior of the coach. "May I give the driver an address?" he queried.

There was only a slight hesitation before Jessica answered clearly, "The Green Dragon."

She watched carefully for his reaction. He merely raised an eyebrow and then passed the information on to his driver. The Duke climbed in beside her, then there was a slight lurch as the carriage started up.

Feeling the need to say something to him, she said shyly, "I hope I am not taking you too much out of your way, Your Grace."

"It is never out of my way to help a beautiful woman," he answered with a grin, as he turned those damnable green eyes on her. "I understand you rarely lose at cards. Were you so troubled tonight because your husband will beat you for losing so badly?"

Jessica's look was sharp as she answered, "I have no husband."

"Really?" the Duke murmured. "How long have

45

you been a patron of Madame's establishment?"

"About six months."

"Your parents do not object to their daughter frequenting such a place?"

"I really do not believe that should concern you, Your Grace, but since you ask, both my parents are dead," she answered coldly. This man was infuriating. He had discovered more about her in a few short minutes than any of the other patrons of Madame's had discovered in all the time she had been going there.

"I am sorry," he said simply.

His apology surprised her into one of her own. "You are forgiven, sir, provided you forgive me for being so sharp with you. I have no right to offend someone who is kind enough to offer me a ride to my door." Her smile was genuine, and it charmed him.

"You need do nothing more than smile, m'lady, and all is forgiven." He watched her dimples deepen at his compliment, and decided he had never met a more intriguing woman. His curiosity piqued, he ignored her obvious reluctance to speak about herself, and asked, "You live with your guardian at the Green Dragon?"

Jessica's smile faded quickly as she stared at him. The man's tenacity was incredible. Her temper flared at his question, yet she had enough common sense to realize that she should not anger him. He was a Duke, powerful and influential; and he was a man, strong and muscular. She was alone with him in his carriage, a dangerous circumstance.

"Please," she said firmly, "I would rather not discuss it."

He raised an eyebrow at her tone. "Of course," he acceded coolly. He allowed her this victory because he had learned a great deal about her already. He knew she was unmarried, probably unattached to

46

any man. Most likely, she was living by her wits, for no lady of wealth would live in the squalor of the Green Dragon. And she hid some secret, for her reluctance to speak of herself was more than some artifice to keep men's attention. He watched the darkened streets as he considered the woman beside him.

Jessica watched the Duke stare out the window and was greatly relieved for his silence. He appeared to be ignoring her, and she was just as happy to be left to her own thoughts. His presence beside her made her uncomfortable, and that alone gave her pause. No man had ever had that effect on her. What was it about him that made her afraid of his glance and shy away from his touch?

Hoping that the journey to the Green Dragon would be over soon, she sat tensely against the soft leather cushion and clasped her hands together in her lap. The Duke rode easily with one booted foot up on the seat across from him. Damn him for being so relaxed! she fumed. What did he care that she had lost a small fortune this night? He did not have a furious stepmother to face if he did not have enough money to bring home. Or the threat of marriage to someone who repulsed him. What did he know of bill collectors and creditors? What did he know of grief at losing a loved one? Jessica turned and stared out her own window.

The coach stopped before the inn. Jessica did not let on that she actually lived in the rooming house next door. She had decided that if this man wished to come looking for her, he would not find her where he thought she would be.

In silence, the Duke helped her from the carriage. His hand remained on her elbow even after Jessica stood firmly on the ground. She could feel its warmth through her cloak and dress. Taking a step back so that he was obliged to drop his hand, she boldly looked up into his face. Once again, that strange mingling of fear and fascination slid through her. Quickly, she lowered her eyes.

"Thank you for your kindness, Your Grace," she murmured. "I should still have been left at Madame's if you had not happened along." She smiled shyly up at him.

"It was my pleasure to help a fair maid in distress," he answered with a smile. "It was certainly a much better ending to the evening than I had anticipated. Having been so long away from home, I have lost track of many of my friends."

"How lonely for you. Certainly, you will reacquaint yourself with them after a short time. After all, the season will be starting soon."

"Yes, that is true. Perhaps I will make your acquaintance again at one of the balls or masques."

Jessica laughed at the irony of his statement. If her family had not fallen on such hard times and it had not been for Margaret, it might have been very possible that she would have met this man during the upcoming season. "Hardly, Your Grace. My name does not appear on any invitation list."

"If I knew what your name is, I could change that," he offered, knowing the name she used at Madame's was a false one.

Becoming immediately wary, Jessica stiffened at his gentle probe. "That, Your Grace, is none of your business," she huffed. "Do not presume that because I accepted a ride from you, I am of easy virtue. I thank you for your generosity, and I bid you good night." Nodding once, she turned on her heel and stalked away into the shadows. It did not even occur to her that she had completely passed by the door of the Green Dragon.

Damien watched her disappear, and he stood staring after her for several seconds before he climbed back into the carriage to be driven home. She was a puzzle, but the most intriguing puzzle he had ever met. He had listened to the gossip about her at Madame's, but had not really believed any of it. Until he met her. She was obviously well bred and cultured, but as for her being the daughter of an earl, he was doubtful. She had played cards too well this evening. Oh, yes, he had beaten her, but he had seen the skill with which she played. No titled gentleman would allow his daughter to gamble, and certainly not at Madame du Barré's. The chit had to be an adventuress, albeit a very desirable one. He could still envision her sitting next to him in the coach. His hand reached out and rubbed the leather cushion where she had sat. Her fragrance lingered in the air. She would be a delightful diversion, just the thing to make him forget the hardships he had endured. The Duke smiled to himself in anticipation.

Jessica slowly climbed the stairs to her room. Things had gone very badly this evening. It was not possible to give up, however. She would have to go back to Madame's the following evening. There was no other place for her to go. She would not be allowed entrance to any of the clubs or private homes where the stakes would be high enough for her to regain what she had lost, and the other gaming houses would not accept her. In dejection, she pushed open the door to her room.

Donny could tell at a glance that Jessica had lost. There were no words exchanged, but the little woman immediately set about helping her mistress get ready for bed. After Jessica's warm nightgown had been slipped over her head, her shoulders suddenly straightened.

"Damn him!" she exploded, as her fist banged against the bedpost. "I will not allow him to mock me!" She turned to face Donny; her blue eyes blazed. "I'm going back, Donny. I will show him

49

that I am not to be trifled with. Do you know, I believe he dismissed my carriage this evening so that I would have to ride home with him? The audacity of the man!" Fuming, Jessica lapsed into silence.

Donny did not pursue the matter, even though she was intensely curious. After brushing out Jessica's hair and tucking the girl into bed, she slipped from the room. When she left, Jessica's eyes were burning holes in the ceiling.

Chapter Four

Damien stood before his cheval mirror and examined his reflection critically. His wine-colored, superfine jacket and buff-colored riding breeches fit perfectly. His boots gleamed softly, and his stock was tied in an intricate new fashion. Wilson brushed the shoulders of his jacket once more and stepped back.

"If I may presume to say so, Your Grace, you are looking like your old self again," the valet offered.

Damien's eyes were mischievous as he caught Wilson's in the mirror. "And what, pray, did I look like before, Wilson?"

Wilson coughed uneasily as he tried to think of some tactful answer to give. In truth, the Duke had looked wretched when he had first arrived home a week ago. He had appeared haggard and much too thin. Now, however, the bounce had returned to his step and the twinkle to his eyes.

Damien watched his man for a moment, then relented. "That bad, eh? Well those days are gone, Wilson. Where's my hat?" He turned and his valet handed him a tall beaver hat, soft leather gloves, and riding crop. "I have a fitting this afternoon with my tailor, and tonight I believe I will be going to dinner with the Viscount Whitehead and the Earl of Shatley."

"Very good, Your Grace," Wilson bowed. "I will

have everything ready."

Damien threw him a quick smile. "Good man," and he went out the door and down the stairs.

As he reached the bottom of the winding staircase, Jacobs was waiting for him.

"General Drayton is here, Your Grace," he informed the Duke. "He is waiting for you in your study."

Damien's eyebrows lifted slightly. "General Drayton, you say? How curious. Thank you, Jacobs." He handed the man his hat, gloves, and riding crop, then headed for his study.

Upon entering the room, he was met by a grey-haired gentleman who wore his soldier's uniform with distinction. He bowed formally to Damien. "Good morning, Your Grace," he said.

Damien hid a smile of amusement at the man's formality. It was strange how roles could be reversed so quickly. "Good morning, General." He held out his hand to his former commander and smiled warmly.

Grateful that the Duke was dispensing with formality the general shook Damien's hand. "It appears that retirement agrees with you."

"It is so much easier than living in a hovel." Damien motioned to a chair and the two men sat. "Can I offer you some refreshment?"

"No, no. Thank you just the same. My visit here will be brief."

"Ah, I see," Damien nodded. "I take it this is not a social call, then? You have not come to discover how I have fared since returning home?"

The general cleared his throat. "No, I am afraid this is not a social call. We have a problem, and you are the only man who can help us."

The Duke raised a cynical eyebrow. "I seem to remember hearing that somewhere before, George."

General Drayton smiled. He had used the same words when he had first recruited Damien Trevor as a spy for England. "The—ah—problem, if you will, is here in London," he went on. "Madame du Barré to be exact."

"The Barré, you say!" Damien exclaimed. He shook his head. "A loss to the men of London."

"I daresay," the general agreed dryly. "Well, she is spying for Napoleon. We know it, but we can't prove it. She rarely, if ever, leaves London, so we know she has someone relaying information to the coast. We captured her last courier, but the devil tried to escape on the way back to London, and he was shot by one of his guards."

"God's blood, George, how do you expect to win this war with numskulls in your command?"

General Drayton looked pointedly at the younger man across from him. "That was my thought, exactly."

Damien sighed. "So you want me to find out who the Barré is using as a courier and capture him for you."

"If you could, it would help us greatly." The general leaned forward in his chair and spoke earnestly. "Damien, you know I would not ask this of you, if there was any other way. You are known at Madame's, and so would not arouse suspicion. My other men, well, they are not suited to this sort of thing as you are."

"Spare me the arguments, George," Damien interrupted caustically. Then in a milder tone, he went on, "I will do this one more thing for you, General, but I can not afford to spend any more of my time in the service of His Majesty. I have to see to my own affairs, which I have neglected for too long. Besides, it has become too dangerous. I can not jeopardize the lives of my men. Fouché has come too close to discovering my identity and that of my men."

General Drayton nodded. "I understand perfectly, Your Grace." He stood up to leave. "Thank you, Damien. If there is ever anything I can do for you, please let me know." As Damien stood the general shook his hand. "Don't bother to see me out. I will find my own way." He turned and left.

Damien sank back down into his chair and stared thoughtfully after him. This assignment would not be all work. It might even be enjoyable. Although he regretted that London would lose a witty, entertaining lady in Madame's arrest, he knew that before that could take place, he would have to spend many nights at her establishment, a not unpleasant task. There was also a certain young lady with eyes like sapphires and hair like ebony, whom he had met at Madame's. He smiled. At least he could live in comfort and enjoy his pleasures while he accomplished his task. Whistling, he left the house for his ride.

During the week after her encounter with the Duke of Wyndham, Jessica had frequented Madame du Barré's every evening. She had won back all she had lost, plus a sizable amount more. Several nights earlier, she had made the sum of the stipend for her stepmother; she was now playing to once again solidify her reputation of a shrewd gambler. She would be leaving for Braeleigh on the morrow, so this would be the last time she would be going to Madame's for several days.

"Be extra careful with my hair, Donny," she said as the woman arranged her shimmering, black tresses. "I want to look special tonight. I want the men at Madame's to remember me."

Donny snorted. "Haven't I been doin' yer hair since ye was a babe? An' I don' see how they could ferget ye at that place. Ye've been there every night fer the past six. Sit still, or I'll havin' to be doin' yer hair all over again." This last comment came as Jessica squirmed to see better what Donny was doing.

"There. An' if that don't suit ye, then nothin' will."

Jessica looked critically at herself in the small mirror and smiled. "It's perfect, Donny. Thank you."

The little woman said nothing, but Jessica could tell she had been pleased with the compliment. Donny walked to the bed and picked up a flow of blue silk. "Come on, then," she said. "I'll help ye with yer dress."

Donny had made the gown Jessica was wearing this evening, as she had made all the girl's gowns. It was the same clear blue as Jessica's eyes and showed off her small, perfect figure. The bodice was cut low and the skirt was composed of tiny, vertical pleats that rippled and clung to her body as she walked. It was a sensuous dress, made to cause heads to turn and keep men's minds from the cards in their hands.

Jessica was finally satisfied with the way she looked and was ready to leave. Donny handed her a warm, woolen cloak that she placed about her shoulders. Pulling the cloak's hood over her hair, Jessica said, "Don't wait up for me," and walked out the door.

When Jessica arrived at Madame's, it was somewhat later than her usual arrival time. After paying her respects to the owner of the establishment and receiving the woman's approval of her appearance, she went to the private room where she would be playing cards. There was a game already in progress. One chair was empty, its back to the door. She recognized all of the players but one, who was in the chair to her right. Before she had time to speculate on the identity of the man, however, the round ended and her presence was noted. The gentlemen stood up as she approached the table.

"Good evening, gentlemen," she smiled as she glanced around at them. She turned to the man to her right to introduce herself. Her smile froze on her face as she recognized the two green eyes watching her. Recovering quickly, she nodded a greeting.

"Your Grace," she murmured.

"Ah, good show!" Lord Patterson exclaimed. "You two children have met."

"Yes," the Duke answered. "The lady and I spent a most interesting evening together."

Jessica did not miss the interested glances that were passed about the table at the Duke's loaded remark. Not wishing to enlarge on the subject and cause more gossip, she remained silent. However, much to her dismay, it was Wyndham who helped her into her chair, not Lord Hoxly who was to her left. Why did the Duke have to be here tonight of all nights? Jessica fumed angrily to herself. One more evening and she would have been gone for several days. He could have come to Madame's then. Besides that, he was sitting right next to her. It just was not fair!

As Jessica waited while the cards were being dealt, she noticed there was a considerable pile of money before His Grace. Did he never lose? Well, tonight, she was ready for him. Tonight, she would win.

Play continued for several hours. Except for an occasional witty or charming remark from the other players at the table, the time seemed to drag on forever for Jessica. The pile of money before her became smaller and smaller, while that before the Duke grew. Becoming desperate, Jessica decided to do something she had never done before at Madame's: cheat. Her father had taught her how to cheat when he had taught her to play cards, only because he wanted her to know when other people were doing it. She had become so proficient at it that even her father had been unable to tell when she had dealt from the bottom of the deck. She doubted that the Duke, who was her only target, would be able to catch her.

It was Jessica's turn to deal. She held her breath as she dealt the cards around the table. The Duke said nothing. He merely picked up the cards before him.

Bets were placed and play went on. Jessica won the hand; the Duke lost.

The turn to deal travelled around the table twice more. Each time it was Jessica's turn, she won and the Duke lost. She was convinced he did not realize what she was doing. It was so easy. Perhaps she should have tried this before.

It was her turn to deal again. She picked up the cards, shuffled them. Just as she was about to deal them out, a darkly tanned hand snaked out and grabbed her by the wrist. With wide, frightened eyes, she looked up into twin shards of green ice.

"It would seem that the lady is dealing from the bottom of the deck," the Duke said. His voice was quiet, menacing.

Jessica blinked, but had the presence of mind not to display her intense fear. "Of what are you accusing me, Your Grace?" she asked innocently.

"I think that is quite evident," he told her. "I believe it is called cheating."

"How dare you, sir!" she demanded hoarsely. The only thing to do was to bluff her way out. She jumped up, knocking over her chair in the process. She was hoping he would let go of her wrist and allow her to leave, but his grip became even tighter.

"But I do dare, my lady," he answered in a still quieter voice. "You see, I have been watching you. It is only to me that the cards come from the bottom of the deck. Would you care for a demonstration?"

One of the other men at the table cleared his throat and tentatively suggested, "I really don't think that is necessary, Your Grace."

The Duke acted as if he had not heard. Never taking his eyes from Jessica's face, he turned the deck of cards face-up and began to recite each card as he took it from the top of the pile. "Four of hearts. Seven of spades. Jack of spades. Trey of diamonds. Shall I go on?"

Jessica's eyes closed and she turned several shades paler. Suddenly, he was on his feet. He seemed to tower over her.

"If you were a man, I would demand satisfaction with weapons tomorrow at dawn," he told her roughly. "But since you are a woman, there will have to be another way." He paused for a moment, then his voice became silky. "I believe I have just the solution." One arm went about her waist and pulled her close against his unyielding body. He forced her head back with a thumb under her chin as if he meant to kiss her. "Perhaps Madame would not be pleased to discover that one of her patrons has been cheating in her house."

Jessica's eyes widened in fright. "No, please!" she gasped.

"Then you will have to convince me otherwise," he told her coldly.

Lord Hoxly leapt to his feet. "This has gone far enough, Your Grace," he said stiffly. "I demand that you leave the lady alone."

The Duke's chilling glance fell on the man. "You 'demand' sir?"

"Yes." Lord Hoxly stood at his full height. "If you require satisfaction from this young lady, I will gladly stand for her."

Jessica glanced from one man to the other in uncertainty. She was relieved that someone at the table saw fit to protect her from the rogue who held her, but she did not wish anyone harmed because of her. Before she could gather her wits enough to speak, she saw the Duke's eyes narrow dangerously.

"This does not concern you, Hoxly, nor any of the other gentlemen present. If you value your life, I would suggest you remain silent. You know I do not speak idly if I tell you that I will call out every man at this table if there is a hint of rumor concerning this night. The insult was to me and me alone, and the satisfaction I demand will come only from this lady. I presume I make myself clear, gentlemen?"

His glance swept around the table, and the men seated either nodded or lowered their eyes in acceptance of the situation. Even Lord Hoxly sank back into his chair. When he was convinced there would be no further interference from the others, the Duke turned back to Jessica.

His thumb casually caressed her cheek as he murmured, "Remember, my sweet, persuade me." He released her without warning and strode from the room.

There was deathly silence for several seconds after his departure. Suddenly, Jessica swayed on her feet. As Lord Hoxly reached out to steady her, everyone came to life and began talking at once. Hoxly helped her into his chair.

"Are you all right, my lady?" he asked solicitously.

Jessica managed a weak smile for him. "Yes, thank you. It was merely a slight dizzy spell. The man frightened me."

"He is, indeed, a very frightening man," Hoxly agreed. "Allow me to get you something to drink." Jessica nodded.

She heard Lord Patterson complain, "Good heavens, Wyndham was nasty. Not a word of this, he says. What fun can we have if we don't gossip?"

Jessica's attention was drawn to a servant who slipped into the room and gathered up the Duke's winnings along with her own, then left as unobtrusively as he had come. By the time Lord Hoxly had returned with a glass of brandy, her mind was racing. She had to get out of there and speak to the Duke. How long would it be before he relayed what went on tonight to Madame?

She took a small sip of the brandy, sighed deeply, and stood up. "If you will excuse me, I think I will leave. Thank you for your kindness, my lord."

"Of course, my dear, not at all," Hoxly said with fatherly concern. "May I escort you to the door? Or perhaps to your home?"

"No, please don't trouble yourself," she told him. "I feel much stronger now, and I am sure the Duke will not bother me any more this evening. Good night, sir." The other gentlemen were deep in conversation, so she was able to slip out unnoticed.

She walked quickly to the door, collected her cloak, but before leaving, she asked Jacques if he was acquainted with the address of the Duke of Wyndham's residence. After she told him it was to return something the Duke had left behind that evening, the majordomo gave her the address. Then she went out into the night. Her coach was there waiting. She gave the driver the address, and they sped off.

As the coach drove up to the house, Jessica saw it was in darkness. Perhaps, she thought, he had not come straight home, after all. Well, she was prepared to wait for him all night if necessary. She dismissed the carriage and walked up to the front door. It was slightly ajar. She thought that a bit strange, but terribly convenient. At least she could wait for him inside without waking the household. It did not occur to her that there might be others, like parents or siblings, living in the house who might discover her.

Without another thought, she pushed open the door and walked in. She was in a large foyer, but it was dark, and she could not see any of its details, yet she could feel its size extend above her head and stretch out before her. Looking about, she spied an open door. Knowing that creeping about a strange man's house in the middle of the night was the ruination of whatever shreds of a decent reputation she had, she nonetheless only had the slightest hesitation in crossing the threshold. This room, too, was dark, but there was a fire blazing on the hearth. It seemed odd that a fire would have been lit in a deserted house, but who was she to question? The warmth of the flames beckoned to her, and she went to stand before it. She held her cold hands out to soak up its heat.

"I am glad that you came, Jessica," a voice she recognized all too well spoke from her right.

Gasping, she spun around. He was there, sitting in a chair, a brandy in his hand. He had been there all the time! He had been waiting for her! She felt like a small child who had been discovered with its hand in the cookie jar.

To give herself time to regain her composure, she asked, "How did you know my name?"

The Duke shrugged. "A simple matter of asking Madame. She enjoys making love-matches."

Jessica opened her mouth to protest his term for their relationship, then decided she had better keep silent. This was not the time to argue about insignificant things. Turning back to the fire, she took a deep breath to steady her nerves.

"I . . . I had to talk to you," she ventured. When he said nothing, she went on. "Please, you mustn't tell Madame that I cheated. I have never done it before, and I will never do it again. Please." She turned back to face him and tried to read his expression, but his face was in the shadows.

He watched her as she spoke, pleading with him. He was torn between his righteous anger and his foolish desire for her. He had never met such a beautiful creature. She was an enigma, one minute seductive and alluring, the next cold and aloof, the next childlike and innocent. Yet, she had played him for the fool, and for that she would pay.

Finally, he spoke. "How do I know that you will never cheat again? You seem to be quite expert at it, which leads me to believe it is something which you do quite often. For one, such as myself, who has been wronged, you seem to be asking rather much."

Jessica could see this was going to be quite difficult. The Duke was not one to be easily swayed by a coquettish smile or a pouting lip. He was not a man who would forgive easily. She was not going to be able to charm her way out of this predicament.

"What else can I say, Your Grace, except that I am sorry?" she tried. He merely raised an eyebrow. "What do you want of me?" she whispered desperately "I will do anything you ask."

Carefully, he placed his glass on the table beside him. In one graceful movement, he rose from his chair and came to stand before her. Jessica had the courage not to back away. A strange tension enveloped her with his nearness. She fought to keep her feet planted where they were. He gazed down at her a long moment before he spoke.

"Anything, Jessica?" he queried softly.

Her clear blue eyes looked up into his green ones, darkened from the shadows. The firelight played across his face and made it appear demon-like and handsome in turns. She suddenly knew what he wanted, what she would have to pay to keep his silence. A thousand thoughts raced through her mind. Was the price really too high to pay to continue in her current existence? The memory of Sir Percival floated before her eyes, and she knew the answer to her question.

"Yes," she answered him. "Anything."

Reaching out, he untied her mask and slowly removed it from her face. Her beauty was totally revealed to him, and it caused the blood to race in his veins. It was not an ugliness she had been hiding, but rather a perfection that would cause the angels to be jealous. He unclasped her cloak and pushed it from her shoulders. A tremor ran through her body when his hands brushed her skin. He stood gazing at her a moment, drinking in her loveliness. Then, wrapping his arms about her, he brought his lips down on hers, searing them with his passion.

It was her first taste of a man's kiss. It was not totally unpleasant at first. She enjoyed the strong feel of his arms holding her, the hardness of his body against hers, the warmth that enveloped her. Then the kiss became more demanding. Jessica felt as if she was being smothered. He took her breath, and still he did not stop. She began to panic. She had never felt this way before. She began to push against his chest.

"No," she murmured. "Please, stop."

When he released her, a puzzled, annoyed expression darkened his face, but he did not move away.

She gave a small, nervous laugh. "I . . ." she started, then realizing she could not explain her action, merely shook her head in bewilderment. She was too embarrassed to admit she had never before been kissed by a man. Besides, she was supposed to be worldly; that was part of her persona at Madame's.

"I will not force you, Jessica," he told her coldly. "It is your decision. You know the cost of my silence. If you wish to pay the price, you will find me upstairs."

Jessica watched him move with controlled strength and feline grace to the door and out into the foyer. His footsteps echoed in the dark as he crossed to the stairway. She heard him begin to climb the stairs.

She turned back to the fire as she worried her lower lip between her teeth. His touch had been exciting, his kiss frightening. Jessica had known no man intimately, and the prospect of making love with this stranger, handsome and intriguing though he was, struck fear into her heart. Not only that, she also would lose the one thing which she could bring to her husband should she ever marry—the fact that she had saved herself only for him.

Jessica closed her eyes and sighed. It had not been easy living by her wits these last several months. She had been very cautious about becoming too friendly with anyone—male or female. It was self-preservation that caused her to react with coolness toward everyone. Being a lone female in a place like Madame's, without the benefit of protector or benefactor, she had been fair game for any man who wished to try his luck at trying to seduce her. Only Madame's very thin blanket of guardianship had saved her on several occasions. What would happen now if she succumbed to the Duke? Could she pay his price and still remain aloof?

She glanced sideways to the door. She could not allow him to inform Madame of her cheating. Even though Madame was the one person with whom she had a close relationship, she could not impinge on that friendship. Madame did not countenance any form of dishonesty in her establishment. Jessica would be barred from ever playing there again, and she did not have entrance to any other gaming house. She would be unable to pay Margaret. She would be forced to wed Sir Percival.

Jessica came to her decision. There was no recourse but to climb the stairs and go to the Duke. Taking a deep breath, she started on her journey.

As she came to the top of the stairs, she wondered if he often had women guests in his bed. Thinking back on the gossip she had heard about him since his arrival, she thought it very probable that he did. Although not the usual course for a gentleman to entertain his paramours under his own roof, the Duke did not seem to be the usual sort of gentleman. Also, the absence of any servants in the house was quite noticeable. They were probably quite used to his late-night assignations.

There was one door that stood ajar at the end of the hall. Firelight flickered through the opening. She turned in that direction, and before she realized it, had arrived before it. As she hesitated before the dark wood of its panels, she could feel her heart pound a nervous tattoo. She swallowed once, trying to beat down her fear. Reaching out, she placed her hand on the door and slowly pushed it open.

The room that greeted her was a dark, masculine room. It had been subtly lit by a group of candles in one corner on a table. A fire crackled warmly on the hearth. A large, four-poster bed with simple, but elegant, blue velvet hangings dominated the room.

The Duke was sitting on the very edge of the bed and was leaning back against the headboard. He had removed his jacket and waistcoat and untied his stock. His shirt was open halfway down his chest. He rested a casual arm across one knee that he had drawn up. The other long, muscular leg hung over the edge of the bed, his booted foot on the floor. In his right hand was a thin, vicious-looking rapier whose point rested on the floor boards beside his foot. Jessica had never personally met any pirates, but she assumed that, if she did, they would resemble Damien Trevor, Duke of Wyndham, as he looked this moment.

Jessica stopped just inside the door. A chill ran down her spine. It had been a mistake to come to the Duke's bedroom. It was still not too late to turn and run, but somehow, she felt rooted to the spot. Her eyes were riveted on the lean figure who relaxed on the bed.

"Come here, Jessica," he spoke softly from the dimness.

His voice was like a crack of thunder in the silence of the room. Jessica jumped. Slowly, as if drawn by an invisible string, she moved forward, closer and closer, until she reached the foot of the bed. Another few steps and she would be standing right next to him. The Duke raised the point of the sword, stopping her just inches from its tip.

"That is far enough," he told her.

Jessica's breath came in tiny gasps. Her fear ran rampant through her, for she did not know what this man meant to do. He was a Duke, arrogant and powerful, and in comparison, she was a nonentity. If he killed her, there would be no one to question her disappearance. No one but Margaret, who would not care; Jason, who was too young to do anything about it and Donny, who was just as powerless.

Unknowingly, she created an entrancing vision. Damien was stirred by her more than he had been by any woman. His eyes raked over her body, the swell of her breasts, her tiny waist, the curve of her hips. Her thick lashes shaded her clear blue eyes, making them dark in her pale face. Her softly shaped lips were parted slightly in her apprehension. Whether she knew it or not, her whole being beckoned to be loved.

"Undress," he commanded.

Jessica hesitated. She had never been unclothed before any man.

"Take off your clothes, Jessica, or I will cut them from you." The Duke moved the point of the sword threateningly.

Her hands moved to her back to unfasten her dress. She knew he would not hesitate to carry out his threat. She pulled the dress from her shoulders; it fell to the floor with a sigh. Her petticoat followed. Blushing hotly, she stood clad only in her chemise and stockings and shoes. She fought the desire to cover herself.

Indicating her shoes and stockings, the Duke pointed his sword to her legs. "Remove those," he ordered.

She stepped out of her shoes and removed her stockings.

"Take down your hair."

Slowly, one by one, she pulled the pins from her hair and allowed it to cascade about her shoulders and down her back to her waist.

Finally, she was able to find her voice. "Please," she whispered. "Do not hurt me."

At her words, the Duke stood in one swift movement. Defensively, Jessica took a step backward. The Duke's teeth flashed white in a smile. Turning, he placed the rapier across a nearby table.

"Contrary to what you may have heard, Jessica, I do not make a practice of harming beautiful, young women," he informed her as he advanced. "You need not be afraid."

Reaching out, he pulled her easily toward him. He took her face in his hands and kissed her gently. This kiss was closer to Jessica's idea of lovemaking, and she decided that it was rather pleasurable. Perhaps this would not be so terrible, after all, she thought.

The Duke was vaguely aware of her inexperienced response, and somewhere, in the back of his mind, he was surprised. For a woman to be so self-possessed and assured in a place like Madame's and to have had little experience in intimacies with men was most unusual. His mind did not dwell on it, however. He was intent on the sensuous creature in his grasp.

Damien's fingers lost themselves in the mysterious depths of her hair, as he drank in the soft feel of her and the faint scent of jasmine surrounding her like an aura. One hand travelled down her back to her rounded bottom and pressed her close. He wanted to ravage her with wild desire, but something warned him to go gently.

Jessica could feel the warm hardness of him against her thigh. It frightened her, but his hands worked magic on her body, and made it come alive under his touch. Her fear receded with his soft caress. Seemingly of their own volition, her arms crept around his neck. When he raised his head, her eyes had darkened from her aroused passion.

His hand moved from the tangle of her tresses,

down the slim column of her neck, over her shoulder, to one rounded breast. He teased its rosy tip as he kept her gaze locked in his. Her breath came quickly through her parted lips. The sensation of his hand through the thin material of her chemise was more exciting than she had dreamed possible. A wonderful warmth enveloped her. Her lids drooped languidly over her eyes.

He pulled at the ribbons holding her chemise and allowed her breasts to come free. His hand brushed across her softness as he pushed the thin material away. Making her lean back on his arm, his mouth travelled the same path as his hand—down her throat, across her shoulder, to her breast. As his mouth closed on its tip and his tongue flicked at it playfully, her breath caught in her throat. A frisson of excitement ran through her. He retraced the road to her mouth with his own and once again captured it. Instinctively, her lips parted, allowing his tongue to ravage the sweetness they had guarded. Finally, raising his head, with a little smile, he released her. Turning away, he undressed quickly.

Jessica felt suddenly bereft. The feelings he had awakened in her were intoxicating. She wanted more, much more. As he discarded his clothes, she watched him in a trance. She swayed slightly as if she were drunk, as, in fact, she was—drunk on the passion and desire he had aroused in her. Her body tingled all over. Her skin had come alive, responding to his every touch. Never had she realized that the touch of a man could feel so magical.

His body was magnificent, even to her naive eyes. Broad shoulders tapered down to narrow waist and hips. The muscles in his arms and legs were hard and sinuous, and rippled under his skin when he moved. In spite of the heat of embarrassment she felt in her face, she could not look away. She wanted to watch his every movement.

When he turned back to her, her eyes caught on the thatch of golden fur that covered his chest. A thin, white line, from shoulder to breastbone, marred the symmetrical beauty of it. Without thinking, she reached out and traced the scar. Her hand skimmed the softness of hair that spread across his chest, then followed the golden arrow of hair down across his flat stomach that led to his manhood. Suddenly realizing her boldness, she stopped just short of it. She could not bring herself to touch him there.

Glancing up shyly, she caught his amused gaze. Her cheeks flamed in embarrassment, and she jerked her hand away as if she had been burnt. He took her hand and kissed her open palm, then, his arms came about her. Scooping her up, he deposited her gently on the bed.

He leaned over her and kissed her again. Jessica's arms went readily about him. With his tongue, he traced a line down her throat, between her breasts and over her stomach. He lifted her thigh and intimately stroked the silky inner skin with his hand. A sigh of pleasure escaped her when his tongue branded a tattoo in the same spot, but when he came too close to her secret place, she held him away. Fear made her stiffen.

That niggling voice came again in the back of his head to go gently. He wanted to taste her desperately, but he would not force her. He sensed her naiveté. Stretching out beside her on the bed, he nibbled at her ear as his hand again claimed her breast.

"Are you still willing to pay my price, Jessica?" he asked against her throat. He would give her every opportunity to back down.

She let her eyes close. "Yes," she whispered with a sigh.

Jessica did not allow herself to think beyond the immediate present. The Duke, so far, had been gentle, and what he had done to her made her feel wonderful. She had come this far. There was no turning back now. Surprisingly, she found the sensations he aroused far from horrible. In fact, she rather wished they could go on forever.

He explored her body once more with his hands and mouth. She opened to him like a budding flower. Her throaty moans of pleasure aroused him until he could stand it no longer. He covered her body with his, pressing her into the bed. Jessica marvelled at the way their bodies fit together so intimately. His skin against hers made her tingle. She held him close and ran her hands over his back. He buried his face in her hair.

"You are a witch, Jessica," he whispered. Then he drove into her.

The sudden pain caused her to arch up against him and cry out. Confused, Jessica lay very still, her eyes squeezed shut. She had known that there would be pain her first time, but after the exquisite feelings the Duke had aroused in her, she had dismissed the knowledge. Now, the truth frightened her. Would there be more pain if he continued? Would there be pain every time she made love with a man, if, in fact, she ever did again? Not knowing the answers, and expecting the very worst, she prayed this encounter would be over soon.

Damien, surprised at the resistance he had broken through, waited for her pain to subside. The fact that she was still virginal had not entered his consciousness, but as he lay with her, the memory of her nervousness and shyness and unpracticed naiveté returned to him. A pang of guilt surged through him at the thought that he had forced the seduction of a virgin. But then, his hurt pride reared up and changed his way of thinking. She deserved this deflowering. She had made a fool of him. Besides, he had not forced her. And he wanted her.

His thumb found the hardened peak of her breast

and he stroked it gently. Slowly, Jessica began to relax. When his mouth took his thumb's place, Jessica felt the surge of excitement all the way to her toes. The pain the Duke had caused began to recede. She felt a throbbing need to be fulfilled, and she moved hesitantly against him. Her movements fanned his desire, and he held her against him as he began to thrust into her.

Jessica gave herself up to the insistent, driving need that engulfed her. Her mind reeled, and she lost all sense of reality. There was only the man above her in her world. She felt as if she were in a whirlpool, being drawn deeper and deeper into the vortex. Down, down, they fell, clinging to each other, until the bottom gave way and the sudden, great release came. Never in her life had Jessica experienced anything like it. She thought she was going to die. With every ounce of her being, she grabbed at the man who held her.

As the waves of feelings receded and her world tentatively came back into focus, the import of what had just happened hit her squarely. Like floodgates being opened, the sobs came from deep within her. Damien rolled off her and held her close as she clutched at him and cried against his chest.

"Why didn't you tell me you had never been with a man, Jessica?" he asked softly as her tears quieted.

She sniffed and wiped at her eyes. "You would not have believed me if I had." Trying to hide her embarrassment, she sat up quickly and pulled away from him. Shrugging one shoulder, she went on, "What difference does it make now, anyway? The deed is done. You have your payment, Your Grace."

He sat up next to her and made her look at him. "Was it so bad, my sweet? Did you not enjoy giving payment as much as I enjoyed taking it?"

"You are despicable!" she spat at him.

Laughing, he answered, "And you are beautiful,"

and pulled her back down with him.

Jessica glared up at him as he lay above her. "Have you not had enough, Your Grace? You have deflowered a virgin and avenged your honor at the same time. Not every man can make that claim."

Damien winced. "Must you be so crude?"

"Crude?" Jessica echoed. "It was not I who was crude. You were the one to force me into your bed."

"Tut, tut." He tapped her nose. "I did not force you. I asked you. And I did this." He bent his head and tickled her throat with his tongue. "And this." His hand slowly caressed her breast. "And this." He sucked gently where his hand had been.

In spite of herself, Jessica moaned as he began to fan once more the fires of her passion. A part of her brain told her she was crazy to succumb to him again, while the rest of it decidedly ignored its warnings. What this man did to her was exciting beyond belief, and she wanted more of it.

Acknowledging her acquiescence, he made love to her again, bringing her passions alive a second time. When it was over, there were no tears from Jessica. Giving an exhausted, contented sigh, she fell asleep in his arms.

She dreamt of green fields and her mother and father playing with her. She was a young girl again, and there was Braeleigh, and everything was right. But, suddenly, she was alone, her brother was standing next to her, and it was dark; they were lost. Her stepmother's face floated before her; she was smiling cruelly. It was no longer her stepmother, but Sir Percival; he was surrounded by faces she did not know. She was at Madame's and the faces were yelling at her. "Get out! Cheater! Liar! Get out!" Then there was a pair of mocking green eyes. She tried to run away, but she fell. Hands grabbed at her.

"Jessica! Jessica!"

Those eyes! His eyes! Then she realized she was

awake, and he was looking at her. It took a moment to remember exactly where she was.

"Are you all right?" Damien asked her gently. "You're shivering." He held her close and smoothed her hair with his hand until her tremors stopped.

Jessica accepted his gentle comforting. In his embrace, she felt safe from Margaret and her cruel demands. Yet she also realized that even as she felt protected in this man's arms, he also was a threat to her and her precarious existence. Slowly, her strength of will returned.

"I am all right, now," she said, her voice muffled against his chest. She felt foolish for being so afraid of a dream. Turning in the bed, she noticed the sky beginning to brighten. "I have to go."

"Go where?" he demanded. "What do you have to go to?"

Sitting up, she smiled slyly. "I have to go where all creatures of the night go, Your Grace. Back to my lair. You did call me a witch, didn't you?" She glanced back at him under lowered lashes. "Or was I mistaken? Perhaps it was the Devil whispering in my ear."

Running his hand up her back under her hair, he laughed. "It was not the Devil, my sweet, only a man bedevilled by your beauty."

"Truly, sir, you are the Devil, for no mere mortal man could seduce a witch such as I so easily." Sliding out of his reach before she again succumbed to his touch, she jumped out of bed and began gathering her clothes.

Through narrowed eyes, he watched the delightful picture she made in the dim light of the room. She was like a woodsprite as she bent and straightened, retrieving her things. A thought began to form in his mind.

Jessica glanced up to find his eyes on her. Quickly, realizing she wore not a stitch of clothing, she

73

donned her chemise, but her dress was slipped from her grasp before she could put it on. The Duke was standing near her with the ripple of blue silk dangling from his hand.

"Please, Your Grace," she entreated. "My dress." She knew that determined look in his eyes. She was just as determined that he would not have his way with her again.

"Not until you stop calling me 'Your Grace.' My name is Damien. Say it," he commanded arrogantly.

Jessica looked at him with wide eyes. Even after a night of lovemaking, she felt still the tiniest bit of trepidation in being near him. Yet, she did feel a certain sadness in having to leave. But to call him by his given name! He was still the powerful Duke of Wyndham to her.

"Say it, Jessica," he said in a softer tone.

She swallowed. "Damien," she whispered.

"Was that so difficult?" he smiled.

When he smiled at her like that, she found her resolve melting away. Careful! she cautioned herself. You mean nothing to him. With her emotions well under control, she allowed him to slip her dress over her head. He turned her around to fasten the back. Pushing her hair aside, he brushed his lips across her nape. When she felt his caress, she moved away, but was stopped by his hand on her arm.

"Don't be so skittish," he laughed softly. "I promise to behave."

When he finished doing up her dress, she thanked him and walked to the mirror. Her hair was a riot of tangles.

"Will this help?" he asked as he held his brush out to her.

"Thank you," she murmured shyly and began brushing her hair.

While she was occupied, Damien dressed quickly. When he saw that she had finished, he walked to the door and held it open for her. They descended the stairs in silence. He collected her cloak from the floor of the salon where it had been left several hours previously.

As he placed it about her shoulders, he asked, "Will you come again tonight?"

Jessica stepped away and whirled to face him. Her emotions were a jumbled confusion inside her, but what she felt most keenly was that he had received double his due for the injury she had done him. In her mind, his pride had been soothed many times over. It was time she allowed her own self-esteem to emerge.

"Do you think because you have stolen my maidenhood that I will come meekly to you whenever you ask? I have paid your price for silence. I am not your whore." Her anger at his arrogant assumption and all her pent-up, confused feelings were evident in her flashing eyes.

Damien's surprise at her outburst was quickly replaced by anger at her scornful rejection of him. However, he realized she must be very confused, so he struggled to keep his patience. "I am not asking you to be a whore," he answered. "I am asking you to be my mistress, my lover."

Her chin went up proudly. "It is the same thing. I will be no man's mistress."

His resolve to be patient flew out the window at her haughty attitude. She was, after all, only an adventuress. "What man will have you for wife when he finds out that you are no longer a virgin?" he whipped at her. "Or did you plan to never marry and become an old maid, to sit at home and knit for no one but yourself?"

"Who would know that my maidenhood has been taken?" she demanded. "I would not be stupid enough to let on."

The Duke's answer was merely a slight lifting of an

eyebrow.

Jessica felt as if she had been struck. He would not, could not ruin what little reputation she had. He could not possibly be so cruel to gossip about what had occurred in his house this night. Fighting back the tears, she struggled to answer in a level tone.

"I can not keep you from speaking about this night if you wish to do so. I will not beg you to keep silent. I have given you my most precious possession in payment for your silence on another matter. I can not give you anything more."

"Give me yourself, Jessica," he said softly.

"I can not. Why do you want me? There must be hundreds of women in London who would gladly tumble into bed with the powerful Duke of Wyndham. Please, let me be."

"I do not want hundreds of women. I want you," he stated emphatically.

"No."

"I will have you, whether you want it now or not," he went on as if she had not spoken. "Jessica, the Lady Fortuna, will be the sole property of Damien Trevor, Duke of Wyndham. I will make you want it to be."

His arrogance and powerful bearing, instead of frightening her, made her furious. Dear God, she thought. First, he wanted her as his mistress, and now she was chattel, his property! This man was unbearable. What would he ask of her next? She decided not to wait to find out.

"You presume too much, Your Grace, Damien Trevor," she answered haughtily. "You know nothing of my life, nor why I acceded to your will and came to you tonight. One thing you should know, however, is that I will be considered the property of no one—not even you. Now, if you will excuse me, I will be leaving. I am taking an early coach out of London, and I have much to do."

She turned and stalked to the door, into the foyer, and across the floor to the front entrance. It was not until she was outside that she took a breath. At each step she had taken, she had expected a hand on her arm, detaining her.

Jessica walked down the steps and out to the street. There were no carriages in sight. She resigned herself to a long and possibly dangerous walk back to her rooms.

After walking for several long minutes, she heard the clatter of hooves on the cobblestones of the street behind her. They slowed as they came abreast. Looking up in the dim light of dawn, she saw a rider on a magnificent black stallion. Recognition of who it was broke upon her consciousness. She began to walk more quickly.

"It is a long walk back to the Green Dragon," Damien observed. "May I offer the lady a ride?"

"The lady would prefer to walk, thank you," Jessica answered coldly. She pulled her cloak closer about her and lengthened her stride.

Damien made a sudden move. An arm went about her waist, and she felt herself lifted off the ground and seated on the horse in front of the Duke.

"As I said, it is a long walk, and I will have nothing of mine abused," he stated sternly.

"Nothing of yours?!" Jessica repeated incredulously as she twisted about to face him. "I told you, I will not be owned like a piece of furniture. You have no right . . ."

Her words were cut off by his mouth coming down hard on hers. Jessica fumed silently and tried to wriggle free, but his hold on her was too tight. In her mind, she called him every foul name she could think of, and she even made up a few new ones. He had no right to do this to her.

He finally raised his head. Jessica's temper exploded. Like lightning, her hand whipped out to strike his arrogant face. Just as fast, the Duke caught her wrist before she could do any damage. Jessica met his cool, amused gaze with her fiery one. She was so furious she could have spit. Realizing that it would do no good to struggle or berate him, she jerked her arm out of his grasp and faced forward as she tried to ignore the fact that she sat in such intimate contact with the man. They rode in silence until they came to the front of the Green Dragon.

Before she could slip from the horse, he turned her face to him and lowered his lips to hers again, this time with more gentleness. Possessively, he cupped her breast in his hand. It took every ounce of Jessica's will power not to melt against him. His touch could be devastating; his kisses could make her forget who she was. Instead, she held herself stiffly away.

"You will be mine, my sweet. Sooner or later, you will be mine," he whispered against her mouth.

Jessica jerked away. If looks could kill, then Damien would have been dead ten times over from the glare Jessica sent him. He gazed back at her with amusement in his eyes, then guided her as she slipped from the horse. She straightened her cloak, then stalked away, past the door of the inn, with as much dignity as she could muster.

After only a few steps, something landed with a clink in front of her. Looking down, she saw a pouch, and the shine of coins peeked through its opening. Scooping it up, she swung around to face the Duke as he sat smugly upon his horse.

With her cheeks flaming in indignation, she raged, "I will not accept payment for anything I did this past evening. You may keep your money." She lifted her arm to fling the pouch back at him, but his words stopped her.

"You may throw it back at me if you wish, but I would discover exactly what it is you throw away," he shrugged.

Jessica lowered her arm and stared quizzically at him.

"The pouch contains your winnings from this past evening at Madame's. It seems I collected them by mistake," Damien told her with a grin.

"By mistake!" she exclaimed, remembering the servant who collected both her winnings and those of the Duke. "Ooooh! You . . . ! You . . . !" Words failed her in her rage. Stamping her foot, she turned on her heel and disappeared into the shadows.

Damien watched her stalk away without a backward glance at him. The night had turned out to be a great deal more interesting than he would have believed possible. Grinning broadly, he wheeled his horse and headed back home.

Chapter Five

The coach ride from London to Dorset, where Braeleigh was located, was a long one. Jessica would not reach her home until the middle of the morning of the next day. Therefore, she had plenty of time to consider the events of the past several hours.

Jessica was still very confused. She could not understand what had made her give in to the Duke so easily. She had always been so sure of herself where men were concerned. Holding herself aloof and discouraging any advances had usually been enough to keep them at a distance. Those who had not kept their distance had felt the sharp edge of her tongue and had gained her scorn. It had been her only defense in the unconstrained atmosphere of the gaming house.

But last night, she had lost something of herself. More than just her maidenhood, it was some secret part of her that no one else had ever touched before, not even her father. It was quite frightening, to say the least.

So, for most of the trip, Jessica kept her thoughts to herself, and Donny dozed as best she could while being bumped around from the ruts in the road. They were the only two passengers in the coach. Not many people travelled out of London at this time of year. The spring social season was coming up soon and people were preparing for the fetes and balls they would give. The weather was unpredictable, making travel unpleasant, if not actually hazardous. Just that morning, the sky had been grey and angry and had threatened rain before the day was out.

As they stopped at a post station to change the horses, the rain began. Jessica decided that the weather matched her mood perfectly.

After a quick refreshment, they embarked again. It was dark by the time they stopped for the night. They were chilled to the bone by the cold and damp from the rain. Jessica was very quiet during their supper, and Donny began to worry. When they reached their room, Donny confronted her.

"All right, out with it," she demanded. "What be yer problem? Are ye sick? Don't ye feel well?"

"Donny, I feel fine," Jessica protested.

"Ye don't look fine. Ye be glum all day, hardly said two words, ye did. Aye, and I be thinkin' it's got somethin' to do with that man ye met at that gamblin' place."

Jessica forced a laugh. "What man? I have met many men there."

"Don't ye be tryin' t'get out of it. Ye know very well what man I'm talkin' about. That one that made ye lose."

"Oh, him." Jessica pretended innocence. "Whatever makes you think that? I can't tell you the last time I saw him." And that, she thought grimly, was no lie. "Now, are you going to undo my dress, or will I have to do it myself?"

Donny humphed and looked like she was about to say something else, but said nothing. Jessica could tell, though, that Donny did not really believe her. The matter was not discussed any further that night, and they both went to bed.

The next day dawned sunny and bright, a fore-runner of the spring days soon to come. Jessica's mood lightened considerably. Having slept well, her state of mind was quite different from the day before. She was excited about seeing Jason and Braeleigh again, despite the presence of Margaret. The Duke was far away, in London, and had no control over her here. She had a feeling of freedom, a feeling she had not felt in a long time.

Jessica made Donny hurry through her breakfast so that they could wait outside for their coach. There was a cool wind, and the older woman grumbled about the cold making her bones ache.

"Oh, Donny," Jessica laughed. "It's too beautiful out here to complain."

"Hmph. Get yerself in the coach before ye catch yer death."

Jessica laughed and climbed into the coach. In a few hours she would be home. She smiled in anticipation as they started off.

The longer they rode, the more familiar things Jessica recognized. Suddenly, she shook Donny's arm and pointed. "There's the Whittington farm. We get off at the next bend in the road."

She rapped on the roof of the coach, and it began to slow before coming to a halt. She and Donny descended, and their valises were tossed down. They would now have a long walk to get to Braeleigh, unless someone passed by and could give them a ride. Margaret did not see the need to send a carriage to pick up her stepdaughter and a servant.

Jessica and Donny had not been walking long when they heard a horse and wagon behind them. Looking back, Jessica recognized one of the farmers from the area. He pulled up beside them and stopped.

"Good day to ye, Yer Ladyship, Mistress Donlin," he greeted them with a bob of his head and lift to his hat. "Can I be givin' ye a ride to the manse?"

"That would be very kind of you, Mr. Stockham,"

Jessica answered.

"Well, then climb aboard. I be on my way there now with a load of eggs." He helped them clamber to the seat beside him, then clucked to his horse and they started off.

"Home again to visit Her Ladyship, I see," Mr. Stockham observed. "Yer a good child, Lady Jessica."

Jessica smiled at him but remained silent.

"Won't be too peaceful at the manse, I fear," he went on.

"Oh?" Jessica interjected.

"Yep. Her Ladyship be fixin' the ol' place over. Workers there all the time."

"Really?" Jessica said as she exchanged a glance with Donny. "Well, I suppose it needed it."

"Ye know that better'n I, Yer Ladyship."

Mr. Stockham lapsed into silence then, and Jessica sat and wondered what Margaret was up to. Several minutes later, the wagon turned into the drive of Braeleigh. It was not an overly large house in comparison to other country manors of the nobility, but it was old and had an honorable history. It had been built by the first Earl of Braeleigh. The land had been bestowed on him by Edward III for the earl's heroics in the battle of Agincourt during the Hundred Years' War. The original square stone structure had been added to with a wing on each side, yet it still retained its charm. It was built of stones of an unusual tan color, and sitting on a rise as it did, it was visible from a great distance. A parapet topped the roof of the oldest section, where the first earl's men could stand guard, and a moat surrounded the hill where it stood.

As they crossed the small drawbridge that was now permanently lowered, Jessica's eyes widened in shock. There were workmen swarming around the house, and there was a constant coming and going through the great, wooden door. What was Margaret up to this time? she wondered. And where did she get the money for all these workmen? Certainly, the stipend that Jessica brought her every month was not enough to pay all these people.

Jessica and Donny looked at each other in anger and shock, then back again at the house. Mr. Stockham pulled up in front of the door, jumped down from the wagon, and helped the ladies. Tipping his hat, he said, "Good day to ye, Lady Jessica. 'Tis good to have ye home again."

"Thank you, Mr. Stockham," she said and smiled through her embarrassment. It was very obvious to her that the villagers were gossiping about the strange goings on at Braeleigh and the odd antics of Margaret. She even suspected they were aware of why she went to London and came back every month. It pained her to see the dignity of the family title degraded so.

Holding back a sigh, Jessica went to find Margaret to ask her the meaning of all the activity. She had to walk around several ladders and groups of paint cans, and climb over piles of rolled-up carpets. She finally found her stepmother in the study. Various swatches of material were spread out before her, and she was studying them intently. It was several moments before she looked up, condescending to acknowledge Jessica's presence.

"Jessica, my dear, come, sit down and help me decide on a color for my dressing room."

Jessica did not move. Instead, she asked coldly, "Margaret what is all this? What is going on here?"

"Why, I am redecorating, of course," Margaret answered, her voice full of amazement at Jessica's slowness of wit. "Anyone with half a brain can see that."

"Margaret, don't play games with me. You know what I am talking about. Where did you get the money?" Jessica's voice remained hard.

"My, my, your months in London have certainly made you cynical," Margaret observed. She leaned back against the settee and coolly looked Jessica in the eye. "Don't you have a friendly hello for your stepmother whom you haven't seen in a month?"

Jessica was having a difficult time trying to keep her temper in check. "Believe me, Margaret, when I tell you that any greeting I give you will be far from friendly. Where did you get the money for this redecorating?"

Margaret sighed and spoke as if to an impertinent child. "Ah, well, if you must know. It would seem that your father was not such a fool as I thought. He had invested in quite a large parcel of land in that wretched place, America. Land-wise, Jason is a very rich little boy. Since he is too young to control his estate, as his stepmother and guardian, I have taken that worry out of his hands."

"So you are using my brother's inheritance for your own pleasure," Jessica stated as she tried to assimilate the fact that Jason, at least, was no longer poor.

"I am using it only as collateral, my dear."

"When did you discover this land?"

"Why, just several weeks ago, just after your last visit. You don't think I would have kept it a secret from my lovely stepdaughter, do you?"

"To be truthful, Margaret, I do not know what to think." Jessica finally sat down. The shock of the news of the inheritance had turned her knees weak. A thought suddenly occurred to her. "Why didn't we find out about this land at the time of my father's death?"

Margaret raised her eyebrows and asked mildly, "Are you questioning my integrity, Jessica?" Jessica merely looked back at her stepmother without saying a word. "Ah, well, I suppose the young are always suspicious," she mused to herself, then to Jessica she said, "The solicitor arrived shortly after your last visit and informed me that your dear father had large holdings in America. Imagine! And he never even told me, his wife."

There is probably a lot more that he did not tell you, Jessica thought to herself. To Margaret, she asked casually, "Then you will no longer require the stipend that I bring you every month?"

"On the contrary, my dear. And let us not quibble over words. Let us call it what it really is: ransom."

"Ransom?" Jessica repeated, feeling rather stupid for not understanding.

"Yes my dear, ransom. Ransom for your . . . ah . . . freedom."

"Margaret, what are you talking about?"

"Do not act so stupid," Margaret answered in a hard voice. "Do you think I was going to marry you to Sir Percival just for the legal right to get you in his bed? You certainly can not be as naive as that. I want you out of this house, you simpering little fool, and I want Jason out of your influence. You can either get married, or you can pay me every month. Either way, it makes no difference to me. Just remember, I am still your legal guardian. If you find some young buck who is willing to marry you, just make sure he has plenty of money so that he can pay for that dubious honor."

Jessica was stunned by her stepmother's cruelty, yet her thoughts fastened only on the least of Margaret's dictates.

"But Margaret," Jessica protested, "it is I who is supposed to bring a dowry to the marriage."

"Then you do have a problem, don't you, my dear?" Margaret's smile was cruel.

"And what of Jason?" Jessica queried, trying very hard to remain calm. "Will you throw him out also?"

"On the contrary," Margaret answered. "He is the Earl of Braeleigh. He needs guidance and help in running the estate. Who better to help him than his loving stepmother?"

The conversation was making Jessica feel ill, but before she left the room, she had to ask one last question. "Will I still be able to visit my brother?"

Margaret laughed as though she found her step-daughter very amusing. "Of course. How else will I get your payments every month? Our agreement still stands as it did before. It is only the reasons which have changed. Now, be a good girl, and find Clark, the cloth merchant, for me. I think I will do the walls of my dressing room in yellow silk . . . or, per-haps pink brocade."

Margaret again leaned forward and began to study the material swatches in front of her.

Jessica rose slowly from her chair and walked from the room. Ignoring Margaret's demand, she crossed blindly to the stairs and began to climb. Her mind was reeling. She could not believe she had just been thrown out of her own house. Somehow, she had thought that eventually she would have been able to quit her life in London and return to Braeleigh. Now, that did not seem possible while Margaret was still alive.

The cruel words of the Duke came back to haunt her. No man would pay to marry a woman of ques-tionable reputation, especially one who had been thrown out of her own home. Jessica sighed deeply. The prospect of becoming the Duke's mistress did not seem such a terrible fate now. At least, she would be well cared for. Jessica shook her head to dispel her gloomy thoughts. She would not think of these things now. She would fetch Jason, and they would go riding together.

When she reached the door of the schoolroom, she saw Jason in the middle of a fencing lesson. Donny stood just inside the door with her hands over her face, but peeking out with dread. After several minutes, Jason finally scored. The fencing master called out the required, "Touché!" Jessica could sense Jason grinning behind his mask. His eyes finally landed on his sister.

"Jessica!" he exclaimed. He dropped his sword and ran to his sister's side. Jessica put her arm around him and gave him a quick hug.

The fencing master cleared his throat. "I beg your pardon, m'lady, but I am trying to give the young lord his fencing lesson."

"Fencin' lesson!" Donny exclaimed. "Hmph. More like ye was tryin' t'skewer him!"

The master looked pained and turned to Jessica for help. "I am only doing what I have been hired to do, m'lady," he pleaded his case.

"Yes, I know," Jessica nodded with a smile. "Thank you. That will be all for today. You may inform the Earl's other tutors that he will not be at lessons for the rest of the day."

"Yahoo!" Jason yelled. "No more studying today! Thanks, Jess."

The fencing master bowed his acceptance of Jessica's orders and saluted Jason with his sword. Jessica motioned for her brother to return the salute, which he did rather sloppily. When the man left the room, Donny breathed a noisy sigh of relief.

Jason turned expectantly to his sister. "What'll we do, Jess?"

Jessica laughed. "First, you are to change your clothes, then we'll have something to eat, and then we'll go riding. How does that sound?"

"First rate!"

Jason put his sword away, discarded his mask and padded vest and raced out of the room. Jessica watched him, and immediately after he had gone, the smile faded from her lips.

Donny, seeing the quick change in expression, grumbled, "So I s'pose Lady High-and-Mighty was in good health."

Jessica grimaced. "Exceedingly so."

"I wish that woman was rottin' in Hell," Donny observed.

Donny's comment brought a wry smile to Jessica's lips. "I fear that won't be for some time yet. Come, help me change and I'll tell you about it."

After donning her riding clothes, Jessica met Jason in the kitchen. Before she had left Braeleigh, she would very often forego dining in the great, empty, formal dining room so that she and Jason could eat together in the kitchen. There, they would be able to laugh and tell each other stories without incurring Margaret's wrath. Jessica had continued the tradition on her visits home.

After a delightful lunch together with much laughter, the brother and sister headed out to the stables. Their horses were saddled and waiting for them. Jessica's horse, Aphrodite, had been given to her by her father when it was just a foal. Upon hearing Jessica's voice now, the animal whinnied and shook its head.

Jessica greeted her softly and rubbed her velvety nose. She missed not being able to ride while in London, and always looked forward to it when she came home. She and Jason mounted, then trotted out of the stable yard.

When they were out in open country, Jason called to her, "I'll race you to Eagle Rock!" Without waiting for his sister's reply, he dug in his heels and galloped off. Jessica laughed and raced after him.

They both rode very well, but Jessica had the advantage of several years more experience than her younger brother, and she easily caught up with him. They raced side by side until they had almost reached their goal, then Jessica eased up and allowed Jason to win the race.

As they slowed their horses and brought them to a stop, Jason looked at his sister with disappointment.

"Aw, Jess, you let me win," he complained.

Jessica looked aghast. "How can you think such a thing?"

Jason only looked suspiciously at his sister.

They dismounted and allowed the horses to graze. Jessica looked around her and took a deep breath of clear country air. Eagle Rock was an outcropping of several large rocks on a small rise at the edge of the land belonging to Braeleigh. It overlooked the countryside in one direction, and the sea in another. This had been first Jessica's, now Jason's, private spot to think. It was now their refuge away from their stepmother and her servants who always reported everything back to their mistress.

"Everything seems so peaceful up here," Jessica remarked. "This is all yours now, Jason. How does it feel to be an earl?"

The boy shrugged. "All right, I guess. Margaret doesn't give me much time to enjoy it."

"Has she been very terrible?" Jessica noticed for the first time the shadowy smudges beneath his eyes.

"She has me taking fencing lessons, history, French, Latin, Italian, etiquette lessons, and dancing lessons." At this last he made a face. "I wish you could live here with me again, Jess. It's no fun any more." He suddenly looked very sad and young.

Jessica put her arm around his shoulders and sighed. "I know, Jason. It's not really fun for me either. I miss you terribly. But Margaret doesn't like me for some reason, and until I can think of a way out of this mess, we'll have to go along with what she says."

Jason brightened suddenly. "I have scads of money now. Did you know that? I can help you!"

Jessica laughed. "I know you have scads of money, my lord, Earl of Braeleigh."

"Well?" he asked expectantly. "Why can't I help you?"

Jessica shook her head. "It's not that simple, Jason. Margaret has control of your money. She wouldn't let you use it to help me."

"I hate her!" Jason exclaimed.

Jessica gave her brother another hug. "I know," she sympathized, "but for now, we'll have to do as she says. Things won't always be like this. Come on," she said, poking him in the ribs. "Let's go to the village. Maybe the baker has made tarts."

They mounted their horses and rode to the village. They spent the rest of the afternoon there visiting and exploring the businesses and shops. Jason was delighted to watch the blacksmith work. He was fascinated by the rhythmic clanging of hammer against anvil and the change that occurred in a piece of metal as the smithy worked on it. The baker had, indeed, made tarts, and Jessica bought Jason some, which he devoured.

The sun was beginning to set when they finally left. They galloped back to Braeleigh so that they would arrive before it became dark. Jessica guessed that Margaret would be fuming because she had spirited Jason away from his tutors.

When they finally walked into the house, Jessica knew she had not been wrong. They received the message from Barclay, the butler, that Margaret was waiting for them in the salon. Glancing at each other with a knowing look, they entered the room.

"Did you wish to see us, Margaret?" Jessica asked.

Margaret was drumming her fingers on the arm of the chair where she was sitting. "Don't play the innocent with me, Jessica. Where have you been all afternoon?"

"Out riding," Jessica stated simply. Jason edged closer to his sister.

"Obviously," Margaret stated dryly. "You were in the village, weren't you?" she accused. "I have given Jason specific orders that he is not to associate with that trash." Turning to the boy, she said, "You deliberately disobeyed me, Jason. You will go to your room and go without dinner tonight. Tomorrow you will spend at your lessons and will not be allowed to see your sister."

"But Margaret, she's leaving tomorrow!" Jason wailed.

"I can not help that," Margaret said coldly. "You should have thought of that before you disobeyed me. Now, leave us. Jessica and I have some matters to discuss that do not involve bad little boys."

Jason looked to his sister in confusion, tears bright in his eyes. Jessica squeezed his shoulder and nodded that he should do as he was told. She watched as he walked from the room in dejection. Her heart ached at not being able to help him, but she knew that if she had come to his defense, his punishment would have been harsher.

When he had gone, she turned back to her stepmother. "That was a cruel thing you did, Margaret," she stated boldly. "He has done nothing wrong. I was the one who suggested we go to the village."

"It is not your concern any more how I discipline Jason. You are no longer a member of this household. Now, there is the matter of a payment due. I would like to receive it before dinner."

"You will have it," Jessica answered stiffly, as she held her emotions in tight check. "Is there anything else you wish to discuss with me?"

"Yes. If you persist in disrupting this household when you come, then I will not allow you to visit with Jason when you are here."

"You can not mean that!" Jessica exclaimed in spite of her resolve to remain calm.

"Oh, but I do mean it. And I think I will require that you bring me double what you are bringing now. After all, you have had six months of experience, so it should be much easier for you." She flicked an imaginary piece of lint off the skirt of her dress.

"I can not bring you that much money, Margaret. I need money on which to live."

"Then you will have to find another way to raise it." She yawned behind a daintily raised hand. "I believe I will take a short rest before dinner." She rose abruptly and swept from the room.

Jessica stood for a moment, not quite believing the conversation she had just had, then wandered from the salon. Encountering Barclay, she informed him she would be dining in her room. As she slowly climbed the stairs, she could feel the tears welling up in her eyes. Damn! she thought furiously. She was not going to let that woman make her cry.

She ran the rest of the way to her room and closed the door firmly behind her. Jessica undressed down to her chemise and crawled under the covers of the bed. She was so tired. Tired of the gambling, tired of the cruelty of Margaret, tired of the arrogance of the Duke. Why couldn't things have remained as they were? But she knew that could never have happened. Tomorrow, it was back to London. On her way, she had to deliver the letter to Monsieur Montaigne from Madame du Barré. With these thoughts running through her mind, she fell asleep.

When she awoke, it was dark. It took her several seconds to remember why she was lying in bed in her old room. Memory was not sweet when it returned. She still had to give Margaret her stipend. Rising, she pulled on a dressing gown and tied it carelessly. Her hair had come undone during her nap, so she pulled out the pins and ran a brush through it. Then, picking up the pouch containing the money, she went in search of her stepmother.

Margaret was in her room. She was primping before the mirror and did not even look up when Jessica walked in.

"I've brought your money, Margaret," Jessica said as she threw the pouch on the dressing table before her stepmother.

Margaret picked it up and weighed it in her hand. "Is it all here?" she asked sweetly.

"Margaret, I hope you burn in Hell," Jessica stated hotly, then turned and fled from the woman's presence.

Jessica stalked down the hall, her thoughts on what she would like to see happen to Margaret. As she turned a corner, she bumped into a footman, one who had been newly hired by her stepmother. He grabbed her arms to keep her from falling.

"Why don't you watch where you are going?" she berated him.

Instead of apologizing and being chagrined, he stood there holding on to her.

"Well, now, ain't we a sight?" he leered as his gaze focused on her cleavage that was plainly visible beneath her gapping robe.

"Let go of me this instant!" Jessica tried to pull out of his hands. "I'll have you fired for this impertinence!"

"Now, don't go gettin' all upset there, m'lady. How's about a little kiss for ol' Dickie?"

Jessica was momentarily shocked into immobility, and her mouth dropped open. Recovering her wits quickly, she began to struggle away from him. "How dare you! Let go of me!"

The man was strong, and her efforts to free herself proved fruitless. Suddenly, she found herself crushed against his chest. Her head was pulled back by the hair, and he planted his wet, foul mouth on hers. For once, she was grateful for the experience she had gained at Madame's. Using all her strength, she slammed her knee up into his groin. With a yowl of pain, he released her immediately and

94

clutched at the injured area. As she turned to flee, she saw Margaret with a smile on her face. Jessica ran down the hall to the safety of her room with her stepmother's laughter chasing after her.

Locking the door behind her, something she had never done before, she wondered how much of the scene in the hall Margaret had witnessed. She almost believed that her stepmother might have had something to do with it. Matters were getting worse every time she came home. She had to think of some way to get out of this predicament, something that would also get Jason out of Margaret's clutch. Even if she married someone, that would not guarantee her brother's safety, for Margaret would still be his guardian.

Ideas and plans swirled inside Jessica's head all evening. Her dinner came, but it remained virtually untouched. By the time the clock in the hall had struck eleven, she still had not arrived at any solution.

Remembering that Jason had gone to bed without any dinner, she decided to smuggle some food to him. She hoped Margaret had already retired for the night. Carefully she unlocked her door and opened it. The house was quiet. Noiselessly as possible, she made her way downstairs to the kitchen. There, she found some apples, cheese, and bread, tied them in a napkin, and tiptoed back upstairs.

As she opened the door to Jason's room and crept in, a small voice came from the bed. "Who's there?"

"Sh. It's me," Jessica whispered. She crossed to the bed and sat on its edge. "I've brought you something to eat." She placed the napkin on Jason's lap and opened it to reveal her treasure.

"First rate! Thanks, Jess," he mumbled around a piece of cheese.

She waited quietly while he ate his snack, then, when he had finished, she took the napkin and stuffed it in her pocket. "So I won't get you in trouble again," she explained with a smile. Becoming serious, she said, "I won't be able to see you tomorrow. I'm leaving early because I have to visit someone on the way back to London. Besides, if Margaret caught us together again, she would probably tan your hide."

"Can't you take me with you, Jess?" Jason asked wistfully.

For just a moment, Jessica was tempted to say yes, but reality wiped away the temptation. She remembered the first time she had tried to leave with Jason, and Margaret had caught them. Jason had not been able to sit down for a week, and Jessica had been locked in her room and unable to leave for London until Margaret decided she wanted the money more than the enjoyment of watching Jessica suffer.

Jessica shook her head. "Not this time, Jason. But some day, I'm going to bring you with me, and then we won't have to worry about Margaret any more. Until then, I want you to do as she says. She has complete authority over you, so if you disobey her, she can punish you as she sees fit."

"But she's so mean!" Jason wailed.

"I know."

Jessica put her arms around him, and they sat holding on to each other, gaining strength from the other's nearness for several minutes. Her resolve hardened to free her brother from Margaret. After the episode in the hall with the footman, she was not at all sure that their stepmother was completely sane. However, for now, Jason was better off at Braeleigh than in London.

Jason yawned hugely.

"I think it's time that you went to sleep," Jessica commented.

"Stay a few minutes longer, Jess," Jason pleaded.

Jessica shook her head. "I can't. It's late, and you should be asleep. What if Margaret found me in here with you?"

Reluctantly, Jason nodded his agreement and leaned back on the pillows.

"Now, be brave, and I'll be back at Braeleigh before you know it." Jessica leaned over and kissed him on the cheek.

Before she could straighten, Jason put his arms around her and gave her a hug. "I'm going to miss you, Jess," he whispered.

"I'm going to miss you, too." Gently, she disengaged herself and stood up. "Watch from the window early tomorrow. I'll wave to you when I leave."

She left quickly, not wanting him to see how upset she was, knowing it would only make it harder for both of them. Returning to her room, she made sure her door was locked, then climbed into bed. Sleep did not come easily. Thoughts of Jason and Margaret and the Duke kept chasing themselves around in her head. After several hours of tossing and turning, she finally fell into a troubled sleep.

Morning came much too early for Jessica. The sun was streaming through the window when she opened her eyes, but she felt as if she had not slept at all. Knowing she could not remain in bed, she forced herself to rise. Madame's letter had to be delivered before she caught the coach back to London, and she wanted to be away from Braeleigh as soon as possible. She had the feeling that Jason had an easier time with Margaret when he was here by himself.

Dressing quickly, she went down to breakfast. The dining room was empty, for which she was very grateful. She was in no mood to spar verbally with Margaret.

As she was finishing her meal, Barclay entered and announced, "Your horse is ready, m'lady."

"Thank you, Barclay," she answered. "I shall be out presently."

She would ride to Monsieur Montaigne's on horseback to deliver the letter, then ride to the inn where Donny would be waiting for her with their luggage. From there, they would board the coach for the ride back to London. The innkeeper would make sure that Aphrodite would be returned to Braeleigh.

As she was rising from the table, Margaret sauntered in. "All ready to leave?" she asked rhetorically. "What a pity you can not stay with us a while longer. Dickie was so disappointed he was unable to finish what he began last night."

Jessica did not bother to answer. She walked out of the room with Margaret's evil laughter ringing in her ears.

Quickly donning her hat and gloves, she left the house. A stableboy was holding the reins of her horse, and he helped her mount. Glancing up at the front of the house, she saw Jason in a window. She smiled and threw him a kiss, then waved as she wheeled her horse and cantered down the drive.

Being out in the open helped to clear her mind. Her thoughts were still troubled, but she felt a weight had been lifted from her shoulders just because she was away from Margaret. The problem of the Duke that now faced her seemed small in comparison to the villainy of her stepmother. She forced those thoughts out of her mind. She was free for several hours, and she was on her way to visit a very charming gentleman.

After an hour and a half of easy riding, Jessica came to the home of Monsieur Montaigne. It was a neat, compact house, barely bigger than a cottage. Standing on a grassy cliff, it overlooked a stony beach about twenty feet below. A steep path zigzagged down to the water. Except for his housekeeper, he lived alone.

As Jessica dismounted from Aphrodite, Monsieur Montaigne came to the door. "Mademoiselle Jessica!" he exclaimed. "I was hoping you would come today," he said in French. "You look more lovely each time I see you, like a flower ready to bloom."

Jessica laughed. "Bonjour, monsieur, and thank you. Your compliments always make my head spin."

She had answered him in French. Their conversations were always in that language, for Monsieur Montaigne said it made him feel as if he were back in his own country.

After tying Aphrodite to a hitching post, she held out her hand. Monsieur Montaigne bent over it gallantly, then walked with her to his house. Jessica noticed he leaned rather heavily on his cane, and realized his leg was giving him a great deal of pain. He had told her he had been badly injured during the revolt against King Louis. It had not been on the side of the revolutionists that he had fought, however, but for his king. Because of his loyalty to his sovereign, he had been forced to flee France or be executed with the other Royalists. Now he lived in England, an ex-patriot and outcast in his own country.

Jessica stopped to admire the early flowers beginning to bloom beside his door. A movement in the trees beyond the house caught her attention, and she stared in that direction trying to see what it was.

"Mademoiselle, what is it?" Monsieur Montaigne asked.

Jessica squinted against the sun, then turned to her host with an apologetic smile. "I thought I saw something move in the woods, but there seems to be nothing. It was only my imagination."

"Ah, the mind does like to play tricks on us, yes? Come, I will have my housekeeper make you some tea." Taking Jessica's hand, he tucked it into the crook of his arm and escorted her into his house.

Jessica spent a very enjoyable hour with the older gentleman. She always delighted in these visits, for her host was a charming and gallant man. It was easy to understand why Madame du Barré was so fond of him. The time of her departure came much too soon. When she left, she carried a missive back to Madame. She would deliver it the following evening.

Chapter Six

"Excuse me, Your Grace."

Damien glanced up from his breakfast to find Jacobs standing in the doorway of the dining room. The majordomo's face was carefully expressionless, a look he wore when he disapproved of something.

"Yes, Jacobs, what is it?"

"There is a—ah—person here to see you, Your Grace. He says it is most urgent that he speak with you."

"Who is it, Jacobs? You know I dislike having my breakfast interrupted."

"Yes, Your Grace." Jacobs' impassive veneer cracked slightly, and he grimaced. "He would not give me his name. He said it was a question of the utmost secrecy. He is waiting in the front hall."

Damien raised an eyebrow. For Jacobs to leave a visitor standing in the front hall meant he regarded the individual as little better than riffraff from the streets. However, the man must have had some redeeming quality for Jacobs to even allow him past the front door.

The Duke tossed his napkin down beside his plate and stood. "All right, Jacobs. I will see him."

"Very good, Your Grace. I will be nearby should you wish my services."

Damien hid a grin. He would like to see very

proper Jacobs in a tussle with some vagrant. Solemnly, he thanked his butler and went to see about this mysterious visitor.

As the Duke entered the front hall, he saw a man gazing up at a recently acquired painting by J.M.W. Turner. The man's clothes were mud stained, and it appeared he had worn them for quite some time. Mud streaked his face, making him almost unrecognizable. Several days' growth of beard shadowed his jaw. Damien had barely entered when the man swung about, snapped to attention, and saluted him.

"Edward!" Damien grinned as he walked toward the man and held out his hand. "You haven't saluted me in four years, Leftenant. There's no need to start now."

Edward grinned back as he took Damien's outstretched hand. "I like to practice occasionally."

"I didn't expect you until tomorrow. My apologies for Jacobs' inhospitality. He obviously didn't recognize you. Come into my study and I'll pour you a brandy. You look like you could use one."

When the two men had settled themselves and Damien had supplied his guest with a generous helping of his brandy, the Duke gazed at the man who was next in his command in his group of spies. He watched with amusement as Leftenant Edward Johnson took a large gulp of the amber liquid and sighed in pleasure.

"That helps to warm my bones," Edward said. "It's damned uncomfortable living in the woods."

"I thought you enjoyed hunting," Damien suggested.

Edward glared at him. "Not for five days running. I did not expect to be playing the spy in my own country."

"Hmm. Yes, quite an odd situation. Well, what have you found out for us?"

102

The Leftenant began his report. "I watched Monsieur Montaigne's house, as you ordered, for five days—three of which were bloody rainy, by the way. Nothing unusual happened on the first four; no visitors; he and his housekeeper went about their normal routine. On the fifth day, his housekeeper left early in the morning. It appeared she was going to market. While she was gone, Montaigne had a visitor."

"Ahh." Damien nodded in satisfaction.

"How the devil did you know the courier would show up?"

Damien smiled. "Information concerning England's negotiations with Turkey had been revealed to Madame du Barré. We knew she would rush to get this to Fouché."

Edward gave a low whistle.

"Yes, it is incredible, isn't it? Now, about this visitor. Can you describe him?"

It was Edward's turn to grin. "It was not a 'him' at all. It was a woman."

"The devil you say!"

Edward chuckled. It was not often his commanding officer could be surprised. "Yes, a woman."

Damien's eyes narrowed as he remembered his last attempt to get information before he and his men had to flee France. "I don't suppose you could have been mistaken?"

Edward shook his head and snickered. "I was not the one who decided that Madame Duquènes would make a good hostage."

"I seem to recall you agreeing with me." Damien watched his second in command squirm, then said, "Well, what about this one? Could we be mistaken a second time?"

"No, not this time. This was very definitely a female."

103

"All right. Describe her." Damien sighed. He disliked having to arrest women. He felt they should not be involved in something as dangerous as spying.

"She was small, rather young, had jet black hair. She was quite attractive, beautiful, one might say, making your job rather pleasant."

"All I want is a description, Leftenant, not a commentary."

"Sorry," Edward grinned, not in the least repentant.

"What else?"

"From her mannerisms and the way she carried herself, she appeared gentle-born," Johnson went on. "The horse she was riding was of excellent stock, Arabian, it seemed. And she spoke French."

"Could you hear what was said?"

"Only the usual pleasantries, then they went inside."

"Interesting," Damien mused. "Could you discover any clue to her identity?"

"I did visit the local inn. It seems she comes from the area, but does not live there any longer. She visits once a month, usually around the fifteenth, but I could not find out her name, nor where she resides now, nor the purpose of her monthly visit, unless it is merely to act as courier for Madame du Barré. The people in the area are suspicious of strangers asking questions. It seems this woman, whoever she is, is important to them. They appeared to be protecting her."

"Well done, Edward," Damien nodded with satisfaction. "Perhaps *Le Chat* will be riding again soon."

"Here? In England?" Edward was surprised. Damien had told him and the others who rode with them that he was ending his career as the notorious spy *Le Chat.*

"Yes, just this one more time. It takes a cat to catch a rat." He stood to signal the end of the interview when he saw Edward stifle a yawn. "Go home and get some rest, Leftenant. I will contact you when I need you and the rest of the men."

Leftenant Johnson rose also, but not before he tossed down the remainder of the Duke's excellent brandy in his glass. Damien watched him with amusement.

"I will give you a cask of that when this job is over," he told him.

Edward grinned. "It's been a long, wet, cold assignment. And I have always enjoyed your brandy." He added as an afterthought, "Your Grace."

Damien chuckled, and shook his friend's hand, then rang for Jacobs. When the butler appeared, the Duke told him, "See Leftenant Johnson to the door, Jacobs."

He watched his majordomo's eyebrows lift ever so fractionally as the man realized whom he had left standing in the front hall. Jacobs bowed his acknowledgment of the Duke's request, then turned to Edward and apologized with great dignity. At Jacobs' admission of his mistake, Edward lifted a comical eyebrow at Damien, then followed the man out the door.

When the two had left, Damien sank thoughtfully back into his chair. So, it was a woman he was after. A woman of small stature with black hair. One who usually appeared at Montaigne's around the fifteenth of every month.

A tiny, nagging suspicion began to gnaw at the back of his mind. He frowned at his thoughts. It was too easy, too coincidental. There were many black-haired women who frequented Madame's, several of whom were small. But how many of them left

London around the middle of every month? He remembered her words, saying to him that she was taking the early coach out of London. It had been two days before the fifteenth. He cursed under his breath.

The evening of Jessica's return to London found her at Madame's. She had delivered the letter from Monsieur Montaigne, and now she wandered about the establishment. As she watched the play at the various tables and listened to the gossip, it did not take her long to discover that quite a bit of the conversations concerned herself and the game she was involved in the night before she left for Braeleigh. Her sudden appearance again after being absent for three nights after the incident raised more speculation than she cared to think about, especially when her name was repeatedly linked with that of the Duke of Wyndham.

Jessica could not understand her reluctance to leave Madame's this night. She was too tired from travelling to play, yet she lingered among the tables. She watched a game in progress over the shoulder of one of the players. The man was going to lose heavily if he continued to pick at his buttons every time he had a bad hand. It was an easy task for the others at the table to pick up his nervousness.

Becoming bored with the game, she glanced around the room. Then she saw him. The Duke was here, but he was not alone. A young, blonde woman hung on his arm. He leaned close and smiled at something she said. A surge of something that she could not quite put a name to flowed through Jessica. It made her insides contract. How charming, she thought spitefully. He certainly did not waste any time finding someone else to warm his bed.

Well, at least he would not be bothering her any more.

Turning away from the table, she began to make her way to one of the empty private gaming rooms. She had a splitting headache and needed to be away from the noise.

Entering the room, she walked to the table covered in green felt and picked up a deck of cards. She decided she would give the Duke time to become involved in a game and then she would leave. That way, she would be sure of not meeting him again. Absently, she began to shuffle the cards. Again and again the cards slipped together; the monotony of the movement helped to ease the ache behind her eyes. Suddenly, she felt another presence in the room. Looking up, she saw him standing on the other side of the table. He had an uncanny ability to sneak up on her.

"May I sit in on the play, or is this a private game?" the Duke asked with a smile.

Shrugging her indifference, Jessica motioned to a chair across from her. Returning her eyes to the cards in her hands, she asked coolly, "What happened to your companion?"

His smile widened into a grin. "Is the lady jealous?"

"No," she stated flatly, "merely curious."

"Ah, I see," he said, still smiling. He was obviously enjoying himself immensely. "Well, to satisfy your curiosity, my love, she is occupied with trying to lose a substantial amount of coinage I just bestowed on her. And to further assuage your inquiring mind, she is just a friend, someone with whom I occasionally dally, but who means little to me. I do not live the monkish life."

The bluntness of his last statement caused Jessica finally to look at him. "I did not inquire about your *petites amoures,* Your Grace," she said evenly. "We have no commitment to each other."

The Duke sighed. "That is true. Sad, but true." Something I hope to remedy in the near future." He took out a cheroot. "Do you mind if I smoke?" he asked politely. Jessica shook her head. After lighting the long, thin roll of tobacco, he leaned back in his chair and let out a stream of smoke above Jessica's head. "Was your business concluded successfully?" he asked.

"It was," she answered without thinking. Then realizing what she had admitted, she asked suspiciously, "How did you know I was away on business?"

"No one leaves London for only three days for pleasure," he told her. "Especially not at this time of year."

Jessica watched him, waited for him to tell her that he had discovered her identity, or at least to give a reason why he came to speak with her, but he just sat and smoked and looked at her. Finally, she could stand the silence and his gaze on her no longer.

"If there is nothing else you wish to say to me, Your Grace, I would appreciate your leaving me alone," she stated tiredly.

"I have a great many things to say to you, my love," he replied softly, "but this is neither the time nor the place." He paused for a moment as he watched the ash glow at the end of his cigar. Then, in an offhand manner, he said, "I am having a small dinner party tomorrow evening. I would like you to be my guest."

"No." Jessica did not even have to think about her answer.

"Fine," he went on as if he had not heard. "I will send my carriage for you at eight."

Jessica stared at him in disbelief. "I beg your pardon, Your Grace. Perhaps you did not hear me. I said no. I will not be a guest at your dinner party."

The Duke's eyes narrowed dangerously. "You will be there tomorrow," he contradicted her. "You will be ready at eight o'clock, or my footmen will drag you from your lodgings in whatever you might be wearing at the time."

"You have no right. . . !" she began. The forbidding expression on his face made her voice falter.

"I disagree. I would say I had every right to do as I wish with you. I am remaining silent in order that you may continue as a patroness of Madame's house."

"That is blackmail!"

The Duke smiled and nodded. "Precisely." He stood and crushed out his cheroot. "Until tomorrow, m'lady," he said as he gallantly bowed to her. Then he turned and sauntered from the room.

Totally disconcerted, Jessica gazed after him. How was she to get out of this predicament? she wondered. Evidently, the Duke's interest had not waned with her absence from Madame's. Things were not going right at all. She had thought that if she ignored him, he would leave her alone. Obviously, that was not going to work. Damn him!

She sighed and rested her head in her hands. She supposed the only thing to do was to go tomorrow night. There was nothing else she could do. She believed him when he said he would have his footmen drag her out of her lodgings, and the threat of his not remaining silent about her cheating still hung over her. Standing, she decided to leave Madame's and go back to her rooms. She was too tired to really care what he did. Perhaps tomorrow some solution would occur to her.

The following day, Jessica desperately pondered

how she was going to escape being the Duke's guest that evening. When it came time for her to get dressed for the evening, she still had not found any solution. Then, while she was bathing, she suddenly arrived at an answer to her problem. She simply would not be at her lodgings. She would go to Madame's. He would not cause a scene there and drag her out. Madame would not allow it. Jessica smiled triumphantly to herself. Quickly, she finished her toilette. She had to be gone before his carriage arrived.

Finally, she was ready. Donny stood back and critically looked her over. Jessica wore a simple gown of deep red velvet with no lace or frills to hide the plunging neckline. Tiny puff sleeves barely hugged her shoulders, leaving a generous expanse of bare skin. The gold locket that she always wore was her only adornment. Her hair was swept up into curls atop her head, and tiny tendrils escaped to frame her face and tickle her neck. She presented a breathtaking picture.

"Aye," Donny nodded approvingly. "If he catches sight of ye tonight, he'll be eatin' out of yer hand."

Jessica made a face. "I don't want him eating out of my hand, Donny. I don't even wish to see him. If he comes tonight, tell him . . ." She paused, searching for some appropriate reason why she would not be there. "Tell him I am out with another gentleman." Jessica smiled wickedly to herself. That would teach him she was not to be owned.

Donny's look was disapproving. "Ye be playin' with fire, lady fair. He be a duke, a ye don't anger them high-born gentlemen. Besides, ye might be better off if ye was pleasant to him. He might ask ye to marry him."

"Marry? Ha! The last thing on his mind is marriage. Besides, I wouldn't marry him if he were the last man on earth. He's arrogant and overbearing and despicable, and I hate him." Jessica clasped her cloak about her shoulders and carefully raised her hood so it would not muss her hair. "Don't wait up for me, Donny. I will probably be quite late."

"Hmph, I'll wait up fer ye if I've a mind," Donny grumbled as Jessica walked out the door.

Chapter Seven

When Jessica arrived at Madame's, there were very few people about, for it was much too early for the members of society to be there. To pass the time while she waited for an interesting game to begin, she sat on a settee, sipped a cup of tea, and watched the people arrive. As it grew later, games were begun in the main room. Jessica did not join any of these for she would be playing for much higher stakes at a game later in the evening, but she enjoyed going from table to table to watch the play.

Nervously, she watched the clock as eight o'clock came and went, then nine. Gradually, she began to relax. The Duke would not be coming after her. Soon, she would be involved in a card game, and she would be able to forget him altogether.

As she watched a particularly lighthearted match among several men and women, she suddenly felt a presence at her elbow. Laughing, she turned to make a witty comment to the newcomer. Instead of some innocuous stranger, she came face to face with the Duke. The fury on his face was frightening. His jaw was tightly clenched, and his eyes were like ice. Jessica could only stare.

"Where is this 'other gentleman' whom you are

supposed to be with this evening?" His voice was quiet with repressed fury.

Jessica opened her mouth to reply but no sound came out. Desperately, her mind groped for something to say, but all she could manage was a shake of her head. She had never believed anyone could look so angry and forbidding.

"No 'other gentleman'?" he asked as he took hold of her elbow. "Then you have two choices. Either you can come quietly with me, or I will carry you out."

Jessica looked again into those green eyes and swallowed. She knew she had no real choice at all. The game had been suspended as the players had become aware of the drama that was going on near them. The people at the table were drinking in every word, every glance, every nuance that passed between Jessica and the Duke. In order to keep gossip at the minimum, she had to go with him.

Nodding, she allowed him to guide her away from the table and to the door where he collected her cloak. She noticed he had not even bothered to remove his own when he had come in. Outside, he helped her into his waiting carriage, and they drove off.

The ride to his house was made in complete silence. The Duke stared out the window, and Jessica kept her eyes on her tightly clasped hands in her lap. Fearfully, she wondered what would happen to her once they reached their destination. What would the Duke do to her for defying him? He had told her he did not harm young women, yet he was frightfully angry with her. She did not wish to contemplate her immediate future.

After what seemed to Jessica like hours, they arrived at the Duke's house. Again, no words were exchanged as he helped her from the carriage and guided her up the front stairs and in through the door. He took her cloak from her shoulders and handed it to the butler with the directive that they were not to be disturbed. With a firm hand beneath her elbow, he steered her into the salon where he closed the door behind them.

Finally dropping his hand from her arm, he walked several steps, turned and faced her. With an obvious effort to keep his temper in check, he said, "I will not be made a fool, Jessica."

Jessica's temper flared, overcoming any fear she might have felt. What about her feelings? "Then do not order me about, treating me like one of your servants," she spat back at him. "I have told you before. I will not be owned."

The Duke raised an eyebrow, but said nothing.

"I told you last night that I would not come," Jessica stated vehemently.

"It would seem that you were wrong, for you are here now." His tone was sardonic.

"Do not mock me. You know how I came to be here. If I had not come with you, there would have been a scene, and the resulting gossip would have ruined the respect in which Madame's patrons hold me. As it is, it will be difficult to defuse the speculation concerning our relationship."

"Why defuse it at all?"

"Because we have no relationship!" Jessica suddenly realized the house was very quiet, too quiet for there to be other dinner guests. "I thought you said you were having a dinner party. Where are your other guests?"

"There are no other guests."

Jessica's mouth dropped open. "You lied to me!"

The Duke finally smiled, the anger leaving his face. "On the contrary, my love. I said it was to be a small dinner party. I did not say how small it was

114

to be."

Jessica stared at him, not trusting herself to speak. How could he be so arrogant, so insufferable? Finally, taking a deep breath and raising her chin, she said with as much dignity as she could muster, "If you would be so kind as to have your carriage brought around, I will be leaving. If you deny me the use of it, I will leave on my own." She turned and began to walk out of the room.

"Jessica!" The tone of the Duke's voice made her stop, but she did not turn around. There was the tiniest pause before he spoke again, as if what he had to say was very hard. "I apologize for my rude behavior. Have you dined yet this evening?"

She whirled to face him. Was he mocking her again? His expression was earnest.

"I asked you a question," he said softly when she did not answer immediately.

Jessica shook her head. "No." Eating dinner had simply not entered her mind. She had been so anxious to evade him that she had had no appetite.

The corners of his mouth twitched upward. "How fortunate!" he exclaimed. "My chef has created a magnificent feast for my dinner guest and I, but alas, she was last seen heading out the door to God-knows-where. Will you take her place, my lady? Please?"

Jessica smiled in spite of herself. He could be so damned charming sometimes. There he stood, no longer arrogant, but thoroughly engaging, entreating her like some wounded lover to stay and dine. Against her better judgement, she decided to remain.

"You are very persuasive, Your Grace," she dimpled. "How can I refuse such a gallant request?"

The Duke walked up to her and removed her mask. Taking her hand, he smiled down at her.

"You will not be sorry that you stayed, my love." He kissed the palm of her hand, then led her to a small table that had been set up before the fire.

She felt that she really could not eat anything, especially with the Duke sitting so close, but with his teasing and gentle cajoling, she discovered she was quite hungry. The food was delicious. There were many different dishes, and many different wines, all of which the Duke enticed her to try. Although Jessica only sipped a small amount of each, by the end of the meal she was quite light-headed.

As he held her chair for her when they had finished, she lost her balance and grabbed the Duke for support. Giggling, she looked up at him. She was surprised into silence by the intense, hungry look in his eyes. He stared down at her a moment and ran his fingers across her cheek. Then, as if coming out of a trance, he smiled suddenly.

"Come," he said. "Let's sit before the fire and watch the flames dance."

Jessica allowed him to lead her to a settee. She sat in one corner, and the Duke sat very close to her. He draped his arm behind her. She could feel the soft velvet of his coat on the skin of her back. It sent warm tendrils through her. Leaning back, she relaxed against him. She felt comfortable and content. It would be so nice if this night could go on forever, she thought.

She suddenly realized what she was thinking. Would she really want to spend forever with him? She glanced up at him. His profile was turned to her as he watched the flames. It was a strong, aristocratic profile, and now that he was relaxed, it had softened and become gentle. He had shown her a side of himself tonight that was very endearing. Yes, she thought, she would very much like to spend forever with Damien . . . but not as his mistress. She sighed.

Damien heard her sigh and looked down at her with gentle eyes. He had discovered himself quite drawn to this beautiful enigma. "What is it, my love?" His hand moved to her shoulder and pulled her close.

The touch of his hand on her bare skin sent chills through her. She smiled up at him. "I was just daydreaming."

She reached up and touched his cheek. She could not allow herself to become involved with him any more. There was Margaret's demand for money, and there was Jason to think about. But tonight, well, she was here anyway. Her body and her heart were playing traitor to her mind. She was drawn to him like a moth to the flame.

"Make love to me, Damien," she whispered.

He gazed down into her eyes, two bottomless pools of limpid blue, now slightly darkened by her desire for him. He was surprised by her advance and wondered briefly if perhaps this was not some game she was playing. She was, after all, a courier for Madame. Besides the fact that he enjoyed her company, her seduction and subsequent disclosure of information had, of course, been the basic purpose of the whole evening. At least, that is what he kept telling himself.

He had expected some resistance on her part, thereby the large amounts of wine at dinner. Evidently, his plan was working far better than he thought it would. He felt her hand at the back of his neck, her fingers curling in his hair. As she pulled his head down to place her warm, inviting lips to his, he decided that any game he lost this pleasantly was worth the price.

He kissed her deeply, probing her sweet mouth, her tongue meeting his. Jessica's senses reeled, and a fire was kindled inside her. That strange, wonderful pulsing began within her again.

He stood up, pulling her with him. His mouth tasted and nipped along her jaw and down her neck, as he enfolded her in his arms. She felt his hard, muscular thighs against her own soft, supple ones. His hands cupped her bottom and held her tight against him. His need throbbed against her hip. Sweeping her up, he carried her upstairs to his room.

He stood her beside the bed and drank in her beauty. Slowly, she raised her arms and began pulling the pins out of her hair to allow it to tumble down to her waist. Then she held out her arms to him. He took her in his arms and kissed her again. She could not get enough of him. With her arms about him, she pressed close, feeling his hard, unyielding body down the length of her.

When he moved away, she discovered he had unbuttoned her dress. Gently he slid it from her shoulders, and it fell to the floor. Stepping out of her shoes and removing her stockings and petticoat, she stood in nothing but her thin chemise. Then, with her eyes locked on his face, she untied the ribbons holding the chemise and slipped it from her body. Naked, she stood before him and offered herself to him.

Not taking his eyes from her, he removed his clothes. When he had finished, she stood for a moment and admired his magnificent body. In one step, she pressed herself against him and put her arms around his neck.

"Make love to me, Damien," she repeated almost desperately.

Her eyes gazed into his. She knew precisely what she was doing. The consequences be hanged. His lips crushed down onto hers, and they tumbled onto the bed. Their passion carried them far into the night.

It was still dark when Jessica awoke. The curtains had never been drawn, so the moonlight shone through the window. Damien was sleeping soundly, one arm and leg thrown possessively across Jessica. She moved slightly, and he sighed and turned in his sleep. Feeling the need to be away from the magnetism of his body, she eased out of bed. Damien's shirt lay in a white puddle on the floor, so she picked it up and slipped it on as she walked to the window.

Looking out, she saw an enclosed garden beyond. Little was growing there at this time of year, but in a week or so, she knew green shoots would begin to appear. The thought of spring brought a pang shooting through her chest. Spring was for new things and new love, something that she could not have.

Her discovery of her feelings for Damien this night were too much to bear. She could not spend any more time with him. She could not afford to, for there was Jason to consider. Becoming the mistress of the Duke of Wyndham would solve her problem with Margaret, but it would not help her brother, still too young to help himself. Besides, Damien did not love her. To him, she was only a plaything, someone to amuse him while other ladies were not about. To him, she was only the adventuress, the Lady Fortuna. The tears, which she had not allowed herself to shed since her father's death, finally began to fall in silent streams down her cheeks.

A pair of warm arms wrapped themselves around her from behind. "Why are you crying, my love?" he whispered as he held her close.

She had not heard Damien get out of bed. If she

had, she would have made an effort to compose herself. She could not tell him her problems. He would not be able to help her. His arms gave her a sense of security that she knew was false.

Quickly wiping at her cheeks, she turned to face him. "Please," she begged, "do not force me to come here again. There are circumstances about which you know nothing. I can not be your mistress, Damien."

"Tell me about these circumstances," he demanded. "Let me help you."

She shook her head. "No one can help me." She laughed bitterly. "I can't I even help myself." She pulled away from his embrace, and a very lonely feeling enveloped her. She wandered to the center of the room. Her disembodied voice floated back to him out of the darkness. "Things are never as they seem. Events never happen the way they are planned. I am not what you think I am."

Damien thought he understood what she was saying. Yet, there was another dimension to her words that baffled him. He supposed she was speaking of her involvement with Madame, but she sounded as if she was desperately in need of some sort of assistance. What that assistance was and the reason for it eluded him. For some inexplicable reason, he wanted to help her, an adventuress—albeit, a very desirable one—a woman who had made him look the fool and, except for tonight, had rebuffed him at every opportunity.

He chided himself for being soft. Had he not wanted her in just this state so that she would reveal what she knew of Madame and her spy ring? "Tell me who you are, Jessica," he demanded softly. He could just make out the white of his shirt covering her as she stood in the shadows.

"I am the Ice Witch," she whispered mysteriously,

then gave an ironic laugh. "That is what the patrons of Madame's call me, you know. The cold-blooded woman who uses sorcery to make the cards do as she wishes. They are wrong. I am not a woman at all. I am too young. Too young to decide my own fate, to make my own decisions."

She moved suddenly into the moonlight and stood defiantly before Damien. Grabbing the front of his shirt in both hands, she ripped it open down the front and exposed her body to his gaze. "Do I look like a young girl to you, Your Grace, or a woman, fully grown?"

Damien approached her softly. He instinctively knew he would get no other information from her this night, and he knew she needed to be reassured. The information would come once he had gained her trust.

Placing his hand beneath her chin, he tilted her head back so he could look into her troubled eyes. "You are a very beautiful woman, Jessica." His other hand gently moved to cover her breast, his thumb caressing the pink tip. "Let me prove to you that you are no child."

She placed her own hand over his on her breast and made him stop. "Please, promise that after to-night, you will no longer pursue me."

His green eyes glinted in the darkness. "I make no promises that I will not keep, but you have my word that I will not force you to come to me if you do not wish it."

"Thank you," she whispered. She reached up and touched his lips with her fingers, tracing their outline. "Now, make me feel like a woman."

He brushed his lips across her ear and tickled her neck with his tongue. Leaning her back across his arm, he kissed her shoulder, then covered the breast he held cupped in his hand with his mouth. He teased its rosy tip until she moaned.

Jessica gave herself up to the delicious tension he created within her. Her womanly instincts asserted themselves, and she moved her hips enticingly against him. She heard him gasp his delight, and she smiled in satisfaction.

He raised his head and gazed with amusement into her languorous eyes. "No innocent would move like that, my lady," he smiled.

Her dimples deepened, and she pulled away, turned and slowly walked to the bed, his shirt was discarded along the way. Again turning to face him, she stretched, catlike. Her whole body exuded a smoldering sensuality.

"I am no longer an innocent, Your Grace," she teased. "You have seen to that. I am a wanton woman with no good reputation left to my name. Come, let me show you how wicked I have become." She held out her arms to him.

In three long strides, he crossed the space between them. Gathering her to him tightly, he captured her lips. She pulled him down onto the bed. Her hands roved over his strong back, and her legs entwined themselves with his. She could feel his desire for her, hard against her thigh. Her blood raced through her veins; she wanted him, needed him, more than she had ever wanted anything in her life. His hands were everywhere, touching, teasing, making her moan with pleasure.

He paused, and framing her face in his hands, made her look at him. "You are mine, Jessica. You belong to me."

She gazed into his green eyes and knew he spoke the truth. Her only answer was to pull his head down and kiss him passionately. He rolled between her legs, becoming part of her until the world seemed to explode inside of her. Her scream of pleasure was cut off by his devouring mouth. After they parted, they lay still entwined, their fingers enmeshed. Her head rested against his shoulder, her leg intimately laying across his thighs.

"It will be dawn soon," she sighed with regret. "I must leave."

"You could stay, Jessica." His fingers persuasively caressed the back of her neck.

"Please, let's not argue again. You made a promise to me."

"I did, but I don't have to force you to stay." His eyes glinted mischievously. "I can make you want to remain here, if I wish."

Despite his teasing manner, she was alarmed. His words held a great deal of truth, for just a simple caress of his fingers caused her to forget everything. Would he keep her here a prisoner, making love to her whenever she wanted to leave?

He laughed, the noise rumbling in his chest. "Do not look so frightened, my love. I am no fiend who keeps ladies imprisoned to await my pleasure." He gently pushed her into a sitting position. "Go and dress before I change my mind."

Jessica scrambled from the bed and dressed quickly before he did as he threatened. Damien watched her for several minutes, then he, too, got up and dressed. As he reached for his shirt, Jessica grabbed it away. She looked down at it sheepishly. It had not been her intention to rip it when she had put it on.

"I will take this and sew it for you, Your Grace," she told him.

Damien took it out of her hands and held it up. He examined it critically, then handed it back to her with a grin. "I am afraid it is beyond repair, my lady, but if you wish to keep it as a remembrance of my male prowess, I won't mind."

"You arrogant cad!" she exclaimed, as she threw it back at him, then turned her back.

He laughed, grabbed her by the arm, and swung her about to face him. He pushed a wisp of hair away from her face and let his hand linger in her thick mass of curls. "Do you know that you are beautiful when you are angry?"

"How many times have you said that to other women you have held in your arms?" she wanted to know.

"You wound me deeply, my lady," he said in mock seriousness. "I do not pay compliments unless they are true, and with you, my love, I have seen you angry more times than not."

"Then do not goad me into anger, Your Grace, for I harbor a sweet side to my nature, as well as a thorny one."

"I know," he agreed softly, and lowered his mouth to taste her sweetness once more.

When he finally raised his head, she was breathless. "I think you have changed your mind, and mean to keep me here to satisfy your lustful whims," she accused him with a grin.

"Perhaps," he smiled. "I do not think you would mind that overly much."

Jessica feigned shock. "What do you take me for, Your Grace? I am not some strumpet off the street who will covet the body of every man who passes by her. I am a simple maid who fell victim to an unscrupulous knave." With that she gave the hair on his chest a playful tug.

Damien grimaced in pain. "Unscrupulous knave, am I?" He firmly grabbed the hair on the back of her head. "I think, perhaps, the lady needs some manners taught to her. She should not repeat things which are not true, for it was the lady, I seem to recall, who did much of the seducing this evening."

Relentlessly, his mouth lowered, and he kissed her thoroughly.

When she was finally able to catch her breath, she said, "If you do that again, the morning will find us again in your bed, and no closer to going about our separate business than we are now."

"Would that be so terrible?"

"Damien!"

With a reluctant grin, he released her and finished dressing. When they were both clothed, Jessica waited while Damien roused his valet and had him gather the footmen to bring around his coach. Jessica smiled to herself. This departure from Damien's house would be made in more comfort than the last.

It was not long before the coach was ready, and they sat close to each other in the dark interior. Jessica could feel his hard thigh pressed tightly against her supple one; his arm was warm and comforting about her shoulders. It was a bittersweet time for Jessica. She had found something wonderful this night, only to realize that it could never be fulfilled. She relished these last few moments alone with Damien. For once, the silence between them was not strained, but was filled with an easy companionship and contentment.

The trip to her lodgings ended much too soon for Jessica. After Damien helped her down from the carriage, he kept her hand in his. Gazing down into her clear blue eyes, he drew her to him and kissed her sweet mouth.

When he raised his head, he warned quietly, "Do not think this is the last you will see of me, Jessica. I do not relinquish my hold so easily on those that are mine."

Where once she would have rebelled at his words, now they only made her leaving that much more difficult. She put her hand to his cheek and smiled sadly. She could never be his. "Good-by, Damien," she whispered. Pulling out of his embrace, she turned and fled into the shadows.

Chapter Eight

During the weeks that followed, Jessica won a great amount at Madame's. It seemed that no one could beat her at cards. The games in which she played had stakes that were incredibly high, even for Madame's establishment, but Jessica was forced to risk losing everything in order to win the large stipend that Margaret wanted.

The gossip concerning her and Damien had died away, to be replaced by speculation about the games with the tremendously high stakes in which she played. At the end of the evening, everyone would watch as her game finished to see if she had, indeed, won again. There were some who even placed bets on whether she won or lost on a particular evening.

For Jessica, it was very exhilarating, yet, at the same time, she knew her nerves were stretched to the limit. She realized she could not go on in this manner much longer and remain sane. Her one, steadying influence was Damien. She did not talk to him every night. In fact, the most she ever did was exchange smiles with him across the room. He was keeping his promise to her. However, just knowing he was about gave her a sense of security.

On one particular evening, about a week before she was due to leave for Braeleigh, she arrived at

Madame's a bit earlier than usual. After paying her respects to Madame, she wandered to the room where her game would be played. It was empty; not even any of the servants were about. Strolling toward the table set up with new decks of cards, she surveyed pensively her personal battlefield. Tonight, if she played well, she could make the amount of stipend that Margaret had demanded. She took a deep breath to calm her nerves.

"'She hath forsworn to love; and in that vow do I live dead, that live to tell it now.'"

Jessica swung about at the deep voice that quoted Shakespeare's *Romeo and Juliet* and saw Damien standing in the doorway.

"Hello, my love," he smiled.

He looked magnificent. The emerald color of his silk coat enhanced the color of his eyes, his black trousers fit his trim legs closely, his pale yellow waistcoat embroidered in white threads set off the intricate knot of his stock that held a glittering emerald in its folds. Jessica's heart began to hammer in her chest. She felt her throat close up as a delicious thrill ran through her.

Smiling happily, feeling absolutely foolish for allowing her feelings to be so transparent, she managed to whisper, "Hello."

"Is that all I get?" he asked as he sauntered toward her. "Just, 'hello'?"

Torn between her desire to fling herself into his arms and her own restrictions on their relationship, she retreated a step. "You startled me," she defended herself. His nearness was very disconcerting. She retreated another step. Not being able to think of anything else to say, she asked, "You have been well?"

Damien raised an amused eyebrow. "Do I look like I have been ill?" He advanced another step, and she backed away.

Jessica smiled at her own foolishness. "No."

He reached out suddenly and grabbing her hand, drew her to him. "Why are you running away, my love? Do I suddenly repulse you?"

"No, you know that is not true." Feebly, she tried to wriggle out of his embrace, then gave up.

"Then what is it?"

"Please," she pleaded. "I have a game soon. Someone will see us."

"What if they do?" he murmured as he nibbled at her ear and rained light kisses on her neck.

Jessica felt her willpower weakening as the effect of his touch began to take hold of her. "Please, Damien," she tried once more. "Not here, not now. I can not be connected in any way with a man. The gossip . . ."

"The gossip be damned," he growled as he captured her mouth with his.

Jessica resisted for as long as it took to draw a breath. She finally gave herself up to the inevitable and melted against him. It had been torture for her these past few weeks. Seeing Damien every night, knowing he was near, yet not being able to be with him, had been painful. Hungrily, she drank him in, his touch, his taste, his scent. For just a few moments, she would allow herself this tiny glimpse of heaven.

Some sixth sense brought her back to reality. There was a small movement in the room. Jessica stiffened and pulled away from Damien. When she looked up, she saw Charles Bellingham, Marquis of Durham, standing just inside the door to the room.

"A thousand pardons, my lady, Your Grace," he leered as he bowed with sarcasm. "I was under the impression that there was to be a card game in this room this evening. Perhaps I was mistaken."

The Marquis of Durham was the last person she wished to see her with Damien. He was always trying to put his hands on her, but her obvious disdain of a relationship with a man had kept her reasonably safe. Now, she knew, he looked upon her as fair game.

Jessica turned away to hide the deep blush rising in her cheeks, but her voice was cool as she answered, "You were not mistaken, my lord, but the game is not scheduled to begin for another half of an hour. If you would be so kind to find the other players, perhaps we could begin earlier."

"Of course," he agreed smoothly. His eyes flicked to Damien. "My congratulations, Wyndham, on your victory. I should have realized it would be you who would breach the wall."

"Cities have walls, sir," Jessica retorted coldly. "I suggest you review your physiology before you enter the game this evening. You might think it is statues who bet against you."

The Marquis gave Jessica a long stare. Bowing once more, he said again, "Of course. Excuse me." Turning on his heel, he left.

Damien grinned and applauded. "Bravo, my lady. You have put the dog to rout."

Jessica turned on him in exasperation. "You are insufferable!" she raged. "You made a promise to me! I can not abide that man, and now he thinks he is free to impose his attentions upon me. You have ruined everything."

Damien became serious. Taking her by the arms, he said, "If I have ruined anything, I apologize, but I did not break my promise to you, Jessica. I have not forced you to be with me. If you need help, you know you need only to ask for it." He brushed his lips lightly across her mouth. "For luck," he whispered, then he was gone.

130

Jessica put her fingers to her lips where Damien's had touched. Her anger gone, she smiled to herself. It was going to be a very lucky evening. She could feel it.

Damien had used every ounce of willpower he possessed not to carry Jessica off to his home and make love to her for the rest of the night. He berated himself for allowing himself even the one, stolen kiss. But she had appeared so vulnerable, so desirable, as she had shied away from him. He had wanted to envelope her in an invisible cocoon of safety. Instead, he had held himself tightly in check, remembering the true purpose of his watch over her.

Jessica had been in his thoughts almost constantly since the last time they had been together, much to his dismay. Unbidden, her face would appear before his eyes when he least expected. To remedy the situation, he spent hours each day pouring over the accounts of his estate. For the evenings, he accepted practically all the invitations to dinners and other social gatherings that had begun to pour in when news of his return to society had become known. Nothing had helped. Jessica still haunted him.

He made a point of stopping at Madame's every evening to check on Jessica. He told himself it was because of the job he was doing as Le Chat, but he would not admit the truth to himself. He wanted to see her. He found himself comparing every woman with whom he came into contact with Jessica.

He did not know why she bewitched him. He could have almost any woman he wanted. Mothers were throwing their unmarried daughters at him whenever they had the chance; married women were throwing themselves at him. None really interested him. He had decided he was not about to be married to anyone, especially some scatterbrained twit, and the thought of fighting a duel with a jealous husband over some unsatisfied, hot-blooded woman with the morals of an alley cat bored him. Perhaps what intrigued him so about Jessica was that she always seemed somehow remote, that there was a secret side to her that she allowed no one to see. He knew the reason behind her gambling was part of her secret. The reason for her helping a spy — that baffled and angered him.

On the one hand, he wanted to make continuous love to her, and on the other, he wanted to strangle her. He had decided that she was probably in the spying business for the money, although it did not pay as well as her gambling seemed to. Or, perhaps, she was in it merely for the excitement, seeing it as just another game.

He knew women who attempted dangerous liaisons with their lovers just for the excitement of possible discovery by their husbands. He did not think Jessica was that type of woman. Jessica had no jealous husband with which to contend. He surmised there was not even a jealous lover. He had been her first, and as far as he knew, her only one. She could not have time for another, for she spent all her nights gambling. She was an enigma that he could not decipher. Truly, she was the Ice Witch.

His moods swung from elated, to dark and brooding. It was as if he was caught in the throes of some mysterious disease without a cure. His one consolation during these times was his knowledge that he would find out exactly what Jessica's secret was very shortly.

Several days after her meeting with Damien, Jessica was in the middle of a game when she received a message from Madame. The note asked to meet with her in one of the upstairs rooms. Jessica thought the request odd, for Madame never interrupted a card game for anyone or anything. She decided that perhaps Madame wished to see her about the letter she would be delivering to Monsieur Montaigne in a few days.

During a break in the game, Jessica excused herself. As she emerged from the room, she saw Charles Bellingham staring at her. When their eyes met, he grinned lecherously at her. Ever since that night he had seen her with Damien, he had been a nuisance. He engaged her in conversation several times, always when Damien could see him, and usually, his hand just happened to land on her arm or to take hold of her fingers. Jessica tried desperately to discourage him without making a scene, but he would not be put off.

One night, he had gone so far as to corner her in one of the quiet cubicles that Madame had about the main room for intimate conversations. As Jessica tried to get past him, he had ripped off her mask and tried to kiss her. She had slapped him soundly across the face for his efforts. Damien had appeared as she was replacing her mask, and just his threatening presence had made the Marquis scurry away into the crowd. Since then, she had stayed as far away from Bellingham as possible, but his leering, knowing smile followed her whenever their paths crossed. When she saw his lecherous grin on this night, a chill ran down her spine. It was time to speak to Madame about him.

The meeting room was on the third floor of her establishment. Jessica thought this unusual, for these rooms were used for illicit liaisons, liaisons created by a woman losing a bet to a man, or vice versa, or secret liaisons where one or both of the partners had a mate to contend with. Jessica had never been above the second floor apartment in which Madame lived. She supposed the strangeness of the meeting place had to do with the secrecy involved in her acting as messenger for Madame.

When Jessica reached the room, she knocked, but there was no answer. Finding the door unlocked, she opened it. Curiously, she glanced around. It appeared as any other bedroom would. Candles were lit, but the room was empty. Madame was not there.

Thinking that perhaps Madame had been detained, Jessica walked in to wait. A footstep behind her made her turn, but it was not Madame who stood there. Instead, the Marquis of Durham blocked the door.

"Lady Fortuna," the Marquis leered. "What an unexpected pleasure to find you here."

Jessica raised her chin, determined not to show her fear. "I am waiting for Madame du Barré. We have private matters to discuss."

"How mysterious," he observed as he walked into the room. He closed and locked the door behind him.

"What are you doing?" Jessica demanded.

"I do not think Madame will mind if I keep you company while you wait for her."

"Why did you lock the door?" Jessica began to panic. "Madame will be here any moment."

"I think not, my lady." His smile was evil. "You see, Madame does not know you are here in this room. As a matter of fact, no one knows you are here."

Suddenly, her brain started to work. "Then it was you who sent the note."

"How very perceptive you are, Jessica."

"How do you know my name?"

"I have made it my business to know everything there is to know about you, everything, that is, that one can discover about the mysterious Ice Witch. But, to me, you are no mystery. I know whom you see when you leave London. You would have no letters to deliver for Madame if it were not for me."

As he spoke, he began to move toward her. She retreated.

"What do you mean?" she asked. "What letters?" Even though she was trying to protect the secret of Madame's letters to Monsieur Montaigne, her attention was mostly on keeping her distance from the Marquis.

Bellingham ignored her question. His mind was focused on his prey. "Don't run away, Jessica. We can have a wonderful time together."

"Don't touch me, or I will scream," she warned. She glanced around for a weapon of some sort that she could use. There was only a candlestick on a table. If only she could keep him talking until she could reach it. "Everyone will hear, and you will be embarrassed and dishonored."

He smiled complacently. "Scream all you wish. No one will care, that is, if anyone hears you. These rooms are quite soundproof."

As she took one large step toward the table, he lunged for her and grabbed her. Her arms were pinned against her sides. She was helpless in his grip. His cruel lips descended on her tender mouth, crushing her lips against her teeth. She stood as stone in his arms, neither responding nor fighting to free herself. When he became conscious of the fact that she was motionless, he raised his head, but kept hold of her arms. Anger burned in his eyes.

"Am I not good enough for you?" he sneered. "Or do you only tumble into bed for a duke? What does he pay you? I will triple it."

"You are not man enough to polish his boots," she spat.

His nostrils dilated and his eyes narrowed at her insult. "You little slut," he rasped.

His hand slashed out and struck her across the mouth. The blow rocked her head back, but she still remained in his metal hold. She could taste blood. Tears glittered in her eyes from the pain.

"Very well," he said. "I was willing to pay you handsomely, but now you will have to make do with the payment of whatever pleasure you get from our coupling."

Somehow, Jessica's fear did not paralyze her, but made her coldly calculating. If she could reduce his urges to nothing, she would be safe.

"What coupling?" she taunted. "Am I supposed to drool over a eunuch?"

"Eunuch?" he screeched.

With a tremendous shove, he pushed her back onto the bed. She missed the mattress, fell heavily to the floor, and banged her head on the bedpost. Lights exploded in her brain, and momentarily, she was stunned. She felt herself grabbed and thrown back onto the bed. The Marquis pounced on her and straddling her on his knees, pulled up her skirt. She heard the sound of rending cloth.

"I will show you what a true man feels like, you whore," he panted. "We shall see if I am man enough for you." He laughed viciously.

Jessica weakly tried to fend him off, but her head spun from the blow she had received. She was so frightened now that she could not think clearly.

"No," she whimpered. "Please, no."

She felt him between her thighs, and the horror of what was happening to her overwhelmed her. She screamed, and screamed, and screamed.

Suddenly, from far away it seemed, there was a splintering sound. The heaviness of the Marquis no longer held her down. A commotion followed, and when she looked to see what was happening, she saw Damien pinning the Marquis against the wall. Her attacker's feet dangled several inches above the floor. Bellingham's face was beginning to turn purple, for Damien had him by the throat.

"If you even look at her again," Damien warned in a very cold and dangerous tone, "I will see to it that no woman will want anything to do with you again."

Damien loosed his grip quite suddenly and stepped back. The Marquis slumped to the floor. Damien helped him out the door with his foot.

When he was sure the Marquis would no longer bother them, he turned to Jessica. Her eyes were wide and dark in a very pale face. There was a trickle of blood from her split lip, and a purplish bruise was beginning to appear on her temple. Her gown was ripped in several places, exposing skin. She made no effort to cover herself. Removing his coat he placed it about her shoulders and rearranged her skirt to cover her. He sat beside her on the bed and dabbed at the blood at her mouth with his handkerchief.

Jessica allowed him to do as he wished. She had no energy left to dissuade him. In an expressionless tone, she asked, "How did you know where I was?"

"I was just arriving when I saw you go up the stairs," he told her. "Then I saw Bellingham follow you. I did not like his manner, so I followed." He pushed a stray hair out of her face.

Jessica merely nodded her acceptance of his explanation. Her mind was a complete blank. She did not want to think about anything, yet one painful thought kept recurring to her. If Damien had been

137

more discreet on the night he had kissed her when the Marquis had seen them together, or if he had left her alone as she had asked, this would not have happened.

Damien was disconcerted with her lack of tears or any reaction to the horrible ordeal she had just been through. At a loss, he gently turned her face to him.

"Jessica, are you all right? Is there something I can do?" he questioned. He wanted to hold her and comfort her, but her stoniness prevented him.

She lifted deadened eyes to his. "Please," she pleaded, her voice seemingly wrenched from her body. "Leave me alone. You have ruined everything."

Her desperation thrust itself upon his consciousness like a dull blade. Unwittingly, he had caused this to happen to her. Realizing his error, feeling the unfamiliar pang of guilt, he pulled back.

Standing, he said stiffly, "I will send Madame to you." He turned and left her alone.

Madame arrived almost immediately, having learned of the commotion from one of the servants. Under her ministrations, Jessica was made comfortable, then secretly driven to her lodgings so that she would not have to face the curious crowd in the gaming rooms. Donny took over her care when she arrived.

Jessica remained in her rooms for the next several days, as she recuperated from the physical and mental bruises she had received at the hands of the Marquis of Durham. There would be no repercussions from the ordeal except that the Marquis would be barred from Madame's forever. Jessica wished it that way. She had asked Madame to relay a message to Damien asking him not to challenge Bellingham. She wanted the incident to end. A duel

138

would only give the gossipmongers more tidbits to chew over.

She was thankful that she had already made the sum of Margaret's stipend. It relieved her to know that she did not have to return to Madame's until after her return from Braeleigh.

The day before she was to leave, a messenger arrived. He carried a single rose and a note. He did not wait for a reply, but disappeared as soon as the items were in her hands. Jessica thought she knew who had sent them and debated whether to throw them out the window. Resentment against Damien smoldered and sparked deep within her. He had caused her enough problems with his arrogant pursuit of her. As much as it pained her, she wanted nothing more to do with him.

The note and rose remained on her dressing table for most of the morning. Finally, her curiosity overcame her anger, and she opened the note. It read:

A simple rose is not so simple. It hides its essence under many layers. One by one, the petals are peeled away until its heart is laid bare. Beware that all your secrets are not opened to the light. The country is no place for a delicate flower.

The note was signed only with the footprint of a cat.

Jessica realized that she had received a warning of some kind, but the reason behind it eluded her. No one except Madame knew of her secret, and she did not think Madame would betray her identity and the reason for her gambling to anyone. And no one except Damien knew where she lived.

The signature of the cat's paw was another puzzle. If it was Damien, why be so cryptic?

Jessica threw the note and flower back onto the dressing table in impatience. She had enough things to worry about without puzzling over some silly note. She had not bled at her usual time this month. Perhaps it was because of the stress she had been under to meet Margaret's demands. Or perhaps, and this was more likely, she was carrying Damien's child.

If she was truly *enciente*, she would have only another three or four months before she would have to stop her visits to Madame's because of her swollen belly. How would she live after that? Could she swallow her pride and go to Damien to beg for her child? That thought repulsed her. She would not be a kept woman. She knew Margaret would totally disown her when she found out. What, then, would happen to Jason?

Jessica could not arrive at any acceptable solution. Putting the troubled thoughts out of her mind, she decided she would only concern herself with the present. The need for a solution was still several months away. For the moment, all she would think about was leaving for Braeleigh on the morrow.

Chapter Nine

Jessica's arrival at Braeleigh was uneventful. The workers had finished their refurbishing for the most part, and the house was again quiet. Margaret was noxious, as usual. The only change in Jessica's normal routine was that she did not stay the night at Braeleigh. She remained only long enough to give the stipend to Margaret and visit with Jason a short while. Then, she left on horseback to deliver Madame's letter to Monsieur Montaigne. Donny had travelled as far as the inn, where they would spend the night and then travel back to London the following day.

The sun was beginning to set as Jessica rode into the yard of the house belonging to Monsieur Montaigne. She was too preoccupied, her thoughts still on Jason, to notice the unusual stillness, although she did think it strange that the gallant gentleman did not come to the door to greet her as was his custom.

Her horse gave a nervous whinny as she tied it to the hitching post. Jessica calmed it, then walked to the door and knocked. Receiving no answer, she tried the door. It was unlocked, so she walked in. There were no candles lit to dispel the oncoming gloom of dusk. The house was in shadow.

"Monsieur Montaigne!" Jessica called. "It is Jessica!"

There was no reply. she walked several steps farther and tried again.

"Monsieur! Monsieur Montaigne!"

Again there was no answer.

Jessica frowned and began to worry her bottom lip with her teeth. Now, what was she to do? There was no one to whom she could deliver the letter. She could not wait for Monsieur Montaigne's return, for it would be dark soon, and she had to leave for the inn.

As she turned to retrace her steps to the door, there was a movement from the one of the shadows that caught her eye. Glancing in that direction, she saw a form detach itself from the gloom, the form of a man.

He was dressed completely in black, except for his shirt, which was a startling white. His jacket was of superfine, his waistcoat of satin, his breeches of soft, black buckskin, his shirt of silk. His boots gleamed in the dull light, and his hands were covered in tightly fitting black gloves. A long, full cape of the finest wool, lined in fur, fell from his shoulders to the floor. The floppy-brimmed hat of a peasant covered his head and placed his face deep in shadow. He wore a half-mask across his eyes.

He made a sweeping bow, then spoke in French "Bonjour, mademoiselle. Perhaps I can be of some assistance?"

Jessica took a step back. Although his movements had been not in the least threatening, she felt that, somehow, this man represented a danger.

"Who are you, monsieur?" she demanded, also in French. "Where is Monsieur Montaigne? Where is his housekeeper, Madame Souchet?"

The stranger shook his head. "Ahh, I regret they

are no longer here. They were forced to leave on very urgent business. Could I deliver some message, perhaps?"

Something suddenly clicked in Jessica's head. Could this man be after the letter she was carrying? Had he been sent by the enemies of Monsieur Montaigne and Madame du Barré? But why? Who was he?

"No, thank you. That will not be necessary," she answered smoothly. "I came merely to pay a visit to my friend, Monsieur Montaigne. Since he is not here, I will leave." She began to back toward the door.

"I do not think that would be wise, mademoiselle," he said softly in a voice edged with steel.

The dim light that was coming through the open door to the outside was suddenly cut off. Swinging about, she saw a man blocking her only way of escape. She turned back to the caped figure in the room. Panic seized her. Her thoughts turned to a time several nights ago when she was confined in a room with a man against her will. To hide the trembling of her hands, she clutched them together before her. She prayed her knees would not buckle beneath her.

"What do you want of me, monsieur?" She was surprised to hear her voice sounding steady and strong. "I have nothing of value."

"What one person thinks of as worthless, mademoiselle, is another person's treasure. You are carrying something of great value to many people."

Jessica caught the gleam of white teeth as he smiled. She raised her chin in brave defiance. She was not going to be fooled into handing over Madame's private correspondence to anyone, especially this stranger who could be working for Napoleon.

"I believe you are mistaken, monsieur." She

spread her hands before her. "As you can see, I have nothing that could be of such great importance to so many."

The man signalled to his friend blocking the doorway. He stepped back out of the opening and shut the door. Jessica was again alone with the man wearing the cape. He took several steps toward her.

"Perhaps, if I described this important item, you would remember that you carry it," he suggested.

He leaned negligently on the back of a nearby chair. His air of nonchalance did not fool Jessica in the least. Perhaps, however, it would give her a few extra seconds to get to one of the rooms at the back of the house and allow her to make her escape through a window. She backed away a few more steps.

"Yes," she agreed. "If you could tell me what it is you want, then maybe I could help you."

"It is a letter," he told her. "A letter from someone you know in London written to Monsieur Montaigne. Do you know of such a letter, mademoiselle?"

"A letter, monsieur?" Jessica frowned as if in thought. She amazed herself at how easily she was able to playact with this dangerous stranger. She shook her head. "No, I know of no such letter." She edged away a little more. "There must be someone else coming to visit Monsieur Montaigne. He must have the letter you want."

At her last word, Jessica turned and fled. She heard the stranger behind her. If she could only reach that doorway, she could close and lock the door on him. He was so close. Just a few more steps. He grabbed for her. She slipped away. There, into the room. He was too near to shut the door on him. To the window. She felt his hand close about her arm. Her impetus swung her about and slammed her against the wall. Her hands came up to protect her from hitting too hard, but still the wind was knocked from her. He held her where she was, pinned by his body, one hand on either side of her.

She tried to wriggle free, but he caught one of her wrists in each hand and pulled her arms above her head. His grip was gentle, yet she knew he would not let her go. She could feel his heart beating in his chest that was pressed hard against her back. His warm breath caused the tendrils of hair on her neck to flutter.

"I am sorry if I have hurt you in any way, mademoiselle, but it was not a wise thing to do to try to run away," he spoke softly into her ear. "You would not have gone far had you escaped. My men surround the house, and they do not take kindly to people who cause them trouble. Nor do I. Not even someone as beautiful as yourself.

"Now, mademoiselle, you have a choice. Either you give me the letter that we both know you carry, or I will take it by force. I assure you, the first alternative will be more pleasant for you, and the second, well, that will be more pleasant for me, no?"

His last statement sent a shiver down her spine. The thought of having his hands tearing at her clothes was almost more than she could bear. Jessica did not doubt that his threat was sincere.

With her voice barely above a whisper, she told him, "I will give you the letter, monsieur."

"A very wise decision, mademoiselle. However, I should warn you not to try anything foolish that will anger me. You would not like me when I am angry." He released her wrists and stepped back, allowing her movement again.

She swung around to face him. "I do not like

you, now, monsieur," she told him heatedly.

He grinned at her. "I always enjoy a lady with spirit." Becoming serious once more, he said, "The letter, please, mademoiselle."

As she turned her back on him and lifted her skirt over one shapely leg, she prayed that Madame would understand why she had turned over her private correspondence to this outlaw. Tucked into the worn, frilly garter about her thigh was the letter, folded and sealed. Jessica pulled it out, allowed her skirt to drop into place, and faced him again. As she handed the letter to him, she tried to see his face under the hat. There was something familiar about him that niggled at her.

He smiled at her as he took the letter. "Many thanks, mademoiselle. You have saved us both a great deal of aggravation, at least for the moment."

He took her by the elbow and steered her back to the front parlor where they had begun their acquaintance. Stopping before a chair, he gallantly motioned for her to sit.

"Please, be so kind as to remain here, mademoiselle," he requested. "I have had enough exercise for today. I will not be so gentle if you decide to try to escape again."

As he walked away from her to a table across the room, he pulled a pistol out of his belt. Jessica did not doubt that he would use it if she tried to move. Fearfully, she swallowed. Would he release her now that he had what he wanted? Or would he keep her and. . . ? She could not finish the thought.

She watched as he lit a candle. It was almost dark outside, now. He was turned away from her, but the light glinted on his hair that curled below his hat. Golden hair. Jessica's eyes widened as she studied him. He was engrossed in reading the letter. That profile. It could not be, could it?

He finished the letter and turned to face her. The candle threw its light under the brim of his hat. Jessica gasped.

"You!" she blurted. She clutched the arms of the chair. She needed to hold onto something that she knew was solid.

Damien flinched at her word as if he had been struck. The look on her face tore at him. He had hoped to get through this evening without revealing his identity to her. He removed his mask.

"Yes, Jessica," he admitted, once again speaking in English.

"You were the one who sent the warning," she accused.

"Yes."

"But why?" she breathed. "What do you want with Madame's letter? Why are you dressed like that? Why did you do this to me?" The questions tumbled out.

"Do you know what is in Madame's letter?" he demanded.

"Of course not! I do not read other people's private correspondence."

"Perhaps you should." His tone was grim. He walked to the door, opened it, and spoke to someone outside. Then he came and stood over her. "I am placing you under arrest for treason, Jessica."

Jessica's mouth dropped open in shock. Then, almost hysterically, she began to laugh.

"Treason!" she gasped. "Damien, how long did it take you to figure out this little charade to get me to come to you?"

Damien blanched.

"Jessica!"

His voice cut through her laughter like a blade. Her laughter died abruptly.

"I have not broken my promise to you, and I am

not lying." His face was cold.

Jessica stared up at him. Shock turned her expression blank. Deep inside, she knew he was telling the truth.

Damien watched her carefully. Her eyes had gone dead, replacing any expression he might have seen there. She was retreating into herself, protecting herself from any more hurt. He hated himself for what the situation required of him, but he was her jailer now. He had to make her see that.

Grabbing her by the arms, Damien pulled Jessica out of the chair. He knew the signs of shock and hysteria all too well. He could not allow Jessica to fall apart; he wanted to save her.

Giving her a little shake, he commanded, "Listen to me, Jessica. The letters which you have been delivering for Madame contain information which she should not have. You have been helping to deliver information to Napoleon. I am working in secret to stop anyone who is delivering that information. Do you understand me?"

Jessica stared at him as if she had never seen him before. Slowly, her eyes focused and comprehension of what he was saying broke upon her consciousness.

"Treason?" she asked in a small voice.

"Yes."

"I am under arrest?"

"Yes."

When Damien released her, she sank back into the chair. How could this possibly be happening to her? The mess of her life had gone from awful to disastrous. Her mind skittered away from the overwhelming repercussions of her arrest and settled on a rather insignificant question. A tiny frown of curiosity appeared between her brows.

"How can you arrest me?" she asked. "What authority do you have?"

"By the authority of His Majesty the King. I am a colonel in His Majesty's army."

"Then you are not truly a duke?"

"I am that, too."

Jessica was confused. "But why are you both?" she asked. Few men, she knew, bought a commission in the army if they were to inherit a title. Buying commissions was left to second and third sons of the titled.

Damien smiled grimly. "It is a long story."

When he saw that she was beginning to accept the situation and to realize the gravity of her predicament, he turned away and began to collect his pistol, mask, hat, and the all-important letter. He paused beside the table holding the lit candle.

"Come along, Jessica. It is time to leave."

She looked at him a moment as she gathered her strength. Then, slowly, as if she were an old woman, she rose and walked to his side. He blew out the candle and guided her to the door in the gloom. Outside, Jessica saw several other men, dressed similarly to Damien, waiting near their horses. Aphrodite was still tethered where she had left her.

"Who owns the horse?" Damien asked.

In a monotone, she answered him, "She is mine."

Damien raised an eyebrow in surprise. Could this be where some of her winnings were going? he wondered. Was this a clue to her identity?

He merely commented, "You have good taste in horseflesh."

Without thinking, she said, "She was a gift from my father."

Intrigued by her response and hoping to learn more, he inquired, "Where do you stable her?"

Jessica just looked at him without answering. She

had said too much already.

At that moment, one of the men approached. Something dangled from his hand. Jessica heard the clank of metal against metal.

"Excuse me, sir," he said. "Will you be wanting these?" He held up shackles.

Jessica stared at the manacles held together by a heavy metal chain. She could already feel them about her wrists—the hard cold of the iron, the weight of the chain. Again the desperateness of her situation overwhelmed her. A blackness swept over her, and she swayed against her horse.

Damien reached out and steadied her. His concern briefly furrowed his brow, then he wiped it from his face. His training had taught him to keep his emotions under very tight rein.

When he saw Jessica's eyes clearing, he told her gently but firmly, "I will not put these on you, Jessica, if you give me your word that you will not try to escape."

Jessica's eyes reflected her despair. "I have nowhere to escape to," she stated dully.

He nodded and waved his man away. After helping her mount her horse, he and his men did the same. As they rode out of the yard, the men surrounded Jessica. It was done subtly, with no command spoken. Damien rode before her, at the head of the group.

Jessica kept her eyes on his broad back, her mind a complete blank. She could not let herself begin to wonder what would happen to her, or to Jason. It was better just to do as she was told for now. Later, she would begin to think, to question.

The ride to the inn was made in silence. Occasionally, Damien would drop back to ride beside her, but he made no effort at conversation, and neither did she. Jessica found she had nothing to say to him. She could not explain her actions, for she was still dazed from all that had taken place. Assuming Damien now held her in the greatest contempt, she would not make him think any less of her by pleading with him for mercy. With dignity, she rode straight-backed with her head erect.

Damien's men were equally silent. Jessica could not be sure if it was because of their training, or because they, too, despised her for what she had allegedly done. Whatever the reason, she was grateful for the solitude in which they left her.

By the time the party reached the inn, Jessica was exhausted and chilled to the bone. A light mist had begun soon after they had left the house of Monsieur Montaigne and had made the trip seem that much longer and more miserable. Jessica's riding clothes had not been made for long rides in the damp of night, and she was shivering uncontrollably. As Damien helped her down from her horse, he noticed the chattering of her teeth.

"Why didn't you say that you were cold?" His voice held a hint of exasperation.

"You did not ask me." Jessica did have some pride left.

Damien pulled her next to him, covering her with his cloak. The warmth of his body was reassuring; the gesture evoked memories of what once had been. She longed to put her arms around him, but she knew she could not. He was her jailer; she was his prisoner.

They entered the inn together. When Donny, who had been waiting with growing concern for Jessica, saw her mistress come in with a stranger's arm about her and closely followed by a group of men, she immediately came to Jessica's defense.

"Here, now!" Donny exclaimed. "Ye take yer hands off her!" Donny began tugging at Damien's arm to loosen his hold on Jessica. "Ye'll not be puttin' yer filthy hands all over my lady." When her tugging at Damien's sleeve did no good, she tried to wrest Jessica away.

Damien turned cold, green eyes on her. Jessica did not want his anger to spend itself on Donny, so she intervened before he could say anything.

"Donny," she spoke softly. "It's all right. I will explain later."

"Hmph," Donny grumbled. "It doesn't look all right." But she retreated back a step.

Damien took off his cloak and draped it over Jessica's shoulders. He took aside the innkeeper, who had hurried forward at the entrance of the group. While they spoke, Jessica kept her chin up proudly and stared at one of the far beams of the ceiling. Donny warily watched the men who stood stiffly about her. The silence was awkward. When Damien finally returned, Jessica breathed a sigh of relief.

"A meal will be sent to your room," Damien told her. "I understand that your servant has already acquired lodging for you here." At Jessica's nod, he went on, "I took the liberty of ordering a bath for you. It will cure your chill. I will come to see you later."

"Thank you," she answered him. Turning, she started up the stairs with Donny. One of Damien's men followed.

When Donny noticed him, she stopped and blocked his way. "Aye, and where d' ye think ye be goin'?" she accosted him.

Jessica put her hand on the woman's arm. "Please, Donny. It's all right. He will not bother us." She met the man's eyes and gave him a small smile of apology, then continued up the stairs.

Donny was completely bewildered when the man stationed himself outside the door, but she said nothing more on the matter. She knew Jessica would explain eventually, which she did. Jessica told her what had happened at the house of Monsieur Montaigne, and who it was that had brought her to the inn. She only omitted that Damien had been her lover.

Donny listened quietly while Jessica related her story. When she had finished, the little woman asked, "What about his babe that ye be carryin'?"

Jessica stared at her in astonishment. She had not mentioned to Donny anything about missing her time this month.

"Don't ye look so surprised," Donny told her. "I've taken care of ye all yer life. Don't ye think I know what ye be about?"

Fiercely, Jessica warned her, "Donny, don't you breathe a word of this, especially to him, or I will have your hide."

"I can keep me mouth shut," Donny sniffed. "But if ye weren't so proud, ye'd tell him. He might be able t'make things easier for ye."

"No. I will not take his pity. Or anyone else's." The proud set of her mouth discouraged any more conversation. Reluctantly, Donny let the subject drop.

When Damien came to her room, he found Jessica huddled in a chair by the fire. In her dressing gown, her hair hanging loose about her shoulders, she looked very young and vulnerable. He had to fight a strong urge to gather her in his arms and tell her everything would be all right. Instead, he stood cool and remote before her. Despite his clothes, he looked every inch the professional soldier.

"I came to inform you that we will be leaving at dawn tomorrow," he said. "There will be a man posted outside your door tonight. Do not cause him any unnecessary problems."

Jessica gazed up at him. Why couldn't it have been different between them? she cried silently. Why couldn't she hate him?

Instead of speaking her thoughts, she smiled wryly. "I will still be here in the morning, Damien. I think you overrate the ability of your prisoner."

Somewhat pompously, he answered, "The success of what I do depends on my not overrating anyone or anything."

Jessica almost laughed at the ludicrousness of being considered in the least dangerous. Instead, with a mischievous twinkle in her eyes, she said, "Then I suppose I should be flattered that you think me that important."

Damien opened his mouth as if to say something, then closed it again. When he spoke, Jessica knew it was not what he had wanted to say.

"I only tell you this so that you may be warned." Bowing formally, he murmured, "Good night, Jessica."

"Good night."

As he headed for the door, she stood and faced him. "Damien." He stopped with his hand on the latch. "What is going to happen to me?" Her voice was small and frightened.

He did not answer immediately. A muscle twitched in his jaw. Jessica thought she saw a look of compassion—or was it contempt?—cross his face, but it was gone too quickly for her to be sure.

"I believe traitors are hanged," he finally said, then he was gone.

"Oh," she said as she sank back into her chair. His words were like the blows of a hammer. How long, she wondered, before the sentence would be carried out? A month? Two? Certainly not long enough to allow her child to be born.

There would be a trial, she knew. Perhaps she could throw herself on the mercy of the court. Perhaps they would postpone carrying out the sentence long enough to allow her to bear her child. Would Damien accept the child as his? Would he care for it, love it?

Two tears slipped down her cheeks. She supposed it was better that she leave this life. She could never have belonged to Damien the way he wanted, not with Margaret's evil hanging over her head. And poor Jason. Perhaps it was better if he was left alone. Perhaps he could contend with Margaret better on his own. She wondered if Damien would be able to help him after she was gone. Were not the dying always allowed one last request? She would speak to Damien about Jason and about the child, but not now, not until she could wait no longer.

The following morning, another of Damien's men escorted Jessica downstairs and outside where she found a coach waiting. A heraldic device was emblazoned on the door. Jessica recognized it as Damien's.

Damien was speaking with several of his men when she arrived in the yard. He had changed from the dark clothing of the previous night into the uniform of an officer in His Majesty's army. All his men were in uniform. When Damien saw her, he came to speak with her. She felt a catch in her throat at the way he had been transformed. He was just as handsome, just as magnetic, but his bearing had become that of a soldier, a commander of troops, at ease with command.

Without any greeting, he told her, "You will be more comfortable riding in the coach. We will be travelling all day with only a few stops to rest the horses. Since you will not tell me where you stable your horse, we will have to take her with us. Is there anyone in the area whom you wish to inform of your arrest?"

Jessica looked into his face. There was no softening of his features as he said those things. He was merely being courteous. He had become the soldier, her jailer, completely.

Dropping her eyes, she told him, "There is no one."

Nodding his acceptance of her answer, he helped her into the coach. He had not missed the faint, dark shadows under her eyes that spoke of her sleepless night. Evidently, his parting remark of the evening before had done what he intended. She was scared now, as she should be for what she had done. He wanted her to dwell on the consequences of her actions. Treason was a very serious business. By alleviating her fright later on, perhaps she could be persuaded to incriminate Madame. Even if she did not, however, the letter was enough evidence to arrest Madame du Barré, the hub of the spy ring.

As he made his way to where one of his men held the reins of his horse, he considered whether he had made up his mind on Jessica's guilt or innocence. He wanted to believe that she was telling the truth when she said she knew nothing of the contents of the letter. If only she was not so secretive about who she was and where she came from. What was she hiding? Whom was she protecting?

The ride back to the city was agony for Jessica. She conjured up grim and ghastly scenes, most of which occurred in Newgate Prison, and most of which ended in her horrible death. Rejecting even the small, yet very important, fact that the contents of the letters she had delivered were unknown to her, she believed that just the fact that she had delivered them made her guilty of treason. She had been so naïve, so stupid.

By the time they reached the city, Jessica no longer cared what happened to her. She had tried herself and decided she was guilty. She had brought shame and scandal to the family name. Jason was better off without her.

Chapter Ten

It was night when Damien's coach entered the city and finally stopped. Jessica had not given any attention to the areas they passed through. She was too caught up in her guilt and misery to care where she was. When she glanced out the coach window, she expected to find herself in the dark, dreary, prison courtyard. Instead, the coach had stopped before the steps of Damien's house. It was lit as if their arrival had been anticipated.

What was he scheming, now? she wondered in fury. Exchanging a confused, angry glance with Donny, she descended from the coach with the help of one of Damien's men. She knew this man would tell her nothing, so in silence, she allowed him to escort her up the stairs and through the door. Damien was standing, waiting for her, at the bottom of the grand staircase. As she stalked up to him, he bowed gallantly.

"Welcome to my home, my lady."

Ignoring his polite greeting and the guard beside her, she demanded, "What kind of cruel joke is this, Damien? Am I under arrest or not? Why am I here?"

At her words, Damien's face turned stony. "You

are here, Jessica, because I requested it," he answered coldly. "You will be detained here, under house arrest, until your innocence or guilt has been established. At that time, you will either be released or sent to trial. Being the mistress of a duke has its advantages."

Jessica felt as if he had slapped her. How could he say something so cruel before all his men? With her cheeks flaming and her eyes brimming with tears, she opened her mouth to berate him. His icy gaze froze the words in her throat. He turned to a maid who hovered nearby.

"Show Lady Jessica to her room, please, Lucy," he said calmly as if nothing had happened.

Lucy hurried forward and asked Jessica to follow her. Jessica was quite happy to comply. All she wanted at the moment was to be away from the presence of that hateful man. She had been mortified and hurt by Damien's admission of their intimacy before all his men. How could he be so callous? Did he suddenly despise her so much?

What she did not see was the glowering look he received from the man who had escorted her into the house, nor the impatient way Damien had turned his shoulder to him. All she heard was a muttered, "Mind your own business, Leftenant."

When Jessica was halfway up the stairs, he called to her. She stopped and turned slowly, not knowing what to expect, hoping for an apology. She was disappointed.

"Dinner will be at nine o'clock," he informed her. "Please be prompt. My men and I do not like to be kept waiting."

The color drained quickly from Jessica's cheeks. She could not endure sitting through a meal with him. Not tonight. Not with all his men in attendance. Not with all of them knowing of her familiarity with Damien. A black pall suddenly dropped over her eyes and her knees buckled beneath her. She crumpled to a heap on the stairs.

When her eyelids finally fluttered and opened, she discovered Damien kneeling beside her, cradling her head against his shoulder. Blankly, she stared at everyone standing around her. Realizing she still leaned against Damien, she struggled to sit up, but he would not allow it.

"Lay still, Jessica," he ordered. Was that concern she heard disguised in his curtness?

"I'm sorry," she apologized. "I don't know why I fainted."

He raised an eyebrow and one side of his mouth twitched upward. "Obviously, the thought of dining with six men," he commented dryly. Lucy appeared beside him and held a glass of brandy out to him. Taking it, he put it to Jessica's lips. "Drink this. It will put some color back in your cheeks."

Jessica took a sip, swallowed and gasped. It burned all the way down her throat and hit her stomach with a jolt. She coughed and pushed the glass away.

With watery eyes, she looked up at him and said, "I'm better, now. Thank you."

Again she tried to get up. Instead of helping her to her feet, Damien scooped her up in his arms and carried her the rest of the way upstairs.

"Please, Damien, I can walk," she protested, although she appreciated the warmth and strength he emanated.

"Perhaps," he told her, "but I did not bring you here to kill yourself by falling down the stairs and breaking your neck. If I am to hand you over to a judge, I would prefer that you be in one piece. Besides, I like you better alive than dead."

He turned his head to look at her, and Jessica

found her face only inches from his. If she moved just the tiniest bit, she could kiss him, and she very much wanted to do that. Damien had stopped just outside the door to a room. He stood still, gazing at her. Jessica was caught in his intense eyes. Her lips parted, and she saw his head bend ever so slightly toward her.

Donny behind them cleared her throat. Damien blinked. The spell was broken. His spine stiffened, and he entered the room with her. It was a lovely bedroom. As soon as he placed her on the bed, she began to sit up.

"Stay there," he ordered. "I will have your dinner brought up to you." He turned to Donny. "Put your mistress to bed. She seems to be too stubborn to go on her own." With that, he left.

Jessica and Donny looked at each other a moment, each thinking their own thoughts. Donny was the first to break the silence.

"Aye, he's a hard one, that, but he seems fair enough. Ye be lucky he's a duke, and he cares for ye. Ye could be in prison, now."

Sadly, Jessica shook her head. "He does not care for me, Donny. I am only something to amuse him."

"Hmph. Amuse, is it? Ye can't see what's before yer own eyes," Donny grumbled. "Well, come on with ye. Into bed. He'd not like it if ye disobeyed."

Donny helped Jessica get undressed and into bed, then she began to unpack the few belongings Jessica had taken with her to Braeleigh. When she opened the armoire, she saw it already contained a woman's wardrobe. She began to close the door again when something caught her eye. She pulled out a blue silk dress and held it up.

"Look at this," she said.

"Why, that's just like mine!" Jessica exclaimed.

"It is yer dress," Donny replied. "They're all here, all yer clothes."

"But why?" Jessica wondered. "How did he know?"

"He knew. That's all ye need t' know. Ye don't cross a man like that. Ye tell him everything tomorrow."

Jessica's chin went up defiantly. "I'll do no such thing. He will not find out about Jason or the babe from me. He does not have to know yet. And you keep quiet, Mistress Donlin."

Donny's mouth tightened into a straight line. "Aye, I'll keep quiet," she reluctantly agreed. "But ye'll be gettin' yerself into deep trouble with him."

Jessica made no reply. Ending the discussion, she slumped down into the bed and pulled the covers up to her chin.

Lucy came soon after with a light meal for Jessica of broth, fresh bread with butter, and tea. She told Donny there was a meal for her in the kitchen, and that if Donny wished to retire after that, she would take care of the Lady Jessica.

After Donny was gone, Jessica was left alone to think and ponder her situation. The room she had been given was large and expensively furnished. It was evidently one of the better guest rooms. Damien had been quite solicitous of her comfort, at least. It was his manner that baffled her. He had turned so cold toward her, almost cruel. Except for that one moment when they would have kissed. Jessica smiled to herself and put her fingers to her lips. A tingle ran down her spine. She remembered his kisses. The smile faded from her mouth. You are being a fool, she told herself. He despises you now that he thinks you are guilty of treason. That moment might never have happened. It might have only been your imagination.

Sighing, she pushed away the tray and leaned back on the pillows. The food and hot tea had relaxed her. She realized she was very tired. Planning to rest only a short time, closing her eyes, she fell into a deep sleep.

Damien had dined with his men as he had planned, but his eyes had strayed often to the empty chair to his right that would have been occupied by Jessica. His glances had not gone unnoticed by his men.

At the end of the meal, Damien had given them their orders for the following days while Jessica remained his prisoner. It was an easy assignment, to keep a young woman under house arrest, but he had cautioned them against losing their diligence. The men had accepted his warning that they should not be fooled by anything Jessica told them, but he had felt their disapproval in their silence. He had dismissed them in exasperation, not quite sure whether he was angry at the men for having been captivated by this slip of a girl, or at Jessica for arousing their pity, or at himself for being bewitched by such a woman.

He sat alone now, in the dark before the fire. Having gone through a goodly portion of the brandy in the decanter at his elbow, his thoughts chased themselves in circles inside his head. He kept coming back to one simple question whose answer, he knew, was not so simple: Why? He could not find any of the answers that the question prompted. Glancing at the almost empty decanter, he smiled wryly at himself. The brandy certainly had not made him think any clearer, and he was going to have a roaring headache in the morning.

With extreme care, he placed the glass on the table. Pulling himself out of the chair, he stood, weaving slightly, as he lit a candle. He placed a hand on the back of his chair to steady himself, then started for bed.

In the upstairs hall, his feet stopped before the door to the room where Jessica lay. Hesitating only a moment, he opened the door quietly and walked in. He moved silently to the side of the bed and held the candle high, allowing its light to fall on her face.

She was so beautiful, this woman-child, and too young to have become involved in something as treacherous as espionage. He reached out and smoothed a lock of hair away from her face. His fingers trailed down her cheek. She sighed softly in her sleep and, throwing her arm wide, turned onto her back. Her breasts softly thrust against her thin nightrail.

His breath caught in his throat, and he swallowed with an effort. What he wanted to do was climb under the covers with her and make love to her, to feel her beneath him, her body enticing, responding. Biting down on a groan, he lowered the candle and looked away. He could not, not yet. Their positions in this nasty game would not allow it. Quickly, he walked to the door and let himself out as quietly as he had come.

The following morning when Jessica awoke, she thought for a moment she was at Braeleigh, in her own bed. When she opened her eyes and looked about, she realized she was in a strange room, and that room was in the house belonging to Damien.

It was a pretty room, decorated in pale greens and yellows, reminding her of spring. She decided it was definitely better than prison, and was grateful to Damien for using his influence so that she would be allowed to stay at his home. Stretching with feline grace, she luxuriated in the satiny sheets. She felt rested and ready for anything, possibly even a meeting with Damien. As she was lying there, a knock came at the door, and the maid, Lucy, entered with a cup and saucer on a small tray.

"Good morning, m'lady," she smiled pertly. "I brought you some hot chocolate."

Jessica smiled back at the girl. "Thank you, Lucy."

"Did you sleep well? You were already asleep when I came last night to take your tray. Mistress Donlin will be up soon to help you dress." As Lucy talked nonstop, she walked around the room and opened drapes and straightened things. She stopped at the foot of the bed. "His Grace would like to see you in the dining room for breakfast when you are dressed." At that moment, the door opened and Donny bustled in.

"All right, out of bed with ye," she commanded, taking over the situation. "Are ye going t'spend the rest of yer life in that bed?"

Lucy's mouth dropped open at the sight of a servant giving orders to one of the nobility. Jessica gave the girl a grin and a helpless shrug.

Donny turned on Lucy. "They be wantin' ye, girl, in the salon to help with the polishin'." She waited until Lucy had hurried out the door, then she turned back to Jessica.

"Ye be feelin' all right?" she asked.

"I feel fine, Donny," Jessica assured her.

"Good," Donny nodded. "Yer Duke's walkin' around lookin' like a thundercloud. Ye'll be needin' every ounce of yer strength today."

Jessica sighed and climbed out of bed. Suddenly, she was not so ready to meet Damien. She could see it was going to be a very long day.

When Jessica walked into the dining room, Damien was sitting by himself at the long table. He was staring out the window and banging a spoon absently upon the folded napkin beside his plate. Jessica stopped hesitantly just inside the doorway. Finally, he glanced up and saw her.

"Are you going to come in and sit down, or do you think I might suddenly grow fangs and attack you?" he growled.

Jessica frowned at his bad manners. "That is quite possible," she sniffed.

With a look on his face that seemed to suggest he had eaten something rotten, he slowly stood and motioned to a chair at his right. "By all means, my lady, please come in and be seated," he said sarcastically.

Regally, trying not to show that she was in the least intimidated by him, Jessica sailed into the room and waited as he held the chair for her. Her nerves only allowed her to perch uncomfortably on its edge, however, and she ached to slap his face. When Damien had resumed his seat, he rang for the servants to bring in breakfast.

After their plates had been filled, he asked in a more civil tone, "Are you feeling better this morning?"

"Much better, thank you," she answered quietly. Jessica noticed his bloodshot eyes, and could not help adding, "A good night's sleep will cure almost anything."

Ignoring her subtle gibe, Damien said, "I thought I should inform you of what will be expected of you while you are here. You will be allowed the freedom of the house and grounds as if you were a guest. However, if you stray beyond the boundaries, my men have orders to treat you as an escaped prisoner. In other words, they will shoot first, then ask questions. I would appreciate it if you would not put them in that position. They

166

truly do not enjoy shooting women. Do I make myself clear?"

"Perfectly, Your Grace." Jessica could not resist baiting him with the formal manner of address for his outright bad manners.

Damien's eyes narrowed, but he made no answering comment. Instead, he went on, "You will be questioned later on in the morning concerning your activities. Your cooperation, or lack of it, will have a large part to play when your fate is decided."

"What will happen if I do not know anything?"

"Then you have a problem, don't you?" he told her, but her steady gaze disconcerted him. "Eat your breakfast," he said gruffly as he turned his attention to his own plate.

By the time they had finished breakfast, Damien's good humor had begun to return. He held Jessica's chair when she rose from the table and walked with her out of the dining room. She would wait in her room to be summoned for questioning. As she started up the stairs, he caught her hand. She turned on the bottom step.

"It will go easier for you if you tell the truth, Jessica. I will help you all I can."

Being a step below her, Damien's face was level with hers. His expression was intent, serious. Was there a hint of sympathy there, too? Jessica longed to reach out and touch his cheek. Instead, she bit down on her bottom lip to keep her emotions under control.

"Thank you," she murmured, then she turned and fled up the stairs.

About an hour later, the summons came. She was to meet with Damien in the salon. Her nerves were as frayed as the handkerchief that she had picked at while she waited. Soon, she would discover her fate.

There was no one in the room when she arrived. Jacobs told her that His Grace would be with her presently, then left her alone. Jessica sat on the edge of a chair, her hands clasped in her lap, her eyes downcast. With her high-necked, long-sleeved, slightly worn, woolen dress of blue, she presented the very picture of demure innocence. Several minutes went by before Damien entered the room with another man, a soldier, quite a bit older than Damien.

"Jessica," Damien spoke gently, "this is General Drayton. He would like to ask you some questions."

The General bowed over Jessica's hand. He reminded her of someone's grandfather.

"I can not recall ever being presented to so lovely a prisoner," he smiled kindly.

"Thank you, General," Jessica smiled back at him. Perhaps this would not be such a terrible experience, after all.

The General sat down across from her and began. "I am sure you realize that you are in very serious trouble. The more you can help us, the easier it will be for you in the end. We are very willing to be lenient with someone who cooperates. Do you understand, my dear?"

Jessica nodded. Oh, yes, she understood. Her imprisonment would be less of a hardship, her execution would be quicker.

"Good," the General smiled. "Now, suppose you begin by telling us how you came to be delivering messages for Madame du Barré."

Jessica began her story. She told how she had gone to Madame to gain entrance to her house, how Madame had offered her a loan to start gambling. Then she explained the way she was to repay the loan: by delivering the letter once a month to Monsieur Montaigne.

"Did you not think this an odd way to repay a loan?" the General asked.

"Ye-es," Jessica faltered. "But Madame was so nice. I had planned to repay her anyway when I could afford it. Delivering the letters was such a small favor to ask. I had no idea what the letters said."

"Hmm," the General mused. "Why was it such a small favor to deliver a letter every month to Monsieur Montaigne? He lives near the town of Osmington in Dorsetshire. That is a fair distance to travel just to deliver a letter."

Jessica almost blurted out the truth, but she stopped herself in time. Lowering her eyes, she said, "I can not tell you."

"Then tell me, my dear, why a well-bred young woman like yourself would want to have anything to do with a place like that of Madame du Barré?"

Watching her knuckles turn white as she clenched her hands in her lap, she said in a voice barely above a whisper, "I needed a great deal of money."

"Why?"

"I can not tell you." She raised anguished blue eyes to the General.

"Whom are you protecting, Jessica?" The General suddenly did not look like someone's grandfather. He had changed to a steely commander who was not used to being thwarted.

Jessica pressed her lips together and remained silent.

"All right," he conceded. "We will let that go for the moment. Can you tell us if you ever saw anything unusual at Madame's? Was there ever anyone there who did not seem to belong? Or was there anyone to whom Madame was particularly friendly?"

Jessica tried to remember but nothing came to mind. She shook her head.

"I'm sorry," she told him. "I can not remember anything like that. I spent very little time there when I was not involved in a game. I . . ." Jessica's voice trailed off, and she stared off into space.

The General leaned forward. "Yes?"

Her eyes came back to focus on the gentleman across from her. "Charles Bellingham. The Marquis of Durham."

"Yes? What about him?"

Jessica felt Damien's tenseness behind her. "He said something . . . odd . . . the night . . ." She halted, not able to speak of the horrible night the man had attacked her. She had tried not to think of that night, had tried to put it out of her mind. Now, however, the words of the Marquis came to her clearly.

She took a breath and forged on. "Several nights ago, the Marquis told me that if it were not for him, I would have no letters to deliver for Madame du Barré." General Drayton exchanged a glance with Damien, who was no longer lounging on the window seat behind Jessica, but was now sitting forward, intent on every word.

"I knew I should have killed him then," Damien muttered.

The General made a placating gesture with his hand, then turned back to Jessica. He asked, "Did he ever say anything else about these letters that you delivered?"

Jessica shook her head. "No. Just that once."

The General nodded his approval. "I believe you have just given us the name of the traitor in our midst. You see, the Marquis works closely with His Majesty's Foreign Minister. He is privy to

170

many state secrets."

Jessica's eyes widened in shock, but she said nothing. General Drayton went on, "What you have told us, my dear, is a great help, but I am afraid the story of your own involvement in this matter is not very plausible. How can we be sure that you are not lying to us about being ignorant of the contents of those letters? We must have some proof of your innocence. His Grace informs me that you refer to yourself as 'Lady Jessica'. Are you, in truth, the daughter of some lord?"

"Yes."

"Then who is your father?"

"My father is dead, sir," she answered quietly.

"Then you have my deepest sympathies. However, that does not help. Your family. Who are they? Where are you from?"

Jessica did not answer. She was not going to dishonor her family name by revealing whose daughter she was. She was also not going to give Margaret the satisfaction of knowing what had happened to her.

When the General received no answer, he tried, "Could it be, perhaps — and please excuse my being indelicate — that you are the illegitimate daughter of some lord?"

Jessica felt the heat rise in her cheeks. "No!"

The General sighed. "All right, if you can not reveal your family, then tell us why you have a need for such a large amount of money. I understand that you have won a fortune at cards, yet you live very simply. Where does the money go, my dear?"

Again, Jessica remained silent. How could she explain that her *dear* stepmother was holding her only brother hostage on his own estate? Who would believe her?

She heard Damien move impatiently behind her. Not even his anger would make her reveal her secrets. Let them put her in prison if they wished. She would keep Jason free from scandal.

General Drayton cleared his throat. "I see. You will not tell us. Very well, my dear. I feel I must warn you that your fate still hangs in the balance. If you happen to change your mind and wish to tell us your story, just inform His Grace. Now, if you will excuse us, we have some things to discuss."

So Jessica was dismissed. She had told them everything that she had dared. There was nothing more she could do. Damien impersonally escorted her to the door of the salon and held the door for her. It closed behind her like the door to a prison cell.

She supposed that they would decide to bring her to trial, for she could not expect the General to believe her story. It sounded like a fabrication, even to her. Would Damien believe her? she wondered.

About an hour after the end of her questioning, she watched from her bedroom window as the General left. Several minutes later, there was a knock on her door. Thinking that it was only one of the maids, she called to enter. It was Damien who walked in, however. He looked angry.

"How can someone," he began without any preamble, "who is so shrewd at cards, be so foolish with her own life? You have not helped your cause any by remaining silent about who you are, Jessica."

"I know," she stated simply, and turned back to stare out the window.

Damien crossed the room in several long strides, and taking her by the arm, swung her about to face him.

172

"Why?" he demanded.

Jessica answered his question with one of her own. "Would you dishonor your family, Damien? Would you not prefer to die in obscurity than drag your family name through the mire?"

He dropped his hand from her arm; her words had hit their mark. "Jessica, if your story of your innocent involvement is true, then you have nothing to fear," he said gently. "There would be no scandal, for there would be no trial. General Drayton only needs some proof that you are telling the truth."

"Oh, there would be scandal. How else would Madame be convicted if not with my testimony? How was it that someone like me came to know a woman like Madame? What was I doing in her establishment?"

Damien raised an eyebrow. "Well?"

Instead of answering him, she asked, "Do you believe that I am telling the truth, Damien?"

He stared at her for a moment, then, no longer able to meet her gaze, he turned to look out the window. "I don't know."

Jessica nodded, understanding his indecision. Why should he believe her? He had met her in circumstances that would cause anyone to have grave doubts about her integrity. She had even cheated him in a card game.

"Thank you for being truthful," she told him. Ruefully, she smiled. "I would probably have trouble believing my story, too, if I were not the one telling it."

Damien turned his head to look at her, his eyes for a moment reflecting the pain of his uncertainty; then the instant was gone, and his expression was once more impersonal, that of her jailer.

"I will leave you to think over your reticence," he

said. His tone was cool, detached. "Perhaps you will change your mind. If so, just inform one of the servants. They will know where to find me." Bowing formally to her, he left.

Chapter Eleven

Jessica remained in her room for the rest of the day; she even requested to have her meals there. Damien did not come again, and she did not try to find him. There was nothing left to say.

After the dinner tray had been taken away, she wandered to the window. She seemed to spend a great deal of time standing, staring out at the drive, seeing nothing, thinking less. Her mind was brought back into focus by the arrival of Damien's landau on the drive. She saw him emerge from the house and enter the carriage. He was dressed for the evening. He looked stunning. His evening cape swirled about his legs and reminded her of how he had been dressed when she had been arrested.

A strange feeling swept over her as she realized she was actually a prisoner and could not come and go as she wished. Possibly, never again, would she be able to see London at night, to mingle and converse with interesting men and women, to see Braeleigh. With a sigh, she turned away from the window. She wondered where Damien was going to spend his evening, then put the thought from her mind.

Go to bed, she told herself. Don't think about anything. Sleep.

She rang for Donny to help her undress, and was

soon in bed, but she could not sleep. For hours, she lay listening to the house become quiet as the servants retired. She knew Damien had not come home, for she had not heard the carriage on the drive. Tossing and turning, unable to sleep, she decided to go in search of something to read. She had not seen a library in the house, but perhaps there would be books in Damien's study. Slipping into her dressing gown, taking a lit candle, she started her exploration.

On the bottom floor, Jessica opened several doors before she found the right one. As she walked into his sanctuary, she felt her pulse quicken. Here was where Damien ran his estate, conducted his business. Another side of him revealed itself in this room.

Holding up her candle, she looked around. There were no lamps lit, but the fire burned brightly. Evidently, this was where he would come when he returned home. It was a typically masculine room with walls panelled in rich, dark mahogany and the floor covered in a deep red Persian rug. The various chairs, large and comfortable looking, were covered in red or black leather. Along one wall, from floor to ceiling, were bookshelves filled with books. In a corner of the room was a massive desk. A portrait above the fireplace caught Jessica's eye, and she went to examine it more closely.

The man portrayed in the painting bore a marked resemblance to Damien. Except for the color of the eyes and the wig the man wore, it could have been Damien. Even the expression was similar; she had seen Damien's eyes glint in just that way. The nameplate attached to the frame told her that this was the fifth Duke of Wyndham, Damien's father. She wondered if this man had been as adventurous as his son.

Jessica turned her attention to the books. For a small collection, it was very diverse. It contained many works of the older writers, as well as those of the modern period. She took down a volume by Sir Walter Scott. It had been signed by the poet with a personal inscription to Damien. She replaced the book on the shelf. One of Shakespeare's comedies was what she needed to lighten her spirits. Curling up in one of the chairs by the fire, she began to read.

Several hours later, a noise startled her awake. Looking about, she realized she had fallen asleep in Damien's study. She was about to uncurl from the chair and scurry back to her room when the door opened and Damien walked in. His gait was careful, as if he expected to step on something at any moment. Jessica realized he had been drinking heavily.

As he came to stand before the fire, Jessica stood, the book falling unheeded from her lap. She wanted to leave as quickly as possible. He swung about in a crouch, ready to pounce, in his surprise at finding someone else where he thought he had been alone. A small, sharp, deadly-looking stiletto appeared as if by magic in his hand. Jessica remained pinned where she stood.

When Damien realized who had startled him, he straightened, and a slow grin spread across his face. He pushed the stiletto back into his sleeve where Jessica assumed he must have had some sort of sheath. His eyes travelled to the book lying at her feet.

"What is this?" he drawled. "A raid on my library? Or were you waiting up for me?"

Jessica could smell the brandy he must have been drinking all night. She wanted to get out of his way. His mood was dangerous.

"I could not sleep, so I came to find something to read," she explained as she began to edge away. "I only meant to stay for a little while." Out of his reach, she turned to leave.

"Wait!" he ordered.

She stopped.

"Turn around."

Slowly, she did as she was told. Jessica did not really believe he would harm her, but it was better not to take any chances.

"Why do you still wear the nightclothes of a young maid?" he demanded. "Is it to disguise yourself, Witch?"

Jessica's mouth dropped open at his unexpected question. She watched him approach her and did not move as he untied her dressing gown and unbuttoned several buttons down the front of her nightrail.

"There," he breathed. "That is better."

Jessica immediately began to rebutton her gown. She could not endure the bittersweetness of another night of lovemaking with Damien.

"I think I had better leave," she told him firmly.

"Why? To recite your incantations and weave your spells, Witch?"

"Damien, you're drunk."

He grinned. "I know. You should feel great remorse, Witch, for it is because of your sorcery that I am in such a sorry state."

"I am going to bed," she stated, ignoring his comment.

"Ah, now that, Witch, is a very good idea." He put his arm around her shoulders. "I believe I will come with you."

She slid out of his grasp. "Damien, please."

" 'Please'? 'Please' what? Do you not wish me to see your cauldrons boiling with your magic brews?

Are you afraid to let me see your lair, Witch?"

"This is your house. You may go where you wish." She stood coolly before him and hoped her manner would dissuade him from any nocturnal activity of which he might be thinking.

"You are right," he agreed. "It is my house, and I wish to walk with my arm about you up the stairs to your room. You have fallen into your own trap, Witch." He smiled triumphantly and chucked her under the chin.

Jessica ground her teeth together in aggravation as he put his arm around her shoulders once more. His grip was tighter this time, and she knew he would not let her go again. She glanced up at him from beneath her lashes.

"Beware, lest I turn you into a toad," she warned. She could not help the flutter in the pit of her stomach at his nearness.

He chuckled. "So, the sorceress shows her true colors. Perhaps it is you who should beware. Being a toad, I could give you warts." He laughed at his own cleverness.

Jessica groaned, but made no comment. They climbed the stairs together, and she brushed his lips away from her neck several times before they reached her room. He walked in behind her and closed the door.

"This is a very pleasant room," Damien observed. He took off his coat. "I believe I will spend the night here." He removed his stock and unbuttoned his shirt.

"Oh, Damien," Jessica said in dismay. "Please, don't."

She began to rebutton his shirt. Afraid because she very much wanted him to spend the night with her, her fingers shook. He caught her hands to stop their clumsy fumbling.

"Look at me and tell me no," he ordered quietly.

She looked up into his eyes. "Please," was as far as she got. His mouth stopped any other words she might have said.

Jessica melted against him. She hungered for him, wanted him so badly. Her mind told her that she was being stupid, that she would despise herself in the morning for being so weak, but she did not care. Urgently, she helped Damien out of his clothes and removed her own. As they snuggled under the covers, Damien gave a huge yawn.

"I fear my endurance is at an end, Witch," he said. "What spell did you put on me to make me so weak?"

Jessica giggled. "How much brandy did you consume this evening?"

"Oh, gallons." He nuzzled her neck and held her close. "Stay with me, my love," he whispered.

As Jessica held him close, a soft snore reached her ears. Smiling, she herself fell asleep.

The next morning, Jessica awoke with a wonderful feeling of well-being. The other side of the bed was empty, but the pillows gave testimony that Damien had slept there. She ran her hand over the sheet beside her, remembering the night before. It had been wonderful just sleeping the night in Damien's arms. If only it could be like that forever. Knowing that it could never be, her feeling of well-being faded somewhat, but did not disappear completely.

Damien had already breakfasted and was about his business by the time Jessica arrived in the dining room. However, the room was not empty. One of Damien's men, the man who had escorted her into the house, was seated at the table. He rose when she entered the room.

"Please," she smiled. "Sit down and finish your

meal." She slid into a chair across the table from him. "I hope you don't mind sharing the table with your prisoner."

"Not at all, Lady Jessica," he replied. "It is a pleasure to share the table with one so lovely as yourself."

"You are very kind, sir." She glanced at him from under her lashes. "I feel I am at a great disadvantage, for you know my name, yet I do not know yours."

"Forgive me, my lady. I am Edward Johnson, Viscount of Winslow, third son of the Earl of Mark, Leftenant in His Majesty's Army."

Jessica smiled at his thorough introduction of himself. "Then I am very happy to make your acquaintance, Leftenant. You must find the duty of guarding one woman rather tedious."

"As I said, my lady, with one so lovely as yourself, the duty is a pleasure."

He smiled back at her, making crinkles around his hazel eyes. Jessica decided she liked this man.

"But would you not prefer to be attached to some unit that is fighting Napoleon in Austria? Or perhaps Italy?"

"We have been fighting Napoleon, my lady, but not in the manner you suggest," he replied, then grinned. "This duty is much more pleasant than some others I have been assigned."

"Oh? Have you been under the command of His Grace for very long?" she queried.

"As long as I've been in the army," he replied. "About four years."

"Then you must know him very well."

The soldier shook his head. "Not as well as you might think, but better than most, I suppose."

"Do you know why he joined the army? It is so unusual to find a duke with a commission." Jessica knew she was prying, but she thought she might have a wonderful source of information on Damien sitting across the table from her. She was not about to let it disappear.

Leftenant Johnson gazed at her for a moment, obviously trying to make up his mind how much to tell her. Finally, he said, "He was not supposed to inherit the title. He had an older brother."

Jessica blinked. "Had?"

"Yes, he was killed in a duel about four years ago, just after I entered the army."

"How terrible!' " she exclaimed. She shook her head. "Duelling is such a waste. Why can't men find some other way to settle their differences?"

"Perhaps because men often duel over women," the Leftenant offered. "Someone has to be the victor and take possession." His smile was mischievous.

Jessica smiled back at him. "I think you have been with His Grace too long, Leftenant. You sound suspiciously like him."

"I consider that a compliment, my lady."

Jessica regarded him seriously. "You respect him a great deal, don't you?"

"It is deeper than respect," the Leftenant told her. "He has saved my life several times, as I have saved his. That creates a very strong bond between men." He drained the last of his coffee and stood. "If you will excuse me, my lady, I must attend to some things."

Jessica nodded and watched him leave the room. She remained at the table and played thoughtfully with the food on her plate. So, Damien had an older brother who had been killed in a duel. She remembered her father had been in a duel once, when she had been much younger. She was not supposed to have known, but she had heard her father and Margaret arguing about it. Jessica had never heard him so angry. Evidently, it had been because of Margaret that he had been forced onto the field of honor. At the time, she thought duelling to be very romantic. Now, she knew it for what it was: a stupid tradition. Her heart ached for Damien. What a terrible way to inherit a title!

Her appetite having left her, she got up from the table and decided to retrieve her book from Damien's study. The door to the room was closed, and she listened a moment to see if she could hear if anyone was inside. Hearing nothing, she knocked to make sure. Damien's deep voice bade her enter.

Opening the door quietly, she stepped inside. "I'm sorry to disturb you," she apologized.

Damien leaned back in his chair and smiled. "I wish all my interruptions were as pleasant." He held up her book. "I was wondering when you would come to get this."

Jessica walked to the desk and took hold of the book, but he would not let it out of his grasp. Instead, he grasped her hand with his free one and guided her around the desk so she stood at his knees. Embarrassed because of her obvious desire for him that she had revealed in their kiss of the night before, she kept her eyes on their hands.

"I only came to retrieve the book, Damien. I did not know you were here," she spoke softly.

"I will not keep you from your reading. Witch." This last was whispered.

Thinking perhaps he was mocking her, she raised her eyes, but instead, his gaze glowed with his want. She turned away quickly, her cheeks flaming.

"Do not look at me so. Someone may come in."

"I will look at you any way I wish, but if I embarrass you, we can retire to an upstairs room," he suggested.

"No!" She took a breath to steady herself. "Please,

just let me have the book."

"You did not wish to read last night," he reminded her.

He gave her hand a tug, pulling her off-balance into his lap. She tried to wriggle free, but he would not let her up.

"Damien, please, let me up."

"No one comes in here unless they are bid." His voice soothed as his hand slid up her side and cupped a breast. "There is no need to worry about discovery." His free hand went to the back of her neck and slowly brought her lips down to meet his own.

Wonderful sensations coursed through her body at his caress, but she knew that unless she did something immediately, she would end up making love to him right there. Gently, she pushed herself upright.

Running a finger down his cheek and over his lips, she sighed with a pout, "Oh, Damien, you do not play fairly." When she saw that his attention was on her finger, she jumped up quickly and moved out of his reach. "Neither do I," she laughed lightly. She blew him a kiss as she hurried out of the room. She took her book with her.

As she closed the door behind her, she heard Damien call good-naturedly, "Witch!"

Chapter Twelve

Later that morning, as she sat reading by the window of her room, a coach drove up to the front of the house. Curious, Jessica watched as a woman alighted from the vehicle. She had hair streaked with grey, yet she had the carriage and figure of a young person. Jessica's eyes sought out the crest emblazoned on the door of the coach. Her heart sank when she recognized it. It was as she feared. The crest was that of Damien's family. The woman was his wife.

Jessica remained at the window to see if there were any children who would appear from the coach, but there were none. Perhaps, she had left them at Wyndham, or perhaps—and Jessica hoped for this—there were no children. If his wife were barren, then at least Jessica could give him a child.

Confused at the appearance of the woman, she could not remember hearing anything about a wife in the gossip she heard concerning Damien. It had always seemed that the women spoke of him as if he were an eligible bachelor. Perhaps his marriage was only one of convenience, an arranged marriage between families; perhaps Damien and his wife had an agreement and each went their separate ways and took lovers. It was certainly not unheard of in the London ton. In any case, Jessica's relationship with Damien would now change. He was her jailor, nothing more. No longer could she hold the dream that someday he would marry her. Yes, she had to admit it finally. It was a hope she had held close to her heart.

Straightening, she turned away from the window. Now, more than ever she had to be strong and resist his devastating good looks, his seductive touch. There would be no more secret trysts.

Not wishing to intrude into the private lives of Damien and his family and feeling very uncomfortable in her situation, Jessica remained in her room for the rest of the morning, not even leaving for the midday meal. By the middle of the afternoon, however, the sunshine and spring weather began to beckon to her. She decided if she were careful, she could get to the enclosed garden in the back of the house without being noticed.

It was a lovely garden, even now, before the flowers were in bloom. She always enjoyed the spring and summer months. Everything was so alive.

She had been reading for a while when she noticed the woman she had been trying to avoid walk into the garden. The Duchess had not seen her, for Jessica was sitting partially hidden by a bush. Jessica studied her as she came closer. The Duchess was much older than she had guessed at first. She was, however, quite lovely, a woman of ageless beauty.

The Duchess looked up suddenly, surprising Jessica into a blush for staring at her. The lady smiled and advanced, her hand extended.

"You must be the house guest whom Damien mentioned," the woman said. "I am Lydia, Duchess of Wyndham."

Jessica took her hand and curtsied. "It is a pleasure, Your Grace." She wondered fleetingly if Damien had informed this woman what type of house guest she was.

"We missed you at lunch," the Duchess went on warmly. "Were you not feeling well?"

"I did not wish to intrude. I understand that you have not seen Da . . . His Grace for some time."

"How thoughtful that was of you! Yes, I have not seen him for a very long time." Her tone was wistful, and Jessica wondered at that. "But, we will have plenty of time to catch up on each other's news. Promise me that you will not stay away at dinner."

As she absently agreed not to miss dinner, Jessica noticed the Duchess had green eyes, like Damien. It was odd that two people who were married should both have uncommonly green eyes.

"Damien will be pleased," the Duchess was saying. "He was disappointed that you did not come to table. I will see you then." She began to turn away to leave, then turned back suddenly with a laugh. "I am very sorry. My manners are not usually this bad. I did not give you a chance to tell me your name."

Jessica smiled. She liked this woman in spite of who she was. "Jessica Carlton, Your Grace." She did not know what prompted her to give her full name. It slipped out so easily.

The Duchess stared for a moment, then asked slowly, "Daughter of James, Earl of Braeleigh?"

"Yes," Jessica answered, puzzled and surprised that this woman would know her father.

At Jessica's response to her question, the blood drained from the Duchess' face. Her eyes became glazed, and she swayed as if she might faint any moment. Concerned, Jessica helped her to a stone bench so that she might sit.

"Your Grace! Are you all right?" Jessica asked. "Can I get you something?"

The Duchess did not answer. She only stared back at Jessica.

When she got no response, Jessica told her, "Stay here. I will get help."

Jessica ran to the kitchen door, which was not far away, and called to the cook and several maids who were there. "Please! Come quickly! The Duchess is ill!"

The cook told one of the maids to fetch Jacobs, then she and the others followed Jessica out to the garden. The Duchess was sitting where Jessica had left her, her face white and drawn. The cook and maids fussed about her as they tried to get some color back into her cheeks. Jessica felt she was only in the way, and that somehow, she had caused the attack or whatever it was. Quietly, she slipped away and returned to her room.

She heard the commotion several minutes later when the Duchess was brought upstairs. An unreasonable pang of jealousy seized her when she realized how well liked and well cared for the Duchess was. Jessica herself would probably never know that respect and love. A single tear rolled down her cheek. Angrily, she brushed it away. She would not give in to tears, now. There was no point in crying, for her fate had already been decided.

About an hour later, Donny came into Jessica's room with some clean linen. She glanced sympathetically in Jessica's direction.

"Have you heard how the Duchess is feeling?" Jessica asked her.

"Aye," Donny answered grimly. "She be fine. Just a touch of the vapors."

"Then why are you looking so glum?"

Donny turned to face her. "Ye be in fer it, that's

why. When His Grace found out who ye be, his eyes went all hard. Gives a person the creeps, it does. He's in with her, now. Seems they be talkin' about ye. The Duke is lookin' t' tear ye apart. But it seems the Duchess be on your side. I told ye, didn't I, t'tell him everythin'."

At that moment, a knock came at the door. Before either woman could make a move to open it, Damien walked in. His eyes were as Donny had described them, glittering and cold. He turned to Donny.

"Leave us, please," he said in a voice to match his eyes. "I have some things I would like to discuss with your mistress."

Donny sent a questioning glance at Jessica. She would defy the Duke and stay if Jessica gave the slightest hint she wanted her. Jessica only shook her head. With a distrustful look at the Duke, Donny did as she was asked.

Damien closed the door very softly behind her, then crossing his arms across his chest, he leaned against it. No one was going to get in to defend Jessica.

Jessica noticed he was attired for riding. His breeches fit him like a second skin; his dark green jacket made his eyes piercing in their brightness. He carried a short quirt in his hand. Swallowing, Jessica decided to take the offensive.

"How is the Duchess?" she asked.

"She is fine, now, though a bit shaken, no thanks to you."

"I am sorry. I don't know what I did to upset her."

"Don't you? Lady Jessica Carlton." Her name became a sneer on his lips.

Jessica's head went up proudly. "Who I am does not concern you."

189

"I disagree." Damien pushed away from the door and began to advance toward her. "It concerns me a great deal. Not only am I harboring a traitor under my roof, but now I discover she is the daughter of a murderer and the stepdaughter of a whore." He stopped barely a foot away from her.

Jessica's reaction was too quick for him to stop her. Her hand flashed out and connected soundly with his cheek. The blow rocked Damien's head to one side. When he turned back to her, there was a savage smile on his lips.

"How dare you!" she gasped. "What are you saying?"

"You know what I am saying, my sweet," he answered with mock gentleness. "Margaret has schooled you well in the wiles of allurement. How she must have clapped her hands in glee to discover the second brother had fallen so easily into her clutches."

Jessica backed away in horror at what he was saying. "I don't know what you are talking about."

"No? Playing the innocent to the very end, Jessica? I must admit, you do it very well. You are quite convincing. That little story you told General Drayton was so touching. You even had me convinced you were protecting your family name." He barked a short laugh. "What a fool I was."

Jessica took another step back. Damien stopped her with a soft touch of his quirt on her shoulder. "Do not back away, my sweet," he told her menacingly. "It is too late to run."

Jessica was dumbfounded and totally confused at his manner, what he was saying. What was going on?

"Damien," she tried to reason, "I have never lied to you."

"Perhaps not," he allowed. "But that is a very

small point in your favor. Those monthly visits to Monsieur Montaigne were conveniently scheduled to coincide with a visit to Margaret, were they not?"

"Yes," Jessica answered miserably.

"Ah, now we get the whole truth. She must have gone into fits of laughter when she heard her protegée had made me the fool."

"She has no idea that I know you. I have never spoken your name to her."

He brought his quirt down with considerable force on the arm of the chair next to him. Jessica flinched. His blow had left a sizable mark on the wood.

"Do not play games with me, Jessica," he warned. "You told me you have never lied to me. Do not start now."

Jessica's chin went up defensively. "I have not lied to you. I do not know what this is about, but what I have said is the truth."

Damien's eyes narrowed at her words, and a muscle twitched in his jaw. "Very well, if that is how you wish it." He turned and walked to the door. He turned with his hand on the handle. "While my mother is here in residence, you will remain cloistered in your room. There will be a guard posted at your door at all times. Your presence here has greatly upset her." He turned on his heel and left.

Jessica sank into the chair upon which Damien had vented his anger. Of all the things he had said, there was one that had imbedded itself in her mind. It was his mother whom she had met in the garden. His mother! Not his wife. And she had introduced herself as the Duchess of Wyndham, not the Dowager Duchess, which meant that Damien was not married. He had no wife!

No wife. And from the way he had just left, he hated the very sight of her. Life seemed to be playing one huge joke on her. Now that she knew he was free, he no longer wanted her. His reasons were beyond her understanding. Something about Margaret . . .

Donny came back into the room. She puttered about, not saying anything until Jessica realized she was there. Donny might know what this was all about. She had been with the family since Jessica had been a babe.

"Donny, he said my father was a murderer," Jessica stated. Her tone was strangely unemotional. "What did he mean? And he said something about Margaret getting her clutches on the second brother."

Donny stopped her fidgeting and came to sit in the chair across from Jessica. She had been afraid of this moment from the time she discovered the name of the man who had such a hold on her charge. It was not a nice story.

"Aye," Donny said. "There was a scandal. Be about four years now, maybe a little more. And Margaret in the middle of it. Seems yer papa found out she be seein' another man. This time weren't the first, but he found 'em together in his own bed. Margaret was the clever one, though. Made yer papa believe she'd been forced. Said th' other man had some hold over her family. Nothin' else yer papa could do but challenge th' other man to a duel. He be a young 'un, too. Well, yer papa shot 'im. Didn't die right away though. Lingered for a few days. Yer papa weren't never the same after that. The man he killed was th' Duke o' Wyndham."

Jessica sat with wide eyes as she listened to Donny's tale. She felt sick with regret. It had been Damien's older brother whom Margaret had cuckolded and her father had killed in a duel. No wonder when the Duchess had heard her name, she had become ill.

Jessica got up and wandered to the window. The futility of her situation overwhelmed her. Leaning her forehead against the glass, she said, "He thinks I am involved in some sort of plot with Margaret to destroy him."

As she stood there, she watched Damien ride out proudly on his horse. The soldier standing guard at the gate saluted him as he rode past. An ache so deep she almost sobbed grabbed her heart.

"I have to be alone for a while, Donny," she said in a strangled tone. "I have to think."

Shaking her head, Donny got up and left. There was nothing she could do to help Jessica.

Jessica spent the afternoon in despair. She realized nothing she said or did would convince Damien of her innocence. He was so caught up in his grief and his contempt of her family because of what Margaret had done that he would never see that she had been an unwitting pawn. It was almost teatime when a knock came at her door. Damien had not returned from his ride, so it could not be him. With a sigh, Jessica went to open it. Lucy, the maid, stood there. The soldier standing guard outside her door watched them curiously.

"May I come in, my lady?" Lucy asked. "I think I left my duster in your room when I was cleaning."

With a disinterested gesture, Jessica allowed her in. She could not remember seeing any duster, and she could not imagine any maid in this house being so careless. Lucy closed the door carefully behind her once she was in the room. Instead of looking about for her duster, she held out a note for Jessica.

"A messenger brought this for you, my lady," Lucy told her. "He said it was from His Grace and not to let anyone know about it."

Jessica took the note. She thought the messenger's

request rather curious. Why would Damien send her a note and be so secretive about it? He could have easily sent the message through one of his soldiers. She opened the note and read:

Jessica,
Damien has been badly injured. He is here with me. Come quickly.

A. du Barré

Damien hurt! She had to go to him. Of course the note had to be secret. Damien's men would never allow her to go to Madame du Barré's if they knew. Now, she just had to figure out how to escape from the house.

Lucy had seen the Lady Jessica's cheeks pale when she read the note. Despite what she had heard about her in the kitchen, she liked the lady. With concern, she asked, "Is there something wrong, m'lady? Can I get you something?"

Jessica stared at the girl a moment, wondering how much she could trust her. She decided there was no other way. "I have to leave," she said. "It is a personal matter."

"But, m'lady, the guards," Lucy protested.

Jessica waved away her argument. "I know. I am under arrest. I'm not supposed to go anywhere, but I have to attend to this. It is a question of life or death. His Grace is not here for me to ask permission, and the guards won't allow me to leave if I tell them. You have to help me escape." She grinned conspiratorially. "Do you think you can help?"

Lucy looked doubtful. "Well . . ."

"I give you my word that I will return as soon as I can."

Lucy nodded. "All right."

"Good. Is there another door to the house that is

not so well used as the front or kitchen doors?" Jessica asked.

Lucy thought for a moment. "There are French doors in the salon, but they lead to a veranda, not to the ground."

Of course! Jessica remembered them now. "Those are perfect. Now, all I have to do is get to them."

It was Lucy's turn to grin. "If you mean the handsome soldier standing outside your door, I can take care of him."

Jessica almost hugged the girl in her relief. Instead, she smiled and said, "You are very brave for helping me, Lucy. I am sure, when His Grace finds out about this, he will reward you handsomely."

"Oh, pooh," Lucy said, embarrassed. She turned to leave, but stopped to say, "I hope everything is all right, m'lady."

"I'm sure it will be," Jessica assured her, hoping that she was telling the truth.

Lucy opened the door, saying as she did, "I'm sorry to have disturbed you, m'lady. I can't understand what happened to that duster." As she began to close the door, Jessica heard her say, "Sergeant, since you're so strong, do you think you could do me a tiny favor and help me move a chair?"

"Well, miss," the sergeant answered, "I'm not supposed to leave my post, you know."

"Oh, Sergeant, please? I have to clean under it, and I just can't move it myself. If I don't do it, Jacobs will have my head. It will only take a minute, Sergeant. Please?"

"Well, just for a minute."

As Jessica heard them move off down the hall, she quickly changed into her riding clothes, leaving her dress where it fell. Bless that girl, she thought. The note, she left in a conspicuous place. There would be no suspicion that she had tried to escape from Damien's loose confinement.

She waited until she was sure that Lucy and the sergeant were gone, then she slipped out of her room and down the hall. She stopped to listen at the top of the stairs. Hearing no one near, she glided down the steps and across the hall. Outside the door to the salon, she stopped again. Hopefully, there would be no one inside at this time of day.

Opening the door slowly, she peeked inside. The room was empty. Slipping inside, she closed the door quietly behind her and looked around. There were the French doors, just as she remembered them. She ran lightly across to them and tried the latch. It turned smoothly. She stepped onto the veranda.

The veranda was situated on the side of the house and overlooked a small orchard. Through the trees, she could see the street and the iron fence that surrounded Damien's property. The fence appeared to be about four feet in height. She would have to jump it, for she could not risk going past the guard at the gate. She hoped the shock of seeing a woman on horseback jumping the fence would cause his aim to be off the mark.

Walking swiftly to the railing surrounding the veranda, she looked down. It was not too far to the ground. Climbing over, she let herself drop. Time was now working against her. It would only be a matter of a few more minutes before her escape was discovered. Not even bothering to be careful, she ran to the stables. She could not waste the precious minutes in stealth.

Aphrodite's stall was at the back of the building. Fortunately, there were no stablehands about. So far, her luck had held. Quickly, she saddled her horse and led her to a low stool and mounted. Jessica leaned over and patted the silky neck as she spoke a few words of encouragement, both to her horse and to herself.

"All right, girl, it's now or never."

She dug in her heels and they took off at a gallop. As they reached the fence, she glanced over at the guard at the gate. His mouth hung open in amazement.

"Halt!" he called.

Jessica and Aphrodite sailed over the fence with ease.

"Halt!" he called again. This time, a shot was fired behind her. The ball whizzed past above her head. Fortunately, by the time he could fire another shot, she would be out of sight.

She did not slow down as she rounded the corner of the street, for she knew the soldiers would be after her very soon. If she could just reach Madame's, she would be safe. Damien's men would not come after her there for fear of ruining all their hard work in incriminating the woman. Besides, that was where Damien was. She would still be his prisoner.

As she galloped through the streets, passing coaches, making people jump out of her way, her mouth tightened. She had a few questions for Madame herself. It had certainly not been fair for Madame to involve her in such treason. As far as Jessica could see, she had done nothing to Madame to make the woman wish to entangle her in her crimes. But first, Jessica wanted to see Damien, to be sure that he was all right.

It did not take her long to reach Madame's. Throwing herself from her horse, she ran up the steps and pounded impatiently on the door. It seemed a lifetime before Jacques came to the door and showed her into the salon where Madame was pouring tea.

Jessica did not bother to greet her. "Damien," she blurted breathlessly. "Where is he?"

"Ah, *ma petite*," Madame smiled. "Come, sit down. Calm yourself."

Jessica walked several more steps into the room, but she did not sit. "Where is Damien? I have to see him. How badly is he hurt?" The thought crossed her mind that Madame's was a strange place for Damien to come for help if he had been injured.

"He is upstairs. He is being tended by the doctor," Madame tried to calm her. She poured another cup of tea. "Please, Jessica, sit down. Have some tea. You may visit with him later. There will be plenty of time when the doctor has finished."

Jessica finally perched on the edge of a chair across from Madame and accepted the cup offered her. She took a small sip. "How did it happen?" she wanted to know.

"A fall from his horse." Madame shook her head. "The poor animal stumbled and broke its leg. It had to be destroyed. Damien must have hit his head. He was . . . How do you say? . . ." She searched for the word.

"Unconscious?" Jessica offered.

"Oui, c'est ça. Unconscious."

So, that was why his horse had not been out front, Jessica thought. What a shame that such a magnificent animal had to be destroyed. Absently, she took another sip of tea. She noticed it had an odd taste, but attributed that to Madame's French chef. No one made tea like the English. She glanced nervously toward the door of the room. How long was that doctor going to be? She drank some more of the tea.

Suddenly, a thought occurred to Jessica. If Damien had been unconscious when he was brought here, how did Madame know that she had been under arrest at his house? Damien certainly could not have told her. She glanced at Madame. Something was not right. The woman was watching her closely, almost as if she were waiting for something to happen.

Casually, Jessica placed her cup on the table and stood up. Trying desperately to act nonchalant, she walked around to the back of her chair. For some reason, she felt the need to put something solid between herself and Madame. Her knees felt strangely weak, but she thought it was only because she was nervous.

Jessica suddenly wanted to get out of this house. There was something very wrong. As she stood with one hand on the back of the chair, a wave of dizziness swept over her. She ran her hand over her eyes. What was happening to her? Madame was looking very smug about something.

"Are you not feeling well, *ma petite?*" Madame asked, but her expression showed not concern, but triumph.

Suddenly, Jessica knew. It was the tea.

"What did you do to me?" she demanded weakly.

Madame smiled. "It was only something to make you sleep for a little while. You will feel better when you wake."

"Damien is not here, is he? It was a trick to get me here," Jessica accused.

"Non, he is not here." Madame watched as Jessica swayed and caught herself by grabbing the chair. "Do not fight it, *ma petite*. It will do you no good."

Jessica heard her voice as if from far away. She felt herself falling, then blackness.

Chapter Thirteen

Darkness had fallen by the time Damien returned home. He was not in the best of humor, having spent the afternoon trying to convince General Drayton to leave the arrest of Madame du Barré to him and his men. The General was of the mind that since Damien had captured Madame's courier, it was no longer necessary to involve himself in the case. Damien, on the other hand, was not content to allow the matter to be taken out of his hands so easily. He felt he knew Madame's wily tricks and trusted no one but himself to bring her to justice. The argument had ended in a stalemate. Add to that the fact of just who it was he had under house arrest, and his mood was as black as it ever had been. When he found no guard at either the gate or the front door, his temper boiled over. He knew something had happened in his absence, something he did not want to hear. Leftenant Johnson met him in the foyer as he walked in the door.

"Edward, what the devil is going on?" he demanded harshly. "Where are the guards? Why is there no one on duty?"

Edward Johnson cleared his throat nervously and walked to the door of the salon. "I think you had better come in here, sir," he told Damien with unaccustomed formality. He opened the door for his commanding officer.

Damien glared at him, but he walked through the doorway. As he entered the room, all his men jumped to attention. Damien's eyes narrowed dangerously. He had taught his men never to come to attention when he walked into their midst. It had been too dangerous for any remnant of army etiquette to appear while they had been in France.

Damien sat on the arm of a chair and looked at Johnson. "All right, Leftenant," he said quietly, holding his temper in tight check. "Perhaps you had better tell me what this is all about."

Johnson picked up a note from a nearby table and handed it to Damien. "I think you'd better read this, sir."

As Damien took the note from Johnson, he realized his men were still standing at attention. "Dammit, sit down!" he barked at them. They immediately sank onto chairs.

He was beginning to get a cold feeling in the pit of his stomach. The feeling became worse when he read the note that Jessica had left behind for her guard to find. What Jessica had not known was that he had placed guards on her not only to keep her from trying to escape from him, but also to keep her safe from Madame. He had expected the woman to try to get to Jessica, and through her, to him. At least in this, he had been proven correct. But that did not absolve his men for allowing it to happen. He ran his gaze around the room, meeting the eyes of each of his men.

"Do you mean to tell me, gentlemen, that one, rather tiny woman outwitted five of the best men in His Majesty's Army?" he asked scathingly. There was no answer, only a general uncomfortable shifting under their commander's scrutiny. "How long ago?" he wanted to know.

"As near as we can tell, about three hours, sir," Johnson answered.

Damien looked up at him where he stood beside the chair. "Hmm," was all he said. His mind had already jumped ahead.

Absently, he rose and walked to the very French doors through which Jessica had made her escape. Staring blindly out into the darkness, he crushed the note in his hand. The little fool! How could she fall for such a ruse? Did she not realize what a cleverly dangerous woman Madame du Barré really was?

He stood lost in thought for several minutes. His men nervously waited for him. When he swung around, his face was hard with determination.

"It seems, gentlemen, that Madame du Barré has played her trump card. By taking the Lady Jessica, she has nothing else to do but run for the coast. I believe she has played right into our hands."

"How has she done that, sir?" a young man asked.

"She will have to come out into the open to make her escape, Wells," Damien answered. "We will capture her, retrieve the Lady Jessica, and then lay *Le Chat* to rest."

There was a general murmuring as the men approved of Damien's plan. Dropping the note he still held on a nearby table, he went on, "Now, I suggest that we change for the evening meal and discuss this over dinner. There is nothing we can do but wait until Madame sends us some indication that she has the Lady Jessica".

Resigned, his men dispersed to change for dinner, then reconvened soon after about the dining table. Almost immediately, Damien explained his plans.

"Madame most assuredly will send some sort of indication that she has the Lady Jessica for, I am sure, she expects us to follow. As soon as she does that, she will begin her escape to France, but not too quickly;

she does not want to lose us. I believe, however, she would prefer to have us catch up with her on French soil, rather than on English. It would be a victory for her if she could capture us as spies, instead of the other way around.

"I assume she has more than one escape route to France. We know of at least two. One of them was from the beach at Montaigne's house. She won't use that one; now that we know of it, it's too risky. She must have another from somewhere around Dover, for when she is pressed for time." He glanced around the table at his men. "Any other ideas where she might cross?"

"Someplace in Cornwall, sir," the sergeant who had been guarding Jessica's door offered. "Smugglers land in those coves as if they were free ports."

Damien nodded. "You are probably right Higgins, but Cornwall is too far away for Madame's purposes. Remember she has a hostage with her. She would have us on her trail for too long."

"If I were her," Johnson said thoughtfully, "I'd head for Dover. It's the quickest way out of England and closest to France. There would be more people about to see her, so she could leave a visible trail for us to follow."

"That seems to be the logical way for her to run," Damien agreed. "Something tells me, however, that she will not do the logical thing. I don't think we should trust to luck on this. Higgins, I want you to watch Madame's house. When they leave, follow them to the edge of the city and observe which road they take. Then wait for us there. Wells, go with him. When Madame leaves her house, come back and let us know. We can't lose any time in following. I will wait here with the rest of you for Madame's message that she has the Lady Jessica. Any questions?"

"What about taking her now, in her house?" Wells wanted to know.

"That would seem to be a good idea, Wells, but the house is a fortress. The walls are twice as thick as an ordinary house, and the doors, although decorative, could belong to a vault. Madame probably has built several escape tunnels. She would slip right through our fingers. Any other questions?"

"Suppose she has already left for France?" a young man named Walker asked morosely. "Suppose she doesn't want us to follow?"

Damien had already thought of this, but had determinedly tried not to dwell on it. If it was true, and Madame reached France secretly, then any chance of ever recovering Jessica was lost. Despite his rage and mistrust of her, he could not bear thinking about never seeing her again.

Slowly, he answered, "We have to assume that Madame has not done that, Walker. I truly don't believe she has. Madame wants me to follow her. She has a score to settle with me for fouling up her plans. We have to work on the assumption that she will be trying to lure me—all of us—to France so that we can be captured as spies. For that reason, we will have to be very alert if we wish to come out of this alive.

"Any other comments?" There were none. "All right, gentlemen, you know what you have to do."

The men dispersed to their various duties: Higgins and Wells to change from their uniforms to their less conspicuous peasant garb and then to leave to watch Madame's; the other men to change and ready the horses and other gear they would need. Damien remained at the table for some time, hoping that he was correct in his assumptions, hoping that Jessica had not been harmed, that he would find her safe and be able to free her from Madame's clutches. Finally, he went to wait for word that Madame did, indeed, have Jessica as captive.

Jessica returned to consciousness very slowly. She became aware of lying on a bed long before she was able to open her eyes. Her eyelids felt heavy, almost as if they were glued shut, and her head felt as if it were stuffed with cotton. Several minutes after lying still, listening for sounds that would tell her where she was, she forced her eyes open and looked around. The room she was in was dark, the only light coming from a crack beneath the door. She heard the faint sounds of many people, as if they were far away. Memory rushed back. She was at Madame's, and she had been tricked into escaping from Damien's house. The thought made her grimace. Damien must surely think of her now as a traitor and a deceitful woman. What a mess.

As her mind began to function, she realized the only thing she could do was escape from Madame and turn herself in to Damien. She gave no thought as to why Madame wanted her as captive, but she was sure it had something to do with this spy business the woman was involved in. Jessica wanted nothing more to do with it.

She tried to move her arms, but a sharp pain made her stop. Her wrists had been tied together, and her arms pulled above her head and tied to the bedpost. Moving her legs experimentally, she discovered that her ankles were bound, also, but had not been tied to the bed.

Turning onto her side, she attempted to sit up. She thought she might be able to loosen her bonds with her teeth. When she finally reached a sitting position, nausea gripped her insides. Slumped against the headboard, she fought down the waves of sickness. As she felt stronger, she tried to pull herself up more so she could reach the knot in the rope. The knot about her wrists was just out of reach. With a groan of frustration, she slumped down again to a prone position.

Jessica lay on the bed for what seemed like hours. She heard people walk past the door. Occasionally, she heard a woman giggle. No one came in, however. No one answered her calls for help. Eventually, she dozed.

She did not know how long she slept, or what it was that woke her, but she was suddenly completely alert. She lay listening. It was very quiet. It had been the silence that had awakened her. In that silence, she heard footsteps approach and stop before her door. A key turned in the lock, and the door swung open. Jessica had to close her eyes against the sudden light.

She heard Madame's voice. "So, *ma petite,* you are awake finally, eh? *Bon,* it is just in time. We have to go on a little journey."

Jessica struggled to open her eyes against the glare. "Where are you taking me? What do you want with me?"

"Ah, always the questions. First, eat a little something, and then I will tell you." Madame turned to Jacques who had come into the room with her. "Untie her and bring up the tray I prepared."

Jacques took out a knife and cut the ropes binding Jessica's hands and feet, then he left. Jessica sat up and rubbed her hands and feet as her circulation painfully came back. Madame came to the bed and sat on its edge. She took one of Jessica's hands and began to massage it.

"That oaf," she complained. "He does not realize that a woman does not have to be tied up like some angry bull. It is painful?"

Jessica nodded. "Madame, why are you doing this?

I have done nothing to harm you."

"Nothing, *ma petite?* Do you mean that you have said nothing about the letters you have delivered for me?"

Jessica lowered her gaze before the woman's accusation.

"Ah, well, I expected that. You are the innocent. It is too bad you became involved with *Le Chat.*"

"Le Chat? Who is ... ?" Jessica started to ask, then as she met Madame's eyes, she realized who it was. Damien, of course. The warning he had sent her had been signed with the paw print of a cat.

Jacques returned at that moment with a tray of food and some wine for Jessica. He placed the tray on the table beside the bed, then left once again. Madame poured a glass of wine and handed it to Jessica.

"Drink this, *ma petite,*" she told her. "It will warm you. We have a long, cold journey ahead of us."

Jessica took the glass but did not drink. She remembered all too clearly what Madame had done to the tea. "Where are we going?" she asked, trying to delay drinking the wine.

"To France, of course. Drink your wine, *ma petite.*"

"But I don't want to go to France. Please, can't you leave me here? I would not tell Damien anything."

Madame laughed. "Foolish girl. Of course you would. *Non.* That is quite impossible. You will come with us. Now, drink the wine." Madame's voice became hard.

Jessica was beginning to be more than a little afraid. If Madame took her to France, who would know where she was? What would become of her once she was there? How would she ever get back to England? Still she did not drink the wine.

Madame sighed in exasperation. "Jessica, please drink the wine. It will not make you sleep. It will only relax you. I wish for you to be awake when we leave. If you will not drink it, there are other, more unpleasant things that I will use to keep you calm. The choice is yours."

Jessica stared at Madame as she weighed what the woman said. Somehow, she did not doubt for a moment that she would do as she said. Deciding she had no other choice, Jessica drank the wine.

When she had finished the glass, Madame handed her a plate of food and remained with her while she ate. By the time she finished eating, a warm, languid feeling began to spread through her. It was quite pleasant; she felt very relaxed. Madame handed her a second glass of wine, and this Jessica drank with no questions. With a tiny part of her brain, she realized she was in a great amount of danger, but for some reason, she did not care. Nothing at that moment seemed to bother her. She smiled as she handed the glass back to Madame.

Madame stood and tilted Jessica's face up. "You are a good girl, Jessica. You will stay here for a little while. Do not try to get away. I will be back soon."

"Yes, Madame," Jessica answered obediently. She watched as the woman left, locking the door behind her.

As Jessica waited for Madame to return, she felt the effects of the second glass of wine begin to take hold. The small part of her brain that had told her she was in danger had been silenced. She felt nothing, wanted nothing. All her emotions had been numbed. She did not care what happened.

When Madame returned, she had two of her maids with her. She carried a bundle of clothes and a pair of scissors.

Handing the clothes to one of the maids, she said, "Put these on her."

The maids helped Jessica stand. She remained

quiet as the two girls undressed her and replaced her own clothes with those Madame had brought. When she was dressed, Madame removed the pins from Jessica's hair and allowed it to tumble about her shoulders. Taking the scissors, she proceeded to cut off Jessica's beautiful, long tresses. When the woman had finished, Jessica's hair was a mass of short curls. The clothes she now wore consisted of trousers, shirt, and jacket. With the help of a hat and cape, Jessica had been transformed into a boy.

Madame removed Jessica's locket and retrieved a long lock of hair from the floor. Giving a satisfied smile at the transformation she had performed on Jessica, she told the maids to bring her downstairs.

Jessica had become a puppet, doing as she was told, moving as she was guided. After waiting for some time in one of the rooms where she had once played cards, she suddenly found herself sitting astride Aphrodite. Her wrists had once again been bound together before her, and her ankles were tied together by a rope that ran under her horse's belly. Madame came to inspect the knots that Jacques had tied.

"Imbecile." Madame berated him. "These are too tight! I do not want her marked." She moved aside as Jacques came to remedy his mistake. She ran a hand down Jessica's thigh and smiled slyly. "She will make a lovely demimondaine and fetch a very lovely price, eh, Jacques?"

Jacques grinned back at her in anticipation of his share of the profit they would see from the sale of the girl. He helped Madame, who was also dressed as a man, mount her horse, then he did the same. The group of riders, about eight strong and all dressed as men except for two of them, began their flight to France.

Chapter Fourteen

When Damien finally rose from the dining room table, he retreated to his study to wait. He knew the message from Madame would not come until very late, so he stretched out on the sofa and tried to sleep. Sleep would not come, however, for a pair of clear, blue eyes haunted his thoughts; the touch of silky skin heated his blood; the memory of inky, thick hair made his fingers itch. She was a witch to so prey on his mind.

He thought back on their conversation of that afternoon. He had been merciless with her and unforgiving. Yet in spite of that, when she had thought him injured, she had gone to his aid. Doubts plagued him. What if she had been telling the truth, that she knew nothing of Margaret's evil duplicity? If he allowed Madame to take her to France, he had a fairly certain idea of what would happen to her. Then he would never know the truth about Jessica.

Eventually, he dozed, his dreams uneasy. He was not sure how long he slept, or what it was that awakened him. He lay quietly, listening, every muscle tense, waiting. Then, like an explosion, a window that faced the front of the house shattered. Something heavy landed in the middle of the floor.

Damien bounded off the sofa where he lay and scooped it up. A rock was tied to a small, unmarked package. Sitting back down, he placed the package on the table before him and untied the string. Dread hung over him at what he might find and made him pause.

Collecting himself after a moment, he opened the package. Inside, was a gold locket and a long, black lock of hair that curled about itself. There was no note or message, only the two items. He picked up the hair and placed it in the palm of his hand. It felt soft and alive, and it brought to mind several nights when he had lost his fingers in hair such as this.

A sudden anger possessed him as he realized that Jessica was being controlled and spirited away from him. She was his. He had claimed her as such. Although he still felt rage against her for who and what she was, he had not yet relinquished his hold on her. Unconsciously, he clenched his fist about the length of curl in his hand.

Leftenant Johnson appeared at the door to check on his friend and commander. He had heard the commotion of the breaking glass. Upon realizing he was not alone, Damien stood up and allowed the silken coil to spill from his hand.

"We have received Madame's message," Damien told him. "Higgins should be returning soon with the information that they have left. You had better inform the men that we will be moving out." His face was a study in impassiveness.

Johnson stayed a moment in the doorway as he watched his friend. He had not missed the distraught expression on Damien's face when he had come upon him. "We will get her back, Damien," he said quietly.

Damien nodded absently. Then, annoyed that he had allowed his thoughts to be so visible, even to this man, Damien snapped at him, "We will not get anyone back if you stand there yapping about it."

Johnson smiled, saluted casually, and left to arouse

the other men. Damien went to change his clothes.

Several minutes later, *Le Chat* and his men waited in the dark stable for Higgins to bring the news that Madame had, indeed, begun her escape. They did not have a long wait. The clatter of hooves on the road reached their ears, and soon after, Higgins rode into the stableyard. Damien, leading his horse, went out to meet him.

"They have gone, sir," the young man panted. "There were eight of them. Two women."

"Good work, Higgins. And Wells?"

"He is following them."

Damien nodded, motioned for his men to mount, then he followed. He led them out of the yard and into the street. They rode without speaking, each man harboring his own thoughts about what this night might hold.

Upon reaching the outskirts of the city where the road forked, they stopped and waited. Damien gave a low whistle. An answering whistle came, then a man on horseback emerged from behind a hedgerow and approached the group.

"Which way did they go, Wells?" Damien asked.

"They broke up into two groups, sir," Wells told him. "Five of them took the road to Dover. That was with the two women. The other three took the west road to the coast."

"Then it's to Dover," Johnson stated.

"No, wait." Damien stopped him as he thoughtfully stared down the empty road. "Can you describe the three that took the west road?" he asked Wells.

"Two men and a boy, it looked like," Wells answered.

"That's it," Damien said grimly. "The group on the Dover road is a lure. Once we caught up with them, we'd discover we had followed the wrong group. We would never be able to catch up with Madame. We'd be forced to cross into France. Come on! A cask of Mr. Napoleon's finest brandy for every man if we can make it to the coast before her." He spurred his horse and raced off, his men following close behind. What he did not tell them was that he might be forced to cross into France anyway.

They skirted the road, not wishing to come upon Madame unexpectedly, and arrived at the coast well in advance of the woman. It took a little searching to discover the exact cove from which she meant to leave, but eventually, they found the small boat riding at anchor a few feet from shore. A man sat waiting at its tiller.

Quietly, Damien and his men dismounted, tethering their horses where they would not be seen. Then, melting into the shadows, they hid themselves behind boulders that were strewn about the beach.

They did not have too long to wait before they heard the sound of approaching hoofbeats. Three riders came into view and rode onto the beach. Damien waited until they had dismounted, then he stepped out from behind the rock.

"*Bon soir,* Madame" he greeted her pleasantly. He brandished a pistol in his hand. "Are you taking a late-night sail?"

At his words, three people turned to face him. Madame had her hand on Jessica's arm. She appeared to have to guide her. In the moonlight, Jessica's eyes stared at him blankly. What was wrong with her? Damien wondered.

Madame recovered quickly from the shock of seeing Damien. "So, we are finally met, eh, my friend, *Le Chat?*"

Damien bowed gallantly. "At your service, Madame."

Madame glanced around. "Is it possible you are by yourself? You are the foolish one."

"Hardly, Madame." Damien's tone was dry.

As he spoke, his men stepped out of their hiding places and formed a semicircle, effectively blocking any means of escape by land. It would be foolhardy for Madame to try to outrun them to her boat in the opposite direction.

"Now, if you would be so kind as to allow the young lady to move to this side of the beach, we can conduct our business," Damien suggested.

Madame only paused a fraction before she shrugged and dropped her hand from Jessica's arm. Jessica did not move. She stood staring at Damien as if she did not see him.

"Jessica." Damien tried to gain her attention. Why wouldn't she come to him?

Madame smiled. "If you want the girl, Monsieur Le Chat, you will have to come get her."

Damien's eyes narrowed. There was something . . . Then it dawned on him. Jessica had been drugged! She would not be able to react quickly enough to save herself or allow him to save her if the situation demanded it. One of his men began to edge toward Jessica. Madame turned back her cape to reveal a tiny pistol pressed against Jessica's side.

"You will tell your man to move away, Monsieur Le Chat. The young lady is in danger of losing her life. I know you do not wish that to happen. So, you will let us wade out to our little boat and sail away."

As she spoke, she began to back away, taking Jessica with her. The other rider, Jacques, hurried out to the boat. As Madame reached the water, she turned and ran the few feet to the boat. She dragged Jessica with her, effectively keeping the girl between herself and the men on shore.

As Jessica was pulled through the water, she turned around once to look at him. Madame roughly forced her into the boat, but as soon as Jessica was aboard, her eyes again sought the men on the beach. Damien saw her lips move once, then again as her face finally broke the mask of the drug she had been given.

"Damien!"

Her scream of fear wrenched at him. Jacques shoved her down into the boat. Damien watched in silence as they began to sail away. The only clue to his feelings was a tightness about his mouth and a muscle that twitched in his jaw. Inside, a part of him was screaming in rage and anguish. Higgins, who was standing next to Damien, raised his gun.

"Let me get off a shot at her, sir," he pleaded.

Damien put a hand on the young man's arm to restrain him. "No. There's too much risk of hitting the Lady Jessica."

Without another word, he stuck his pistol into his belt and strode up the beach to where the horses had been tied. Leftenant Johnson reached Damien just before he swung himself into the saddle. Damien turned to look at him. Even in the dark, the Leftenant could sense his friend's remorse and determination.

"Madame won this time, Edward," Damien said quietly. "I allowed her to escape and take Jessica with her. Arrange for transportation to France for me for tomorrow night. I have to go after Jessica."

"All right," Johnson agreed. "I'll tell the others."

"No," Damien told him firmly. "I'm going alone. It's too risky for you and the others to come. We just barely made it out with our lives the last time. You will not tell the others of my plans."

Johnson said nothing as Damien mounted his horse. The other men arrived, bringing the abandoned horses with them. Damien gazed down at his friend a moment.

"That's an order, Leftenant. Not a word to the

215

others," he said sternly. Wheeling his horse, he rode off.

It was two hours after midnight the following night when Damien rode onto the old, little-used dock just outside the port of Dover. A small bark was riding the gentle swells at the end of the wooden structure. The dock had originally been built for much larger ships, so it was above the level of the deck of the tiny ship that rose and fell at its end.

The whole area was deserted, and the sound of Apollo's hooves on the wooden planks of the wharf seemed unnaturally loud in the stillness. As Damien dismounted, a figure detached itself from the shadows on the boat.

"You're late," Leftenant Johnson accused Damien with a touch of humor in his voice.

Damien grinned down at the man standing at the boat railing. He was not really late, but it was a greeting they had often used in France when they had become separated while carrying out their mission.

"I was unavoidably detained." Damien gave the accustomed answer.

As Johnson vaulted to the dock, a group of riders could be heard approaching. Damien scowled in frustration. There was nowhere to hide, and the last thing he wanted was to be seen by anyone. His trip across the Channel could be delayed because of these intruders.

The riders came closer and then rode onto the dock. Damien stood his ground, but loosened the pistol from the waist of his breeches. In the dark, he was unable to discern faces. They kept coming. He pulled out the pistol and held it down beside his leg. The group stopped several feet away and dismounted.

Damien swung about on Johnson. "What the devil is this, Leftenant? A bloody going away party?" he growled. "I told you I was going alone."

Sergeant Higgins cleared his throat where he stood with the rest of the men in Damien's command. "We didn't think you should, sir," he ventured.

Damien turned on him in a rage. "*You* didn't think. . . ?" He took a deep breath to calm himself, then swung about to Johnson. "Leftenant, I gave you an order."

Johnson shrugged and grinned, unaffected by Damien's anger. "You have always told us to be resourceful. Have me court-martialled."

Damien's eyes narrowed. "I may just do that." He returned the pistol into his waistband with a sigh of exasperation. "As long as you are here, you might as well come along." He threw the reins of his horse to Johnson. "Since you brought so much help, you won't need mine to get the horses aboard."

He jumped down onto the deck of the ship and found a comfortable spot to relax while his men boarded and they made the crossing to France.

Chapter Fifteen

"Fouché, never before have you questioned my intentions. Why do you start now?"

Madame du Barré paced before the fireplace in a small, ornate sitting room. In a chair, was a slight, handsome man watching her with the eyes of a fox. He was Joseph Fouché, the very powerful Duke d'Otrante, Minister of Police under Napoleon.

"Adèlée, I am not questioning your intentions," he answered smoothly. "I merely asked if it was wise to sell the girl at auction. She is, after all, the daughter of an earl. We are having enough problems with England as it is, without causing an international incident over some chit."

Madame waved her hand impatiently. "Her father is dead, and her stepmother does not care what happens to her. The auction is the best way to flush out The Cat. You do wish to capture him, do you not?"

Fouché bowed his agreement. "You are so sure he will come after her?"

Madame stopped her pacing and looked confident for the first time since Fouché had arrived. "He will come after her. Come, I will show you."

She led him to a door across the room and into another small room beyond. The two walked to the bed and gazed down at the unconscious girl laying upon it.

"Lovely," Fouché conceded.

"There is another reason for him to pursue her," Madame told him smugly. "She has been examined. She carries his child."

Fouché raised his eyebrows in curiosity. "How can you be so sure it is his?"

"It is his. In things such as this, I am never wrong."

Fouché turned and began to walk back to the sitting room. "It will be much to your advantage if you are again correct, Adèlée. I was not overly pleased to discover that you had to flee England in order to save your precious skin."

Madame followed the man back out to the sitting room. "It was because of that man that I was forced to flee. He will follow me here. He will come looking for the girl. I know he will. When he does, he is lost."

Madame smiled wickedly and flexed her fingers as if they were claws. She gave Fouché an intent look.

"You must allow me to make the arrangements for his capture. Revenge for his meddling will taste very sweet."

Fouché picked up his walking stick in silence and walked to the door that led out to the hall. With his hand on the latch, he said coldly, "You may make the arrangements. Keep in mind that the fool who allowed him to escape from France the last time has not been heard from since. I do not tolerate mistakes." Then he was gone.

Madame sank into a chair with a sigh of relief. He was such a difficult man, and a ruthless one. A smile of anticipation soon appeared on her face, however, as she contemplated the capture and eventual demise of the man who was known as The Cat.

When Jessica awoke from her drug-induced sleep,

the sun was high in the sky and streaming through the window beside the bed. The room was unfamiliar to her, and she wondered where she was. She stretched, feeling the stiffness in her arms and legs that indicated she had been unconscious for some time. Easing herself to a sitting position, she swung her legs over the side of the bed. She drew deep breaths as she tried to calm the dizziness and nausea that swept over her. As she sat with her head lowered, she realized she was wearing boy's clothing. Absently, she picked at the breeches while she wondered what had happened to her own clothes.

Her last clear memory was of having tea with Madame du Barré. Everything that took place after that was an indistinct blur or a complete blank. There was one moment in time that she remembered vividly. It was of Damien, standing on a beach, surrounded by his men. He did nothing; he just stood there, watching her. Yet, she could not be sure that she had actually seen him or had just been dreaming.

She stood up and slowly wandered about the room. It was not an unpleasant room, even though it was sparsely furnished. There was a curious arrangement of four metal rings attached to one wall, two at arm's length above her head and two near the floor. She did not wish to think what they were used for. A small shiver of fear ran down her spine. She repressed her apprehension with the thought that, up until now, she had not really been treated badly.

Her head felt strangely light, and she put her hand up to discover why. The scantiness of her once long tresses made her gasp. She rushed to the tiny mirror above the dressing table and peered at herself. As the truth was revealed to her, she stifled a groan. Her hair had been cut off! Turning and twisting to see better, she pulled at several curls. Sighing in acceptance of something she could not fix, she realized the reason for her haircut and the boy's clothing. Madame had disguised her.

She walked to the door and knew before she even tried it that it would be locked. As she stood there, she heard two people coming. She listened as they walked past. It was two girls, probably maids, and they spoke French. Jessica leaned against the door to remain upright as she realized what had happened. Madame had brought her to France. She frowned as she tried to remember the journey. There was a vague memory of being in a boat, and Madame making her drink more wine. After that, she remembered nothing.

Jessica rubbed her hands across her eyes. Why was she here? What did Madame want with her? She wandered over to the window and looked out. The fleeting thought of escape died when she saw the long drop to the ground and the wrought iron work across the window. She could hear the sound of carriages and people from somewhere not far away, but if she could not get out, no one could help her.

The door opened then, and Madame du Barré walked in with another woman. The woman was about the same age as Madame, but that was where the similarity ended. This woman was dressed gaudily, with an overabundance of frills and bows on her gown that was just able to contain her very ample bosom. Her hair was a vivid, violent red-orange color. Jessica warily watched them approach.

"Well, little one," Madame began, speaking in her native language. "I see you are finally awake." She indicated the other woman. "This is Madame Rousse. She is kind enough to allow us to stay in her house for a while. She does not mind that you are here, but you must behave yourself. You will remain in your room at all times, no matter what you hear. If you do this, no harm will come to you. If you try to escape, or if you wander out of your room, there will be some suitable punishment. Do you understand?"

Jessica looked from one woman to the other. She understood all too well. Madame was not the kind woman she had led Jessica to believe she was. Jessica should have paid attention to her father's warnings about not going near the woman or her establishment. There was danger here. Jerkily, she nodded her understanding of Madame's threats.

Madame Rousse turned to Madame du Barré. "Are you sure you will not sell her to me, Adélée? She is lovely. She would be very popular with my customers."

Madame du Barré shook her head and smiled slyly as she tilted up Jessica's face. "I am sorry, Colette, but I have other plans for this one. I will give you a share of what I get for her at auction because you have been so kind. She should bring a handsome price, don't you think?"

Madame Rousse appraised Jessica critically. She nodded her approval. "She will bring a very handsome price, indeed. A pity you will not sell her to me. Ah, well. I must attend to my girls. I will see you later, Adélée."

Jessica watched the woman disappear through the door. In confusion, she turned to Madame.

"What is going on, Madame?" she asked. "What auction? What are you going to do with me?" Apprehension wound itself about her insides.

Madame smiled. "You always were the curious one. You, little one, are bait to catch a very large fish. Or rather, I should say, you are the fish to trap a cat."

Jessica frowned, not quite sure what the woman was talking about. Then, suddenly, her meaning became clear. Damien! Jessica's eyes widened as she stared at Madame in horror.

Madame laughed. "Yes, that is right. Your handsome Duke. Such a pity. He is such a handsome devil."

Jessica shook her head. "He will not come, Madame. He hates me."

"Ah, you are so innocent, Jessica. Love and hate are so closely bound together that, at times, one can not tell them apart." Madame's voice turned cold. "He will come."

"And if he does not? What will happen to me?"

Madame shrugged. "Whether he comes or not, you will be sold at auction to the highest bidder. You will become whatever your owner wishes, and I will make a considerable profit. Your Duke will have no need of you in Hell."

Jessica felt a cold weight in her middle. Despite Damien's contempt of her, she could not allow Madame to kill him. She loved him!

Grasping at anything, she ventured, "You could send me back to England. I could pay you a fortune. You know how well I gamble."

"Pay me?" Madame asked incredulously. "With what? Where would you play? And what of your stepmother and your poor little brother?" She laughed shortly. "I am not so stupid, little one. No, I am afraid you will remain in France. Resign yourself that you will never see England again." She walked to the door. "I will have some food brought to you. Do not concern yourself with your future. It is out of your hands."

Jessica sat down on the bed as soon as Madame was gone. Feeling very alone and very afraid, tears welled up in her eyes. She fell back onto the pillow and sobbed until she could cry no more.

When the tears finally stopped, Jessica felt drained. As she got up and walked to the washbasin to splash cold water on her face, she decided it was better not to feel anything at all. That way, nothing could hurt her.

It was too much to hope that Damien would come after her and actually rescue her. If he came, he would be walking into a trap, and there was no way she could warn him. The most she could hope for was that Damien would not come and whoever bought her would be kind and not hurt her.

As she dried her face on the thin towel, the door opened and a maid entered with a tray of food. She said nothing to Jessica, but left the tray and hurried out, locking the door behind her. Jessica wandered over to the tray and played with a croissant, but she had no appetite. She wished she could take a bath. She knew it was an incongruous wish considering the trouble she was in, but thinking about mundane things seemed to help her remain calm. Throwing herself onto the bed, she stared up at the ceiling.

The maid came after a while and removed the tray. Jessica tried talking to her, but the maid just looked frightened and hurried away without a word. No one else came to her room. Twilight softened the shadows.

Jessica's appetite returned somewhat, and she ate a little of the evening meal the maid silently brought her. The food was actually quite good—sausage, cheese, fresh bread. Jessica did not drink any of the wine. The maid entered again to take away the tray. Jessica gave up trying to talk to her.

With the night came noises of people laughing and talking. Several times, Jessica heard couples passing her door. She was grateful, then, for being locked in. It had not been hard for Jessica to discover exactly what type of establishment Madame Rousse owned by listening to conversations of those who walked by her door. The girls were *filles de joies,* paramours, whores. Jessica felt compassion for them. After the auction, she would belong to their society.

After she had learned where she was, Jessica turned away from the intimate, seductive bits of conversation that floated to her ears through the wood. She found other ways to amuse herself. As the night wore on, she counted all the cracks in the ceiling; she knew how many steps it took to cross the room from wall to wall. Finally, the boredom lulled her to sleep.

The next day was no different than the previous one. She saw no one except the silent maid who brought her meals. Since she was unable to have a bath, she stripped and washed as best she could with the stale water in the small washbasin. After she had dressed, she went back to counting the spaces between the floorboards.

Jessica passed the next five days in this manner. She knew by heart every inch of the room. Occasionally, she would try the door to see if someone had accidentally forgotten to lock it, and several times, she banged on the door and yelled to see what would happen. Nothing. It was as if she did not exist.

During the afternoon of the sixth day of her captivity, the door opened and Madame walked in. She was followed by the fattest man Jessica had ever seen. He waddled sideways through the opening. Rolls of fat hung over the neck of his huge, velvet tunic he wore in place of shirt and coat. His arms were twice as thick as Jessica's waist. Tiny pinholes showed where his eyes were in his bulging cheeks. His face had the appearance of unkneeded bread dough with a dot of strawberry jam in the middle where his mouth should be. He and Madame approached Jessica where she was standing in the middle of the floor as she counted the number of steps from the bed to the washstand.

"You see, Le Cochon," Madame was saying. "She

is small, but very well proportioned. You must sell her as your last item. It will be worth a great deal to your purse."

The man reached out with his sausage-like fingers and grabbed Jessica's chin, turning her face this way and that. In disgust, she jerked out of his grasp. He threw up his hands in dismay.

"Madame, how can I make a judgement if the chit can not even hold still for me to look at her. And these rags! They must come off." His voice came out in a high sing-song.

Madame turned to Jessica. "Take off your clothes," she ordered.

Jessica, who was still awestruck at the immensity of Le Cochon and not quite sure she had heard Madame correctly, asked, "I beg your pardon?"

"I said to get undressed," Madame said testily.

Jessica shook her head and backed away a step. "No."

With an exasperated sigh, Madame explained, "Jessica, either you take off your clothes yourself, or I will have someone take them off for you." She turned to the fat man. "She will be more amenable by the time of the auction, I assure you."

"There are those who prefer their purchases to have spirit, Madame," Le Cochon said. "Do not break her."

Jessica felt the fear tighten inside her. She stared from Madame to the fat man and back again. If only there was some means of escape . . . Her eyes drifted to the doorway, and she realized Madame had left the door open.

The invitation to freedom was too great to let slip by. She did not know where she would go once she escaped, but she decided to worry about that later. With one leap, she jumped out of Madame's reach and bounded out the door. There was a set of stairs to the left, and she ran down them, two at a time. In the far wall was a door leading to the outside and freedom. Keeping her eyes on that door, she ran lightly across the thick rug. It was a mistake not to see if there was anyone else about.

A very large body hit her from the side and threw her to the floor. The wind was knocked out of her. When she turned her head, she looked up into the grinning face of Jacques. Jessica groaned her deep disappointment as he hauled her to her feet. To struggle against him was useless. Pulling both her arms behind her, he held her wrists together in one large hand and propelled her back up the stairs.

Madame and Le Cochon were waiting at the top of the stairs. When they saw that Jessica had been successfully recaptured, they returned to the room that was Jessica's prison. Jacques followed with his prize.

"That was a foolish thing to do," Madame told Jessica after she had carefully locked the door behind her. "You are fortunate that the auction is tomorrow night, and there will be little time for bruises to heal. Otherwise, the consequences of your attempt to escape would not have been pleasant. Perhaps, though, we can still find a suitable punishment." She turned to Jacques. "Strip her."

"No." Jessica cried and struggled to free herself from Jacques' grip.

Her struggles only seemed to aid him in his task. She was soon left panting from her exertions and without a stitch of clothing on her body. Powerless and humiliated, she kept her eyes on the floor. She would suffer in silence any punishment Madame might devise.

Her head snapped up in shock when she felt the fat man touch her arm. He squeezed her flesh, touched her here and there, smoothed his hand across her stomach and her bottom, but when he pinched the sensitive tips of her breasts, she cried out and backed away. She was brought up short by the formidable bulk of Jacques behind her. Le Cochon turned to Madame with a satisfied nod.

"She is valuable property," he said. "Beauty, good skin, responsive, spirited. It is a shame about her hair, but it will grow. I can start the bidding very high."

"How high?" Madame wanted to know.

He turned back to Jessica and regarded her thoughtfully. "We will start at five hundred guineas."

Madame's eyes gleamed with avarice. "You will be well rewarded, Le Cochon. Come down to the kitchen. I believe the cook was baking fresh pastry." As they walked to the door, Madame told Jacques, "Tie her to the rings. I will decided what to do with her later."

As the door closed behind Madame and the fat man, Jacques dragged Jessica over to the wall where the four metal rings were attached. He held her against the wall with his body as he tied each of her wrists and ankles to the four rings. When he had finished, she was spread across the wall and unable to move anything except her head. As Jacques stood back and admired his work, Jessica realized how completely vulnerable she was. How many women had suffered through men's atrocities and perversions in this position? she wondered.

Something of her fear must have registered in her eyes, for Jacques caught her gaze and grinned lasciviously. Jessica locked her knees to keep them from buckling beneath her. Tensely, gripping the velvet cords that bound her so hard her knuckles were white, she waited for Jacques to do something to her. She clenched her teeth together and raised her chin. Whatever he did, she would keep her dignity as long as she could.

Slowly, the grin died on his face. He had seen something in her face that had dissuaded him from whatever it was he was going to do. His face twisted into a snarl.

"Poule!" he spat. Whore.

He turned on his heel and stomped out the door.

Jessica released the breath she was holding and slumped against the wall. She had no idea what he had intended to do, but she had learned something from the encounter. If she showed no fear, she would more than likely be able to dissuade anyone from touching her. It was the fear that made her vulnerable.

She turned her attention to the knots that bound her and tried to work them loose. After several minutes, she realized her efforts were useless. Nothing she did made any difference. The bonds remained tight and secure. With a sigh of resignation, she leaned her head against the wall and let her mind drift. Thoughts of Damien filtered through her head: Damien whispering to her, Damien touching her, Damien loving her. The memories were all she had now. The memories and the child she carried.

She was brought back to reality by the door opening. The shadows on the floor indicated it was late afternoon. She had been bound for several hours. The silent maid who delivered her meals entered with a kettle of hot water. Pouring some into the wash basin, she brought the basin, a washcloth, towel and soap over to where Jessica was tied.

"Madame du Barré told me I was to wash you," she told Jessica timidly. She glanced at the door as if she expected it to open any minute. "If you promise not to try to get away, I can untie your hands so you can wash yourself," she whispered. "Please, don't get me into trouble."

Jessica's heart went out to the maid. The girl was obviously deathly afraid of being punished, yet she took the risk of being kind.

Jessica nodded. "I promise." As the girl untied the cords from about her wrists, Jessica asked, "What is your name?"

"Marie."

"Why didn't you talk to me before, Marie?"

Marie looked around again at the door before she answered. "Madame Rousse told me not to speak to you or she would beat me. Please, I should not be talking to you now."

"Just one more question," Jessica persisted. "Why is Madame so concerned suddenly with my toilette?"

Marie sent Jessica a compassionate glance. "I heard Madame Rousse and Madame du Barré discussing what to do to you because you tried to escape. You are to be put on display."

Jessica handed the towel back to Marie after drying herself. "On display?" she repeated weakly.

Marie nodded and handed Jessica a brush. "Madame Rousse does that to the new girls to allow the customers to see them." Marie's voice became soft and strangled at the end of her explanation, as if she were holding back tears.

"Have you ever been . . . on display, Marie?" Jessica asked gently.

Marie nodded without meeting her eyes. "Once. It was awful. The men . . ." Her voice trailed off as she shivered in disgust. Then regaining her composure as if no confidences had passed between them, she took the brush from Jessica and said, "I have to tie you to the rings again."

Jessica only paused a moment as she weighed the possibility of trying to convince Marie to escape with her. Realizing the futility of such a thought, knowing that Jacques was on watch for just such a thing, she rejected the idea. With resignation, she nodded. She watched absently as Marie tied first one wrist, then the other, expertly copying the knots that Jacques had tied. How, she wondered, would she be able to cope with the humiliation and degradation of the coming night? She swallowed back the fear that threatened to overwhelm her.

"Thank you for being kind," Jessica said as Marie finished her task. She gave the girl a smile that was braver than she was feeling. Marie smiled back and cleaned up the washbasin and other things.

Before she left, she whispered, "Don't let them know you are afraid."

The sun set and evening fell. Dinnertime came and went. No one came to Jessica's prison, not even to bring a meal. She tried to imagine all the things that could possibly happen to her that night, but she did not have enough experience in the ways of men. Just the fact that she would be on display like some article in a shop window caused her stomach to knot in fear. Time passed slowly, and it became very late. Still, no one came. She began to hope that, perhaps, Madame had changed her mind.

Her rising hopes were soon dashed when the door opened to allow in Jacques and Madame du Barré. A wicked smile crossed her face as she walked up to Jessica.

"So, little one," she smirked. "Have you decided to behave?"

"I will not try to escape again, Madame," Jessica told her meekly with her eyes lowered.

Madame grabbed Jessica's hair and jerked her head up. "You do not fool me with your meek words, little one," she said cruelly. "It is time you were taught some obedience and learned a few lessons for your new profession. Your pride and willfulness will only get you beatings where you are going. The men who buy girls from the auction block have no patience with those who do not perform well." Roughly, she released Jessica's hair.

"Do you have firsthand knowledge of that, Madame?" Jessica asked with mock sweetness.

Jessica thought the woman would strike her. Her eyes blazed and a flush of anger colored her cheeks. Her anger was gone in seconds. Instead, she smiled.

"You are not going to goad me into marking you, Jessica. You will be sold tomorrow night, as perfect and unharmed as you are now. Only by tomorrow night, you will be wiser." She turned to Jacques. "Untie her and put this on her." She gave Jessica a cruel smile. "We do not want our prospective buyers to see everything before the auction."

Jacques untied Jessica and slipped the garment over her head. It was a long, silky shift with full sleeves and a high neck. In spite of its modest proportions, it made Jessica feel naked. It clung to every curve of her body. Roughly, he tied her again.

With a vicious grin, Madame and Jacques left. Deliberately, they left the door wide open. In spite of her comparatively modest dress, Jessica felt horribly vulnerable. There was nothing she could do to protect herself from whatever any of the customers wished to do to her. The thought sickened her. Swallowing hard, she leaned her head back against the wall.

Marie's words echoed through Jessica's head. Don't let them know she was afraid. Jessica knew there was wisdom there, for that was exactly what Madame du Barré wanted: for Jessica to be afraid, to show her fear and feel degraded.

As the night wore on, Jessica knew Marie was correct. Men walked into her room, came up to her, stared at her, touched her. Jessica allowed none of them to see her feelings. In this, her gambling helped her immensely. She kept her face expressionless, her eyes cold, in spite of wanting to scream her repulsion and fear. The men became bored with trying to arouse a woman of ice. They left her alone. Occasionally, Madame entered the room, sat in a dark corner and observed the men with Jessica.

Several hours after midnight, the house became quiet. Almost all the girls had retired to the rooms upstairs with their customers. Madame du Barré appeared suddenly before Jessica. Her face was ugly in her rage and disgust.

"You are a fool, little one," Madame spat. "You have done nothing to help your cause. One of these men might have bid for you had you acted like a woman tonight. Instead, you turned them away with your cold eyes. If you do not bring a high price tomorrow night, I will sell you to Madame Rousse. Then we shall see what will happen to the proud Lady Jessica." She turned to Jacques who had come up beside her. "Untie her." She gave Jessica one last, piercing glance, then she stalked away.

As Jacques untied Jessica's wrists, she slumped to the floor. She had been in the same position for so long that her legs could not carry her weight. Leaving her where she lay, he turned on his heel and locked the door as he left.

Jessica crawled across the floor to the bed. With a stifled cry of pain as her sore muscles complained, she pulled herself up onto its relative security and climbed under the covers. Only a few tears of desperation escaped beneath her lids before she fell asleep.

Le Cochon, propped up on many pillows because of his enormous weight, slept the sleep of the innocent. Snoring thunderously, he did not hear the muffled scrape of a boot on the parquet floor of his bedroom. Nor did the soft hiss of a dagger drawn from its scabbard awaken him. Two dark shapes watched him sleep, one from beside the bed, the other from deeper shadows in the corner of the room. It was not until one of the shapes knelt on the bed beside him and pressed the cold steel of a knife against his throat that he became aware that he was not alone.

With a snort, Le Cochon reluctantly opened his eyes. He had been dreaming of roast pheasant with chestnut stuffing, of puff pastry filled with orange-flavored cream. It had been a wonderful dream. Now he was awake, and hungry. He felt the blade nestling between folds of skin on his neck and realized it was not morning; he would have to wait before he could eat again.

"What do you want?" he demanded testily. He was not afraid. There were few who wished him harm. He was too valuable a source of information.

"Please, Le Cochon," a silky voice entreated from a black corner of his room. "A little civility would be appreciated."

Le Cochon knew that voice. It was the only one that could inspire fear in him. That voice had kept him hungry for two days. Two whole days! Gingerly, because of the dagger at his throat, he turned his head toward the shadows and tried to make out the figure who lurked there.

"Monsieur Le Chat," he placated, "please forgive me. I did not expect to ever see you again."

Le Cochon felt, rather than saw, the cold smile that appeared on those handsome lips.

"Ah, you heard, then, of our misfortune, of our betrayal. Did you truly believe I had used up all of my nine lives, Le Cochon? Perhaps you know something more about the trap Fouché set for us?"

The knife against Le Cochon's throat pressed harder. "No, no, monsieur, nothing. I know only what I hear in the streets, in the bistros." Le Cochon sent a pleading glance at the shadow hovering over him. The pressure against his neck lessened.

A movement from the black corner drew his attention. Le Chat stepped forward onto the Aubusson carpet. He appeared to drift above the floor like some dark angel.

"Fortunately for you, Le Cochon, I have not come seeking revenge," Damien said. "I came for information. There is a woman. Small, beautiful, with raven hair and eyes like sapphires. I want her."

Le Cochon swallowed against the knife. He should have known the girl belonged to someone of significance, especially because of the lack of secrecy involved. They wanted her to be found. If he told this devil where the woman was, he would lose the tremendous profit he had been expecting to get for her, and he would gain the wrath of that bitch, du Barré. The knife wiggled against his throat, and he felt a sliver of pain as his skin was broken. There was still a way he could make this venture worthwhile.

"There will be an auction, Monsieur Le Chat. She is to be sold to the highest bidder." Becoming cagey, Le Cochon added, "The rest, monsieur, you will have to pay for."

Le Cochon felt the anger emanate from the dark figure standing across the room. For a moment, he thought he had pushed too hard. Then, he sensed the tension release.

Damien had expected to have to pay this pig. He had used him as a source of information before, and had been forced to pay dearly for it. The information always had been accurate, however, so he had paid. Now, he prayed that it would be so again. If it was wrong, then he and Jessica and all his men were lost.

"You will get your payment at the auction, Le Cochon," Damien said. "I will bid for the girl. And I will win her. You will get more than what you dreamed possible. Now, where is the auction to be held, and when?"

Le Cochon hesitated only fractionally before he announced the information. He had no doubts that Le Chat would appear at the auction. He had seen the girl; she was exquisite. He assumed that Le Chat had more than a nodding acquaintance with her. Why else would the devil risk returning to France? As for his payment, he knew he would receive that, also. Le Chat harbored an unusually honorable streak for such a ruthless rogue.

As soon as Le Cochon had given them the time and the place of the auction, Damien and Edward Johnson slipped out of the bedroom door. They had no fear of being discovered, for they had incapacitated all of Le Cochon's servants, having either knocked them unconscious, or tied them up.

At the bottom of the stairs, they turned toward the back of the house. The rest of Damien's men lounged outside, waiting. As Damien emerged, Higgins pushed away from the garden wall.

"The cook's been tied up and hidden in a stable a few houses away, sir," Higgins reported.

"And the food?" Damien asked.

Higgins grinned. "Distributed to the poor of the city, sir."

Damien gave an answering grin. His revenge for the possibility that Le Cochon had been involved in his betrayal to Fouché was to deprive the man of any way to assuage his enormous appetite for a while. "Good. Let's leave here, gentlemen, and get some sleep. We have work to do tomorrow night."

Chapter Sixteen

When Jessica awoke, it was early afternoon. Marie
and another maid were preparing a bath. For a moment, Jessica wondered at the sudden kindness of Madame du Barré, but then realized the reason for it.
That night was the auction. She would be put on display like some piece of merchandise and sold to the
highest bidder. It would be to Madame's advantage to
have her merchandise as attractive as possible.

Marie looked over to the bed then, and seeing that
Jessica was awake, smiled. "You are to have a bath as
soon as you have eaten." She indicated a tray of food
on a table beside the bed.

Jessica picked at the food. She had little appetite.
However, she did look forward to her bath. It would be
the first time she would be completely clean in a week.

By the time Marie and the other maid had finished
Jessica's toilette, it was quite dark. They left her with a
smile of encouragement. Naked, Jessica sat huddled in
a blanket as she waited for the hour of her degradation. The minutes seemed to crawl by. She prayed for
the night to be over quickly, so that the pain of the
unknown would vanish. Finally, she heard the scrape
of a key in the lock, and Madame du Barré entered. She carried a white garment over her
arm.

Madame smiled. "It is almost time to go, little one.

Stand up and let me look at you. And take off that hideous blanket."

Jessica's eyes travelled past Madame to Jacques, who hovered just behind the woman. His face was expressionless. He appeared to care little if Jessica was clothed or not. Raising her chin proudly, she stood and allowed the blanket to drop. There was no point in fighting. Her fate was already sealed.

Madame nodded in approval as she studied Jessica. "Very good. Marie has done well. I will have to tell Madame Rousse to commend the girl. Now, for the finishing touch."

She shook out the white material that had been draped over her arm. It was not a garment at all, but a large square of diaphanous, white silk. She wrapped it about Jessica, pulling it under one arm and tying two corners at the other shoulder. It concealed and revealed at the same time, for it remained open down one side of Jessica's body.

Madame stood back to survey her work critically. When she was satisfied, she held out her hand to Jacques who gave her a warm cloak. This she carefully placed about Jessica's shoulders and pulled the attached hood over her head. No one would guess that Jessica wore next to nothing.

"Now, you are ready, little one," Madame told her. "Just a short ride, and then you will enter a new life."

Jessica gazed impassively at the woman. She was determined not to reveal her awful fear. Don't let them know you are afraid, she kept telling herself.

They descended the stairs and left the house by a side door. A coach was waiting for them. Jessica breathed in the chill, night air. She relished the tiny feeling of freedom it gave her. It had been so long since she had been outside, that the fresh air made her slightly giddy. Slowly, she entered the coach, followed by Madame and Jacques. With her head bowed, she sat quietly in the corner of the seat and prayed that fate would not be too cruel to her this night.

"For whom are you praying, little one?" Madame sneered. "For yourself, or for your lover, Le Chat?"

Jessica's head snapped up at the mention of Damien. What diabolical scheme had Madame planned? Did she really believe that Damien would come after her?

Madame laughed. "Oh, yes, little one. He will be there tonight. Feast your eyes when you see him, for it will be the last time you will be able to gaze upon his handsome face." Madame sadly shook her head. "Such a shame to kill such a perfect male specimen. Ah, well, perhaps he will not have to be killed right away. Perhaps I can persuade him to remain in France. I have always wondered what it would be like to have my own love slave."

Jessica bit her lip to refrain from making a reply. Invoking Madame's anger now would serve no purpose and would, perhaps, lessen any chance she might have to warn Damien of a trap. Once again, she lowered her head.

The auction was to be held in a country house several miles outside the city. It was a spot less likely to be discovered by the authorities. Jessica wondered what type of person actually attended these affairs and purchased a white woman. She knew, of course, of black slaves, and she had heard whispered rumors of the slave markets of North Africa where white women from captured European vessels were sold, never to be heard from again. Would she disappear into oblivion, also?

As the coach pulled around to the back of a large manor house, her heart quickened its beat and her hands began to shake. She was determined not to show her fear, and she clenched her fists to hide her tremors. Keeping her face expressionless, she descended from the carriage. With Madame on one side of her and Jacques on the other, she walked through the door to meet her fate.

They entered through the kitchen and passed down a long hall into a small sitting room. Jessica counted nine other girls waiting to be auctioned. They were all dressed in a similar fashion to what she wore. Some sat waiting quietly, some cried, the rest looked as if they were in shock.

Madame took the cloak from Jessica's shoulders, and then she and Jacques went out the door. Jessica shivered in the chill air. There was no fire in the fireplace. Glancing about, she realized that even though she had been left alone, there was no need to even think about escape. A very large, rough-looking man stood to one side of the door. He watched everything with an attentive stare. Jessica found an empty chair in a corner and sat down to wait.

It was not long before the door across the room opened and a woman beckoned to a tall, buxom girl. Before the girl went out the door, she turned and waved to the others waiting. "Good luck, my friends," she called.

So the auction began. One by one, each of the girls was taken out the door to meet her master. At last, only Jessica remained. The door across the room opened again, and the woman who had been escorting the girls entered. She held a length of long, white, satin ribbon in her hand. She stopped before Jessica.

"Hold out your hands, child," she said kindly.

Jessica gazed at her in confusion and did as she was told. The woman wrapped the ribbon about Jessica's wrists and tied them together, leaving a length of ribbon trailing on the floor. None of the other girls had been bound. Jessica raised questioning eyes to the woman.

"I was told to tie you," the woman said. "I do not

know why. We only tie those who have been unruly."
She gave Jessica a sympathetic smile as she finished.
"Come along. It is your turn, now."

Jessica knew that Madame du Barré had something
to do with her being bound. Why else would she have
been the only one?

The woman led Jessica through the door and into a
room filled with people. The crowd was mostly made
up of men, but there was a scattering of women among
them. A raised platform stood between Jessica and the
crowd. The woman handed the end of the ribbon tying
Jessica's wrists to Le Cochon. He led her onto the platform.

The fat man began the bidding. "Our last sale of the
evening, ladies and gentlemen. A lovely pearl from the
shores of England. Gently born and raised. Intelligent,
yet endowed with spirit, guaranteed to make bedding
her an experience to remember."

At this last, he winked and grinned at the crowd,
then placed his fat hand on one of Jessica's breasts and
pinched her. Jessica gasped in pain. Knocking away
his hand, she swung both fists and hit him in the arm,
then moved as far away as the length of ribbon allowed. The crowd laughed and applauded. Jessica
stared stonily at a spot in the wall straight ahead.

"The opening price is five hundred guineas." Le Cochon announced. "Who will bid?"

"Five hundred!" came a bid from the right side of
the room.

"Seven hundred!" a man sitting directly before the
platform bid.

"One thousand!" a third man bid.

So the bidding went on: eleven hundred, twelve, fifteen hundred, two thousand, up to three thousand
guineas.

"I have a bid of three thousand guineas," Le Cochon
told the crowd. He gazed out over the faces expect-

antly. "Come, come," he exhorted them. "Is that all you will bid for such a creature of beauty?"

He reached out and tugged at the knot at Jessica's shoulder holding her garment in place. It fell to the floor with a sigh. The people murmured with approval at Jessica's nakedness. She shivered, but continued to stare straight ahead.

Le Cochon gave the crowd a sly look. "I have heard it rumored that she is the mistress of Le Chat. Gentlemen, does that not fire your loins? Imagine, having this beauty under you, moaning, knowing that you are taking the place of that devil Le Chat."

"Four thousand!" a dark haired man with small, evil eyes offered.

"Forty-five hundred!" another bidder called out.

"Five thousand!" the dark haired man returned.

Le Cochon waited a moment, but no other bid was offered. "I have five thousand," he said. "Is there another bid?"

He raised his walking stick to finalize the sale, and Jessica's heart sank. She knew the dark haired man would not treat her kindly.

Before Le Cochon's stick hit the floor, a deep voice from the far corner of the room called out, "Ten thousand."

Jessica's eyes immediately sought out the source of the voice. It *was* Damien! He leaned against the wall with his arms folded across his chest, appearing bored with the proceedings. He was dressed as Le Chat.

The crowd babbled excitedly and someone exclaimed, "Le Chat!" Le Cochon smiled happily at the large bid and rapped his walking stick several times to regain order. When the crowd quieted down, he looked questioningly at the dark haired man.

"Do you wish to bid against the rightful owner of this piece of fluff, monsieur?" he asked.

The man scowled and shook his head. Le Cochon

242

brought his walking stick down sharply.

"Sold, to Le Chat, for ten thousand guineas," he announced.

Damien pushed away from the wall and made his way to the platform. He tossed two pouches, heavy with coins, at the feet of the auctioneer.

"You may count it if you wish," Damien drawled, daring the man to do so.

"That will not be necessary, monsieur," Le Cochon replied quickly. "You have always paid me fairly in the past."

A glance full of meaning passed between the two men. Damien finally smiled, without humor.

"You would do well to remember that, Le Cochon," he said.

Le Cochon passed the end of the ribbon to Damien. "You have made a wise purchase, monsieur. There are those who would use the mademoiselle against you."

Damien's eyes narrowed at the oblique warning, then he turned to Jessica. Placing his hands around her waist, he swung her down from the platform. He removed his cloak, placed it over her shoulders, then guided her through the crowd and outside. He stopped just outside the door of the house and untied her wrists.

Jessica remained silent as she watched his fingers work at the ribbon. Her feelings at seeing him, being near him, went so deep she did not trust herself to speak. She shifted her gaze to the dark beyond the lamplight to help herself keep her equilibrium. Some movement caught her attention out of the corner of her eye. There was a dull flash as the light reflected off a metal object.

Turning her head to see more clearly, she saw Madame du Barré aiming a pistol in their direction. Jacques stood beside her, also with a pistol. As Jessica watched, Madame raised the gun and pulled the trigger. Time seemed to slow down to a crawl. Damien had not seen the danger. Screaming his name, she launched herself at him, knocking him off balance. There was an explosion. She felt a thud against her shoulder, then a white-hot pain. A second explosion rang in her ears, and she watched through a blur as Jacques crumpled to the ground. Madame disappeared into the woods.

Damien regained his balance from where Jessica had pushed him against the wall of the house, and held her away from him so he could look down at her. Her face had gone very pale, and her eyes were glazed.

"Are you all right?" he asked.

"Yes." Jessica's voice was weak, but impatient. "Please, you have to get away from here. Madame was trying to kill you. Leave me here and go!"

"Not bloody likely," he ground out between clenched teeth. "Do you think I came all this way to leave you?" He grabbed her by the arm and hurried her down the steps and over to a stand of trees. In its shelter were two horses, one already with a rider. Jessica recognized the bulk of Leftenant Johnson as he held the reins of Damien's huge stallion. Damien mounted, then helped Jessica up to sit before him.

Waves of pain and blackness washed over Jessica at every movement. As they galloped off, she tried desperately to remain conscious. She knew Damien did not need to be hampered with her inert form before him on the horse. Each time the horse's hooves hit the ground, however, a shooting pain radiated out from the wound in her shoulder. She could feel the warm trickle of blood down her side.

She was not really aware of where they went or how long they rode. At best, she remained only half conscious. It was only because of Damien's arm about her that she stayed on his horse.

Finally the horses slowed and came to a stop, blow-ing heavily after their gallop. Damien dismounted, but as he took his arm from about Jessica, she slipped sideways from the horse. Damien caught her before she fell. His hand slipped against her skin, wet and sticky.

"God's teeth," he muttered as he realized it was blood.

With his mouth in a grim line, he picked her up and carried her into the tiny cottage where they had stopped. He placed her gently on the one small cot in the single room. Pulling the cloak away from her shoulders, he saw the round, dark hole surrounded with a smear of blood where she had been shot. He covered her with a blanket, then went to start a fire in the fireplace. As he coaxed the kindling into flames, Leftenant Johnson entered.

"We will have to stay here longer than I had planned," Damien told him. "Jessica has been shot. I want the others on lookout duty, two on, two off, at the usual places."

"They are already posted," Johnson said. "Is she hurt very badly?"

"She was hit in the shoulder. I think the ball is still in the wound. I couldn't see very well." Damien straightened. "I'll need some water and something for bandages."

A sound between a moan and a sob came from the cot. As Damien hurried to Jessica's side, Johnson discreetly disappeared out the door. Taking the lamp that Johnson had lit, Damien knelt beside Jessica and gazed down at her face, now pale and moist from her pain. Something inside him tightened. She was so small and delicate, yet she had pushed him out of the way of a bullet that might very well have killed him. Gently, he smoothed the sweat-dampened curls back from her face.

At his touch, Jessica's eyes fluttered open. Seeing Damien made her panic. She had to warn him!

245

Grabbing his coat, she told him urgently, "Madame has set a trap! She means to capture you! Damien, you have to get away!"

Damien smiled and disengaged her fingers from the front of his coat. Holding her hand he said comfortingly, "It's all right, Jessica. We're safe for now. Rest for a while."

He held her hand until he saw that she understood. The pain took her over, then, and she fell once more into blackness.

Johnson returned with a bucket of water and a handful of cloth strips. Damien helped him empty the bucket into a kettle hanging over the fire, then he took him to a corner of the cottage away from Jessica's cot.

"We have to be away from here by dawn," Damien said. "Any later than that and we could be discovered. We will need a wagon to get Jessica to the coast. Have Higgins take one of the others and see what he can find. Tell them to be very careful. I am sure Fouché is rather upset at our escape. He will no doubt have patrols all over the countryside. After you have spoken to Higgins, come back here. I'll need your help."

Johnson nodded briskly and left. Damien returned to the cot. He unclasped the cloak from about her throat and pulled it off her shoulders. There was an ugly, little hole where the ball had entered her soft flesh. He tucked the blanket more securely around her. When he had finished, he put his hand to her cheek.

"Jessica," he said softly.

Slowly, she opened eyes clouded with pain. Despite the shafts of white heat that lanced through her, she could not have been happier. Damien had come after her. He was here, with her. She tried to smile at him.

"Jessica, I have to remove the shot from your shoulder. Do you understand?"

Damien's voice sounded strange, as if he had been hurt, too. "Are you all right, Damien?" Jessica asked.

246

"Did Madame shoot you, too?"

Damien smiled at her. "No, love, Madame did not shoot me." He touched his fingers to her cheek. "It will hurt when I remove the shot. I'll try to be careful."

Jessica nodded and closed her eyes. She was content that Damien would care for her. If only she did not hurt so much. She wanted to put her arms around him and tell him . . . something. There was something she needed to say to him, but she could not think past the pain in her shoulder. Slowly, she sank back into unconsciousness.

Damien stood and scowled darkly at the wall before him. He was torn with guilt and apprehension, feelings that had never assailed him before. His guilt arose from his desperate desire to help the wounded girl who lay before him, the girl whose family had inflicted so much pain on his own. If he had harbored any sense of justice, he should not have followed her into France. He should have let her go, gaining satisfaction from the fact that justice had been done. Instead, he found himself aching with a need to heal her, to escape with her back to England.

It was up to him to get everyone safely out of France, but he felt very unsure about the outcome of this venture. He had never worried about such things before. A favorable outcome had always been assumed. He knew his talents and those of his men and used them accordingly. He had trained his men to be resourceful in an emergency. With Jessica injured, their progress to the coast would be slow, giving Fouché time to catch up to them. Resourcefulness could not make up for lost time. Since this slip of a girl had entered his life, he found he could not be sure of anything.

He looked up as Johnson returned to the cottage. Forcing his dark thoughts aside, he prepared for the ordeal of removing the shot from Jessica's shoulder. As the Leftenant held a light above Jessica, Damien cleansed the wound with some of the water that had been heating over the fire. Since Jessica was so small, there was not much flesh around her shoulders, and Damien could see the ball just below the surface of her skin. Fortunately, it had almost spent itself by the time it entered her shoulder. Taking his knife, he held it in the fire to clean it. As Johnson leaned across Jessica, holding her down with his weight, Damien pried the ball from its soft resting place. In her unconscious state, Jessica cried out once, stiffened against the pain, then lapsed deeper into the blackness that clouded her brain. Damien pressed a pad of cloth against the sudden flow of blood from the wound, then washed and bandaged her shoulder tightly.

Sitting back on his heels, he let out his breath in a rush. Looking up, he met Johnson's concerned eyes. He frowned to cover his relief and stood up.

"Shouldn't you check on our lookouts?" he asked, irritated that once again his feelings about Jessica were so transparent to this man.

"If they see anything, they will report," Johnson told him with a shrug. He knew Damien understood that as well as he did. "Why don't you try to rest? You haven't slept in two days. I can watch the lady."

Damien glared at him. "The only way you would have known about my sleeping habits recently would be if you had not slept either, Leftenant. Will you please stop mothering me?"

Johnson grinned. "Yes, sir." He reached into a pocket and pulled out a silver flask. Tossing it to Damien, he asked, "Would your mother have thought to bring some of this along?"

Damien caught the flask. Opening it, he sniffed its contents. The pungent scent of his best brandy assailed his nose. Raising the flask to his lips, he took a generous swallow, then poured a liberal amount on the bandage covering Jessica's wound. As the alcohol painfully sterilized her wound, Jessica protested in an unconscious mumble. Damien capped the flask and tossed it back to Johnson.

"At least you are good for something," he grumbled as he felt the brandy begin to quell the nervous flutterings that had suddenly appeared in his stomach since working on Jessica.

At that moment, Walker burst into the cottage. "Sir!" he exclaimed breathlessly. "A patrol passed me on the road, headed this way."

"All right, then we will have to move. Where is Higgins with that wagon?" he chaffed.

As he spoke, the sound of horses drawing a vehicle, probably a coach, definitely not a wagon, could be heard approaching. It stopped before the cottage. The three men stared at one another in dismay, then at a flick of Damien's hand, they moved quickly. Donning their masks and drawing their pistols, they took up positions of defense about the cottage. Johnson and Walker stood against the wall on either side of the door. Damien stood in the corner before Jessica's cot. The door creaked open, and a man filled the opening.

Chapter Seventeen

Just as Johnson was about the bang the man on the head with the butt of his pistol, the intruder spoke. "I've found us some fancy transportation back to the coast, sir."

"Higgins!" Damien exclaimed. "You almost received a nasty bump from Johnson there. Next time, give us the warning so we know it is you."

Higgins swung around as Johnson lowered his pistol. The Leftenant grinned at the Sergeant. "I almost ruined my pistol on your hard head, Higgins."

As Higgins was about to retort, Damien interrupted him, "Let's see this fancy transportation that you found."

He followed Higgins out the door and stopped. Sitting incongruously before the cottage was a very expensive coach and four. The coach door opened and a portly gentleman descended with his hands held above his head. He was followed by young Wells who held a pistol aimed at the man's back.

"Good evening, sir," Wells grinned. "This is Citizen Boudreau. He has graciously allowed us the use of his carriage this evening."

Damien grinned and bowed before the man, whose jaw had dropped open. "Citizen Boudreau, a pleasure to meet you, sir. Allow me to introduce myself."

"I know who you are!" the man blurted. "You are

Le Chat!"

Damien raised an amused eyebrow. "You know of me, then, monsieur?"

Monsieur Boudreau did not answer Damien's question. Instead, he protested, "I know nothing, monsieur. I am just a poor merchant. I will give you all the money I have with me."

Damien looked askance at the coach. "Just a poor merchant, monsieur?" He shook his head. "If you are poor, I would like to see what you consider rich." Becoming stern, he said, "We do not want your money, monsieur, nor do we wish to hear unimportant rumors. What we want is your carriage and your silence and your cooperation. Now, kindly return to your carriage and wait. One of my men will wait with you so that you will not feel lonely."

He motioned for the gentleman to return to the coach. As the man turned away, Damien winked and nodded his approval at Wells. Higgins retrieved a bundle from under the driver's seat and handed it to Damien.

"We borrowed his footmen's clothes, too, sir," he told his commander.

Damien smiled wryly. "I don't suppose your extra efforts had anything to do with having the Lady Jessica along?"

Higgins looked embarrassed and mumbled something about not being appreciated. Damien laughed and slapped him on the back.

"Go put on one of the footmen's livery, Higgins. You can drive the coach." As Higgins began stripping off his clothes, Damien turned to Johnson. "We have to get out of here," he said urgently. "Take over from Wells and have him put on the other livery. We'll pick up Carpenter on the way." He called to Walker, who had remained at the door of the cottage, "Walker, collect the horses. We're leaving."

251

Damien returned and strode to the cot. Jessica was still unconscious. He felt her forehead and frowned. Her skin was hot. She was developing a high fever. He had to get her home quickly. Checking her shoulder, he was satisfied that the bleeding had slowed considerably. He wrapped her in another blanket, then went to douse the fire with the remaining water in the kettle and scatter the ashes. He wanted to leave as little evidence as possible. Returning to the cot, he picked up Jessica and glanced about the room once more. Satisfied that everything was in its place, he left.

Damien laid Jessica gently on the empty seat of the carriage. Seeing that everyone was ready, he gave the word to leave, then climbed into the coach himself. He placed Jessica's head in his lap and gripped the edge of the seat. His arm lay protectively across her body so that she would not be bounced about too much. Glancing up, he caught the sick expression of Monsieur Boudreau.

"Is there something wrong, monsieur?" Damien asked mildly.

"What did you do to her, you fiend?" the man demanded.

"Do, monsieur? I did nothing to her."

The man gestured at Jessica's unconscious body and stammered, "But-but . . ."

"She was shot, monsieur, and, I assure you, not by me." Damien gazed at him steadily.

"There was a rumor of a shooting at the auction, but I thought . . ." The man's voice trailed off once again.

"Ah, you were at the auction this evening," Damien observed. Monsieur Boudreau looked frightened to death. Tiny beads of sweat popped out on his forehead. He mopped his brow with a lace-edged handkerchief. If this outlaw allowed him to live, his wife would have his hide when he finally returned home. She would never believe him when he told her he had been waylaid by Le Chat.

Damien watched the man as he nervously wiped the palms of his hands, then wiped his forehead a second time. He decided to give the fellow a little more to tell his friends.

"What were you doing at the auction, monsieur?" Damien asked suddenly. "I did not see you bid on any of the merchandise."

Monsieur Boudreau stared in fear at Damien. "I . . . Well, I . . . I . . . ," he stammered.

"Yes?"

The man swallowed. "I just went to watch, monsieur," he whined.

"To watch?" Damien repeated. The stiletto appeared in his hand. The blade caught a glint of moonlight as he leaned forward and placed its point beneath Monsieur Boudreau's many chins. "To watch whom?" he demanded threateningly.

"No one!" the man exclaimed. Then realizing his mistake in lying, he amended, "I mean, the girls. I went to watch the girls." He gestured slightly in Jessica's direction.

"The girls, monsieur?" Damien asked, disbelieving. "I think not. I think you were there to watch me."

"No! No, no, Monsieur Le Chat!" He shook his head as vigorously as he dared with the threat of the knife so close. "Only the girls." Then again realizing he had made another mistake because of the unconscious girl before him, he pleaded, "Please, monsieur, I am a married man with children."

Damien sat back, but the stiletto remained in his hand. "I do not like others ogling my woman," he stated as his hand possessively lay on Jessica's arm. "I do not think I like you, Monsieur Boudreau."

"But Monsieur Le Chat, I did not know she was

yours," the man tried to placate. "I only heard . . ." His voice trailed off as he became afraid to repeat what had been told to him.

"What did you hear, monsieur?" Damien asked, very interested.

When the man did not answer immediately, Johnson nudged him in the ribs with the barrel of a pistol. Monsieur Boudreau jumped.

Quickly, he answered, "Only that there was to be a special item at the auction tonight. That you would be there."

Damien met Johnson's eyes in a knowing, silent exchange. Quietly, he stated to his prisoner, "Then you were not disappointed, monsieur." Indicating Jessica, he said, "She is a special item, is she not?"

"Yes," the man answered. "She was—is—exquisite."

He closed his eyes, deep in fear, for he thought he had angered Le Chat again. Yet, the vision of the girl who lay on the seat across from him was vividly etched in his mind. She was a glorious creature, a gorgeous piece of fluff. With her, it might almost be possible for him to become potent once more. The presence of the dangerous man in the coach made him block her memory from his mind. He wondered why the man had paid an enormous sum for her.

Damien broke in on his thoughts. "You are troubled by something, Monsieur Boudreau? You are uncomfortable, perhaps?"

The man shook his head.

"Then please, enlighten us about what bothers you. After all, you have offered us the use of your coach. We would not wish to leave you with unanswered questions." The irony in Damien's words and tone was heavy.

The man shook his head again, but his eyes dropped to Jessica's face and revealed his curiosity.

"Ah, you are wondering why I paid for her," Damien stated with uncanny insight. "There is a certain honor among thieves, monsieur, and I wanted her back. If something you valued highly were stolen, would you not do everything in your power to retrieve it?"

"Yes," Monsieur Boudreau answered. "But ten thousand guineas! Monsieur Le Chat, it is an incredible sum!"

Damien allowed himself a slight smile. "Come, come, monsieur. You saw her this evening. Do you not think she is worth it?"

Monsieur Boudreau shook his head as he thought of his wife. "No, monsieur. No woman is worth that much." When he noticed the dangerous glint in Damien's eyes, he added quickly, "But, of course, she is very beautiful."

"Silence!" Johnson roared suddenly and once again poked the man in the ribs with his pistol.

Monsieur Boudreau cast a frightened look at Damien. Damien smiled wryly and shrugged as he returned the stiletto to its hiding place inside his sleeve.

"You have upset my friend. He has a very short temper."

"I am sorry. I did not mean . . . ," their prisoner began.

"Silence!" Johnson repeated, and Monsieur Boudreau immediately became quiet.

Nothing was said after that. Damien listened to Jessica's sometimes irregular breathing. Never had he felt so helpless. He prayed they would reach the coast without mishap. That was not to be, however. After they had ridden for quite some time, the coach slowed down and stopped. Damien and Johnson exchanged worried glances.

"Monsieur," Damien told their captive in a low voice, "you will find out the cause of this delay and get rid of whoever has stopped this coach. Do not try anything foolish. Remember that my men are sitting above and will hear everything that is said. There will be a pistol trained on your back at all times. If there is any killing tonight, be assured that the first to die will be you." He motioned for the gentleman to get out.

Johnson carefully looked out and reported on what was taking place. "A patrol. I can see five, no, six men. Boudreau is talking to them. They seem to be accepting what he is saying. He's coming back. The patrol isn't leaving."

Monsieur Boudreau opened the door and stepped into the coach. He wiped his brow with his damp handkerchief.

"The sergeant insisted on accompanying me to my home," he told Damien. "He said the notorious bandit, Le Chat, was in this area, and it was not safe to be out alone."

Damien smiled widely, appreciating the irony of the situation. "I am glad he was so solicitous of your welfare, monsieur. It is too bad he will never know that he escorted 'the notorious bandit, Le Chat' to safety. Is there a house close by?"

Boudreau looked out the window to gauge his surroundings. "I think there is one about a mile up the road."

"Good. We will pretend it is yours." Damien opened a tiny door used to communicate with the driver and informed Higgins of the plan. He sat back after that and appeared to enjoy the ride. Actually, he prayed fervently that one of the soldiers did not look inside the coach before he could be rid of them. He glanced down at Jessica and caressed her forehead. She was not doing well. With relief, not too long after their stop, he felt Higgins turn the coach into a drive.

"Thank the soldiers, monsieur," Damien told their

prisoner quietly. "Do it quickly and get rid of them."

Monsieur Boudreau stuck his head out of the coach and called his thanks to the patrol. Higgins started up again very slowly. He stopped around a curve in the long drive. They waited there to allow the soldiers to ride away. Finally, he turned the coach about, and they drove off at a brisk pace.

They rode without another stop until dawn, when they halted in a small field beside the road. A stream meandered through the grass, and they were able to get a drink and water the horses. The animals needed to be rested before they could continue their journey, so Damien allowed Monsieur Boudreau to get out of the coach. He was kept under the watchful eyes of Leftenant Johnson. The others went to relieve themselves and catch a short nap. Walker would take over guard duty after he had rested.

Damien brought water to Jessica, who was still unconscious. The fever had risen. Her skin was hot and dry to the touch. He bathed her face with the cool water and forced a few drops through her cracked lips. As he did so, her eyes opened and she stared up at him. They were glazed from the fever and an incredible, bright blue.

"Papa?" she asked in a small voice. Her eyes cleared suddenly, and she reached up and touched his cheek. "Oh, Damien," she sighed. "Don't let the baby die. It's your baby. Don't let it die." She closed her eyes and a tear slipped out from beneath her lashes.

Damien gently pushed her hair away from her face. "The baby won't die, Jessica. I promise, the baby won't die."

She sighed, content in his reassurance, and fell asleep.

Damien sat back on his heels and frowned. A child? Not once had the thought entered his mind. He felt very stupid. He should have known she would conceive. She had been untouched when he took her, but all he could think of was how he had felt with her near him. He shook his head at himself. He could not dwell on that now. He had to get them out of France.

Pushing all other thoughts out of his mind, he inspected her shoulder. The bleeding had almost stopped. After washing the wound, he changed the bandage quickly, then gathered everyone together. They had to move on. Until they reached the coast, they would not be safe.

By late afternoon, they sighted the English Channel. It was a relief for everyone. They were all exhausted, and Monsieur Boudreau grated on already frazzled nerves. He had grumbled constantly until Johnson finally appropriated one of Jessica's clean bandages and gagged him. Damien had grown grimly silent during the ride as Jessica slipped in and out of consciousness. He now sent up a private prayer of thanks at the sight of blue water.

They waited at the edge of the beach for Carpenter and Walker who had brought the horses and rode several minutes behind the coach. Damien descended from the carriage to reassure himself that all was well. Their small bark was anchored several yards out from shore, just where they had left it, and the woods and fields in the other direction seemed quiet. As he sauntered to the water's edge, Higgins and Wells disappeared into the woods to attend to nature's call.

Damien watched the bark rise and fall gently on the swells. A sense of urgency made him impatient. They would not be safe until they were on board and sailing away from shore. Having come this far without being captured, he would be bitterly disappointed if they were caught.

A sound behind him made him swing about. The

sight that met his eyes made his stomach drop, yet it was not totally unexpected. Madame du Barré sat atop the dunes on a horse surrounded by eight soldiers. They each held a rifle aimed at him. Two more soldiers were on each side of the coach, and they had guns trained on the occupants. Damien glanced quickly toward the woods where Higgins and Wells had disappeared, but there was no sign of them. Walker and Carpenter had also not yet arrived. After Madame was sure he had seen her, she rode down onto the beach followed by the soldiers.

Damien strolled toward Madame and bowed. "Good afternoon, Madame," he greeted her. "Did you come to see us off on our voyage?"

Madame laughed lightly. "You are a brazen rogue, Monsieur Le Chat. Always ready with a quick wit, eh? But, I do not think you will be taking any voyages for a very long time. As you can see, you are greatly outnumbered. I do believe you have used all of your nine lives."

Damien grinned. "Do not be so sure, Madame. Did you know that this spot is called Witch's Cove? Witches are known to have supernatural powers and are always associated with cats." As he spoke, he moved closer to Madame's horse.

"Stay where you are, monsieur," she warned. "These men may get very nervous if you come any closer."

As she finished speaking, an eerie wail, ending in unearthly laughter came out of the woods. The horses bobbed their heads and pranced nervously. The soldiers fought to keep them still and exchanged frightened, worried glances.

"You will not fool me with your tricks, Monsieur Le Chat," Madame told Damien sternly.

"Tricks, Madame?" he queried. "I have used no tricks. You have watched me. I have been standing

259

here before you in full view."

As he spoke his last word, the sound of horses could be heard in the woods. They thundered across the ground, sounding as if they would burst out of the woods in a huge herd. The soldiers with Madame watched expectantly for this large group of riders to emerge from the woods, but none appeared. Then, as suddenly as the sound had begun, it stopped. There was no fading of the sound into the distance, it merely ceased. There was deathly silence. Even the waves crashing on the beach seemed muted.

"Ghosts!" one of the younger soldiers exclaimed.

"Witches," another mumbled.

"Captain, contain your men," Madame ordered to the officer beside her without taking her eyes from Damien.

Before the captain could open his mouth, the spectral laughter sounded again from the woods. A few of the soldiers exchanged frightened glances a second time, wheeled their horses and bolted. Damien raised an amused eyebrow at Madame.

"Hold steady, men," the captain commanded.

"What are those noises, sir?" a very young soldier questioned.

"Quiet, soldier!" the captain barked.

Three huge, black crows flew up out of the trees, circled, and, cawing loudly, swooped past the group on the beach.

"Mother of God," one of the soldiers who was guarding the carriage mumbled. "A witch's messenger." He dropped his rifle and galloped away, followed by two more men.

As the soldiers and Madame watched the birds, Damien dug the toe of his boot into the sand and flung it up in front of Madame's horse. The animal reared in fright. Madame fought for control, but without success. She was unseated and fell heavily to the beach. Damien quickly dropped to one knee beside her and held his stiletto to her throat.

When the soldiers' attention again centered on him, he spoke. "If you do not wish to see this woman's throat slashed, gentlemen, I suggest you retreat back to Paris."

"Shoot him!" Madame screamed. "Forget about me and shoot!"

"I am afraid I can not do that, Madame," the captain told her with regret. "I have received other orders from Monsieur Fouché." He turned to Damien. "You win, this time, monsieur. You are fortunate in that Madame du Barré has outlived her usefulness." He saluted and rode off with the remainder of his men following.

"Coward! Fool!" Madame screamed after him. "You will live to regret this!"

Damien smiled coldly down at his captive. "I think, rather, it is you who will live to regret his actions, Madame. It would seem that Fouché no longer requires your services."

He stood and pulled the woman up with him. Whistling sharply, he waited as Higgins, Wells, Carpenter, and Walker emerged from the woods with the horses. Madame glared at Damien at the appearance of his men.

"You have not won yet, Monsieur Le Chat," she spat at him. "You will never see me go to trial."

Unmoved by her anger, Damien turned to his men. "You have the makings of evil spirits within you, gentlemen," he smiled.

"I thought the crows were a nice touch," Higgins grinned.

"You can't take all the credit," Carpenter complained. "I was the one who found the nest."

"I liked the wailing myself," Wells added.

"You sounded like a sick pig," Walker told him as

the others guffawed.

"Speak for yourself," Wells told him. "Your laughter sounded like a billy goat."

"All right," Damien chuckled. "Enough, gentlemen. Higgins, tie her up." He handed Madame over to the Sergeant. "Wells, tie up Monsieur Boudreau and start his coach back on the road to Paris. Someone is sure to find him sooner or later. The rest of you, start boarding the horses. We have to get out of here quickly. Fouché may change his mind about letting us go."

He strode to the coach and checked inside. Jessica was mumbling in her delirium. Johnson was holding her on the seat of the carriage with one hand, and with the other, he pointed his pistol at Monsieur Boudreau. The Leftenant smiled with relief when he saw his commanding officer.

"You ought to teach those goblins some manners," he quipped as Damien entered the coach to take over the care of Jessica.

"I thought they acted rather well, myself," Damien remarked with a grin, then turned his attention to the feverish girl on the seat before him.

It was nearly an hour later, as Damien watched the shoreline of France recede, that he gave a small sigh of relief. Mentally, he discarded the character of Le Chat. This last episode in that disguise had nearly cost him his life. It could still reach out and claim Jessica's. The thought pained him more than he cared to admit. Determined that he would do everything he could to keep her alive, he turned with resolute steps away from the rail to tend the sick girl who lay in a bunk below.

Chapter Eighteen

When Jessica opened her eyes, she discovered herself in the soft bed in a room of Damien's house. The window had been opened to allow the gentle spring breezes into the room. She felt strangely weak and tired. It was not until she tried to move and felt the pain in her shoulder and the tight bandages restricting her movement that she remembered she had been shot. The horror of her capture by Madame and the events that followed crowded her mind. With an effort, she shut them out. She wondered how she came to be safely back in Damien's home. A movement from the corner of the room drew her attention. She watched with some trepidation as the Duchess of Wyndham came forward.

"I am glad to see that you are awake, Jessica," she said gently. "You had us all quite worried. You were very ill when Damien brought you home."

"I am sorry I caused you any inconvenience, Your Grace," Jessica murmured.

She was embarrassed that it should be this woman, whom her family had wounded so deeply, who had been forced to take her into her home and care for her. She began to sit up.

"Please, don't move," the Duchess told her. "You will open your wound and make it bleed."

"But I . . . ," Jessica began.

"Jessica, lie still," the Duchess ordered as she pushed her gently back to the pillows. "It is no inconvenience to have you here. I would not have forgiven my son if he had not brought you here to recover. Are you hungry?"

"Yes, a little," Jessica admitted.

"Good. That is a good sign. I will have Aggie make up a tray for you. Now, stay there and rest. Donny will be back soon to sit with you."

With a smile, she left the room. Jessica mused over the kind attitude of the Duchess. The woman seemed sincere in her concern, yet Jessica could not help but feel uneasy in her presence. Having been the victim of two other women who had appeared kind at first then had turned loose their true, cruel nature, Jessica was hesitant at accepting the Duchess' kindness. She somehow felt that Damien's mother was not like Margaret or Madame du Barré, but she was determined not to be taken in again.

Her musings took a different route when she wondered where Damien might be and what he might be doing. She decided he was probably quite happy to have his mother take over her nursing. She was even rather surprised to find herself not in jail, although she guessed that not even Damien would have put anyone who had been wounded in jail.

As her thoughts centered on the master of the house, she heard a horse and rider arrive on the drive. Damien's voice drifted through the window as he spoke to one of the grooms. He sounded energetic and well rested for one who had obviously travelled all night and a good part of the day to flee France. With a peevish movement, she put him out of her mind. If he wished, he could sprout horns and a tail if given the proper provocation.

The door opened and Donny entered with a tray. Her eyes crinkled at the corners as she tried without success to hide a smile.

"I see ye finally decided to wake up," she grumbled. " 'Tis bad enough ye try t'escape, but then t'get yerself shot . . . !" Her voice trailed off in an unspoken accusation as she shook her head. She helped Jessica prop herself up, then placed the tray across her lap. "Had us all worried to death, ye did. An' His Grace havin' t'go t'France after ye."

"He doesn't seem any worse for the adventure," Jessica observed wryly. "I just heard him arrive home, and he sounded very fit, as if he had just had a wonderful night's sleep."

"Aye, and that he has," Donny nodded. "The first in six nights. Yer fever broke last night, and he finally left yer side and went t' his bed t'sleep. Wouldn't leave ye no matter how much Her Grace asked."

Jessica stared in astonishment at Donny. Damien had remained with her the whole time she had been ill. Did that mean that he cared for her, at least a little?

Donny looked at her closely. "Ye be all right?"

Not wanting to reveal her hope or her feelings about Damien, Jessica asked instead, "Did you say he hadn't slept in six days?"

"Aye, brought ye here six days ago, he did, not lookin' much better than ye did."

Jessica closed her eyes and leaned her head against the pillows, as the ramifications of the length of her imprisonment, kidnapping, and illness struck her. It had been slightly longer than a fortnight since she had made her last payment to Margaret. It would take her another week, at least, before she would be well enough to venture out at night. Since Madame du Barré's establishment no longer existed, she would have to find another at which she would be accepted. Margaret's deadline would pass without her returning to Braeleigh with the stipend.

"What is it?" Donny demanded with worry.

Jessica opened her eyes and muttered, "Margaret."

"Aye. Well, don't ye fret none about her. Just get yerself better. Th'rest will take care of itself."

Suddenly, another worry entered Jessica's head. "Donny, the babe. Is it . . . ?"

"It lives." At Jessica's sigh of relief, Donny nodded briskly. "Eat yer broth. I'll sit with ye until ye finish."

Jessica ate most of the thick broth that Donny had brought, but before she had finished, she found she could not keep her eyes open. With the spoon still in her hand, she fell asleep once more.

For the next three days, she had no strength to do anything but sleep and eat. Donny remained with her most of the time, and the Duchess visited her often. Damien, however, was conspicuously absent. Occasionally, Jessica heard him arriving or leaving; she could even hear his voice in the hall, but he made no effort to visit her.

She wondered if he had been told of her recovery, but then realized that his mother must have said something to him. No doubt, he would be very relieved to have her move out from under his roof. It would certainly ease her mind considerably to be away from his house. He had made his feelings for her quite apparent before she had been captured by Madame. It was her intention to be away from this house as soon as she was able. Her only problem was where she would go. She had no money. Deciding she would give herself a few more days to recuperate, she put off making a decision. Of course, in a few more days, she could find herself in jail.

On the fourth day after her fever broke, she began to feel stronger and was able to remain awake for most of the day. The following day, she was allowed to sit in a chaise in her room, and the day following she was allowed to take some air in the garden.

Jessica regained her strength quickly over the next two days. She roamed the house freely when she was not being fussed over by Donny or Aggie or Lucy or the Duchess herself. Her guards had completely disappeared, and she assumed that Damien counted on her weakened condition to keep her close to the house. During her wanderings, she never encountered the master of the house. He was either out, or sequestered in his study. Occasionally, she would hear his voice as he arrived home, or his footsteps as he passed her room. One night, quite late, she thought she heard him stop outside her door, but she could not be sure.

While she had been recovering, she had done quite a bit of thinking and had come to a decision regarding her future. Of course, her future depended on what Damien and the courts decided to do with her, but if she was found innocent, she had a course of action planned. She had made the acquaintance of many men when she had been at Madame's. She would prevail upon one of them to gain her entrance into another gaming house. She knew the cost would be high; she was not the innocent fool she once had been. It would mean the ruination of her reputation and her self-respect. Yet, if becoming a paramour would save Jason, then it was worth the price. After all, had not Damien taught her well?

As she stepped from her bath that day, a knock came at her door, and it swung back unceremoniously. Damien leaned against the doorframe as he puffed on a cheroot. As Donny jumped to stand in front of Jessica to hide her nakedness, Jessica clutched a towel to cover herself.

"Yer Grace!" Donny gasped in shock at his untimely intrusion. "M'lady is bathing."

Totally unruffled by the discomfort of the two

women, Damien glanced at her through a puff of smoke. His gaze went past Donny to rest with obvious pleasure on Jessica.

"I would not deem it improper to pay my respects to my fiancée," he smiled lazily.

At his words, Jessica's mouth dropped open. It was some moments before she was able to repeat in a croak, "Fiancée?"

"Yes, my love," Damien answered, enjoying the effect of his words. "Fiancée: that term which is applied to one betrothed to be married."

"Married?" Jessica again repeated his last word.

"Married," Damien nodded. "I believe it is customary that a couple who are to be parents should be married. Do you not agree?" When Jessica did nothing but stare, he went on, "Is it not your wish to have a legitimate father for the babe?"

"Babe?" Jessica squeaked. How did he know?

"Yes, babe." Damien's eyes narrowed. "You have thirty minutes to make yourself presentable, then I wish to see you in my study. I would also appreciate a slightly more liberal use of the English language. You are beginning to sound like a parrot."

At his last words, Jessica's temper flared. How dare he come into her room and announce that they would be getting married! He could not even summon the courtesy to propose properly. She picked up the closest thing at hand, a bar of soap, and flung it at him. He had seen her intent and quickly ducked out of the doorway. The soap hit the door as it closed behind him. She could hear him chuckling as he strode off down the hall.

Immediately, Jessica turned on Donny, "You told him!" she accused. "You broke your promise!"

Donny shook her head. "Nay, child. I not be the one to tell His Grace. Ye be the guilty one."

"Me?"

268

"Aye. When ye be sick, ye said much ye had kept in yer heart."

Jessica groaned and sank to the stool near the tub. "But how did *he* find out? Were you not the one to tend me?"

"He was with ye from the time he brought ye through the door until yer fever broke, don't ye remember my tellin' ye? Her Grace would make him leave to get some sleep during the day, when she would stay with ye, but he'd be back again in an hour."

Jessica's heart lifted slightly at the thought that perhaps he did care something for her if he had been so reluctant to leave her during her illness. Her mood immediately plunged back to the depths with her next thought. He probably only wanted to be sure his heir did not die with its mother. She was good for nothing more than to give him a child. Well, if that was what he wanted, she would give him the child, but there was nothing to guarantee that it would be a boy. She smirked at the thought. Outside of rape, she could foresee no possibility of his having another offspring by her. She would teach this arrogant duke a few things about manners and women.

Although Jessica had been ordered to appear before Damien in thirty minutes, she took her time getting dressed. Besides wanting to defy him, she decided that she would have something in her favor if she looked her best. So, an hour after Damien had left her room, she stood before the door to his study. She wished she could have had something new to wear. Her dress revealed its age if one looked closely. Yet, the high neck and long, tight sleeves of the black-striped, grey taffeta gave her a feeling of modesty after Damien's intrusion into her privacy. Steeling herself for whatever he had planned, she knocked softly on the door.

Damien's voice bade her enter. When she walked into the room, she discovered that he was not alone. A rotund little man with twinkling eyes stood as she entered.

"It seems that my fiancée has finally decided to grace us with her presence," Damien drawled with ill-concealed annoyance. "She has not yet learned the value of being prompt, I'm afraid." He then turned to the introductions. "Jessica, this is John Soames, the family barrister. Soames, my fiancée, Lady Jessica Carlton."

Jessica extended her hand and murmured, "Mr. Soames."

The little man bowed over it gracefully. "A pleasure, my lady."

Turning to Damien after seating herself, she smiled through clenched teeth and told him innocently, "I am sorry I took so long, Your Grace. I only wished to look my best."

Damien's brow drew together. "Jessica, Soames has drawn up a statement concerning your involvement with Madame du Barré. I took the liberty of giving him the information from what you had told me before. Since you have been ill, we will try to have you excused from appearing at Madame's trial. This statement will be submitted in your absence. However, it is necessary that Soames asks you questions and then you read over the document to be sure it is accurate. Then you must sign it before witnesses."

"Madame is going to trial?" Jessica asked. "She is here in England?"

"Yes," Damien answered. "She found it expedient to return with us."

Jessica could not imagine how Damien had possibly managed to get Madame to return. From what she remembered, it had been they who had been trying to flee from her, not the other way around.

At Jessica's prolonged silence, Mr. Soames said, "It need not be done immediately, m'lady. The trial will begin four days hence. You may have the next two days to gather your thoughts."

He cleared his throat. "May I remind you, m'lady, that your refusing to give a signed statement to the court could be construed as collaboration with the enemy. There would be a lengthy trial which you would have to go through, and, I am afraid, your wedding plans would have to be postponed, perhaps indefinitely."

Jessica smiled at the man. "Since I was only informed an hour ago of His Grace's intentions, I am afraid we have no wedding plans as yet. However, I have no wish to spend any time in prison. I will do as you ask, sir. I will answer your questions and sign your statement."

Mr. Soames beamed his approval. "Wonderful! I will return later this afternoon with several witnesses and a clerk to record your answers, if that is agreeable." He turned a questioning look upon the Duke. At Damien's nod, he went on, "We will take your statement then." He stood up and offered his hand to Damien. "My congratulations again on your forthcoming marriage, my boy. Your father would have been pleased with your choice. Your lady is most charming, most charming, indeed." He bent over Jessica's hand, then was gone from the room with surprising alacrity for one so portly.

There was a moment of silence in the room after the barrister's departure, as Jessica and Damien gazed at each other. Finally, Jessica lowered her eyes. The return of the barrister in the afternoon gave her a perfect excuse for leaving.

"If you no longer need me, I will return to my room," she spoke softly without raising her eyes.

She needed to be away from his presence. She was

still angry with him for his arrogance, but her feelings were mixed with gratitude for sheltering her from the ordeal of a trial, and something like excitement rippled through her at the prospect of being married to him. Confusion was rampant in her brain, and she needed to think.

"I would like you to stay for a moment, Jessica," Damien answered. He pulled a small object out of his pocket and placed it in her lap. It was a tiny velvet box. She looked up at him curiously.

"Open it," he instructed her gently.

She did and gasped. Nestled amidst the folds of black velvet in the box was an exquisite sapphire and diamond ring.

"It is beautiful," she breathed. "I have never seen anything so lovely."

"It is yours," he said brusquely as he turned to gaze out the window.

"I can not accept such a gift." She closed the box and held it out to him.

"It is the custom in our family for the Duke's fiancée to receive this ring upon their betrothal," Damien informed her. He turned back to face her. With a strange glint in his eyes, he stated, "I see no reason why you should not accept it."

Jessica stood and placed the box in his hand. She had come quickly to a decision. Raising her chin proudly, she informed him, "I will give you the best reason of which I can think: I am not going to marry you, Your Grace."

Damien's eyes became hard, and a muscle twitched in his cheek. "You are a fool, m'lady. I offer security for you and the child for the rest of your life. How can you refuse?"

"Very simply, Your Grace. I merely say no."

Damien was very quiet for a moment before he spoke. His tone was dangerously soft. "You can not say no. I will not have it."

Incredulous, Jessica's brows went up. *"You* will not have it? It takes two *consenting* people to have a wedding, Your Grace."

Damien's temper finally got the better of him. "I will not have my child born without a name!" he thundered.

"You forget the child is also mine!"

"You are a fool!"

"You are an arrogant bore!"

Blue eyes met green and clashed. It seemed impossible that only several weeks before, these two wills had meshed as one in a night of passion. Now, the distance between them was greater than that between earth and sun.

Damien's breath hissed between his teeth and his eyes narrowed suddenly. "How do you propose to live?" he asked. "What will you use to live on?"

"I will live the same way I did before you disrupted my life," Jessica informed him haughtily.

"Madame's is no longer in existence. Do you have entrance to any other gambling establishment?"

Jessica shrugged and turned away. "I met many gentlemen at Madame's. I am sure one of them could gain me entrance to another establishment."

"Ha! For what price? I remember hearing you declare that you would be no man's mistress."

Jessica flinched as her words were thrown back at her. "I am sure I can find an honorable gentleman who would not require that I go to bed with him merely for the small favor of an introduction," she said with more conviction than she felt.

Damien snorted his disbelief. "You are more a fool than I thought."

Jessica turned on him. "Not so much a fool, Your Grace, as to marry an arrogant, tyrannical boor," she snapped back.

273

Damien took a step toward her and she braced herself as if for a blow. His words hammered themselves into her brain. "You may defy me, now, my lady, but marry me you will. Before the week is out, you will have this ring on your finger." He held up the velvet box, then placed it on a corner of his desk as if throwing down the gauntlet of a challenge.

Jessica groaned her aggravation and impatience, then turned on her heel and stalked out of the room. Upon reaching the security of her own room, she gave full vent to her anger and frustration. She paced from wall to wall as her emotions reached the boiling point. Stopping before the bed, she glared at the offending piece of furniture, then she dropped to her knees and banged her fists upon it until she was exhausted.

It was not fair, she thought. She had gained her heart's desire only because of a sense of duty on the part of Damien. She would not be trapped into a marriage with a man who did not love her. He did not even have the courtesy to ask her to marry him, but rather informed her she had no choice. He could not even bring himself to be polite to her. He must despise her that much. Dear God, it was just not fair! Laying her head on her arms, she cried her frustration until she fell asleep.

Damien had watched Jessica leave. He stood now with his hands clenched tightly at his sides. He wanted to throw something, anything. That girl would drive him crazy. Perhaps she had already. What was he doing forcing her into marriage? Her family had brought such pain to the Wyndham family. Now, he wanted to marry her? She was obstinate, outspoken, proud. She was soft, vulnerable, desirable. He threw himself into a chair, leaned his head back and closed his eyes.

You really messed things up, he told himself with disgust. What happened to your manners and that charm that gets you any woman you want? God's teeth, he had been a boor! If only she wasn't quite so lovely, or quite so naive, maybe he wouldn't feel so honor bound to wed her. But he knew that was not true. His honor would dictate that he do the right thing no matter what Jessica was like. It was an added bonus that he found her so desirable, which was why he found himself in this position in the first place.

He had wanted to be gentle with her. Her illness and her pregnancy made him want to protect her. Yet, her relation to Braeleigh and Margaret grated upon him every time he looked at her. While he felt himself aroused by the sight of her and the thought of her passion, he felt more keenly the pain and anger caused by her family. What a mess!

He opened his eyes, and his glance fell on the little velvet box. He had to talk to someone. Edward was still in London. He was staying at his family's town house before returning to his duties. Rising swiftly, Damien scooped up the little box and deposited it in his pocket as he strode out the door to go call on his friend.

Chapter Nineteen

That afternoon, Jessica was summoned to the salon. Mr. Soames had arrived to ask Jessica questions. He had several clerks with him to take down what she said and to witness her answers.

As Jessica reached the door, Damien arrived at the same time. They stood, not moving or speaking. She glared at him; he raised a sardonic brow at her. Finally, Damien backed up a step and bowed mockingly.

"After you, my lady," he said.

Jessica could smell brandy on his breath. It was only early afternoon. "You've been drinking!" she hissed.

Damien gave her a benign smile and swayed slightly. "I believe I have. Leftenant Johnson was most free with the cask of Mr. Bonaparte's brandy I had given him upon the completion of his guard duty here."

Jessica primly compressed her lips and turned up her nose as she waited for him to open the door. With a snicker, Damien obliged and allowed her to enter before him.

After they had both greeted Mr. Soames and the introduction of his clerks had been made, Mr. Soames suggested, "Well, shall we begin?"

Damien settled himself on the far side of the room

in a high backed chair. He rested his elbows comfortably on its arms and stretched his long legs out before him with his ankles crossed. Jessica frowned disapprovingly at him, but he only gave her a beatific smile. Her attention was soon captured by the barrister, however, and so she paid Damien no more heed.

After Jessica and Mr. Soames had been absorbed for about an hour, there was a strange rumbling that distracted her. After another few minutes, she heard it again. This time, she glanced questioningly in Damien's direction. He had fallen asleep and was snoring!

Mortified, Jessica's cheeks turned pink, and she tried to see if anyone else was aware of Damien's rudeness. No one appeared to notice, but her attention was distracted when Mr. Soames asked her the next question.

For the next half hour, the barrister's questions and her answers were interspersed with the low rumbling of Damien's slumber. When he finally roused himself, she sent him a dark frown. He only smiled at her innocently, as if there had been no breech of manners. It was another two hours before Mr. Soames declared they were done. Jessica was relieved for more than one reason. She was exhausted, and her shoulder ached interminably, but she also could not wait to give that arrogant boor a tongue lashing.

When Soames and his clerks had gone, she turned on Damien like a hurricane. "How could you be so rude! You fell asleep!"

Damien shrugged. "I was tired." He yawned behind his hand.

"You snored!"

Damien grinned. "Did I really? How amusing."

"It was ghastly. It was mortifying! I was never so embarrassed in my life!"

"Ah, Witch, weren't your potions working?" He

reached out and tugged at a curl.

Jessica slapped his hand away. "You are insufferable. How could I have ever thought—?"

Jessica caught herself just in time. She had almost revealed that she had loved him.

"Thought what, Witch?" Damien asked.

"Nothing," she mumbled. "Excuse me, I am very tired." She swung about and hurried out of the room, away from his presence.

When she returned to her room, she was so exhausted she could not even think about what had gone on that afternoon. Stripping off her dress without even waiting for Donny's help, she climbed into bed and fell asleep.

She awoke with Donny standing over her, looking down at her with a worried expression. Jessica stretched and yawned.

"When is dinner?" she asked. "I'm starved."

"Ye missed dinner," Donny informed her. "And breakfast, too. Are ye all right? Are ye sick again?" Donny felt her forehead.

"I'm fine, Donny." Jessica pulled herself up. "I guess I was just very tired."

Donny gave Jessica a skeptical look. "Are ye sure?"

"Yes, Donny, I'm sure."

Satisfied, Donny nodded. "Good. Then get yerself up. Her Grace would like to see ye in the salon. She has a dressmaker here so ye can be measured for ye weddin' dress."

Jessica groaned and flopped back onto her pillow. Evidently, the Duke had received his domineering traits legitimately from his mother.

"Tell Her Grace there is to be no wedding," Jessica instructed Donny. "Therefore, I will have no need of a wedding dress."

Donny gasped at Jessica's impertinence. "Are ye out of yer mind? I can not tell Her Grace that."

"Why not?" Jessica demanded. "You've never been shy before."

Instead of answering, Donny asked her own question. "Why ain't there goin' t'be a weddin'?"

Jessica sighed. "Because I am not going to marry a man who does not love me."

"Hmph. Then fool ye be," Donny stated with certainty. "I ain't goin' t'tell Her Grace no such thing."

Jessica glared at her nanny, then relented. "Then tell her I am not feeling well and can not come down. Tell her anything, but I will not be measured for a wedding dress I am not going to wear."

Donny hmphed again and mumbled something about the blockheadedness of young people as she went out the door. Jessica sighed and climbed out of bed. Pulling on her dressing gown, she went to sit on the chaise near the window. She needed to sort out her thoughts.

It was imperative that she leave as soon as possible. Of that much she was sure. But where would she go once she had left? It would have to be some place where Damien could not find her—some place she could afford. That did not leave her much choice.

She also had to decide who would be the man to gain her an introduction into a new gambling house. Jessica sobered as the impact of what she was planning suddenly struck her. Had she become so depraved that the thing that she had sworn not to do was now a welcome escape? She was not fool enough nor so naive to believe there would be no repayment of her favors to the gentleman she selected. Leaning her head back against the chaise, she covered **her** eyes with her hands, trying to shut out her thoughts with the light.

It was no use. As distasteful as her plan of action was, it was the only way to avoid the agony of being married to Damien. That was something she could not bear. As angry as she was with him, she found she could not hate him. Her love was still a strong spark in her heart, but it was a spark she would have to keep hidden. She could not bear having it extinguished by Damien's hate for her.

As Jessica sat with her musings, a knock came at the door. She was not willing to entertain anyone, especially Damien, and having lost her appetite, she did not wish to eat anything that Aggie might have sent up to her, so she did not answer. The knock came again, this time with more persistence, and a voice called out her name.

Jessica recognized the voice of the Duchess. That was one person whom she could not ignore. Slowly, she rose and went to the door to open it. The Duchess stood on the other side. Concern showed on her face.

She inquired, "May I come in?"

Jessica stood aside and allowed her to enter the room. Jessica closed the door softly, then stood before it in apprehension. The Duchess sat on a chair next to the chaise that Jessica had just vacated.

"Donny told me you were not feeling well," the Duchess began. She patted the chaise next to her. "Come, sit here and tell me about it."

Jessica went to stand before Damien's mother, but did not sit down. She found she could not lie to this woman. "I am well enough, Your Grace. Perhaps your son would be better able to tell you why I am troubled."

The Duchess smiled gently. "I have asked him already. He told me that you would be able to enlighten me better than he."

Jessica made an impatient gesture and sank to the chaise. "I am not surprised that he places the blame for this confusion on me," she muttered, more to herself than to the woman sitting near her. Looking

280

straight into the Duchess's eyes that were so much like her son's, Jessica stated bluntly, "There is to be no wedding, Your Grace."

The Duchess nodded. "I had guessed as much. What has Damien done that has caused you to be so angry?"

Jessica dropped her eyes to her fingers entwined in her lap. What had he not done? "It is not what he has done, but how he feels," she answered quietly. "I can not marry a man who hates me."

"Oh, dear Jessica," Her Grace exclaimed as she placed her hand over Jessica's. "He does not hate you. Please, believe that. He cares a great deal for you."

Jessica shook her head in disagreement. "I have to believe what my own eyes and ears have told me, Your Grace." She raised tear-brightened eyes. "It is not possible for him to feel any differently."

"That my son took advantage of you was despicable, but he is an honorable man and will set it right. His feelings for you at this moment are clouded by his grief for his brother and the horrible events that led to his brother's death. My two sons were very close, and Damien has not been able to put away his hatred for the creature who manipulated such a tragedy. His work in France has also made him hard; it has made him forget his softer side. He needs a woman such as yourself to cause his gentler nature to reemerge."

Jessica shook her head again. "I do not want to marry a man because he feels it is the right thing to do. I want him to love me for myself. Is that so wrong?"

The Duchess smiled. "That is not wrong at all. It is exactly what you should want. But I think you should also consider the child you carry. Do not act rashly, Jessica, so that you find yourself regretting your actions." The Duchess's smile turned into an impish grin. "I would not run away just yet, at least not for another day.

Jessica's eyes widened in surprise as she watched the woman rise and leave the room. How had the Duchess known that she had planned to leave? With a shake of her head, she dismissed her curiosity. There were other things to think about.

Contemplating the words of the Duchess, Jessica sat for a long while after the woman had gone. What she had heard, could, indeed, be the truth, that Damien cared for her. Yet the woman was Damien's mother. Would not her idea of the truth concerning her son's feelings be somewhat clouded by prejudice?

Jessica was more confused now than ever. She liked the Duchess a great deal. Yet, the fact remained that this woman had lost a son who had been killed by Jessica's father. Because of this, Jessica felt a certain reticence in trusting her. Perhaps, though, she would heed one small piece of advice that the Duchess had given her. She would remain in Damien's house until the morrow.

Jessica passed the remainder of the day in her room. She took some time deciding which belongings she would take with her when she left. After that, she slept, or stared out the window trying not to think too much about what she was going to do.

As the dinner hour approached, the maid, Lucy, appeared at her door. She seemed nervous about something.

"Excuse me, my lady," she began. "His Grace wishes you to join him at the dinner table this evening."

Dining with Damien was not how she wanted to spend her evening. "Tell His Grace that I have no wish to upset his digestion," Jessica told her. "I will dine in my room."

Lucy cleared her throat in agitation. "Excuse me, my lady, but His Grace said to tell you that if you refused to come down to dinner, he would come to get you."

Jessica drew in her breath sharply in anger. Would he never leave her alone? She knew it would do no good to defy him. He had come after her before; he would do it again. She glanced at Lucy who was moving nervously from foot to foot. Relenting, she smiled at the girl sympathetically. It was not fair to blame her for the boorishness of the Duke.

"Tell His Grace I will be down as soon as I am dressed," Jessica told her.

Still, Lucy did not leave. "My lady?" she ventured.

Jessica sighed. She knew Damien would leave nothing unsaid. He would make sure he had complete control over her.

"What else did he say, Lucy?" she asked, resigned.

"He told me to tell you—begging your pardon—that dinner is at eight o'clock, and if you are not downstairs at that time, he would bring you down even . . ." Lucy's voice faltered and trailed off.

Jessica knew what was coming next, but she decided she had better hear it anyway. "Even what, Lucy?" she prompted.

Lucy swallowed and finished in a rush, "Even if you are not dressed."

Jessica's teeth clamped together in her anger. It was as she had thought. He was being as arrogant as ever.

"You may tell His Grace that he need not worry. I will be on time for dinner."

Lucy left, relieved that she had completed her errand without getting her ears boxed. Jessica set about getting changed for dinner. She rang for Donny, then turned to the task of deciding what to wear. She finally settled on the black dress she had worn the first night she had met Damien. Since this would be the last night she would spend in his house, she decided it was only fitting to wear it.

As the clock was striking eight, she arrived at the door of the salon. Damien leaned negligently on the mantle with one elbow. He glanced up as she entered and saluted her with the glass he was holding. She felt his glance pass over her in appreciation like a warm breeze.

The Duchess rose and came to greet Jessica. "I am so glad you could join us for dinner this evening, Jessica," she said warmly. "Are you sure you are feeling well enough?"

"Yes, quite well, thank you."

Jessica glanced over the lady's shoulder at Damien, who had obviously not informed his mother of his threat. He smiled innocently and shrugged. Jessica turned back to the Duchess who was asking if she would like a glass of wine before dinner.

"No, thank you, Your Grace," Jessica answered politely.

"Well, then, let us go in to dinner," the Duchess suggested. She linked arms with Jessica and guided her to the dining room. Damien was left to follow by himself.

Dinner turned out to be a pleasant affair, and Jessica enjoyed it despite the presence of Damien. The Duchess was a practiced conversationalist and storyteller. With a sharp wit, she related gossip she had heard during the day, and Jessica found herself laughing for the first time in months. Damien and his mother also kept up a lively banter which Jessica delighted in. It had been so long since she had taken part in a family dinner where the people around the table actually enjoyed each other's company. She covertly watched Damien during the meal and noticed the softening of his features as he spoke to his

284

mother, and the crinkles around his eyes when he laughed with her. How wonderful it would be to have him look at her with love, she thought to herself.

When the meal ended, the Duchess excused herself to write some letters. Jessica and Damien were alone at the table. An awkward moment of silence ensued. Jessica stood suddenly, deciding it was time for her to leave.

"I think I will retire. I wish to finish the book I am reading," she told him lamely.

Damien had stood also, and he approached her and took her hand. "Don't go just yet, Jessica," he told her. "Come into the salon. I would like your company for a while longer."

When she did not object, he led her out of the dining room and into the salon. There, a table had been set up with two chairs and a deck of cards in its middle. She glanced at him questioningly.

"I thought perhaps we could spend some time playing cards," he said. "That is, of course, if you are not too tired."

"No, I am not too tired," she answered with a small smile.

"Splendid!" Damien exclaimed. "We will play for. . . ." He glanced about the room. "Rose petals!" Pulling a deep, red rose out of a nearby arrangement, he ordered, "Hold out your hands."

Laughingly, she did so, and he pulled the petals from the flower and dropped them into her cupped hands.

"And you, Your Grace?" she dimpled up at him. "What will you use to gamble with?"

Damien smiled mysteriously. "Oh, I will find something."

He seated her at the table, then took the chair across from her. Pulling several coins out of his pocket, he placed them on the table before him.

"It is not fair that you should use money while I have only flower petals to wager," Jessica protested.

Damien reached out and captured her fingers. As he brought them to his lips, he murmured, "Flower petals from your hands are worth far more than the few miserable coins from my pocket, my sweet. I consider it an honor that you will accept my small stakes."

Jessica laughed at his outrageous flattery. "You will not consider it such an honor when you have won nothing but a withered petal."

"Who is to say that I will win anything? Perhaps you will bereft me of all my riches."

Jessica shook her head. "I do not believe that."

"We shall see," he said with a strange glint in his eyes.

They played cards for well over an hour. At first, Damien won most of the hands. The flower petals piled up before him. Then, his luck seemed to change. Finally, he had nothing before him with which to bet. The round had not ended, but Jessica was willing to cease their play.

"I have a document here that I will wager, if that is acceptable to you," he told Jessica as he reached into his pocket and drew out an official looking parchment.

"I do not wish to take important papers from you, Damien," Jessica told him earnestly. "This game was only in fun. I am sure your document has great value."

"Its value is an arbitrary matter," he shrugged. "Will you accept it or not?"

"Well, if it means so little . . . ," she began.

"Ah, but I did not say that," Damien interrupted. "I merely said that its value was arbitrary. Its worth is determined by the person who holds it." He held it up and raised a questioning eyebrow.

"All right. I will accept it."

They played out the hand and Jessica won. She put the document before her without opening it. Damien leaned back in his chair and lit a cheroot.

"I think you had better see what you have just won, love," he told her through a haze of smoke.

Jessica opened the document and carefully smoothed it with both hands. As she glanced through it quickly, her eyes widened. What she read stunned her into momentary speechlessness. It was a document, signed by her stepmother, giving Margaret's permission for Jessica to marry the Duke of Wyndham in return for a small fortune. It nullified the need for Jessica to continue to give Margaret her monthly stipend.

"How . . . ? When . . . ?" she stammered. "Oh, no," she cried softly. "No."

Damien reached out and placed his warm hand over her ice-cold one. "Why is it no, Jessica?" he asked gently. "Do you hate me that much for what I have done to you?"

Jessica stared at him, not trusting herself to speak. If he only knew how much she did not hate him. Pulling her hand away, she stood and walked to the window. She looked out into blackness, her mind in a turmoil. What was she to do?

She sensed rather than heard Damien come to stand behind her. Praying he would not touch her, she felt she would dissolve if he placed just one finger on her. Her emotional defenses had been shattered with her reading of the document.

Damien waited quietly while Jessica sorted out her thoughts. He knew he had shocked her; that had been his purpose. She had defied him too long, this delectable witch. He had allowed his own rage to cloud his thinking. The rage was still there, but through it, he knew he wanted this woman. He had to make her realize she wanted it, too. The passion that had flared between them was more than a momentary spark.

His eyes travelled over her back and came to rest on a tantalizing spot where the curve of her neck became her shoulder. The spot cried out to be kissed, but he knew that would have to wait. He sensed her reticence and respected it. It was time for discussion.

"Jessica, why do you defy me?" he demanded quietly.

Jessica turned to face him. Her gaze was determined, as if she had come to a decision at his question. "I can defy you no longer, Your Grace," she stated coolly. "You have seen to that. You have bought me. You have won."

Damien was taken aback by her hardness, but he did not allow it to ruffle him. "You will not be sorry that you agreed to become my wife," he murmured as he raised her chin with one finger and began to lower his lips to hers.

Jessica stopped him with a hand on his chest. "I will be your wife in name only, Your Grace," she informed him. "I will be mother to your child, hostess in your house, and convenient companion if you wish to go out in public, but you will not buy my body as that of a whore. I will have none of it."

Damien straightened during Jessica's little recitation. When she had finished, a muscle twitched dangerously in his cheek, and his eyes glinted coldly as he regarded her in silence. The moment seemed an eternity. Finally, he too, appeared to come to a decision. He nodded once.

"All right," he agreed. "I will grant you this one concession—for now. We shall see how long you will be able to hold to your own demand."

"Do not threaten me," Jessica warned.

"One thing I never do, my love, is threaten. I state

288

facts."

He took her hand and held it palm-up in his own. Reaching into his pocket, he pulled out the small, velvet box that contained the betrothal ring that she had refused. He placed the box in her hand and closed her fingers around it.

"Wear it," he commanded. "It belongs to you, and I want to see it on your finger. Always."

Jessica's temper flared once again at his arrogance. "You do have a way with words, Your Grace," she snapped with her eyes flashing blue fire. "I will wear the ring, as you so kindly suggested, on the morrow. Now, I find that I am quite fatigued. I bid you goodnight."

Damien bowed mockingly, a smile causing one corner of his mouth to lift. Jessica swept from the room in a swish of skirts, her temper again at the boiling point. Never had a man so enraged her as this damnable Duke could.

The man was infuriating. Even when she believed she had the upper hand in a situation, he always managed to come out the winner. She could not even rile his composure with a denial of his connubial rights. He had the impudence to suggest that *she* would be the one to break the agreement. How utterly absurd!

When she reached her room, she threw the little box onto the chaise with such force that it popped open and the ring fell out. She stood glaring at it as if, by her heated gaze, it would disappear. When the door opened behind her and Donny walked in to help her undress, she finally moved away with a stiff back and clenched fists.

Donny glanced from the ring to her mistress and deduced correctly what had taken place. Without a word, she put the ring back in its box and placed it on the dressing table. Then she helped Jessica undress for bed.

It took a long time for Jessica to get to sleep. Her thoughts shunted between the two men who mattered most in her life: Damien and Jason. Damien, with his outrageously large dowry payment for her, had indirectly seen to the monetary well-being of her brother. What she was concerned with was his emotional well-being. He was trapped with Margaret at Braeleigh. She could see no way to get Damien to agree to taking over the care of the son of the man who had killed his brother. His contempt of her because of her family was only momentarily subjugated by his lust for her. She was not so stupid to believe he loved her. The wedding would be a farce, held only to give his offspring a legitimate name. When she finally drifted off to sleep, she had terrible dreams and nightmares, all of which contained monsters with green eyes.

Upon rising the following morning, Jessica was horribly, violently ill. She was dizzy and weak, and waves of nausea washed over her. Her shoulder ached abominably. Several times she tried to rise, and each time she fell back against the pillows with a hand to her head and a groan. She wanted desperately to appear at breakfast, to be calm and remotely cool to Damien, to prove to him that she had meant her words of the night before, and to show him she would wear his damnable ring and keep her part of the bargain.

Donny was the first to enter and discover that Jessica was not feeling well. She made clucking noises as she went about straightening the room.

"It's the babe," she nodded several times. "It will pass." Then she disappeared out the door.

Lucy was the next to appear with a tray of tea and toast for Jessica. She made sympathetic noises as Jessica turned her head away from the food and told her to take it away.

"Her Grace will be in to see you soon," Lucy told her as she set the tray on a table in the far corner of the room. Then she was gone.

Just as Jessica was weakly climbing back into bed after being sick once more, the Duchess walked in. She, also, was sympathetic, telling Jessica to remain in bed and rest for the day; the dressmaker would come the next day to measure her for her wedding dress. It would be necessary to finalize the wedding plans immediately.

As Jessica opened her mouth to protest that she did not require an elaborate wedding, the Duchess smiled her disagreement. One did not wed the Duke of Wyndham without some pageantry.

Jessica had hoped for a quiet ceremony, for she and Damien to go about their lives afterward without notice. She supposed she should have known better, that this was not to be the case. Nothing in which Damien was involved ever went the way she wished.

As her nausea began to subside, her thoughts turned to Jason. Dear Jason. There had been nothing in the document about her brother. Gloomily, she recalled the scene in the salon the night before. Because of her own pride, she had sealed the fate of her brother. Damien would not concede to any more requests or demands. Instinctively, she knew that she could not expect to get anything from him without somehow giving something of herself first. Jessica sighed. Jason would just have to wait. It would take some time before she could bring herself to swallow her pride and approach Damien. Just the thought made her feel like a whore.

Although her state of mind was no better, by afternoon, she was feeling physically stronger. She climbed out of bed and wandered over to the dressing table. Unconsciously, she reached out and opened the little velvet box. She had told Damien she would wear the ring today. Even though she knew he would not come to her room, she took it from its place and slipped it on her finger. She stared down at her hand. The large stones winked coldly back at her, reminding her of the aloofness of the man she was to marry. Had he only voiced some little feeling for her, she would not have felt so alone. As it was, she felt he only wished to own her, body and soul.

Sighing, she went to sit on the chaise. Leaning her head back, she closed her eyes. She was always so tired lately.

Chapter Twenty

Jessica awoke with a start. With bleary eyes she looked about the room. The sun was no longer shining through the windows, which meant it was already past the middle of the afternoon. She had slept for several hours. Someone had come and placed a light throw over her. As she pushed herself up her on the chaise, a voice she knew very well spoke from her left.

"Good afternoon," Damien greeted her pleasantly. "I was beginning to wonder if my fiancée had turned into Sleeping Beauty and could only be awakened with a kiss."

"There is no kiss needed, thank you very much," Jessica answered briskly. Now, thoroughly awake and alert, she would not let down her guard for an instant.

"Ah, my loss," Damien lamented.

"What are you doing in my room?"

Damien rose and came to stand over her. Her eyes travelled over his broad chest covered in its sheath of white silk up to his mouth—oh, Lord, that mouth!—to his eyes. They told her nothing, so she forced herself to look away.

"I have something to tell you," he said.

His tone was serious, and brought her gaze back to his face. She waited for him to continue. He appeared uncomfortable, as if he were not quite sure how to say what he had to tell her.

Covering up her apprehension with sarcasm, she asked, "What is wrong, Your Grace? Do you wish to tell me that you no longer wish to travel with me down the road of wedded bliss?"

Damien grinned. "Hardly, my love. I look forward with eagerness to the day when you will become my wife." He sat on edge of the chaise. "No, what I have to tell you is of a sad and depressing nature."

Jessica, at the moment, could think of nothing more depressing than being forced to marry Damien, but she remained silent.

Taking her hand, he said seriously, "There will be no need for you to worry about your statement for Madame's trial."

Jessica's alarm showed in her face. Did this mean that she was to be brought to trial? That Damien no longer believed in her innocence?

"Jessica." Damien's voice brought her racing mind back to the present. "Madame du Barré is dead."

"Dead?" she repeated, not quite comprehending.

"Yes. It seems someone smuggled poison to her in prison. She was discovered this morning."

Jessica was quiet for a moment as she assimilated this information. Then, covering her face with her hands, she said softly, "She killed herself. Oh, God."

Damien pulled her hands down. "Jessica—"

"She was so kind to me when I first came to London," Jessica said as if Damien had not spoken her name. "I know she only used me, but she was the closest thing to a friend I had. Why did she have to be a spy?"

"She did what she felt was right," Damien answered gently. "I think her suicide was for the best. She had been disowned by her superior for failing to capture me, and she knew she would find no mercy here."

Jessica nodded sadly. "You are probably right. Thank you for telling me."

They sat looking at each other, and in that moment, there a closeness that bound them together. It felt comfortable for Damien to be holding her hands, to have his strength flow into her. Absently, his thumb smoothed her knuckles. As she gradually became aware of the tingling warmth his touch produced, she disengaged them. Damien's mood changed at her movement, and he grinned.

"I have also come to change your bandages."

Jessica gazed at him suspiciously. "Donny can do that. There is no need to concern yourself about me."

"Why should I not be concerned about my future wife?" he asked. Without waiting for an answer, he said, "Donny has gone out shopping with my mother."

"Then Lucy, or one of the other maids can do it," she offered.

The last thing she wanted was to sit half undressed before him. She was too well aware of what his touch could do to her. She could not take back her demand of the night before.

"I have given many of the maids the afternoon off. They will be working long hours soon enough in preparation of our wedding. The other servants are busy." He dismissed any further argument by beginning to untie the ribbons on her dressing gown.

Panic gripped her. She was practically alone with him in house. What did he mean to do?

Damien chuckled at her expression. "Believe it or not, love, I am not an ogre. I merely came to change your bandages and spend some time with you. We have had little time getting know one another. You are, after all, my betrothed, and I have seen you without your clothes. Be a good girl and unbutton your nightrail."

Jessica looked down and realized he already had her dressing gown untied. While she tried to decide whether or not to comply, he waited patiently. He had agreed to her demand of the night before, and her bandage did need to be changed. Yet, had he really given the servants time off to be generous?

She gazed into his face to try to guess his true intentions. His eyes locked with hers, and she could feel herself falling under their spell. With a great amount of effort, she managed to look away. The barrier that she thought she had erected about her emotions was not as strong as she had believed.

"Jessica," he said kindly, "I will not harm you."

She finally nodded her assent and unbuttoned her gown. He helped her pull it off her injured shoulder. Unfortunately, it was necessary to lower it to her waist for him to remove her bandage. Staring straight ahead, with blazing cheeks, she sat quietly as he removed the old dressing.

His hands were gentle and not unpracticed at their task. Yet, the touch of him against her skin made her flinch more than once. She wanted to relax into him, to feel his fingers travel up her neck, and down across her breasts. Gritting her teeth, she suppressed a moan of desire that clogged her throat. How was she ever going to keep to her demand?

She glanced up at him surreptitiously to gauge his response to their closeness. He seemed unconcerned, concentrating on his task. What she did not know, was that Damien was keeping his own desires tamped down with a great deal of effort.

The sight of her breasts, creamy-skinned and becoming heavy with her pregnancy, laid bare before him, almost made him come undone. He had agreed to Jessica's preposterous demand of the night before because he could see that was the only way to get her to be his wife. By being his wife, he could get her back into his bed, and he wanted that more than anything. He had never wanted a woman so much in his life. And he wanted this woman. With more self-control than he thought he possessed, he kept his eyes, after one quick glance, on the strips of cloth. He was damned if he would be the one to break their agreement.

With a flourish, he tied off the bandage and sat back. Relieved of the tension of being so near, they both found themselves breathing harder than normal. Jessica busied herself with pulling her clothes back on. Damien helped where she was still a bit stiff and confined by her bandage. When she was dressed again, she looked up at him with curiosity.

"You seem very familiar with the changing of dressings," she observed. "Are you a student of the science of medicine, as well as a soldier and a spy?"

"When one is a spy, an outlaw in the enemy's country, one tends to learn how to care for one's own hurts," he smiled. "I have had a great deal of practice in wrapping and unwrapping bandages, as well as a small amount of experience in surgery."

"Were you in France when you received the scar across your chest?" she asked. The thin, white line was etched vividly on her memory. She could still feel it under her finger as she had traced it that first time she had gone to his bed.

He shrugged. "It was a minor disagreement with a gentleman who refused to allow us to kidnap his mistress. He was an excellent swordsman."

Jessica's eyes widened. "How terrible! You could have been killed!" she exclaimed without thinking.

Damien lifted an amused eyebrow. "I did not think you concerned yourself overly much about my health."

Jessica blushed red at her mistake, but kept her voice cool as she returned, "I am concerned about

297

the pain of all God's creatures."

"How humanitarian of you," Damien observed dryly as he rose and walked to the window. He stood gazing out at nothing in particular as he said, "Then you will be very distressed to learn that the gentleman who gave me the scar is missing the last finger of his right hand."

"Oh, no," she breathed, and covered her eyes as if to blot out the vivid picture that came to mind. Feeling he was deliberately trying to shock her, she could not understand his coolness at the obvious cruelty he had inflicted. "How could you do such a thing?" she demanded. "How can you remain so unmoved at what you did?"

"Unmoved?" he echoed, as he swung around to face her. "I am far from unmoved at the things I have been forced to do to remain alive. I am not cold and heartless. I am, rather, well aware of man's cunning and deceit. Perhaps too well aware of it. I have practiced it too long myself. I have not always enjoyed the role I played."

"Yet, you remained in it for several years," Jessica accused.

"Ah, yes, the contradiction," he smiled ruefully. "I think I can explain it best by asking you a question, Lady Fortuna. Did you always enjoy your role of adventuress at Madame du Barré's?"

"But that was different," she protested. "I never hurt or maimed anyone."

"No? Were all those gentlemen with whom you gambled so wealthy that they could afford to lose the exorbitant sums that you won from them?"

"I did not ask them about their financial stability when they sat down to play cards," she stated haughtily. "If they had the money on the table, then I considered it fair to try to win it. If they did not lose to me, it would have been to someone else. I could not afford to be altruistic."

Damien smiled at her as she realized her own logic had lost the debate for her. "We are not so different, are we, my love?" he asked rhetorically. He moved easily to the chaise and cupped her chin in his hand. "Perhaps our marriage will be a good one after all." He dropped his hand and ambled to the door. With his hand on the latch, he turned. "Rest for the remainder of the day. I believe an appointment has been made with my mother's dressmaker for tomorrow. I do not wish to dally any longer over the plans for this wedding than is necessary. I should think a fortnight would be long enough to ready yourself." He opened the door but did not leave immediately. Instead he paused, and, in a softer tone, said, "I enjoyed this discussion, Jessica. I hope to have many more with you after we are married." Then he was gone.

Jessica sat for a long while staring at the closed door. She had a vague feeling of disquiet at Damien's last comments. The thought that he was somehow manipulating her was uppermost in her mind. Yet, she could not understand why he would want to do such a thing. She had agreed to marry him. What more did he want? She finally dismissed the idea as pure nonsense.

The following afternoon, the dressmaker arrived. She came with two assistants who were loaded down with designs and sample materials. Jessica discovered that, not only was she to have a new gown made for her wedding, but she was also to receive a whole new wardrobe. When she cast a questioning glance at the Duchess, that lady merely smiled and nodded. Jessica's feeling of being manipulated again surfaced. She intended to put an end to it before it went any further. Excusing herself, she went in search of the Duke. She found him in his study.

Without a greeting, she stated heatedly, "I think you presume too much, Your Grace. I am not some pauper you have picked up off the streets. I have my own clothes."

Damien leaned back in his chair and regarded Jessica coolly. "I do not wish my wife dressed as a poor relation, nor as a woman of the evening. Your present wardrobe leaves much to be desired. The only clothes that you have that are decent are those which you wore to Madame's. The rest are hardly worth a farthing."

"Then I will make my own clothes," she stormed. "I do not want your charity."

"It is hardly that," Damien told her dryly. "I will derive a great deal of pleasure from seeing you well dressed."

Jessica's mouth dropped open at his innuendo. "You arrogant . . . arrogant . . . !" Words failed her. He was so impossible.

Damien smiled without humor. "Yes, I suppose I am, but like it or not, you will wear the clothes that I purchase for you."

"You can not force me to wear them," she stated decisively.

Damien shrugged. "I would be very embarrassed to walk about as naked as the day I came into the world, if I were you."

Jessica's eyes widened at his effrontery. He would not throw out her old clothes. Or would he?

Damien turned his attention to the papers on his desk. "If you have finished, Jessica, I have to complete these reports for General Drayton and the Prime Minister."

She was dismissed. There was nothing for her to do but return to the morning room where the dressmaker waited and get measured.

She sighed quietly as she stood raising first one arm, then the other, turning this way and that, as the woman took down her dimensions. Having a new wardrobe would be a luxury. She only wished it had not been forced upon her, but given with a feeling of love.

The rest of the day, she spent picking out designs that appealed to her and matching them with swatches of material from which the new clothes would be made. She took great pleasure in choosing expensive material for the dresses, coats, nightclothes, and underthings. Devilishly, she decided if Damien wanted to enjoy seeing her well dressed, she would give him something to look at. She made sure the undergarments and nightclothes were of the sheerest, finest, silkiest cloth, and that several of the evening gowns were cut daringly low at the bodice or made of clinging, soft material. There were still several months before she would swell in her pregnancy, and she would taunt Damien with his own arrogance.

The Duchess sat through the whole procedure with a small smile twitching the corners of her mouth. Jessica realized that she knew exactly what her future daughter-in-law was about. The Duchess said nothing, however, and for that, Jessica was grateful. She felt she had found a friend in Damien's mother.

Chapter Twenty-one

The morning of the wedding dawned clear and bright, a distinct contrast to the weather that had preceded it. The birds chirped merrily and the sky held no hint of rain. Jessica was awake early enough to watch the sky turn from soft grey to blush pink to bright blue. She listened as the house began to come awake and relished her last few minutes of solitude before Donny and the other maids descended on her to ready her for the day. Thankfully, her stomach was behaving and she was not queasy or feeling ill as she had on many of the mornings past. Her eyes travelled to her wedding gown that had arrived from the dressmaker's the day before. In a few short hours, she would be dressed in it and walking down the aisle to become Damien's bride.

The thought excited and frightened her more than just a little. It was what she had dreamed of, seemingly so long ago. Yet, she had come to know him better since then. The man she knew now was not the man of that night of soft sighs and urgency and tears. There was dread mixed in with her feelings.

A knock came at the door, and it opened to admit Donny followed by two maids carrying steaming kettles of water for her bath.

"Aye and tis a fair day for yer weddin'," Donny beamed. "A fair day, indeed."

She bustled about straightening the bedclothes, fluffing the pillows, flicking an imaginary piece of dust there, repositioning a perfume bottle here. Jessica could not remember ever seeing her with such a big smile.

"Donny, if you do not slow down, you'll be too exhausted to watch the wedding," Jessica observed dryly.

"Aye, 'twould be well if the bride showed a little more excitement about her wedding," Donny retorted. "Ye were more excited when yer papa gave yer that horse for yer birthday."

Jessica shrugged. "I like horses."

Donny hmphed and turned to direct the maids in readying Jessica's bath.

The rest of the morning sped past. There was not an inch of her body that was not pampered or perfumed. She felt somewhat like a pagan virgin being made ready for sacrifice before a heathen god. She gazed at her reflection in the mirror and realized the comparison was not far from wrong. Damien was very capable of cutting out her heart with just a glance from those damnable green eyes.

She wondered suddenly where he was and what he was thinking. She had not seen him since yesterday afternoon. In a sudden panic, Jessica tried to guess what she would do if he was not at the altar waiting for her. Realizing he had gone through too much trouble to get her there, she decided the question was ridiculous.

Finally, Jessica was ready. She stood before Donny and the other maids as they inspected her for any flaw.

One of the maids spoke suddenly, "Lawr, just like a fairy princess!"

Jessica did look beautiful. Her gown was made of creamy satin and fell to the floor in simple lines. The toes of her matching shoes poked out at the hem. The neckline was cut low enough to tease, but high enough to retain her modesty. The long sleeves puffed at the shoulders and then tightly hugged her arms to the wrists. A train of the same material as her dress fell from her shoulders, held on by ties knotted in bows. Her hair was pulled up into little ringlets by a simple gold band studded with tiny diamonds. It had been a gift from Damien's mother. Covering her head and face and trailing down her back to the length of the train was a veil of Spanish lace.

As she stood there, a knock came at the door and the Duchess entered. She smiled warmly when she saw Jessica.

"You look lovely, Jessica," the lady said. She handed Jessica a white leather case and told her, "Damien asked me to give this to you."

Jessica accepted the case and opened it. She gasped when she saw its contents. Inside, lay a magnificent necklace of sapphires and diamonds with earrings to match.

"It is the customary gift of the Duke of Wyndham to his bride on their wedding day," the Duchess explained.

"But I can not accept these," Jessica protested. "These are your jewels."

The Duchess shook her head. "Not any more. In a short while, you will be the new Duchess of Wyndham. These are not mine any longer." She grinned then. "Besides, they will look much better on you than they ever did on me. They always clashed with my eyes."

The Duchess took the necklace out of the case and clasped it about Jessica's throat. It seemed to reflect the color of her eyes in its sparkle. Then she clipped the earrings on her ears. Standing back, she inspected her handiwork.

"Perfect," the Duchess smiled. "Well, we should go now. We have kept my son waiting long enough."

Jessica's heart fluttered fearfully, but she followed the Duchess out the bedroom door. She wondered how Damien was feeling at this moment. Was he as nervous as she? No, that man was never ruffled. He would be cool and remote, as he always was.

She descended the stairs slowly, trying to give herself time to gain some composure. There seemed to be confusion everywhere she looked. Guests would be coming back to the house after the ceremony for a banquet and dancing. The dining room table was being readied with food, and the ballroom was receiving a last minute touch up. Trunks containing her and Damien's clothes were standing in the front hall. They would be loaded on the coach after she left for the church. There was one trunk that was quite a bit smaller and older than the others. This contained her old clothes. Damien had not done what he had threatened and thrown them out. She wondered fleetingly at that. It was the only threat he had not carried out.

Jessica stepped out into the sunshine and she climbed into carriage. The Duchess and then Donny followed. Her nanny would take care of any last minute primping that had to be done. The carriage moved off, and she sat back to contemplate her fate.

The ride to the church seemed an eternity, yet not long enough to suit her. Upon entering the vestibule of the cathedral, she could hear the massive organ being played. Its lofty strains sent icicles of fear through her heart and made her shiver.

The Duchess sent her a worried glance. "Are you all right?" she asked. At Jessica's faint nod, she whispered, "Be brave, Jessica," and gave her a quick hug. "It will be over sooner than you realize." Then she turned and walked down the aisle to take her place at the front of the cathedral.

Jessica watched her retreating back with a wistful glance. The lady was so poised and self-possessed. Why was it she could not be so self-assured? Her heart fluttered and her knees shook so badly she was sure she would not be able to walk.

Donny fussed with her veil and her train. Someone came up to her and put a single, white rose into her hands and told her it was from His Grace. The organ music changed, and she sent a pleading glance at Donny. The woman just smiled broadly and motioned for her to start walking.

Jessica gazed down the length of the cathedral. She swallowed hard, and somehow, her feet began to move her forward. Her one, clear thought was that she could never walk the entire, long distance from the back of the church to where Damien stood waiting for her at the front. She had a fleeting impression of many curious and smiling faces, but the main focus of her attention was the man dressed in elegant black velvet and white silk who watched her approach with cold, green eyes. Beside him stood Edward Johnson, the witness to the wedding. His smile was friendly and warm, and gave Jessica a small feeling of assurance.

Damien held out a darkly tanned hand to her. As she placed her small one on his, she looked up into his face. He raised a mocking brow, then turned to lead her to where the priest stood waiting. Inwardly, Jessica sighed. Damien had finally won what he had wanted from the beginning. It was too late to back out now. The urge to flee, screaming, back down the aisle was almost too great, but she repressed the feeling with the thought of the child she was carrying. She would at least give it the name and heritage it deserved.

She knelt quietly beside Damien as the priest said a short prayer, then stood to exchange vows with the man beside her. She listened intently as he stated his vows.

To love, honor and protect. ". . . and I pledge thee my troth." His voice was firm and low, and he sounded as if he meant every word. Would it not be wonderful if he really did? Jessica thought to herself. Before she had time to dwell on the thought any further, it became her turn to say her vows. Somehow, she was able to repeat them in a clear, soft tone, and managed not to stumble over the words. Then it came time for Damien to place the ring on her finger. Her hand was cold in his warm one as he slipped the wide, intricately carved, gold band on the third finger of her left hand. She stared down at the symbol that told the world she now belonged to Damien. She doubted she would ever become used to the idea or the feeling of the ring about her finger.

She was brought back from her musings by the priest giving them a final blessing. The ceremony was over. She was officially the wife of Damien Trevor, Duke of Wyndham. She belonged to him until death parted them. The thought sent a shiver down her spine.

Damien turned her to face him and folded back her veil to reveal her face. She looked up into his hard features, and her mind froze. All her thoughts and doubts were stilled as her senses were overpowered by the man before her.

Damien gazed down at her, this witch-woman who was now his wife. Her eyes were wide and her lips parted in her apprehension. Something stirred inside him, making him aware of feelings he thought he did not possess. The thought ran through his mind that she was an innocent still, even after all she had been through. Yet, her willfulness was as strong as ever.

She had fought him every step of the way, but he had finally won. She was his. One corner of his mouth twitched upward.

"I believe," he said quietly, "that it is customary for the groom to kiss the bride at this point."

His arm went about her, pulling her close. She braced herself for the ravaging of her mouth that she had come to expect, but instead, his lips came down on hers softly, gently caressing and surprising her into a response. The world seemed to spin around her, and her knees turned to jelly. She held onto his coat with both hands and swayed against him for support. Her lips parted, inviting him, beckoning. All thoughts of their bargain died as he leisurely accepted the invitation and tasted her.

She had no idea how long they remained in their embrace. The priest clearing his throat finally brought her back to reality. As Damien raised his head, his green eyes glinted mockingly. They seemed to say, The bargain will be short-lived, my love, and it will be you who will break it.

With an effort, Jessica forced herself to stand on her own two feet. Blushing furiously, she turned away. How could she have allowed her feelings to be so apparent, and in front of all these people? She could not have been more embarrassed if her dress had suddenly fallen from her.

Damien held out his hand to her. She was forced to accept it. Together they walked back down the aisle. It had only been short while ago that she had walked this path alone. Now, she was a member of a lifelong partnership. Strange, how a few minutes of time could completely alter one's life. Before, she had been the poor daughter of a deceased earl, thrown out of her own home by her stepmother. Now, she was the Duchess of Wyndham, wife of a very powerful and very rich man.

They came out into the late afternoon sun and hurried down the steps and into the waiting coach. A curious crowd had gathered outside the church, and there was much shoving and pushing to see the new wife of the Duke. Once inside the coach Jessica sat as far into the corner as possible. She was suddenly afraid and very shy of her new husband.

Damien was unable to sit very close to her because of the long train of her dress. The creamy satin billowed around his feet and up over his knees. He pushed at it ineffectually and smiled ruefully.

"I think wedding dresses are designed specifically to keep husbands away from their new wives as long as possible," he complained with a good-natured grin. His eyes softened as he glanced at Jessica and he reached for her hand. Kissing her open palm, he murmured, "You look beautiful today, my love. Witch turned into fairy princess."

Jessica pulled her hand away. She was furious at him for the kiss at the altar, angry at herself for responding, afraid of the feelings that he had stirred up inside her.

"I do not feel like a fairy princess Your Grace," she stated with bad humor. "I feel like a puppet, forced to dance at the puppet master's will."

"I see," Damien said, feigning seriousness. "And I suppose I am the puppet master?"

Jessica said nothing. She merely glared at the man sitting next to her on the seat.

Damien placed a finger under her chin and raised her head to look into her eyes. "My love, one thing you will never be is a puppet," he stated with a smile. "No other woman could have brought me to the altar as you have. It is I who is the puppet. You have merely to tug on the strings, and I will dance to whatever tune you wish."

"You speak with honeyed words, now, Your Grace,

309

but will you be as pleasant several months from now when our bargain has begun to wear on you?" she asked waspishly.

Damien shrugged nonchalantly, his mood changing abruptly as he leaned back in the seat. "There are many women who are willing to assuage the needs of a duke whose wife is not a true wife in all ways."

Jessica gasped in fury at his cruel bluntness. "You would not dare!"

He gazed at her from under lowered lids, his features stony. "It is you who dare me, Your Grace," he told her coldly, using her new form of address with sarcasm. "Do not press me too far. You will not like the results."

Jessica turned away quickly, her eyes stinging with unshed tears. They had come unexpectedly to her eyes, brought by the pain Damien had inflicted with his words. It appeared he had a talent for making her cry. She looked down at the gold band on her finger and wished, somehow, she could make things different between them. It seemed they were always at odds. One tear escaped and slid down her cheek.

It had not gone unseen by Damien. He had watched her reaction to his words with mild amazement. Not ever expecting tears from this strong-willed witch, he was unprepared for the guilt he felt at causing her pain. Contrite, he resolved not to mar the day any further with sharp words.

Jessica felt a handkerchief put into her hand and heard Damien tell her gruffly, "Dry your eyes, Jessica. It would not do for a bride to be seen crying on her wedding day."

Jessica did as she was told and handed a slightly damp handkerchief back to its owner. "Thank you," she murmured gratefully.

The coach had been moving through the streets and now rounded the corner onto the avenue where

Damien's house was situated. The next ordeal of the day would soon be upon her. Jessica would have to meet all of the invited guests, few of whom she knew. The Duchess had asked her if there was anyone whom she wished to invite, but Jessica had told her there was no one. She would have loved to have had Jason present, but she was sure Margaret would not have allowed him to come.

The coach pulled up before the door, and Damien descended, then turned to help Jessica. As she stood beside him, he bent down and whispered in her ear, "Do you suppose we could have a game of cards?"

Jessica smiled up at him. "Only if you let me win," she whispered back. Her eyes shone gratefully into his. She realized he had broken the tension between them in honor of the day. Together, they walked up the stairs and into the house.

Upon entering, they discovered all the servants lined up waiting for them in the front hall. Jacobs cleared his throat, then announced, "Their Graces, the Duke and Duchess of Wyndham." At that, all the servants cheered and applauded.

Damien thanked them, then smiled down at Jessica, whose color was high in her cheeks "It seems they have accepted you as their mistress," he observed.

With apprehension, she answered, "I hope I do not disappoint them."

The applause died, and Jacobs shooed the servants back to their duties, then he turned to Jessica and Damien. "May I extend my congratulations and best wishes to Your Graces," he said with a formal bow.

"Thank you, Jacobs," Damien answered. "That is most thoughtful of you."

Jacobs snapped his fingers and Lucy appeared with a tray upon which was a snifter of brandy and a steaming cup of tea. "I took the liberty of preparing a small libation for you both," informed them.

"Oh, Jacobs, you are a dear!" Jessica exclaimed as she her took her cup.

The butler looked rather aghast at her classification of him, but was very pleased that she was so grateful. "Thank you, Your Grace," he almost smiled. "Now, if you will excuse me, I must attend to my duties." Bowing again, he left.

Jessica and Damien were alone, but only for a very few moments. Damien's mother arrived along with Donny and Leftenant Johnson. The Duchess and Donny hustled Jessica upstairs to divest her of her veil and train, while the Leftenant took Damien into the study to have a brandy with him before the guests arrived.

Chapter Twenty-two

The next several hours were a complete blur to Jessica. She met and greeted innumerable people. Some were genuinely happy for her and Damien, some were curious to see what woman had finally been able to get Damien to the altar, and some were jealous that they or their daughter had not been chosen. She was grateful that Damien had not left her side.

The banquet had ended and the musicians struck their first chords as Damien led Jessica to the middle of the ballroom to begin the dancing. She had always enjoyed dancing, and she discovered to her delight that Damien was an excellent partner. His hold was firm, but gentle, and after her initial nervousness, she began to relax. The music seemed to float around them, and she felt as if she were drifting on a cloud. Damien never took his eyes from her face, holding her gaze as if she were hypnotized.

"You dance beautifully, my love," he smiled down at her.

Jessica playfully batted her eyelashes at him. "Thank you, Your Grace. You make this poor, innocent girl's head swim with your compliments."

"Not so poor and not so innocent any longer," Damien observed with a grin.

Jessica sighed dramatically. "You are right. I have

been ravaged by a rogue."

"But by a most generous rogue."

Jessica sighed again. "That is true. I can not help myself when he showers me with his gifts."

"Perhaps it is the rogue who can not help himself. Perhaps you have put a spell on him, Witch," Damien suggested.

Jessica gazed up at him, trying to read between the lines of his banter. Did he truly mean that he felt something for her? His eyes bored into hers, but she could not let herself believe what she most wanted to believe. In dismay, she felt herself blush. Lightly, she told him, "Do not look at me so, Rogue. Witches are not supposed to blush. I guess that means I am not one." He gazed down into her eyes and saw there all he needed to know. What he wished for would not be too long in coming.

Answering her, he said, "Who else but a witch could have caused me so much trouble, bargained with me, and from whom I still can not turn away? You weave your spells too well, Witch." His eyes glinted mischievously. "Weave your spells on the guests, Witch, and leave your poor, miserable slave alone for a short time."

"Never a slave, Your Grace," Jessica laughed.

"More a slave than you know, Jessica," he murmured.

At that moment the dance ended. He tilted her chin up with one finger, and Jessica thought he was going to kiss her. She wanted him to very much, but her bargain stood like a wall between them. Instead, he merely smiled and brushed his lips chastely across her cheek.

Applause erupted about them, and Jessica blushed as she realized that only she and Damien had been dancing. As they walked from the middle of the floor, the musicians began another melody, the guests began to dance, and Damien and Jessica became separated as they were wished well.

It was some time before Jessica saw Damien again. While he had been gone she had told her life story at least twenty times and had danced with at least half of the male guests. She had warded off several improper advances, and her toes had been stepped upon innumerable times. Her face ached from smiling so much, and her feet hurt. She discovered a seat in a corner of the room, partially hidden by a flower arrangement, and went there to escape for a few moments. From this spot, she could watch the whole room without being observed.

Across the room, Damien was the center of a group of his contemporaries. She saw his eyes slip away from the group several times probably in search of her, but she just wanted to rest a few moments. One member of the group in particular caught her attention. It was a woman, several years older than herself, but not quite as old as Damien, and extremely attractive.

She had been introduced to Jessica as the Marquessa d'Avilon, a widow. Jessica watched as she wrapped herself about Damien's arm and saw him smile down into her face. A sick feeling erupted in the pit of her stomach as the two moved out to the center of the floor to dance.

When Jessica had been introduced to her, the woman had seemed vaguely familiar. Now, seeing her with Damien, she realized she had seen them together before at Madame's on the evening that Damien had invited her to his dinner party. Jessica had the most incredible urge to scratch out the Marquessa's eyes.

Jessica desperately scanned the crowd to find someone to rescue her from her primitive urges. It was with relief that she was able to catch the eye of

Leftenant Johnson.

As she linked her arm through his and almost propelled him onto the dance floor, she explained, "I apologize for being so forward, Leftenant, but I find I am without a partner for this dance."

The Leftenant looked puzzled, then grinned as he caught sight of Damien dancing with the Marquessa. "You don't have to apologize. I've known several women who would like to scratch out the Marquessa's eyes. I do have my price for rescuing damsels in distress, though."

"What is that, sir?"

"You have to call me Edward," he told her with mock severity.

Jessica smiled. "I will pay your price only on the condition that you call me Jessica. Agreed?"

"Agreed," he nodded.

Jessica had noticed Edward paying particular attention to a young girl who danced past them in the arms of an older gentleman. "Who is that?" she asked now.

"Catherine McCall." Edward answered. "Her father owns the property adjoining Wyndham."

"She is lovely."

"Yes, she is." Edward's eyes wistfully followed the figure of Catherine.

Jessica smiled. "Have you told her how you feel about her, Edward?"

The Leftenant looked shocked. "How do you know?" he blurted. "I haven't told anyone, not even Damien."

Her smile widened. "Women can see these things. I would very much like you to come visit us at Wyndham, Edward. I am sure Damien would not mind if I also invited Catherine and her parents to visit."

"You are a very gracious lady, Jessica. Thank you."

316

The dance came to an end. Jessica thanked him for his company then said she was going outside for some air. The garden was quite dark by now. The lights from the house only illuminated a small area, but the moon was full. It lit quite well the path to the stone bench at the back of the enclosure.

Having picked a time when no one else was in the garden. Jessica wandered leisurely along the path and breathed in the fragrance of the spring plants. She needed the time to be alone, for the sight of Damien dancing with the Marquessa had greatly upset her. The two had appeared to be very familiar with one another. Would the Marquessa be the one to whom Damien would turn when their bargain had begun to wear on him? Sitting on the stone bench, she stared up at the night sky.

Beside her, a dull thud startled her. Looking up, she saw the dim shape of a man standing beside her. Thinking at first it was one of the guests, she opened her mouth to greet him, then realized he was not dressed for a wedding. He wore no coat, his stock was untied, and his hair was disheveled.

"Well, well, what is this? The bride all alone in the dark?" he spoke with a sneer. "Where is your brave, new husband?"

Jessica stood and backed away a step. She could not make out his features in the dimness. "Who are you?" she demanded. "What do you want?"

"Jessica, do you not recognize me? I am crushed." He took a step toward her, into the moonlight.

She realized immediately it was Charles Bellingham, the man who had tried to rape her!

"What are you doing here? If Damien finds you here, he will kill you," she warned.

The Marquis smiled wickedly. "He does not know that I am here, dear Jessica. And I know you will not tell him. You would not wish to make your husband jealous on your wedding day."

"Do not be so sure of yourself," Jessica told him. "He would not believe that I willingly had anything to do with you." She began to edge away.

"I have the feeling that this marriage is not as idyllic as it appears," he observed. "Remember that I know where you spent your evenings for the last several months. And I know what was written in those very private letters you delivered to the coast every month. A word or two whispered in the right ears and you would be arrested and brought to trial quicker than you could blink. It would become known that the Duke of Wyndham wed an adventuress. Do you think your brave Duke would want you then? Do you think he would tolerate the scandal?" He moved toward her.

"I am innocent, sir," Jessica retorted haughtily.

"Perhaps. But does Wyndham truly believe that? What if he awakens some morning and decides you are guilty? He will throw you out without a farthing." He took a step closer. Jessica moved away.

"He won't."

The Marquis shrugged. "You delude yourself, Jessica. I am going to France. Come with me. You will be safe there. I will see to it."

"Ha! How can I be safe with a man who beat me and then tried to take advantage of me?" Jessica sneered.

Jessica could retreat no farther, for she had backed up into the garden wall. The Marquis quickly covered the ground between them. Reaching out swiftly, he grabbed her wrist in a grip of iron.

"You can not run away from me, Jessica," he told her with a laugh. "You will come with me to France."

"Let go of me or I will scream," she threatened, as she struggled to free herself from his grasp.

"Don't," he warned. "I did not come here to hurt

318

you."

"Then let go of me. You are hurting my wrist."

"Jessica, do you think I am fool enough to let you go once I have caught you? You would be gone from here in a moment and I would not get what I came for. I want you, Jessica." His lust for her was evident in every word he spoke.

Jessica could see no way out of the situation. She was becoming more terrified of the man every moment. Taking a deep breath, she opened her mouth to scream, but before any sound came out, the Marquis slapped her hard across the face.

Her head rocked back on her neck, and red flashes zigzagged across her eyelids. If the Marquis had not had a hold on her, she would have fallen. In the seconds it took Jessica to recover from the blow, the Marquis had pulled her to him and wrapped his arms about her. He forced her head back with his hand at her throat and a thumb under her chin. Her arms were pinned between them against his chest. He had her so tightly that she could not move, and she could scarcely breathe.

"Please, Charles, no," she pleaded, gasping.

He ignored her. Lowering his mouth to hers, he kissed her savagely, brutally, forcing her mouth open and bruising her lips so badly she could taste blood. She struggled to free herself, but it was of no use. He was too strong, his hold on her too tight. In the back of her mind was the fear of Damien finding her in this position with the Marquis. She was not sure her new husband would believe any explanation she gave.

As the thought formed, she heard Damien's voice, heavy with sarcasm, from beside them. "I hope I am not interrupting anything."

The Marquis lifted his head slowly, like one returning to consciousness after a pleasant dream. He regarded Damien with an insolent stare, but he retained his hold on Jessica.

"As a matter of fact, you are interrupting," he informed Damien with a leer. "I came to claim what is rightfully mine." Jessica tried to shake her head in denial, but the grip of the Marquis about her throat made it impossible.

"Bellingham, I told you I would kill you the next time you touched Jessica," Damien snarled.

The Marquis smiled his amusement. "I do not think that would be wise, since you would harm your lovely wife in the process." His hand caressed her neck, then stopped, his thumb at her throat.

"You swine! Let her go and stand up to me like a man!" Damien took a step forward.

"Do not come any closer," the Marquis warned. His thumb tightened against Jessica's throat. She gave a small whimper of fear.

Damien's eyes flicked to Jessica, then back to the Marquis. He appeared to relax suddenly. "You realize, of course, that I can call for help from the house. My servants would be out here before you could think about doing any harm," he informed the Marquis.

The Marquis smiled craftily. "What could they do to me as long as I have the lovely Jessica to protect me?" He shook his head. "Sorry, Wyndham, I'm afraid you have lost this game." He began to drag Jessica back toward the outer wall.

Jessica unable to breathe properly with Bellingham's hand about her throat, was not about to be become his pawn. Twisting around, she dug her elbow as hard as she could into the man's middle. With a gasping rush of air the Marquis doubled over, pushing Jessica to the ground as he did so.

What happened next was almost too quick for her to follow. As he straightened, he pulled a pistol and began to take aim at Damien. There was a flash, and the Marquis made a gurgling sound. When Jessica looked up at him, she saw Damien's stiletto buried in the man's throat. He toppled heavily upon her. Smothered by his weight, horrified, Jessica screamed and pushed frantically at him.

Damien rushed to her and pulled the dead man from his wife. Helping her to her feet, he held her tightly as she buried her face against his shoulder. He felt her shudder beneath his arms.

"It's all right, Jessica," he murmured into her hair. "It's all over. He won't bother you any more. Did he hurt you very much?"

Jessica shook her head. "No. I'll be all right in a few minutes." She drew a shaky breath and tried to smile bravely.

Damien held her in silence for a few moments. Finally, he turned her gently away and back toward the house. As they entered, they met Edward and Catherine on their way out to the garden. Damien stopped them and spoke quietly to Edward for a moment.

"I will take care of it," Edward assured him.

With a quick smile at his friend, Damien guided Jessica to the stairs. They did not escape unnoticed, however. Damien's mother met them just as Jessica was about to flee up the stairs.

"There you are," she exclaimed. "I was beginning to wonder what happened to you both. It is almost time for Jessica to change so that you may leave." She took a closer look at Jessica and noticed her disarray and the red marks across her cheek. "Jessica, what happened?" When Jessica did not answer immediately, she turned a worried look on her son. "Damien?"

Not wanting to worry the Duchess, Jessica said quickly, "I fell in the garden, Your Grace. I'm afraid I was quite clumsy."

As Damien threw a grateful look at his wife, his mother exclaimed, "Good heavens, child! Well, thank goodness you didn't do any more damage to yourself!" Linking arms with Jessica, she steered her up the stairs. "Come along. We will fix your hair and take care of that cheek." After they had ascended a few steps, she threw over her shoulder, "Damien, go change and take this child on her honeymoon."

Chapter Twenty-three

The coach sped through the dark countryside. The city's lights had been left behind more than an hour ago. Outside the coach window was moonlit darkness, relieved only by an occasional spark of light from a lonely farmhouse. The trees were great, hulking shadows, sentinels by the side of the road.

Jessica leaned back against the seat. She allowed the swaying of the carriage to lull her into semiconsciousness. Her thoughts were vague, grey things that flitted through her mind like transient ghosts. Her relaxed state came not so much from a sense of well being, but rather one of exhaustion and resignation.

She and Damien were finally alone as husband and wife, a fact she would have to deal with many times in the future. It was these times of being alone together that would be crucial to their marriage, that would make the difference between their living together as a family, or living together in their separate hells.

She had resigned herself to the fact that Damien had won her as his wife. She felt the future was in his hands. It was up to him to prove to her that he truly wanted her as a whole person, not just her body. She would be wife to him in every way except in his bed until she felt he really cared for her. He had been kind and sweet at the ball following their wedding, and he had been brave and protective in dealing with the Marquis, but she wondered how long his feeling of triumph and euphoria would last.

She glanced at him, barely making him out in the dark. He gazed out the window into the blackness beyond, and occasionally the tip of his cheroot would glow red as he puffed on it. He had been silent since leaving London, lost perhaps in his own thoughts of their coming life together.

Jessica longed to reach out to him, to touch his hand and have it close, warm and firm, around her own. She wanted him to turn to her and smile, to have his eyes crinkle at the corners. She wanted to feel his hands on her body, to work their magic and make her forget everything, everything but his desire for her.

Trying to shut out the thoughts caused by her rebellious heart, she closed her eyes tightly. Remember the bargain, she kept telling herself. Remember the bargain. She fell asleep in the middle of her musings.

A low voice speaking in her ear woke her. "Jessica, we've stopped."

Jessica mumbled incoherently and snuggled further against the warm, strong shoulder where her head rested. She was too sleepy to move. This spot was too comfortable.

A warm, strong shoulder?!

Jessica sat up, fully awake. "Oh, I'm sorry," she apologized, flustered. "I did not realize . . . I'm sorry."

Damien smiled, amused at her embarrassment. "I did not mind in the least," he told her warmly. "As a matter of fact, I rather enjoyed it."

They had stopped at an inn to spend the night. Damien descended from the coach and turned to help Jessica. His eyes glinted triumphantly as he watched her descend. Jessica felt there was something he was not telling her.

The innkeeper greeted them warmly. Evidently, Damien stopped here frequently on his trips from London to Wyndham. The man showed them upstairs to their room and asked if there was anything he could get them.

"I think a bottle of your best Madeira would do nicely, Harris," Damien told the innkeeper.

Harris hurried out to get the wine, and Damien began removing his coat and untying his stock. Jessica did not move. She chewed her bottom lip, uncertain what to do.

Finally, she announced, "There is only one bed!"

Damien gave the room a casual perusal. "So there is," he agreed. He turned back to unfastening the neck of his shirt.

Jessica decided the only way to handle this was to take the initiative. "Well, you will just have to speak to the innkeeper about this. He will have to give us a second room."

Damien turned slowly and regarded Jessica a moment. He uttered only one word, but it spoke volumes of his displeasure with her. "Why?"

Jessica turned a deep crimson at his unspoken rebuke, but she would not be put off. "Well, we certainly can not sleep in the same bed."

Damien strode up to her and stood facing her with his hands on his hips. His eyes narrowed dangerously, "And where do you propose that we sleep?"

Jessica took a deep breath. He looked for all the world like a pirate with his shirt undone down the front, his tight breeches and high boots, and he looked just about as dangerous.

She knew she was treading on perilous ground, but something made her suggest boldly, "You will have to sleep in a chair."

"A chair?!" Damien repeated incredulously. "Madame, you may sleep anywhere you like, but tonight, I am sleeping in that bed." He jabbed a finger in the direction of the piece of furniture that was causing the problem.

"But the bargain," Jessica weakly tried to remind him.

"The bargain be damned!"

Jessica flinched at his tone. "You do not have to shout at me," she stated as she turned her back on him and moved off to remove her hat and pelisse.

A knock came at that moment, and Harris entered with a bottle and two glasses on a tray. He had timed it perfectly, for it distracted Damien and prevented him from getting the last word in their argument. When Harris left, however, she could feel Damien's eyes boring into her back. She took a deep breath and turned to him with a dazzling smile.

"I would love a glass of wine, Damien," she said brightly. "Could you pour one for me, please?"

As he turned without comment to do as she requested, she released a silent sigh of relief. One disaster averted, she thought to herself. She would have to be more careful in the future not to upset him. The topic of sleeping in the same bed would have to die an ignominious death if she was to keep peace between them. The last thing she wanted was to anger Damien to the point where he would not honor the bargain they had struck.

What she did not see was the gleam of triumph in Damien's eyes. One night in bed together, no matter how chaste, could lead to others. He would make this witch forget there ever was a ridiculous bargain.

Jessica kept up a constant chatter while they drank their wine before the fire, but soon she had exhausted all subjects, as well as herself. She tried to stifle a yawn, but it did not go unnoticed by Damien's amused watchfulness. He stood and took the glass from her hand, then pulled her to her feet. Gently, he turned her around and began unfastening her dress.

"You can not talk all night, Jessica," he told her with laughter in his voice. "And I do not think you really wish to spend the night in a chair."

Silently, Jessica agreed with him. She was just too tired to fight the inevitable. The bed was too inviting.

She felt his hand brush the length of her back, but she could not tell if it had been accidental. She dared not say anything for fear of pricking his ire any further this night. She could not afford to have him lose his temper when they would be sleeping in the same bed. The consequences could be devastating.

Since her dress had been undone for her, the next logical thing was to change her into her nightclothes, but she had misgivings about doing it in front of Damien. Walking to her trunk, she pulled out her nightrail, not one that he had bought for her but one of her old ones. She clutched it to her as she turned to face him. He was watching her with an amused gleam in his eyes.

"Please," she asked softly. "Turn around."

"Why?" he wanted to know, his teeth flashing in a smile. "I have already seen you unclothed."

Jessica blushed and frowned, not sure how to combat his argument. Damien watched the indecision on her face. Finally, he relented. Chuckling, he went about the room and turned down the lamps. The moonlight coming through the window was the only illumination in the room.

"Since you have suddenly become so modest, I trust the darkness will satisfy you," Damien suggested.

Without a word, Jessica hurriedly undressed and

crawled into bed. She watched from under the covers as Damien approached, divesting himself of his clothes as he came. She could just make out his form in the dark. Feeling his weight on the bed, she moved as far as possible to the opposite edge. She did not wish to place temptation any nearer than she could help.

His voice came out of the blackness. "Good night, Jessica."

"Good night," she answered.

Jessica lay awake a long while as she listened to his even breathing while he slept. His closeness to her made every nerve in her body tingle with awareness. What she was experiencing was not what she had always dreamed her wedding night to be. The thought caused a painful tightening in her chest and brought tears to her eyes. Silently, she cried herself to sleep.

She felt encircled in a protective warmth, and she snuggled closer. It was pleasant and cozy, and she wanted to remain forever, but something nagged at her. Reluctantly, she opened her eyes to be confronted by a wide expanse of chest covered in golden fur. Her eyes travelled upward to behold white teeth exposed in a grin and green eyes sparkling with satisfied humor.

"Good morning," Damien greeted her.

Jessica was appalled when she realized her head was against his shoulder and her right arm and leg were draped intimately across his body. She sat up abruptly, causing the bedclothes to fall away and reveal that Damien had slept without a stitch of clothing.

"Oh!" she exclaimed, her cheeks flaming, as she struggled to pull the covers back over Damien.

Damien watched with amusement, but he did not make a move to help her. In her struggles, her night-dress crept up to reveal a shapely thigh and a glimpse of a very attractive rump. He remembered the feel of that bottom beneath his hands, and his glance became warmer.

Somehow, the blankets had become caught around Damien's legs, but he did nothing to aid her efforts to untangle them. Finally Jessica turned to him with exasperation.

"Well, you could help!" she pouted.

At that Damien laughed outright. "Why should I help you spoil my fun? You create such an attractive display of bare limbs that I find myself dazzled."

At his comment, Jessica suddenly realized where the hem of her nightrail was. If possible, she blushed even more as she tried to pull it down discreetly. She sat immobile as she tried to decide how to get out of bed with some semblance of modesty.

Damien finally resolved her dilemma by throwing his long legs over the side of the bed and getting up. With no selfconsciousness, he walked across to where his breeches lay across the arm of a chair. After her first glance, Jessica studiously kept her eyes averted. She wanted desperately to feast her eyes on his magnificent body, but that would be an invitation to Damien to end their bargain.

"If we are to make Wyndham before nightfall, you had better get up and get yourself dressed," he told her.

As he spoke, he pulled on his breeches and a clean shirt. Leaving the shirt open at the neck, he sat on the bed to pull on his boots. Jessica watched the play of muscles across his back under the silk shirt. She longed to reach out her hand and feel the strength that lay dormant in that body. Damien finished with his boots and stood. After running a brush through his hair, he walked to the door.

"I am going to make sure the coach will be ready when we wish to leave, and to see about some breakfast," he said. "I would appreciate it if you could be ready when I return." Then he left.

Jessica took the opportunity of being alone to quickly jump out of bed and get dressed. Since Donny and Damien's man, Wilson, had left well before them, she was forced to manage her own toilette. However, she could not fasten her dress up the back. She would just have to ask Damien to help.

Gathering together their belongings, she packed away those they would not need for their trip. Damien had placed his stock, waistcoat, and jacket casually over the back of a chair. Jessica replaced the stock with a fresh one and smoothed the waistcoat and jacket. His clothes still held the scent of him — the pungent smell of the cheroots he smoked, the exotic, clean aroma of the sandalwood soap he used. He did not use heavy colognes or perfumes as many men did. She buried her face in the fine wool of his jacket, and for that quick moment, felt close to him.

Hearing a footstep outside in the hall, she hurriedly replaced the jacket on the chair. Angrily, she chided herself. If she went on this way, she would surely be the one to break the bargain. As the door opened to admit Damien, she was fussing with the trunk containing her clothes. She stood as he entered, and she walked up to him.

"I can not fasten my dress," she told him. "Could you help me, please?" She presented her back to him as she tried to ignore his grin of pleasure.

"It would be my pleasure," he replied warmly.

Jessica pointedly ignored his innuendo and remained silent.

He finished the last fastener, but his hands, instead of moving away, landed lightly on her shoulders. Jessica closed her eyes as she gathered the strength to move away. The brush of his fingers along her back had made her grit her teeth to keep her equilibrium.

Now, with his hands on her shoulders, she felt dizzily rooted where she stood. If only he would not touch her, she would not have to battle so hard for her sanity. Taking herself in hand, she stepped away and threw him a look of exasperation. She picked up his stock and handed it to him.

"I suggest that you finish dressing," she prompted. "I recall that you were anxious to begin the last leg of our journey."

Damien did not answer, but his eyes spoke volumes. Jessica was not sure she had done the right thing by hurrying him. He was as adept at undoing her dress as he was at fastening it. Living with the wolf in his own den was a dangerous thing to do.

She was relieved when he slipped his stock from her fingers and turned to the mirror to tie it. He was soon dressed, and they went down to breakfast. They ate at a table in the corner of the common room downstairs. By the time they had finished, Damien's driver came in to tell him that the coach was ready and they could leave whenever he wished. They were on the road, soon after.

After they had ridden for several miles, Damien turned to Jessica. "I have something for you," he told her solemnly. He reached into his waistcoat pocket and pulled out a shiny object that dangled on a chain.

"Oh!" she exclaimed. "My locket!" She took it from Damien and gazed down at it. "I never thought I would see it again," she said softly. "I thought I had lost it when Aphrodite and I jumped . . . when I was at Madame's." She had almost mentioned her escape from Damien's house from under his men's noses. She had a feeling that it was not a wise thing to do to remind him of that incident. "Where did you find it?"

"Madame sent it to me as proof that you were with her," Damien explained. "It must mean a great deal to you."

"My parents gave it to me when I was a little girl," Jessica said as tears sprang to her eyes.

"The woman's portrait is of your mother?" he asked.

Jessica nodded.

"She was very beautiful. You look just like her." His voice was without emotion. He turned away and stared out the window.

Jessica saw his slight frown. She knew it had taken a great deal of effort on his part to even mention any member of her family. It had probably taken even more of an effort not to destroy the locket, for there was another miniature portrait inside it—that of her father.

Jessica sat watching Damien for several moments, but he did not move, and his expression did not change. She wished there was something she could do to ease the pain he felt. Finally, she, too, turned to look out her window and left him to his thoughts. It would take time to heal the hurt that had been inflicted on him.

Chapter Twenty-four

Jessica sat on a quilt on the warm grass under a tree. Her needlepoint had fallen unheeded to her lap. She gazed back at the house—Damien's house—proud and regal in the sun.

They had arrived at Wyndham a fortnight ago. Vividly, she remembered her first impression of the house. The sun was setting, and it cast a golden glow over everything. The house seemed to be made of gold filigree as it sprawled across her field of vision. Upon seeing it, she felt the same way she had when she had first met Damien—frightened but fascinated.

The long ride from the inn had been made in almost complete silence. Damien had seemed to shut her out, his gallantry and charm of the day before had disappeared after he had given her the locket. The small piece of jewelry had appeared to remind him once again of who she was and what pain her family had inflicted on his. Jessica knew what demons he was battling, and it bothered her that she could do nothing to help. She realized that she had precipitated his mood by her presence.

When they had finally drawn near to Wyndham Damien seemed to relax, and she noticed he watched for her reaction. The expression on her face had evidently been the one expected, for he smiled slightly and commented, "It appears to affect everyone that way the first time."

Duchess or no, she could not help but stare wide eyed with her mouth hanging agape. She had never seen such a huge, magnificent house. She could not comprehend fully the idea that she would actually live in this place and be its mistress.

The house was built in the shape of an H, with the main entrance in the center of the crossbar. To reach the doorway, one had to climb a wide, sweeping flight of stairs. The large, open foyer, which was two stories high, was actually on the second floor of the house, along with the ballroom, the main dining room, the salon, and various other rooms for entertaining guests. The bottom floor contained a smaller, more intimate dining room where the family ate when not entertaining, the extensive library, Damien's study, a morning room, and a parlor. On the opposite side of the crossbar were the kitchen and the other rooms necessary for the mundane running of the mansion. The two wings contained bedrooms and the staff living quarters.

It had taken Jessica the better part of a week to inspect the house, and even then, there were parts she did not see. She had gone through the house with the thought that she might have some reorganization ahead of her, but from what she saw, she judged that everything was running smoothly without her intervention. There was little for her to do. Out of deference to her position in the household, Hobbs, the majordomo, asked her opinion on the menus and the linen to be used on the table, but he was so competent that she felt superfluous.

Damien had not spent much time with her. Having been away from his estate for so long, he was immersed in reacquainting himself with it. Occasionally, he would ask her to go for a ride in the curricle, but these outings seldom occurred. Their conversation would center mainly on the sights or history of the part of the estate through which they travelled. He had become distant since their arrival.

She felt a prisoner, for she was never allowed to go out of the house alone. Damien made that rule very clear. Donny or one of the maids always trailed along behind her. She was not allowed to go riding. Damien had forbid it because of the babe she carried. In short, she was bored.

She sighed heavily. The young maid who was sitting several feet away got up and came over anxiously.

"Is there something wrong, Your Grace?" she asked. "Are you feeling ill?"

Jessica smiled to belay the girl's fears. "No, Mary, I am not ill," she told her. "I think I have done enough needlepoint for now. I am going back to the house."

The girl helped Jessica gather up her things, then walked with her back to the house. At the doorway, Jessica asked the girl to put her needlepoint away for her, then she made her escape to her bedroom.

The master bedroom suite consisted of two bedrooms that were connected by a large sitting room. Each bedroom also had its own dressing area. Jessica's rooms were decorated in shades of light blue and white. It was a pleasant room, situated on the back of the house and looked out on formal gardens.

Damien's room, which she had only seen once, and that very quickly when she had toured the house, was on the side of the house, facing rolling lawn and forest beyond. His room was done in shades of darker blue and gold. The connecting sitting room was situated on a corner of the house, thus having two walls with windows. This room combined the colors of the two rooms on either side. Jessica liked this room, but found herself apprehensive about using it. She was always afraid she would meet Damien in it. For some reason, she felt it was his room, and did not wish to tread on his territory.

Now, however, she had no thoughts of going into the sitting room. Damien was nowhere in sight, and her plan had become more enticing the more she thought about it. She would go riding, by herself, one last time before the child was born. After all, her pregnancy was barely noticeable, even when she was naked, so what harm could be done if she was very careful?

Thankful she did not need help to dress, she quickly changed into her riding habit—her old one. Quietly, she slipped down a set of side stairs. As she ran lightly across the grass, she prayed no one from the house would see her. Reaching the stables, she was pleasantly surprised to find no one about.

She quickly located Aphrodite's stall. In minutes, she had mounted and was heading toward a trail that ran into the woods.

Jessica had not gone unnoticed. Damien happened to glance up from his desk just as she disappeared among the trees. He stood quickly and searched for the groom who should have been with her. Seeing no one, he swore and ran out of the room.

Jessica cantered along the broad path that ran through the woods. She drank in the beauty of her surroundings and enjoyed her freedom. After a short ride, she came to a trail that veered off to the left. It was overgrown, but still visible enough to follow easily. She decided it was worth exploration.

The trail seemed to have no destination, for it twisted and turned upon itself. She followed it for quite a while and was about to turn back when she noticed it opened into a clearing ahead. Curious, she decided to see what it was.

The trail ended at a glade with a noisy little brook

running around one side. In the center of the clearing was a strangely shaped tree and beneath it, a table of sorts constructed out of flat stones.

Jessica crossed the brook and dismounted near the table. Allowing Aphrodite to graze, she examined the stones. There were strange carvings all across the top stone.

The legends of the Druids came to mind. She wondered what ancient rites were performed on this spot, and what sort of people performed them. She ran her hand over the stone and felt the roughness of the carvings. A chill shivered down her spine.

"Are you contemplating the sacrifice of anyone in particular?" a voice asked from behind her.

Gasping, Jessica swung around to confront an icy pair of green eyes and a jaw hard with anger.

"Damien!"

He raised an eyebrow. "You do remember me then?" he inquired sarcastically. "Perhaps you also remember that you are not to leave the house alone? And that you are not to be out riding?"

Jessica knew she was wrong for disobeying him, but his commands grated on her, and she was angry at him for sneaking up on her. She shrugged a shoulder.

"I was not aware that you cared so much for my welfare, Your Grace," she told him coolly. "You seem to enjoy the company of your overseer and his books far more than you enjoy mine."

Without a word, Damien took the two steps required to bring him near Jessica. Taking her by the elbow, he forcibly steered her over to Aphrodite, and lifted her into the saddle. His expression was unfathomable as he looked up at her.

"If I had known you craved my company so much, I would have visited you last night in your bed," he said silkily. "Then you would have seen what it

337

means to ride."

Jessica gasped at his crudeness. Swinging Aphrodite around so quickly she almost bumped Damien, she rode off. She was fuming, and if it had been possible, she would have goaded her horse into a gallop. The trail was too overgrown for that, however, so she went as fast as she dared. She could hear Damien on his huge stallion crashing through the undergrowth close behind her.

It seemed to take an eternity to reach the end of the trail, but soon the trees opened up, and she entered the wider trail that led back to the house grounds. Digging in her heels, she galloped off. She wanted to reach the house and be safe behind the door of her room before Damien had another chance to confront her.

Jessica had a head start on Damien, and her mare was very swift, but she was no match for the huge stallion that Damien rode. The stallion had caught the mare's scent, and when he reached the wider trail, Damien gave him his head. The Duke had not finished with his headstrong wife.

Jessica arrived in the stableyard seconds before Damien. She slipped from Aphrodite's back and tossed the reins to one of the stableboys, who stared at her with his mouth hanging open. Jessica gave him a quick smile.

"Give her a good rubdown," she requested. "She's just had a fast run."

Damien arrived just as Jessica finished speaking. Jessica turned and hurried toward the house as he dismounted and tossed his reins to the same stableboy, whose mouth dropped open even farther. The Duke caught up with his wife and took her elbow.

He walked Jessica to the house without a word. Jessica was so furious, she barely felt his touch on her arm. Whatever he had to say to her, she was ready for it. Oh, yes, she was ready.

Damien guided Jessica into his study and closed the door quietly behind him. He stood looking at her. His eyes snapped and the muscles in his jaw worked.

Finally he spoke. His voice was soft, but Jessica could hear his rage behind the words. "Are you so bent on destruction that you must go racing off into the woods by yourself? Are you so unaware of the danger of being abroad by yourself? It is for your own safety that I requested that you not go out alone."

Requested? Jessica thought to herself. More like commanded. Pulling off her gloves, she tossed them negligently on a chair.

Throwing caution to the winds, she retorted, "I am a big girl, now, Your Grace. I am a married woman. I no longer need a chaperone everywhere I go."

Damien strode up to her. His eyes narrowed as he warned her, "Do not flatter yourself. You are only half married, and you act like a child. As to your needing a chaperone, I disagree with you. You do need a chaperone everywhere you go, and you shall have one. Do I have to remind you that you were accosted in a private, enclosed garden on the day of our wedding? There are poachers about in these woods. They are not as civilized as the Marquis was. Or perhaps you enjoy the uninvited advances of men who jump on any woman they come upon."

"How can you say such a thing?" Jessica demanded angrily. "You know I do not. But you are little better than he was. He wished to have me against my will, and you keep me under watch as if I were your prisoner. Well, I am not your prisoner, and I will do as I please."

Damien grabbed her by the shoulders. "You dare to compare me to that degenerate?"

Jessica only stared silently at him.

"You fool."

"No fool, Your Grace. I know quite well what it means to be a prisoner."

"You are not my prisoner, but I will treat you like one if you persist in this foolishness. You carry my child; you are my wife, until such time as I decide otherwise. Until then, you will do as I say. Is that understood?" He gave her a shake that was so hard that it made her teeth snap together.

"Yes," she grated out. "It is very well understood, Your Grace. From now on, I will take very good care of your property. You need not worry that it will be damaged in any way when you wish to exchange it for something more to your liking."

Jessica's eyes had turned to blue ice at the hurt he had inflicted with his words. Silently, they measured each other. She felt his hands convulse on her shoulders. Finally, his hands dropped away. She took the opportunity to gather up her gloves and make a dignified exit from the room. As soon as she had closed the door behind her, however, she broke into a run and dashed up the stairs and into the haven of her own room where she threw herself on the bed and sobbed until she was exhausted.

Damien watched her leave without a word. He had wanted desperately to stop her, to take back the ugly words they had spoken to each other, but somehow, he could not bring himself to do it. Never before had he been so tongue-tied with a woman. Never had he been so cruel. With Jessica, he was like a young swain out for the first time in society. Why did it hurt so much?

Walking to the fireplace, he leaned on the mantel and stared down at the cold hearth. What was wrong with him? He wanted her more than he had ever wanted a woman, yet all they did was fight and pull farther apart. After several moments of not finding the answer, he banged his fist against the marble and swore long and colorfully. Feeling only slightly better, he strode to his desk where he threw himself into the leather chair behind it. For the rest of the afternoon, he stared out the window.

Dinner was a silent affair. Neither Jessica nor Damien had anything to say to each other, and the only conversation was between Hobbs and whomever he happened to be serving at the time.

As soon as she could, Jessica escaped upstairs to her room. She decided a book would be much better company than her silent, overbearing husband. Damien retreated to his study, where he befriended a full decanter of brandy and determined that the two would become very close before daybreak.

It was near dawn when a noise outside Jessica's bedroom door awakened her. She lay quietly and listened. It came again, a shuffling noise, then her door handle slowly began to turn.

"Who is there?" she called.

At her words, the door was flung wide, and Damien stood swaying in the opening.

"You are a witch!" he shouted. "You have worked your spells too well, Witch!"

Jessica jumped out of bed and hurried over to him. Her heart began pounding in her chest. Whether it was from fear or anticipation, she could not tell. Her only thought was to get him out of her room and into his own before he decided to do something to break their agreement, or before he woke all the servants and caused a scandal.

"Damien, you're drunk," she scolded.

"Um hmm," he agreed as he draped his arm heavily across her shoulders and pulled her against him. "I want a kiss, Witch."

Before Jessica could protest, his mouth descended

and captured hers. Caught off guard, still groggy from sleep, Jessica allowed herself to be seduced. Warm tingles of sensations ran through her and curled her toes. Even drunk, Damien did not lose his magic touch.

Finally raising his head, he grinned down at her. "Good night, my Witch," he whispered. Then he turned away and swerved down the hall bellowing for Wilson as he went.

After returning to her bed, Jessica lay awake pondering her husband's strange behavior. Surely the argument they had had that afternoon could not have upset him so that he got himself drunk. He had made it quite clear that he cared little about her, even mentioning the fact that he would discard her when he grew tired of her. Yet, the kiss he just bestowed upon her was warm with feeling. What was he thinking? Her lips still throbbed from his stolen caress. Turning impatiently in the bed, she tried to block out her confusion. Sleep did not come easily for the rest of the night.

The next morning, Jessica found the dining room empty when she came down for breakfast. She had almost finished her meal when Damien entered and sat gingerly in his chair at the head of the table. He moved as if every gesture were painful. His complexion beneath his tan was very much the same color as his eyes — pea green. When Hobbs came in to serve him, he asked only for coffee, then barked at the butler for making so much racket.

Jessica tried to hide a smile behind a sip of tea. His feeling so ill was just payment for causing her so much pain and aggravation. Damien happened to glance up and caught the merriment in her eyes before she was able to lower them.

"What are you looking so damned pleased about?" he growled.

"Good morning to you, too," she greeted him. "Did you not sleep well, Your Grace? Are you ill?" she asked innocently.

Damien just grunted as he added a liberal amount of brandy to his coffee. The decanter was almost empty.

"Hobbs, I thought you filled the brandy decanter only yesterday," Jessica observed.

"Yes, Your Grace, I did," Hobbs answered.

"Then how did it come to be almost empty so quickly?" she wondered aloud. "Damien, did you have guests last night after dinner? You should have informed me. I would have helped you entertain them."

Damien glared at her. She felt that if the table had not been between them, he would have hit her he looked so murderous. With some coffee in his system, his normal color was beginning to return. Jessica decided it was time to leave.

"Well, perhaps next time," she offered. "If you will excuse me, Damien, I have things to attend to. I am so busy, you know."

She began to get up, but a voice from the other end of the table commanded quietly, "Sit down."

Jessica dropped back into her chair. Nervously, she chewed at her bottom lip as she waited for another tongue-lashing from her husband.

Seeing he had her full attention, he asked, "What are you trying to do to me, Jessica? I have honored your damn bargain. What more do you want?"

Jessica sat and looked at him. Evidently, he did not remember the kiss of the night before. Thoughts raced through her mind. She could tell him what she really wanted, that she wanted his love, but that would be like rubbing salt across the open wound of her heart. That would never do.

There was something that she had wanted to speak

343

to him about since their wedding day, but had not found the right time or the right words. It concerned Jason. Damien had power and influence; perhaps he would be able to help her brother. Yet, she was not about to relinquish her superior position in the battle of wits with her husband.

Looking suitably puzzled, she asked sweetly, "Why Damien, whatever do you mean? Have I intimated that you have been anything less than agreeable to live with, gracious, or honorable?"

A pained expression flitted across Damien's face before he warned, "Do not play games with me, Jessica. I feel bloody awful, and I have very little patience this morning. You know I can make you tell me what I want to know."

Having Damien's attention in spite of his poor disposition, she decided to take advantage of the opening he provided. Jessica sat back in her chair and ran her finger thoughtfully along the edge of the table as she searched for a way to begin. The best way, she decided, was to be direct.

"I have a brother," she began. "He is younger than I, too young to shield himself completely from Margaret's influence. He inherited the title of Earl of Braeleigh upon my father's death, and several months ago, we learned he also inherited a substantial land holding in America. But he is Margaret's ward. She has control of everything—the money, the estate, and him."

"Fascinating," the Duke murmured.

Jessica glanced down the table and caught his icy gaze. Her family was not his most favorite topic of conversation. Undaunted, she pressed on.

"Could you do something about the situation? Could you take over as my brother's guardian?"

Disbelief registered immediately upon Damien's face. He responded with an incredulous question of his own. "You are asking me to become involved with *another* member of your family? Have you no sense of justice, Jessica? Or is this further punishment for what I have done?"

Jessica answered him with only one word. "Please?"

Damien's face closed over his emotions. Sardonically, he asked, "You would trust me more than your own, dear stepmother?"

Jessica answered coldly, "I would not trust Margaret to tell me the correct time of day."

Damien did not answer right away. He sat staring at her for so long that Jessica began to fidget in her chair. What was going on behind those cold, green eyes? she wondered.

Finally, his voice stony, he said, "I can do nothing for your brother."

He rose, apparently deciding the conversation was at an end. Jessica had one more thing to say.

"Then I will write to him."

Damien stopped dead and turned to her. "You may write to the Devil for all I care!"

Jessica watched him stride angrily from the room. Stupid! she chided herself. She should have known he would want nothing to do with her family. It had been her deep concern for Jason's welfare that had prompted her to make the request in the first place, but it had been too soon to ask. Now, she was not certain if she had spoiled her chances of ever getting Jason away from Margaret.

Well, at least she could write to him. She had refrained from writing to him since before her wedding out of deference to Damien's feelings. She had sent him only one, short note informing him of her marriage. Now, she would write to him regularly, whether Damien liked it or not. She only hoped that Margaret would not intercept the letters.

Chapter Twenty-five

It was three days before Jessica was able to write to Jason. A myriad of tasks occupied her as she learned how to cope with the running of a house as large as Wyndham. Having finally found enough time in which to compose her letter, she sat at a small desk in the morning room, a cozy sitting room situated at the southeastern corner of the house.

She had just begun her letter when she heard a commotion outside the room. A short time later, a discreet knock on the door heralded the entrance of Hobbs.

"Begging Your Grace's pardon," he began. "The men have captured the poacher."

Puzzled that the majordomo should be telling her and not Damien, Jessica commented, "That is good news, Hobbs. Has His Grace been told?"

"His Grace is still out searching the grounds."

Jessica finally realized why Hobbs had come to her. Damien, who had gone out with several of his men to hunt down the poachers, would not return until late that evening, and the butler wished to know what to do with the culprit.

"Well, then, tie him up and keep him under guard in the stables. His Grace will deal with him when he returns."

Hobbs discreetly cleared his throat. "Begging Your

Grace's pardon, but I believe you would prefer to deal with this yourself."

Intrigued by the butler's suggestion, Jessica tossed down her pen and followed him outside. A group of Damien's retainers stood about a small, bedraggled fellow. As Jessica approached, they parted to allow her through. A pair of dead rabbits lay at the poacher's feet.

"What is the problem, Hobbs?" Jessica demanded. "You caught the fellow red-handed."

At her words, the poacher raised his eyes and stared sullenly at Jessica. She was taken aback to see a smudged, pixie face glaring at her.

"Why, it's a girl!" Jessica exclaimed.

"Ain't she the smart one," the poacher said sarcastically.

The footman, who had been holding the girl by the arm, gave her a shake. "Watch yer mouth, wench. This here's the Duchess o' Wyndham."

"Well, la-di-dah," the girl sneered.

Before the footman could throttle the young girl for her insolence, Jessica held up her hand to stop him. "What is your name?" she asked her. "Where's your family?"

The girl just hunched her shoulders and stared at the ground. Jessica glanced around at all the hostile faces of the men and suddenly had an inspiration. Putting her arm about the thin little shoulders, she said gently, "Come sit over here with me. We'll talk, just the two of us."

The girl resisted at first, but then she allowed Jessica to lead her to the step before the door. They sat down together as if they were equals.

"I bet you're hungry," Jessica observed. Without waiting for the girl's reply, she said, "Hobbs, get something to eat for this child."

Hobbs quickly brought a plate of food, and Jessica

watched the girl devour it. When she had finished, Jessica managed to drag out of her that her name was Mae, and she and her grandmother lived alone. Mae was the provider for both of them.

"Well, Mae, how would you like to come to work for me?"

The girl looked at her suspiciously.

"You can work in the kitchen. We will pay you fair wages, and enough food to feed yourself and your grandmother."

"Will I have to live here?" Mae asked.

"No, you can sleep at your grandmother's, but you must be back here every morning to do your chores." Jessica watched Mae think over her offer. Finally the girl nodded. "Good. Hobbs, get Mae cleaned up and put her to work in the kitchen. She is going to work for us."

Jessica watched with amusement as Hobbs distastefully told the girl to follow him. She had to hurry to keep up, and Jessica heard Mae complain, " 'Ey, you ol' coot, wait up!" With a smile, Jessica returned to the house. Her letter to Jason was forgotten.

Damien did not arrive home until much later that night. Jessica had not felt like eating alone in the dining room, so she had skipped dinner altogether. He found her at the large, worn, kitchen table with a crusty loaf of bread, a hunk of cheese, cold ham, and a large dish of strawberries spread out before her. She had poured wine into a crystal goblet.

"A feast!" he exclaimed as he sat beside her at the table. He looked exhausted.

Jessica smiled at him in greeting and poured him some wine. "Did you catch the poachers, Your Grace?" she asked.

He shook his head in disgust. "No. But I understand from Hobbs that you were quite successful." Damien placed his hand over hers and said, "You did well today, Jessica. I am very proud of you." He lifted her hand to his lips and kissed her fingertips.

She blushed at his praise. "Thank you," she murmured, "but I only did what I felt was right."

Damien looked at her earnestly. "Jessica, I . . ." he began, then stopped and shook his head.

Jessica waited for him to finish, but he stared instead at his glass of wine and said nothing. Her eyes widened as she thought she saw a hint of color rise across his cheekbones.

"Damien?" she questioned.

"Have a strawberry," he offered as he quickly reached out and placed the bowl of fruit before her.

Puzzled at his strange behavior, Jessica did as he suggested and decided not to press him. Diplomatically changing the subject, she began discussing her plans for a new garden. The rest of the meal was spent in pleasant conversation as they discussed the events of the day. Jessica cherished each moment, for companionable times with her husband were very rare.

They retired early that night, for they were both exhausted from the day's events. Damien left her at the door to her room with a chaste kiss upon her cheek. Jessica felt that a permanent, warm glow would forever claim that spot. Reluctantly, she closed her door as she entered her room alone.

She climbed into bed expecting to fall asleep immediately, but sleep would not come. As she lay there, staring up into the darkness, she remembered the unfinished letter to Jason that she had left in the morning room. She decided that since she could not sleep anyway, she would finish it, so it could be sent with the morning post.

When she reached the desk in the morning room, she discovered to her dismay that the letter was missing. She searched around the desk, in the drawer, on the floor, but it was not there. She thought perhaps one of the maids had taken it to her room, so she quickly returned there and began to search frantically. With Damien being so agreeable, the last thing she needed was for him to find the letter and once more be reminded of her family.

As she searched, the door to the sitting swung open and Damien stood in its space. Never had he used that door to enter her room. Something in his manner made her heart begin to pound in fear. He wore a long, dark red dressing gown belted at the waist. She had an uncomfortable feeling that he wore nothing beneath it. He held up a piece of paper. Jessica recognized it as her letter to Jason.

"Is this what you were looking for?" he asked quietly.

Disregarding her initial intuition, relief washed over her at his mild tone. "Oh, you have it," she said. She started toward him to retrieve it.

"Aren't you being rather careless about where you leave letters to your lover?" he asked.

Jessica stopped dead. "What do you mean?"

"Your lover," Damien repeated. He enunciated each syllable clearly. He glanced down at the paper in his hand and read:

Dearest Jason,

I miss you so very much. I wish you could be here with me, now, but I know that is not possible. Perhaps, soon, I will be able to come to you, and we can spend time together, laughing and riding together the way we did before my marriage . . .

He looked up at her. His face was stony. "How touching," he commented sarcastically.

Jessica was devastated at the sordid meaning he

350

read into her innocent words. Damien's manner now was quite evident. He had murder on his mind. She began to back away.

Shaking her head, she told him, "You don't understand."

"I think I understand too well," he grated out. He began to stalk her as she backed away. "You have betrayed me, Jessica. You deny me the right to your bed as your husband, yet you pine to be with your lover."

"No, I—"

"Do not deny it. You have written it with your own hand."

Jessica had backed up into the side of the bed. Damien was so close he only had to reach out his hand to keep her where she was. The look on his face was terrible—a mixture of barely controlled rage and horrible hurt.

"Damien, do not do this," she said quietly.

"No?" he retorted with a humorless laugh. "Why not? Can't you face your own deviousness? What does your lover do to you, Jessica? Does he shower your mouth with hot kisses? Does he caress your body to the point of forgetfulness? Does he excite you to ecstasy?" His voice became deceptively seductive.

Jessica stood shaking her head, her eyes wide and dark in her face. She could not believe what was happening.

Finally, she cried out, "No! No! None of those things!" Then realizing she had come tantamount to admitting she had a lover, she bit her bottom lip. She looked as guilty as the Devil.

"No?" Damien repeated softly. "Then what redeeming qualities does he have?" His eyes narrowed suddenly. "Perhaps none. Would he have chased into France to rescue you? Would he have tended your wounds and nursed you back to health? I doubt it.

Would he have paid a king's ransom, as I did, to get you back? I have paid more for you than this fop probably has to his name. Why have you whored for him?"

Jessica turned white at his words. "I have whored for no one," she whispered hoarsely.

"Then perhaps it is time you did," he told her coldly. "I have paid for you twice and received nothing in return. It is about time that I collected on my investment. How well did Margaret teach you the ways of a whore?"

Jessica could take no more of his verbal abuse. With her appeal to his reason ignored, her hurt turned to rage. He had no right to say such things! Her eyes shooting sparks, she raised her hand to slap his tormenting face.

With lightning speed, he caught her wrist. No more would this woman torment him. He would take her and be done with it. The pain and betrayal he felt upon finding the letter blinded him to see anything beyond what he felt. Her soft words, her denial, her appeals only made him more aware of what she was: Margaret's whore. He thought by marrying her he would find some peace from the hurt that gnawed inside him, but he had been so wrong. His marriage had been a sham from the beginning. Now, all he wanted was revenge.

They stood as statues for several heartbeats. Jessica's surprise at finding her hand stopped made her raise her eyes to his. Morbidly fascinated, she saw a cold rage in their depths, a rage directed at her, and through her at her family. Frightened, yet at the same time unafraid, she met his eyes. She watched as if hypnotized as they changed color from cool green, cold and hard as two emeralds, to a darker shade like that of the sea. His icy rage had turned to a heated desire.

With a gentle shove, he pushed her onto the bed. Leaning over her, he took both her wrists in one hand and pinned them above her head. She closed her eyes, finally able to break the bonds of his gaze. She felt his weight on the bed as he knelt over her.

Jessica swallowed in fear. Her breasts rose and fell with her quickening breaths. This was not how she wished to break the bargain. She did not want him to use her in his anger. She wanted his love, not his hate. Yet, she remained still, unmoving. There were no other weapons left to use in the battle for his love. Time had run out.

Damien's eyes raked over her body. Even in his rage, her seductiveness spoke to him. She stirred him as no other woman ever had. The thought of another man touching her drove him to the brink of madness. She was his and belonged to no other. This night he would take her as his own, brand her, possess her. He would make sure that, always, she would remember it was he who introduced her to womanhood, and he who could make her reach heights of ecstasy.

Jessica felt his lips on hers, rough and demanding. She tried to keep her mouth tightly closed, but it was no use. His tongue prodded and probed until she could do nothing else but part her lips. After gaining his small victory, he became gentler, stroking, nibbling, until she found herself responding to him.

His free hand roamed beneath her robe then slipped under her nightrail until it found the mound of her breast. With his thumb, he teased the pink tip, causing it to harden and swell. Jessica shuddered in pleasure.

The assault on her body was devastating. What she had thought was going to be rape was turning into a seduction she had no power to repulse. He knew what aroused her, what made her mindless, and he used his knowledge ruthlessly. His hand moved over her body and awakened sensations she thought she would never feel again.

His lips moved from her mouth to her neck to her throat to her shoulder, and left a trail of tiny butterfly kisses, making her breath catch in her throat. Somehow, her robe had fallen open and her nightrail had come unfastened, exposing a rosy-tipped breast. His mouth found the spot where his hand had been. A wonderful tingling ran through her body. A sound, somewhere between a moan and a sigh, escaped her lips.

War raged in her brain. Part of her wanted him to stop, afraid of what the aftermath of this assault would be; part of her wanted him to go on forever. Jessica could not act on either decision. She was helpless in his hands. It was as if he had cast some sort of spell over her. She could not break away under her own volition.

Damien's mouth moved back up to her neck. He nibbled at the lobe of her ear. Her head slipped to the side allowing him full access to the spot.

"Do you wish me to stop, Jessica?" he whispered.

The sound of his voice brought her back to reality. The passion in her cooled. Was this the way she wished to end the bargain? she wondered. He was giving her a way out of the situation.

With her eyes closed and her head turned away as if already trying to escape, she whispered, "Yes."

There was a pause before she felt him begin to move away. His weight shifted on the bed as he began to straighten. A feeling of tremendous loneliness washed through her. In that moment, she knew that if he left, she might never get the chance to love him again. She might lose him forever. It was a bet she did not want to lose. She had to take the gamble.

She opened her eyes and turned her head to face him. With a hand on his shoulder, she stopped him

354

before he rose from the bed. Mild surprise showed on his face, and was there not a hint of hope?

"Don't go. Stay with me."

She slid her hand to the back of his neck and pulled him down. Recklessly, her mouth met his, this time inviting him to taste its sweetness. Her fingers curled in the hair at the back of his head, and her other hand moved down his back as she felt the play of muscles under his skin.

She wished she knew what he was thinking, why he had given her the opportunity to stop. He had been enraged with her. He had called her a whore. Yet, he had allowed her the chance to keep the bargain. Why? If he wanted, she would be his whore, but for her, it would be a venting of her love for him.

His hands moved over her freely now, touching the silkiness of her skin. Her nightrail was pulled down to her waist. Both breasts were exposed to his warm gaze and hot touch. He tasted first one, then the other. A heated glow spread through her body.

Damien stood up suddenly and pulled Jessica up with him. Taking her nightrail in both hands, he ripped it to its hem. It fell to the floor about her ankles.

"These are for virgins and old maids," he growled. "You are a woman, and I will not see you in them again."

A blush warmed her cheeks at her sudden nakedness before him. She felt self-conscious with the slight roundness of her belly from her pregnancy. Half turning away from his gaze, she covered herself shyly.

"Don't turn away, Jessica. I want to look at you."

Very aware of his eyes on her, she slowly turned back to face him. He did not take his eyes from her face as he dropped his own robe to the floor. It was as she had thought; he wore nothing beneath it.

Jessica could not tear her eyes away from his body,

the broad expanse of his chest, the muscular sleekness of his hips and thighs, his proud manhood. Taking her by the shoulders, he pulled her against him. He placed a warm, demanding kiss on her lips.

Jessica felt the coiled desire in him. The heat from his body matched her own. His hard thighs pressed against hers; his manhood throbbed along her hip.

"You are a witch, Jessica," he whispered against her mouth. "I want you so badly, I ache."

"Take me, Damien," she whispered back, as her arms tightened around him. "Make me your wife."

In one smooth movement, he scooped her up and placed her gently on the bed. He ran his hand the length of her body, from her shoulder, over her breast, to her slightly mounded belly, to the wellspring of her womanhood. Jessica shuddered and moaned softly. As he stretched out beside her, her own hands travelled over Damien's body and felt the hardness of him. His breath rasped in his throat. She arched toward him as she writhed in her passion. Her shyness disappeared in her desire and she reached for him. She wanted to pleasure him as he was able to pleasure her. He groaned at her touch.

"I need you now, Witch."

Pulling her on top of him, he positioned her gently as he entered her. Jessica's eyes opened in surprise and delight at the wonderful sensations he created. He began to move and she caught his rhythm. They moved as one until a wild burst went surging through them both. Jessica felt as if her world were coming to a spectacular end, that her life's energy was reaching an apex and then being sucked out of her. With a tiny sigh, she collapsed on top of Damien and felt her world come slowly back into focus.

They lay quietly together, gathering their strength after the storm. Jessica rested her head on Damien's shoulder, and he kept his arm about her and held her close. Yet, there was still something between them. She felt it like an invisible wall. He was not totally beside her. A part of him was off wrestling with a demon. Finally, he spoke.

"Does this Jason mean so very much to you?" he asked.

Jessica was taken aback at his question. It was not what she had expected after their lovemaking. She hesitated before she answered.

"Yes," she told him slowly. "He means a great deal to me."

Damien was silent for a moment. When he spoke again, his voice was subdued. "I will not keep you from him, if you truly love him. I only ask that when our child comes, you do not cause it any hardship or distress because of the situation."

Jessica was stunned at his words. Did he despise her so much he would allow her to have a lover? Did that mean he would also take lovers? If that were so, perhaps her plan to gain his love would go awry after all. Even so, she decided one thing had to be set right, and that was his idea of who he thought Jason was.

She sat up and turned to face him. "Damien, Jason is my brother, not my lover."

Damien stared at her as if she had suddenly spoken Arabic. With a jerk, he rose from the bed and went to stand before the window where he gazed out into the night. He stood there, unmoving and silent, for so long that Jessica became uneasy. Was he so furious with her that he could not stand the sight of her? The words that he finally uttered were so unexpected that at first she did not comprehend what he was saying.

"I have been a fool, Jessica," he said. "I had forgotten about your brother. When I saw the letter, I was furious. All I could think of was that you had a lover someplace, and yet, you had married me for some demented reason of Margaret's doing and forced me to accept this bloody bargain. Here you were writing letters to some fop, and I could not even touch you. I was so jealous I could not see what you had told me only days before.

"I do not know the reason for the bargain, although I can probably guess. I can not undo what has already happened, but if you wish to renew the bargain between us, I will agree. Perhaps, in the future, you will come to have some small fondness for me."

He turned finally to face her as she sat on the bed. "I hope you can forgive me for being such a cad."

Tears streamed down Jessica's face as she listened to his words. It was the closest he had ever come to telling her that he cared for her.

"Oh, Damien!" she exclaimed as she slid quickly from the bed and went to stand before him. "Don't torture yourself for something not entirely your fault. There is nothing to forgive. We were both wrong." She put her arms around him and gazed up into his face. "Forget the bargain. It was a stupid idea anyway. I forced you into it to protect myself because I thought you despised me and were marrying me only because of the child. I know now that is not true." Shyly, she lowered her eyes and studiously examined a spot in the middle of his chest. "I love you."

Damien became absolutely still, then with disbelief in his voice, he asked, "What did you say?"

Jessica smiled up at him. "I said, 'I love you!' "

Damien gathered her close and buried his face in her hair. "God's blood!" he whispered. "I never thought I would hear you say that. I have treated you so badly. I thought you hated me and could not bear to have me touch you. That is why you forced the bargain on me. I think I have loved you from the

358

first time I saw you at Madame's, but I was too stupid to realize it or too arrogant to admit it. I was so blind."

Jessica giggled happily and leaned back in his arms. She touched his cheek with her fingertips and gazed lovingly into those green eyes.

"Oh, Damien," she sighed as she hugged him. Then she giggled again and grinned impishly. "You were never blind; you were always ogling me. But I will agree to the arrogant part."

Damien played at being offended. "Ogling you! How could I not help but stare when you always wore those clinging, low-cut gowns to Madame's? My imagination would run wild as I thought of all the things I could do if you were wearing nothing at all."

Jessica smiled an invitation. "I am not wearing anything at all, now."

He ran his hand down her back as if feeling for something. "Hmm," he murmured. "You are right." He grinned. "I guess my imagination doesn't have to work so hard."

He swung her up into his arms and carried her to the bed. Placing her down gently, he suggested, "Shall we see what my imagination can come up with?"

"Mmmm," she purred. Her eyes travelled down his body. "It looks like your imagination has come up with something very useful."

Damien chuckled as he lowered his mouth to hers. He revelled in her compliance. She was his completely, and no one could ever take her away from him again.

Chapter Twenty-six

The days passed quickly for Jessica. The summer months were pleasant ones, for she was happier now than she had ever been. She and Damien spent hours together riding in his curricle, walking hand in hand through his estate, talking about everything, frolicking like two children, or sitting together in companionable silence. Damien was solicitous of her health, and she found him hovering nearby if she needed any help.

There was only one dark smudge on this whole, bright picture. The letters from Jason were becoming fewer, and his tone was different. It was not something she could point to specifically and say, There, you see? He is having a terrible time. But she knew it was there. She discussed her worries with Damien. He told her again, though in much gentler tones than the last time, that there was nothing he could do for the boy. Margaret was Jason's legal guardian, and she had the final say on his upbringing.

Jessica stood facing her husband, now, as frustration made lines appear between her brows.

"Well, why don't we abduct him, then?" she demanded. "I know he would be much happier here, with us."

Damien smiled indulgently. He had had this conversation with his wife several times. "I'm sure he would be much happier, but we can't just ride out to Braeleigh and take the boy," he told her. "Don't you think Margaret would come after him? And if she did, she would have the legal right to take him back. The law frowns on kidnapping."

Jessica walked aimlessly around the room in her frustration. Clasping her hands before her, she stared sightlessly out upon the lawn.

"You are right, of course," she reluctantly agreed. Her mood changed from one of frustration to depression. "I don't think I shall ever see him again." Her voice was wavery, on the verge of tears. "I'm afraid Margaret will change him into a cruel monster, who'll care only for himself and his money and nothing of others."

Damien came up behind her and turned her around to face him. He enfolded her in his arms and held her tightly. As they stood together, an idea began to form in his mind.

"There is one way that we could force Margaret to give him up," he said thoughtfully.

"Tell me," she demanded, eager to hear what plan Damien had in mind.

"I might be able to have her declared unfit to be your brother's guardian and have you named in her place."

"Oh, Damien!" Jessica exclaimed as hope returned to her. "Do you really think you could?"

Damien smiled at her obvious trust in his ability. He brushed his lips across her brow, then became serious once more.

"I can't promise that it will come about," he warned. "It will take a long time, if it ever occurs. All I can do right now is make some inquiries and get the legal work started."

"But at least that would be something!" she protested.

"It will mean I will have to travel to London," he said. "I will have to be gone almost a week."

"Oh," Jessica said, her face showing her disappointment. "You mean I can't go with you?"

Damien shook his head. "There is nothing I would like more than to have you with me, my love, but it would not be healthy for you to be in the city right now, not while you are carrying our child. You will be much more comfortable here, where it is cooler. You're too precious to me. I do not want anything happening to you."

Reluctantly, Jessica agreed. "All right. I'll stay here."

Damien gave her a small squeeze and held her. "Don't be sad, love. I'll try not to be gone too long." He tilted her chin up with a gentle finger. "I will miss you very much."

The following morning, Jessica stood beside him in the early morning mist as he sat his horse. Resting her hand upon his knee, she gazed up at her husband.

"Hurry home, Damien," she told him huskily. "I shall miss you terribly."

Damien placed his hand over hers and smiled warmly. "I will be back as soon as I can."

He touched her cheek, wheeled his horse, cantered down the drive. Jessica watched as long as he was in sight, then, sighing, she went into the house. She missed Damien already.

Five days after Damien's departure, she was sitting in the morning room and embroidering a tiny jacket for the baby. She was restless, and she could not get the stitches even and straight. With a sigh of frustration, she threw down the jacket on the settee beside her and wandered about the room. Stopping before the window, she noted the clouds gathering. Thunder rumbled ominously in the distance.

It would be two days, at least, before Damien's return, and that fact did not lighten her spirits any. Having kept busy, she had done reasonably well in fighting off the depression of loneliness. That morning, she had awakened with an uneasy feeling, but had decided it was only because she had not slept well. The babe's active movements had kept her awake during the night.

A light tap came at the door heralding the entrance of Hobbs. She turned, wondering what problem he had encountered that he could not handle.

"Excuse me, Your Grace," he began. "A letter was delivered for you." He held out a silver tray on which was a rumpled, stained envelope.

Thinking perhaps it might be from Damien, she quickly took the letter and opened it. She read:

Dear Jess,

This will be my last letter to you. I do not know if you received all the others, for Margaret always took them from me to post. Sometimes, she even told me what to write. I asked Dudley, the dairyman, to post this for me so that I would be sure that you received it.

Margaret is sending me away to America with her uncle. She says I should see the land that I own there. I do not believe her. I think she does not want me around. We are supposed to be leaving in a fortnight. I have tried to run away, but she has always caught me. She told me the next time I try, she will lock me in the attic. Please, do not let her send me to America, Jess. I am so afraid.

Your brother,
Jason

P.S. I will understand if you can not help.

Jessica sank down onto a chair. Despair covered her like a shroud. How could Margaret send a young boy to America? What about his schooling? What about Braeleigh? Jessica knew the answer to that last question. Margaret wanted Braeleigh to herself. She had tired of raising the young Earl. Jessica raised her head, and her eyes became thoughtful as an idea began to form.

She rang for Hobbs, and when he appeared, she said to him, "Hobbs, I am travelling to Braeleigh. Prepare the coach for me."

Hobbs looked only vaguely surprised at the request of his mistress, but he said evenly, "Very well, Your Grace. Will there be anything else?"

"No. Yes. I will want strong footmen, men who will not mind a fight."

Hobbs bowed and disappeared to do her bidding. Then Jessica went to find Donny and change her clothes for travel.

As Donny helped Jessica change, the little woman let her know how she felt.

"Ye be crazy t'go there with that woman about," Donny told her mistress. "Ye ought t'wait for His Grace t'come back. He'll take care of it for ye."

"I can't wait, Donny," Jessica contradicted. "Jason's letter said they were leaving in a fortnight, and Margaret might change her mind and send him away earlier. I have already waited too long."

"What about the babe?" Donny tried. "Have ye no thought for him?"

"Donny, I am not an invalid. The babe will survive, and so will I. You may come with me or not, as you wish, but I am going to Jason, and nothing is going to stop me." Softening, she put her hand on the woman's arm. "I have to go, Donny. Jason is my brother. I am his only hope of being saved from Margaret."

Donny merely grunted her disapproval. She knew when Jessica spoke like that, there was nothing that could change her mind.

When Jessica climbed into the carriage, she found Donny already seated. A mischievous smile curved her lips, but she said nothing to her nanny.

Donny caught her smile and grumbled, "Well, ye didn't think I would let ye go into that woman's lair alone, did ye?"

The driver cracked his whip, and they started off. The ride to Braeleigh would take them most of the day. They would not arrive until late afternoon. Jessica remained very quiet for most of the trip. She stared out the window at the passing scenery and unconsciously twisted and worried a handkerchief she held in her hand.

She wondered who Margaret's mysterious uncle might be whom her brother had mentioned in his letter. She had never heard of any relatives of her stepmother. She decided it was probably just some story that the woman had devised to tell Jason.

As they came closer to their destination, Jessica became more anxious. Several times she fretted to the driver they were going too slow. The driver and footmen sympathized with their normally mildly mannered mistress, for they knew something had to be upsetting her terribly for her to be so critical. The driver urged the horses forward with great diligence in order to assuage her worry.

As the coach finally came to a stop in front of Jessica's childhood home, she scrambled out of the coach and almost shut the door on Donny.

"I be comin' in with ye, too," Donny informed her. "I'll not be sittin' out here like a lump while that child is still with that woman."

"No, Donny," Jessica told her. "It will be better if you remain out here with the coach. If I can get Jason away, then I will send him out to you. If something happens to me to detain me, I will meet you at the inn."

Jessica did not wait for any argument from Donny, but left the coach as soon as she finished speaking. Walking boldly up to the front door, she let the knocker fall. She heard it echo inside the hall. Soon, the door opened to reveal, not Barclay, the majordomo who had been with the family since she could remember, but a man she did not recognize.

"Yes?" he queried as he looked down his nose at this young woman.

"Where is Barclay?" Jessica inquired.

"Barclay is no longer employed by Her Ladyship," he informed her haughtily.

Jessica raised her chin and disdainfully brushed past him. "You may inform Her Ladyship that the Duchess of Wyndham is here to see her," she said regally.

The majordomo sniffed primly at such boldness. Jessica ignored him and started toward the salon.

Stopping just before she entered the room when she realized the man had not moved, she prompted coldly, "Well? Will you tell your mistress I am here, or shall I have to find her myself?"

The man bowed, then hurried off to find Margaret. Jessica waited until the man's footsteps had died away before she went in search of Jason. Just as she was about to dash out the door, she heard quick footsteps and the rustle of a skirt coming across the hall. She mouthed a silent oath as she hurriedly sat down in one of the chairs and acted as if she had been waiting for hours.

Margaret arrived, slightly breathless, at the doorway. Her calculating glance landed on Jessica, seated nonchalantly on the settee, as she sauntered into the room.

"Well, well, what is this? Some sort of charade? You are playing at being a duchess now?" she asked sarcastically.

"No charade, Margaret," Jessica answered her stonily. "You know whom I married. You were certainly paid enough by him."

"Ah, yes, I seem to recall now that someone did want to marry you. I could not imagine why the powerful Duke of Wyndham would want to marry such a little slut as yourself, but I suppose you enticed him into your bed. I see you are quite fertile, aren't you?"

"I did not come to trade insults with you, Margaret. I came to see my brother." Jessica could not allow her temper to get out of control if she wished to accomplish what she had come to do.

"Really? Jason is not here at the moment."

Jessica began to panic. What if she was already too late? She forced herself to remain calm.

"Not here?" she asked. "Where is he?"

Margaret waved a hand airily. "Oh, he is out having a riding lesson, and then he was going on a picnic," she answered carelessly. "Or perhaps he was going to visit a friend. It is so difficult to keep track of children."

Jessica knew Margaret was lying. The woman had always kept a very close watch on her brother. She could not imagine Margaret suddenly changing her ways. However, she decided to play along.

"When do you expect him to return?" she asked innocently.

"I really could not say," Margaret answered vaguely. "It really would not be worth waiting for him. He might decide to spend the night with his friend."

"Margaret, I did not travel all the way from Wyndham just to turn around and go back again without seeing my brother." Jessica stood. "I believe I will stay the night and wait for him. You may have my old room made ready. Donny is out in the coach. Would you tell your servants to inform her of my plans? I would like some tea and biscuits, and then I believe I will rest before dinner."

Jessica hoped her imperious manner would fool her stepmother. At the moment, she was feeling anything but imperious. The woman frightened her a great deal. She wandered to the window and looked out, not really seeing anything, but rather, waiting for Margaret's next move.

There was silence from Margaret's side of the room for a moment, then she spoke. "My, my, haven't we become the high and mighty duchess?" she sneered. "Did your new husband teach you those manners? You certainly could not have picked them up in the gutters of London."

Jessica swung around to face her stepmother. "You would know about the gutters of London, Margaret, for I seem to recall that you were the one who told me of the establishment of Madame du Barré."

Margaret laughed evilly. "A word or two about an exciting, seductive place dropped into an innocent ear was all it took to pull Miss High-and-Mighty down from her lily white pedestal. You were so easy to influence, Jessica my dear, that it was almost no fun at all."

Jessica gasped at Margaret's revelation of her manipulation.

Margaret laughed again. "Oh, yes, my plan to get rid of you worked so well." She frowned. "But then you met this duke and landed on your feet again. I will have to think of something else."

"I will leave as soon as you let me see Jason," Jessica told her.

"I have no intention of having you leave, dear Jes-

368

sica," Margaret smiled. "Of course you will see your darling Jason. I may even allow you to travel to America with him." Margaret gazed at Jessica thoughtfully. "Well, we shall decide that later." Margaret took her by the arm.

"Let go of me, Margaret." Jessica pulled out of her grasp.

Margaret's eyes narrowed. "I can call my footmen, if you wish, Jessica. They will not be so gentle with you." She waited until she saw in Jessica's eyes that she would acquiesce. Again taking her arm, she led her out of the room. "You did say that you wished to rest? I have just the place."

Margaret propelled Jessica up the stairs and down the hall to the door of a closet where linens were kept. Unlocking the door, she began to push Jessica through the opening.

"You can not keep me here, Margaret," Jessica warned. "Donny and my footmen are outside. My husband knows where I am. He will be arriving to-night." She knew Damien was still in London, but she hoped the bluff would work.

"Donny and your footmen are well taken care of by now," Margaret told her. "As for your husband, we will deal with him when he arrives. I should not think that will be too difficult."

She gave Jessica a shove. Jessica landed on a stack of blankets. The door closed behind her, and she heard the key click in the lock.

"Have a good rest, my sweet!" Margaret called out.

Chapter Twenty-seven

Jessica heard Margaret's evil laughter float away down the hall, then there was silence. The closet was as dark as a coffin; she could not see a thing except a small crack of light under the door. After making herself comfortable, she sat and contemplated her predicament.

She had accomplished nothing by coming to Braeleigh. Locked up in a closet, she still had not seen Jason and might never see him again. Her only hope was Damien. The bluff to Margaret also had been a voicing of her own hope. Having left word with Hobbs on her whereabouts, she could only pray Damien would return early. The chances of that happening were slim, but it was all she had.

For the moment, she had to try to get out of the closet. Pulling out a hairpin, she slid over to the door and tried to force the lock. Several times, she had to stop when she heard footsteps approach, but finally, by the time the light under the door had begun to turn dim, she heard the lock click open.

Jessica crept out of the closet and carefully closed and locked the door behind her. A clock in the downstairs hall chimed the hour of eight. She made her way stealthily down the hall to Jason's room.

She had little hope of finding him there, but she thought that there might be a clue to his whereabouts.

She arrived, unseen, at his room and entered. The room was full of shadows, but she dared not light a lamp for fear of being discovered. She knew the room as well as her own, and she headed straight for the wardrobe. His clothes were all there, as much as she could tell. Next, she checked the cupboard next to the bed. His favorite books were still there. Jessica knew that Jason would not go anywhere without taking his books with him. She deduced her brother was still in the house or about the estate somewhere. Margaret must have him locked away. She did not wish to consider any other possibility.

Jessica scanned the room for anything unusual, but everything seemed in its place. Sitting down on the edge of the bed, she tried to think of places where Margaret could be hiding him.

As she sat there, a small sound came to her ears. It seemed to come from behind the wardrobe, yet it was not in the room. She walked over to the spot and listened. It was a voice, singing. It was Jason!

She dared not call out to him for fear of being discovered. She had to get to him. She knew he could not be in the next room, because the walls were too thick to allow sound to carry. Suddenly, she remembered. There was a secret room between Jason's room and the room next to it. She used to play in it when she was young. It was an excellent hiding place. There was only one way to reach it, and that was from a garret room on the top floor.

Jessica hurried to the door and opened it cautiously. She checked to be sure the hall was empty, then she scurried quietly to the narrow set of stairs that led up to the top floor. They looked dark and foreboding. Taking a deep breath, she began to climb.

There was a door across the top of the stairs. Jessica pushed against it, and it creaked open. She stepped out into a labyrinth of small hallways and tiny rooms. At one time, these had been servants quarters, but they were no longer used. As she glanced about, she remembered the opening to the secret room was in the floor of a minuscule room to her left.

Feeling her way in the almost complete darkness, it took her several tries to find the right room. When she did, she saw a rectangle of light flicker in the floor. A ladder, the only way down into the secret room, lay beside it.

Jessica sank to her knees beside the opening and peered down. Jason sat on the floor with his back to the wall. There was no table, no chair, no bed. There was one short candle for light.

"Jason," Jessica called softly.

Jason stopped his singing but did not look up.

"Jason," she called again. "It's Jessica."

He jumped up and peered into the gloom above his head. "Jess?" he queried. "Is that really you?"

Jessica's throat constricted at his voice. He was trying to sound brave, but could not completely hide his fear. She smiled widely, hiding her own flood of emotions.

"Of course, it's me, silly," she said with forced gaiety. "I'll lower the ladder down to you."

Dragging the ladder to the edge of the opening, as quietly as she could, she let it down to her brother. As soon as it touched the floor, he scrambled up. The brother and sister hugged each other tightly for a moment, then Jessica held him away from her.

"Are you all right?" she asked. "Has Margaret

hurt you?"

Jason shook his head. "No, I'm fine, really, Jess. I'm just hungry."

Jessica laughed softly. "Then I guess you are all right. I can't get you anything to eat right now, though. We have to get away from here. How long have you been down in that room?"

"Since Margaret caught me giving the dairyman the letter I wrote to you," he said. "I thought I was being really careful. I slipped out of the house when he delivered some eggs a few days ago, and I hid in the bushes until he came out. Margaret came into the kitchen to inspect the eggs and saw me give him the letter."

"Well, I'm here to take you back to Wyndham," Jessica assured him. "All we have to do is find Donny and my footmen and leave."

Sounding much more confident than she actually felt, she knew there was little hope of any of them getting back to Wyndham. She chided herself for being so foolish as to think she could have walked in and just taken Jason away. Once, again, Margaret's evil nature had disrupted her life.

Quietly, they made their way down the narrow stairs to the floor below. Jessica was relieved to find that the hallway was still empty. Creeping to the top of the grand staircase, they stopped and listened. There were voices coming from the salon.

"We will have to use the back stairway," she whispered.

Just as they were about to turn around and disappear, Margaret emerged from the salon. Their movement caught her eye, and she glanced up. Jessica and Jason hurried to get to the other stairway as they heard Margaret call for her footmen.

Reaching the back stairs, they started down, only to be cut off by a large, forbidding shape at the foot of the stairs. They turned and fled back down the hall. Another large man came from around the corner and stopped their flight. They tried the nearest door, but it was locked. There was nowhere left to run. Jessica stood with her arm about Jason and waited for the two footmen to capture them. A third was just topping the front stairs.

One of the men grabbed Jason and threw him over his shoulder. He carried the boy, kicking and yelling, down the stairs to Margaret. The other two each took one of Jessica's arms and led her roughly down the stairs. Margaret watched the proceedings with a triumphant smile on her lips.

When Jessica had reached the bottom of the stairs, the woman spoke. "I have decided what I will do with you, Jessica. A long time ago, I promised you to Sir Percival Lowry in marriage. I think the time has come to keep that promise."

"Do you forget, Margaret, that I am already married?" Jessica reminded her coldly. "The Duke of Wyndham will not stand idly by and watch me wed to another."

Margaret dismissed the problem with a wave of her hand. "Your Duke will not be around to see it happen. I have a score to settle with him. He will be rather unpleasantly surprised when, and if, he comes to rescue you." She turned to the two thugs holding Jessica. "Bring her into the salon." To Jessica she said, "I have someone here who can not wait to see you again."

Jessica was shoved into the salon behind Margaret. The footman holding Jason followed. As Jessica was brought into the room, she was met by the salacious leer of Sir Percival Lowry.

He approached her and bowed. "My dear Jessica, how pleasant to see you again."

His eyes raked over her voraciously. Reaching

374

out, he took her chin in his flabby hand and tilted her face up to his. Jessica tried to turn away, but his grip was too strong.

"Ah, do not turn away, lovely Jessica," he soothed. "You shall have to get used to my face, for we will be spending much time together."

"I would rather die first," Jessica spat out.

"No, no, not now, my lovely. Not yet," he contradicted. "Perhaps at a later time, when I grow tired of you, but not now. We shall have many hours of pleasure before that time comes."

Jessica jerked her head and was finally able to break his grasp. She kept her face turned away from him.

When Jason saw Sir Percival touch his sister, he renewed his struggles. Kicking and punching, he yelled, "Leave my sister alone! Don't you hurt her!"

The man holding him finally dropped him on the floor. As Jason sprawled at the man's feet, he bent over and put a hand over Jason's mouth. "You keep quiet, brat," he warned, "or you're going to lose your teeth." He held up his fist so Jason could see that he meant it. Jason quieted immediately.

Margaret smiled at the boy. "I would pay attention to him, young man, for I have a great desire to thrash you myself."

"He has done nothing to you, Margaret," Jessica spoke up in her brother's defense. "Leave him alone."

"I do so enjoy the family concern you have for each other," Margaret observed sarcastically. "Isn't it heart warming, Percy?"

Sir Percival grinned his agreement. "Very much so, my dear niece."

Jessica's eyes swung around and held on the ugly visage of Sir Percival. He called Margaret his niece!? Margaret saw her expression and came to stand before her.

"You are surprised, Jessica," she noted. "Yes, Percy is my uncle. He has helped me with several unpleasant tasks. You will be his reward." She smiled, then turned away. As she settled herself on the settee, she announced, "I do think we should make ourselves comfortable while we wait for Jessica's gallant rescuer to appear." To the footmen, she ordered, "Tie those two into chairs."

Jessica and Jason were dragged to chairs across the room from each other and tied to them with drapery cords. Jessica smiled encouragement to Jason. Damien was not due back at Wyndham until the morrow at the very earliest. It would be another day before he could possibly get to Braeleigh. She hoped Margaret would not grow too impatient waiting for him.

Sir Percival hovered near Jessica and was constantly touching her arm or shoulder or neck. His touch made her skin crawl, but she gritted her teeth and pretended not to notice. Jason glared at the man's open pawing of his sister, but she warned him to silence with a shake of her head. She did not want Jason to attract any more punishment.

The footmen left the room. Margaret sat in silence as she sipped at a glass of wine. Sir Percival drank stronger spirits. He sprawled next to Jessica so that he could touch her when he wished, which seemed to be always.

The clock chimed nine o'clock, then ten, then eleven. Jessica became stiff and sore from sitting in the same position for so long. Jason's head drooped, and he dozed.

During the last hour, Margaret had become more fidgety. She crossed and uncrossed her legs; she drummed her fingers on the arm of the settee. Several times, she got up and refilled her glass. She

repeatedly licked her lips and clenched and un-
clenched her hand. Finally, she jumped up and
stalked about the room. Stopping before Jessica, she
stood with her hands on her hips.

"Where is this gallant husband of yours, slut?"
she demanded.

Jessica gazed mildly back at her stepmother. "Are
you getting nervous, Margaret?" she inquired. "Are
you afraid you will not be able to do away with my
husband, as you had my father do away with Damien's brother?"

Margaret's eyes narrowed. "How did you come by
that knowledge?"

Jessica shrugged. "It was no secret my father was
in a duel. When I discovered how the present Duke
of Wyndham came into his title, it was an easy task
to figure out the rest. But I am curious about one
thing."

"Oh? What is that?"

"How could you be so sure that it would be the
Duke who would die in the duel, and not my father?"

A conceited, smug smile crossed Margaret's face.
"That was an easy matter to control. Your father
had scruples. I knew he would not really wish to
kill a boy. I merely had Percy hide in the bushes
with a pistol to ensure that the Duke would not
live."

Jessica's eyes widened in shock. "But that is murder!"

Margaret gave an amused chuckle. "So it is," she
readily agreed. "Percy was not very happy with the
plan, but when I promised him a young, beautiful
wench for his trouble, he agreed to my plan quickly
enough."

Margaret looked with disgust at the snoring figure of Sir Percival. He had passed out from his

large consumption of rum. She gave his leg a kick to waken him.

"Wake up, you old fool!"

"Wh-What? Is he here? Where is he?" he asked foggily.

"He could have come and gone, and you would have slept through it all," Margaret complained. Picking up the half empty bottle beside him, she moved it to a table near the fireplace. "No more rum, Percy, until we have finished with this."

"Why do you wish to kill my husband, Margaret?" Jessica asked. "He has done nothing to you."

"Nothing!" Margaret turned on Jessica. "Nothing, you say? His father caused the ruination of my brother, my family! We were made paupers, and my brother was barred from all the decent clubs in London. We were ostracized by society. It was only because of my friendship with several wealthy men that we were able to live."

Jessica stared at her while she wondered how her father could have been so duped by this woman that he had married her.

"Do not forget to tell her, Margaret, that your brother lost your family's wealth at the gaming tables. That he borrowed from my father, and proceeded to lose that, also."

Margaret swung around, and all eyes came to rest on Damien, who had appeared, it seemed, out of nowhere. He stood nonchalantly just inside the doorway. Jessica thought he had never looked so dangerous, nor so wonderful. He held a sword, its point dipped to the floor at the moment. His eyes turned to Jessica, and a message of love passed between them. Noting that she was unhurt, his glance then moved to Jason.

Margaret regained her composure. "That is a lie," she denied.

Damien shrugged. "If you wish," he answered. "But I still hold the note on several thousand pounds sterling with your brother's signature at the bottom."

Jessica could see Margaret knew Damien told the truth.

"If you are dead, it will not matter any longer," the woman sneered.

Damien's lips twitched as if he were enjoying a private joke. "True," he agreed.

Margaret called her footmen, but none came.

Damien informed her, "You will not receive any help from them, I am afraid. They have suddenly become indisposed."

"You murdered them!" Margaret screeched. Her eyes went wild.

"Hardly," Damien answered.

"They may not be able to help, but I can," Sir Percival spoke.

Since no one had been paying much attention to him, he had pulled a tiny pistol from his pocket. Aimed with precision, against a sword, it would win without question. He levelled the weapon at Damien.

Heaving himself up from his chair, Sir Percival unsteadily approached his intended victim. To do that, he had to pass near the table with the rum. His consumption of spirits was his undoing. Stumbling against the table, he fell, hitting his head on the mantle and knocking himself out. The bottle of rum crashed to the floor, spilled its contents on the hearth, and ran into the fire.

As the rum caught fire, Margaret gave a wild, hysterical laugh. Grabbing a candle from a table near her, she ran with it to a window and set the draperies aflame.

"You will not take me from here!" she cried. "I

am the Lady Margaret! I am wife of the Earl of Braeleigh! All this is mine!"

As everyone watched, dumbfounded, she ran about setting fire to the room. Then, without warning, she dashed past Damien and up the stairs to the second floor. Damien did not bother to go after her, but rather, rushed over to Jessica and loosened her bonds.

"Are you hurt?" he asked anxiously.

Jessica shook her head. "I'm fine. Oh, Damien, I am so glad to see you!"

Damien smiled at her and quickly touched her cheek. "I'm glad to see you, too, love." As he went on loosening the knots which bound her, he complained, "I wish you had waited for me."

"I couldn't wait," she explained. "Jason wrote me a letter saying Margaret was going to send him to America. How did you get in without Margaret's thugs getting you?"

"I had a little help," he explained. "I found Donny and the footmen tied up in the stable. I freed them. Margaret's footmen were sitting in the kitchen. We merely showed them that the wisest thing to do was to leave Margaret's employ."

The fire continued to spread as he finished untying her. Jason gave a shout.

"Look out! Behind you!"

Sir Percival had regained consciousness and was pointing his little pistol at Damien's back. Blood dripped from a gash on his head.

As Damien swung about, Sir Percival sneered, "Not so fast. The wench has been promised to me, and I mean to have her." He wiggled his little pistol. "I will not hesitate to use this. I killed your brother; it will not bother me to kill you."

Damien threw an astonished glance at Jessica.

"It's true," she said. "Margaret had Sir Percival

ide in the bushes during the duel between my fa-her and your brother. When they fired their pistols, ae shot your brother to be sure he was killed. My ather never meant to kill him."

Sir Percival snickered. "It was an easy matter," he gloated. "The young Duke was easy prey. He never uspected foul play. Why should he? He was duel-ing against the honorable Earl of Braeleigh." He notioned with his gun. "Stand away from the vench. She is coming with me."

Raising her chin bravely, Jessica declared, "You vill have to shoot me right here, Sir Percival. I will go nowhere with you."

As Sir Percival's attention was on Jessica, Damien gave his hand a little twist, and his stiletto jumped nto his palm. Like lightening, his hand came up and flung the blade at the man. It hit its mark, piercing Sir Percival's upper arm. He cried out in pain, and the gun slipped from his grasp. Jason was quick to kick it out of reach.

By this time the fire had covered one wall of the room and was threatening to engulf the door. Da-mien removed his coat and placed it over Jessica's head to protect her from the flames and heat. With his arm about her, and another about Jason, he hurried them out the door.

When they were safely outside, Damien had Jes-sica and Jason wait, then he returned to the house. Several agonizing minutes later, he reappeared with Sir Percival. Donny approached with the footmen, and Damien handed the murderer over to his men. Sir Percival would be given over to the authorities and tried.

Damien came to Jessica and put his arm about her. "I could not make it up the stairs to Margaret," he said. "She had piled draperies and linen at the top of the stairs and set them alight."

Jessica, Damien, Jason, and the others stood an watched the house burn. There was nothing the could do to prevent the fire from spreading. It ha become too large. It had taken on a life of its own devouring whatever was in its path. The flame caused windows to shatter, and they licked up th side of the structure. Smoke threw a shroud ove the building and reflected the light of the flame back to the ground. The whole area was lit.

As Jessica watched, a figure emerged on the roo and began to walk back and forth along a parapet The figure carried a candle, lit incongruously ami the flames, and seemed not to notice the destruc tion, nor the danger.

"This is mine!" Margaret yelled wildly, throwin her arms wide. "No one will take this from me!"

There was a roar and a crash as a main bean gave way. The whole house shuddered as spark blossomed above her head. With a piercing scream Margaret fell to her death into the house she ha fought so hard to keep.

Jessica watched in horror. Margaret had bee jealous, cruel, and, finally, insane, but Jessica ha never wished such a horrible ending to the woman' tyranny. The house, which held so many happy an painful memories for Jessica was now truly Marga ret's.

Damien watched the tears wet his wife's cheeks His arm tightened about her.

"You have another home to go to, Jessica," he re minded her gently. "One where you can create new memories, happy ones, for our children. When Ja son is older, he can return and rebuild Braeleigh."

Jessica turned tear-brightened eyes to Damien her husband. She smiled. What he had said, in her heart, she knew to be true. The pain of losing her family home would fade, to be replaced by the joy of creating a home filled with love for the new family that would surround her. She had gambled her heart and lost it, only to win more than she had ever expected.

FIERY ROMANCE

CALIFORNIA CARESS (2771, $3.75)
by Rebecca Sinclair

Hope Bennett was determined to save her brother's life. And if that meant paying notorious gunslinger Drake Frazier to take his place in a fight, she'd barter her last gold nugget. But Hope soon discovered she'd have to give the handsome rattlesnake more than riches if she wanted his help. His improper demands infuriated her; even as she luxuriated in the tantalizing heat of his embrace, she refused to yield to her desires.

ARIZONA CAPTIVE (2718, $3.75)
by Laree Bryant

Logan Powers had always taken his role as a lady-killer very seriously and no woman was going to change that. Not even the breathtakingly beautiful Callie Nolan with her luxuriant black hair and startling blue eyes. Logan might have considered a lusty romp with her but it was apparent she was a lady, through and through. Hard as he tried, Logan couldn't resist wanting to take her warm slender body in his arms and hold her close to his heart forever.

DECEPTION'S EMBRACE (2720, $3.75)
by Jeanne Hansen

Terrified heiress Katrina Montgomery fled Memphis with what little she could carry and headed west, hiding in a freight car. By the time she reached Kansas City, she was feeling almost safe . . . until the handsomest man she'd ever seen entered the car and swept her into his embrace. She didn't know who he was or why he refused to let her go, but when she gazed into his eyes, she somehow knew she could trust him with her life . . . and her heart.